The Time of Their Lives

Maeve Haran is an Oxford law graduate, former television producer and mother of three grown-up children. She started her writing career with the international bestseller, *Having It All*, which explored the dilemmas of balancing career and motherhood. Maeve has written eight further contemporary novels, two historical novels and one work of non-fiction.

Her books have been translated into twenty-six languages, two of which have been shortlisted for the Romantic Novel of the Year award. She lives in North London with her husband, son and a very scruffy Tibetan terrier.

The Time of Their Lives

Maeve Haran

PAN BOOKS

First published 2014 by Pan Books
an imprint of Pan Macmillan, a division of Macmillan Publishers Limited
Pan Macmillan, 20 New Wharf Road, London N1 9RR
Basingstoke and Oxford
Associated companies throughout the world
www.panmacmillan.com

ISBN 978-1-4472-5389-1

5 7 9 8 6

A CIP catalogue record for this book is available from the British Library.

Typeset by Palimpsest Book Production Limited, Falkirk, Stirlingshire
Printed and bound by CPI Group (UK) Ltd, Croydon, CR0 4YY

Visit www.panmacmillan.com to read more about all our books
and to buy them. You will also find features, author interviews and
news of any author events, and you can sign up for e-newsletters
so that you're always first to hear about our new releases.

For my four wonderful friends, Alex, Claire, Harriet and Presiley, whom I met on the first day of university and continue to meet every month for friendship and fizz. You have so enriched my life, thank you.

And also for Jane, who asked the question —
'What are we all going to do with the rest of our lives?'
— that sparked this novel.

FOREWORD

When my four friends and I meet up – as we do every month – to drink wine and share confidences, we all agree on one thing: We may not *be* young, but we still *feel* young.

At my age my mother dressed like the Queen. We like to dress stylishly, to go out and enjoy ourselves. As one of the characters in *The Time of Their Lives* points out, 'the only way you can tell a woman's age these days is to look at her husband!'

We are the first generation who may live for another thirty years and sometimes, to the irritation of our children, there's one thing we're sure about – we intend to make the most of it!

'I don't even use the word because, first of all, that's what old people do and, secondly, that's what you do after dinner.'

Dame Marjorie Scardino, ex-rodeo rider and first woman CEO of a British FTSE company, on the subject of retiring.

CHAPTER 1

'OK, girls,' Claudia looked round at her three closest friends who were gathered for their usual night out in The Grecian Grove, a basement wine bar sporting badly drawn murals of lecherous shepherds chasing nymphs who didn't look as if they were trying that hard to get away, 'does anyone know what date it is today?'

To call them girls, Claudia knew, was pushing it. They weren't girls, as a matter of fact, they were women. Late middle-aged women. Once they would have been called old, but now, since sixty was the new forty, that had all changed.

Sal, Ella and Laura shrugged and exchanged mystified glances. 'It's not your birthday? No, that's in February and you'll be——' Ella ventured.

'Don't say it out loud!' cut in Sal, ever the most age-conscious of them. 'Someone might hear you!'

'What, some snake-hipped potential young lover?' Laura teased. 'I would feel I owed him the truth.'

'It's the thirtieth of September,' Claudia announced as if pulling a rabbit from a hat.

'So?' They all looked bemused.

'It was on the thirtieth of September that we all first met.' Claudia pulled a faded photograph from her bag. 'The first day of term at university. Over forty years ago!'

Sal looked as if she might pass out. The others scrambled

to see. There they were. Four hopeful eighteen-year-olds with long fringes, short skirts and knee-length boots, optimism and hope shining out of their fresh young faces.

'I must admit,' Ella said proudly, 'we look pretty good. Why do the young never believe they're beautiful? All I remember thinking was that my skin was shit and I ought to lose a stone.'

Claudia looked from her friends to the photo. At first glance Sal had worn best, with her chic clothes and fashionable haircut, but then she'd never had a husband or children to wear her out. Besides, there was something a little overdone about Sal's look that spoke of trying too hard. Laura had always been the most conventionally pretty, given to pastel sweaters and single strings of pearls. You knew, looking at Laura, that as a child she had probably owned a jewellery-box with a ballerina on top which revolved to the music. This ballerina had remained Laura's fashion icon. Next there was Ella. She had always been the elfin one. Then, three years ago, tragedy had struck out of a blue sky and had taken its toll, but she was finally looking like the old Ella. Oddly, she looked younger, not older, because she didn't try to alter her age.

Then there was Claudia herself with her carefully coloured hair in the same shade of nut-brown she always chose, not because it was her actual colour, she couldn't even recall what that was, but because Claudia believed it looked more natural. She wore her usual baggy beige jumper with the inevitable camisole underneath, jeans and boots.

'It can't be as long ago as that,' Sal wailed, looking as if she could see a bus coming towards her and couldn't get out of its path.

'They were good times, weren't they?' sighed Ella. She knew her two daughters judged things differently. They saw their parents' generation as selfish, not to mention promiscuous and probably druggy. The baby boomers had been the lucky ones, they moaned, inheritors of full employment, generous pensions and cheap property prices while their children had to face insecure jobs, extortionate housing costs and working till they were seventy.

Ella thought about it. They were right about the promiscuous bit. She would never dare confess to her daughters that at the age of twenty she'd prevented a man from telling her his name as they made love, preferring instead the excitement of erotic anonymity. How awful. Had she really done that? Not to mention slept with more men than she could remember the names of. Ah, the heady days after the Pill and before Aids.

Ella found herself smiling.

It had been an amazing moment. The music, the festivals, the sense that the young suddenly had the power and that times really were a-changing. But it was all a very long while ago.

Claudia put the photograph carefully back in her bag. 'I have a question to ask.' She poured them another glass of wine. 'The question is, seeing as we may have another thirty years to live, what the hell are we going to do with the rest of our lives?'

'Won't you go on teaching?' Ella asked, surprised. Claudia was so dedicated to her profession and had been teaching French practically since they left university. 'I thought you could go on forever nowadays.'

'I'm not sure I want to,' Claudia replied.

They stared at her, shocked. 'But you love teaching. You say it keeps you in touch with the young!' Laura protested.

'Not enough in touch, apparently.' Claudia tried to keep the bitterness out of her voice. 'I'm out of tune with technology, it seems. My favourite year group has been reassigned to a younger teacher who gets them to learn slang on YouTube.

It's having an energizing effect on even the slowest pupils according to the deputy head.'

Claudia tried not to remember the deputy head's patronizing tone yesterday, when she had explained, as if talking to a very old person, that Peter Dooley, a squirt of thirty known by the rest of the staff as Drooly Dooley because of his habit of showering you with spit when he talked, would be taking over her favourite pupils.

'Mr Dooley!' Claudia had replied furiously. 'He has no experience of the real France! He looks everything up on the Internet!'

Too late she realized her mistake.

'Exactly!' the deputy head insisted; she was only thirty herself, with an MBA, not even a teaching degree, from a university in the North East – an ex-poly at that, Claudia had thought bitchily.

'But you've always been amazing with your pupils!' Sal defended indignantly. 'Do you remember, years before the Internet, you made tapes up with you and Gaby speaking French to one another? Your pupils loved them!'

Claudia blanched. The deputy head had actually produced one of these twenty-year-old anachronisms during their interview and had had the gall to hold it up and ask in a sugary tone, 'Of course you probably think the old ways are best, don't you, Claudia?'

Claudia had wanted to snap that she was perfectly au fait with modern teaching methods, thank you very much. But the truth was she was beginning to feel defeated. For the first time, since those heady days of the photograph, she had started to feel old. And it wasn't the fault of memory loss or the war with grey hair.

It was technology.

Jean-Paul Sartre might say hell was other people, but he'd

never been to an Apple store on a busy Saturday, only to be told you needed an appointment to talk to a 'genius', one of a thousand identikit geeky youths, before you could ask a simple question.

Nor had he to contend with the horrors of the 'managed learning environment' where pupils and even their parents could go online and access their school work from home. Even the tech-savviest staff found it a nightmare to operate. As if that weren't enough, now teachers were expected to identify their pupils' weaknesses using some hideous software developed by a ten-year-old!

'Snotty cow,' Ella's angry voice echoed through The Grecian Grove in Claudia's defence. 'You're far better at technology than I am. I still think an iPad is something made by Optrex. What are you going to do about it?'

'Actually,' Claudia realized the truth for the first time herself, 'I might even resign.'

'Claudia, no!' Laura was shocked. 'But you love teaching and you're really good at it!'

'Am I? Seriously, girls, the bastards think we're has-beens. Drooly Dooley even said, "If it's any consolation, Claudia, a lot of the older teachers are struggling with the system."'

'Bollocks!' protested Sal, emptying her glass.

'Anyway, another school would snap you up!' Laura, always the positive one in the group, happily married for twenty-five years and a great believer in the virtues of the institution, was attempting to answer Claudia's question. 'You're a wonderful teacher. You'd find something else useful to do. Funny, it only seems the blink of an eye since we first met. We should just keep calm and carry on. It'll only be another blink till we're ninety.'

'Except that this blink will be punctuated by arthritis, memory loss and absence of bladder control,' Sal pointed out laconically. 'And anyway, you should fight back! Don't take ageism lying down. We're not old yet. Not even middle-aged.'

Maybe because she was the one who most needed to earn her living, Sal was fighting ageing the hardest. She had declared war on body fat, laughter lines and any clothing in baggy linen. The dress she wore today was black gabardine, strictly sculpted and teamed with high heels. Ella had given up on anything but flatties years ago, and Claudia was wearing trainers so that she could walk to the tube.

She liked to walk to work on school days. But would there be any more school to walk to? Claudia asked herself glumly, as she poured out the last of the resin-flavoured Greek wine into their glasses.

'You'd definitely find another teaching job,' Laura comforted, with all the encouraging optimism of someone who didn't really need to work.

'Would I?' Despite the jeans, Claudia felt suddenly old. Who would want to employ a teacher on a high pay-scale who wouldn't see sixty again?

'Come on, Clo,' Ella encouraged. 'You're the dangerous radical in our midst. You were in Paris in 'sixty-eight throwing paving stones! You can't just give up because some snotty jobsworth is trying to sideline you!'

Claudia sipped her wine and winced. The trouble was she wasn't sure she wanted to fight back. She was beginning to feel tired. She looked around at her friends. 'A toast.' Claudia raised her glass. 'To us. It was bloody amazing while it lasted.'

'I'll drink to that,' Sal seconded. 'But it isn't over yet!'

'Oh, come on, Sal, admit it.' Ella shook her head. 'We're not middle-aged, we're ancient.'

'No we're not. There's no such thing as old any more. We're YAHs – Young At Hearts. Or maybe we're SWATS.'

'I thought that was a valley in Pakistan,' Claudia giggled.

'Or some kind of police unit,' seconded Ella.

Sal ignored them. 'Still Working At Sixty.'

'If we *are* still working,' Claudia sighed. 'Or in your case, Sal, maybe it's SOTs. Still Out There at Sixty.'

'That makes me sound like an ageing cougar with a drink problem!'

'And your point is . . . ?' Ella teased.

'Now, now,' Laura admonished. 'Don't gang up on Sal.'

'The thing is, we're just not old like people have been old in the past,' persisted Sal. 'At my age my mother looked like the Queen – with a curly perm and twinsets. I wear jeans and shop at H&M!'

'It's true we all look nothing like our mothers did,' Laura conceded. 'The only way you can tell a woman's age these days is to look at her husband!'

'The thing is we may *be* old but we don't *feel* old,' Sal insisted, 'that's what makes us different. We're the baby boomers, the Me Generation. We've always ripped up the rules and done it our way. Ageing isn't inevitable any more, it's a choice! And I, for one, am not choosing it.'

'I don't know.' Ella stretched out the arm in which she got occasional twinges of rheumatism. 'Sometimes I do feel old.'

'Nonsense! We'll never be old. We're the Woodstock generation! What was that Joni Mitchell song?' Sal delved into the recesses of her memory. 'You know, the one about being stardust and needing to get back to the Garden?'

'Yes,' Ella raised her glass. 'Let's just hope the Garden's wheelchair accessible.'

On the tube home Claudia got out her phone and set it to calculator. Yes, she was tech-savvy enough to do that, thank you, even though her daughter Gaby said she only used her phone to send nags-by-text. She roughly added up their major outgoings. If she gave up now it would damage her pension. She couldn't help smiling at Ella's jibe about her throwing paving stones in 1968, when here she was agonizing about pensions. What would the young Claudia have thought of that?

But then she'd only been an accidental anarchist. In fact, she'd really been an au pair, only seventeen, trying to improve her French before A levels, staying with a well-heeled family in the smart sixteenth arrondissement. That's when she met Thierry, best friend of the family's son. It had been Thierry, darkly good-looking with black horn-rimmed specs and an intellectual air, who had persuaded her, on her rare day off, to come and see what the students were doing.

Claudia, from safe suburban Surrey, had been entranced by the heady air of revolution, the witty graffiti daubed on the elegant buildings: *Be realistic, demand the impossible*, *I am a Marxist, Groucho Tendency*, and even more by the alluringly radical Thierry himself.

It had all been so daring and exciting. She had joined hands with Thierry and his clean-cut friends in their corduroy jackets and short haircuts, not at all the standard image of revolting students, to block the Paris streets so that the hated *flics* couldn't pass. She had ridden on his shoulders – like girls now did at music festivals – in the Latin Quarter with hundreds of thousands of others demanding sexual liberation and an end to paternalism.

It all seemed a far cry from today.

She went back to her calculations. How would they survive without her salary? Badly. At this rate, if she gave up teaching, she'd have to get a job in B&Q like all the other oldies! The most infuriating thing was that Claudia knew she was good at her job. She could enthuse her students and she was popular too. But it was true that she didn't use new technology as much as Peter Dooley did. She wondered if she was being a Luddite. *No,* she reminded herself, *I'm bloody good at what I do.* And what if she did give up? She could always coach pupils at a crammer.

But what Ella had said was true; she was still a bit of a boat-rocker and she hated privilege that could be bought by rich parents. *If I give up, I'm bound to pick up some work*, she told herself. But, deep down, Claudia knew that no matter how good she was, her age was beginning to tell against her.

By the time she got home, the brief respite from her problems brought on by wine and friendship had evaporated. She walked up their garden path, noticing that the light was on in the sitting room and that, unusually, her husband Don – also a teacher, in his case of politics – was sitting at the computer underneath the cheese plant, another feisty survivor from the Sixties. The height of fashion in 1969, cheese plants were as quaint as aspidistras now, but Claudia felt an inexplicable loyalty to it and refused to chuck it out.

She had spent most of last night moaning to him about the deputy head. In contrast to her own gloomy mood, Don seemed unusually cheery, which amazed her since recently he had been depressed about his own job. Tonight he seemed a different person.

'Hello, love.' He grinned at her, suddenly boyish. 'I think I may have found the answer to our problems!'

Somewhere deep inside, alarm bells rang. This wasn't like Don. She was always the one who got things organized, made the decisions, rang the changes. Don had always been impractical, disorganized, totally disinterested in anything remotely useful. He was usually far more caught up with how to make the electoral system come alive to bored and phone-fixated teenagers than whether the roof was leaking or where they could get a better rate of interest on their modest savings. These things he left to 'Clever Claudia'.

Their daughter Gaby had followed his example and always turned to her mother, not her father, for loans, advice and late-night lifts.

'OK,' Claudia took off her coat and hung it in the hall cupboard. 'So what *is* the answer to our problems?'

'We'll look into retiring. It'll only be a couple of years early. They always used to be asking for volunteers among the older teachers. We cost more. They can easily replace us with some kid straight out of teacher training, then we can sell this place and downsize to Surrey, near your parents, and live on the income from our investment.' His eyes shone like an early-day evangelist with a new parable to preach. 'You could keep chickens!'

Claudia shuddered. She'd always said retiring was something you did before going to bed, not with the rest of your life. On the other hand, could she stomach Drooly Dooley easing her out of her own department?

She could think of a number of extremely rude French slang expressions to describe the little toad, much ruder than those on the Internet, of which *pauvre mec* was by some way the tamest. What if she protested to Stephen, the head teacher? He was almost her own age. Would that mean he would support her or take his deputy's part? Claudia knew she had a bit of a reputation for arguing. No doubt Stephen would remember it. Besides, the days of mass early retirement for teachers was long gone. Too expensive and too many teachers, worn out by classroom confrontation, had already opted for it. Still, they might be open to negotiation . . .

She'd have to make herself more troublesome.

One thing she knew. She didn't feel ready to bury herself in the sticks. 'But I don't want to keep bloody chickens! And I don't want to move to bloody Surrey!'

'It's only twenty miles down the motorway,' Don placated, his eyes still shining dangerously and his missionary zeal undimmed. 'Half an hour on the train, max.'

'What about me?' demanded a voice quivering with outrage. 'Surrey is the home of the living dead.' Gaby, their daughter, stood in the doorway, her face ashen at the prospect of a rural retreat.

Claudia, who'd grown up there, quite agreed.

Gaby, at twenty-eight, still lived at home. Claudia loved having her. Her daughter was terrific fun and often filled the kitchen with her friends. But she also worried that Gaby really ought to be finding a job that paid enough for her to be able to move out. Gaby's response was that due to the greedy depredations of the generation above she was too broke, but Claudia sometimes feared it was because she wasn't a sticker. She had a perfectly good degree in geography but had thrown herself, in swift succession, into being an actress, a waitress, the receptionist for a vet, a call-centre operative, a circus performer (only two weeks at that), and an art gallery assistant. Recently she had decided she wanted to be an architect. Claudia and Don had exchanged glances and not mentioned the extremely lengthy training. Currently, she was at least working for one, albeit in a very junior capacity.

'We could help you with the rent on a flat,' her father announced, as if the solution were obvious.

Gaby brightened perceptibly while Claudia wondered if Don had lost his mind. 'Somewhere in Shoreditch, maybe? Or Hoxton?' Gaby named perhaps the two hippest areas in the now-fashionable East End.

'I'm not sure about that,' Don began.

'Neither am I,' Claudia agreed waspishly. 'More like in Penge on what our income will be if I leave. But that's because this whole idea of moving is ludicrous.'

'Why?' Don stood his ground for once.

'My job is here. I like London.'

'But as you say yourself, you may not want to go on with your job. What happens if Dooley gets Head of Department?'

Claudia ignored this hideous prospect. 'What about the culture on our doorstep?' she protested. 'Theatres, galleries, restaurants?'

'You never consume the culture. You're always saying theatre tickets are priced so only Russian oligarchs can afford them.'

'Art galleries, then.'

'When did you last go to an art gallery?'

Claudia moved guiltily onwards, conscious that, living in the middle of one of the world's great cities, she rarely consumed its cultural delights. 'And then there're my friends! I couldn't move twenty miles from The Grecian Grove!'

'Don't you think you're being a little selfish?' Don demanded.

'Don't you think *you* are?' Claudia flashed back. 'You've never even mentioned moving before and now it's all *my* fault because I don't want to live in the fake country.'

'Surrey isn't the fake country. Anyway, we could move to the real country. It'd probably be cheaper.'

'And even further from my friends!'

'Yes,' Don was getting uncharacteristically angry now, 'it's always about the coven, isn't it? The most important thing in your life.'

'How dare you call them the coven?'

'Hubble bubble, gossip, gossip. Sal bitching about her colleagues. Ella moaning about the son-in-law from hell, Laura judging every man by whether he's left his wife yet.'

Despite herself, Claudia giggled at the accuracy of his description.

'Thank God for that,' Gaby breathed. 'I thought you two

were heading for the divorce court rather than the far reaches of the M25. You never fight.'

'Anyway, what about *your* friends?' Claudia asked Don. 'You'd miss your Wednesdays at the Bull as much as I'd pine for my wine bar.' Each Wednesday Don met up with his three buddies to moan about their head teachers, Ofsted and the state of British education. But friendship, it seemed, wasn't hard-wired into men as it was into women.

'Cup of tea?' offered Don as if it might provide the healing power of the Holy Grail. 'Redbush?'

Claudia nodded. 'The vanilla one.'

'I know, the vanilla one.'

She kissed Gaby and went upstairs. He knew her so well, all her likes and dislikes over thirty years. They were bonded by all the tiny choices they'd made, each a brick in the citadel of their marriage. But citadels could lock you in as well as repel invaders.

Claudia undressed quickly and slipped into bed, her nerves still on edge.

Don appeared bearing tea, then disappeared into the bathroom.

Two minutes later he slipped naked into bed, the usual signal for their lovemaking. 'I'm sorry. I shouldn't have sprung it on you like that. It was really unfair.'

'Telling me.'

He began to kiss her breast. Claudia stiffened, and not with sexual anticipation. How could men think you could use sex to say sorry, when women needed you to say sorry, and mean it, before they could even consider wanting sex?

Ella got off the bus and walked along the towpath where the Grand Union Canal met up with the Thames. It was a moonlit night and a wide path of silver illuminated the water, vaguely swathed in mist, which reminded her of one of the holy pictures she had collected as a child at her convent school. These holy pictures often featured the effect of light on water as a symbol of supernatural peace. But Ella didn't feel peaceful tonight. It was one of those nights when she missed Laurence.

Any religious faith she'd had had long deserted her. It might have been a help, she supposed, when Laurence had died so suddenly, without her even being able to say goodbye, a random statistic on the News, an unlucky victim of a rare train crash. The safest form of travel. Ha. Or maybe, if she'd had faith, she might have lost it at the unfair nature of his death, away on a day's business, standing in for a colleague, not even his own client.

She thought of Claudia, and Claudia's question. What were they all going to do with the rest of their lives? It was a good question. Work, she knew, had saved her then.

It had only been her job that had got her through the grief when Laurence died. Without work to go to she would have pulled the duvet over her head and never got out of bed again.

Of course, she'd had to be strong for her daughters, but they were grown-up now, thirty-two and thirty, no longer living at home. In fact, another reason Ella had had to be strong was to prevent Julia, her eldest and bossiest daughter, swooping down on her and treating her like a small child incapable of deciding anything for itself.

Cory, her younger daughter, had been harder to console because the last time she'd seen her dad they'd quarrelled over some silly matter, and she couldn't believe she'd never see him again so they could make it up.

That had been three years ago; Ella almost had to pinch herself. The imprint of his head on the pillow next to hers had hardly disappeared. The bed felt crazily wide and every single morning she woke, she heard the empty silence of the house and had to put the radio on instantly. Jim Naughtie had proved no substitute for Laurence but he was better than nothing.

A tactless colleague, whose own husband had left her, insisted that death was better than divorce because at least you had the memories.

But sometimes the memories were the problem. She could still walk into the house, put her keys on the hall table next to the bunch of flowers she'd picked from the garden, and listen, expecting to hear the sound of sport on the television.

Her job as a lawyer had been doubly useful. She had fought the train company for an admission of guilt, not just for her but for the others. And then, when she got the admission, the fight had gone out of her. As soon as she'd hit sixty, she'd retired, just like that. Everyone had been stunned. Perhaps herself most of all.

Now she was crossing the square in front of her house. Even though it was in London it had once been a village green where a market was held, and archery contests. Now it was gravelled over but still felt more a part of the eighteenth century than the present day.

Ella stopped to look at her house, the house on which she had lavished so much care and love, the house where she had spent all her married life.

It was a handsome four-storey building of red brick with square twelve-paned windows and large stone steps going up to the front door. It was this entrance she loved the most, with its elegant portico and delicate fluted columns. Once it had been lived in by weavers, now only the substantial middle class could afford to live here.

She stopped for a moment as she put her key in the door and looked upwards. A jumbo jet was just above her, on its descent into Heathrow. It seemed so close she could reach out and catch it in her hand. Incongruously, these triumphs of Queen Anne elegance were right beneath the flight path. The area where she lived was a tiny enclosure of history surrounded on all sides by towering office blocks benefiting from their nearness to the profitable M4 corridor. The square was one of those little unexpected revelations that made people love London.

Inside the front door she could hear a radio playing and stood stock still, frozen in memory. But it wasn't Laurence, Laurence was dead. It was probably Cory, who had the disconcerting habit of turning up and staying the night if she happened to be nearby. In fact, once she'd got over the shock, Ella was delighted to have her younger daughter there.

'Cory!' she called out. 'Cory, is that you?'

Footsteps thundered up the wooden stairs from the basement and a coltish figure flung itself at her. Cory was a striking girl, slender, with skin pale as wax against a waterfall of dark brown hair. But it was her eyes that arrested you. They were a quite extraordinary bright dark blue. Sometimes they were dancing with light, yet, more often, Ella saw a sadness in their depths that worried her. Cory had so much to feel confident about – an ethereal beauty, quick intelligence, and a job she enjoyed as a museum administrator – but it had only been Laurence who had the capacity to make her believe in herself. When Ella tried to praise her daughter she somehow got it wrong – and Cory would shrug off the compliment, whether to her good taste in clothes, or an acute observation she had made – with a little angry shake, like a duckling that is eager to leave the nest but can't quite fly unaided. Today, at least, she seemed in an effervescent mood.

'Hey, Ma, how are you? I was at a boring meeting in Uxbridge and thought you might love to see me.'

'Did you now?' laughed Ella, taking in the glass of wine in her daughter's hand. She was about to ask, playfully, 'And how is that Sauvignon I was saving?' But she knew Cory would look immediately stricken, so she bit the comment back. 'Don't worry,' Ella shrugged, 'I'd join you but I've been out with the girls already.'

'Speaking of girls, your next-door neighbour is popping back in a mo. She's got something to ask you.'

'Ah. She and Angelo probably want me to water the cat or something.'

'Are they going away?'

'They're *always* going away.' Her neighbours, Viv and Angelo, shared the disconcerting energy of the prosperous early retired. They were both over sixty but had arrested their image at about twenty-six. Viv had the look of the young Mary Quant, all miniskirts, sharp bob, and big necklaces. Angelo had well-cut grey hair, almost shoulder-length, and was given to wearing hoodies in pale apricot. They drove around in an open-topped Mini with loud Sixties music blaring. If there was a line between eternally youthful and weird and creepy, they were just the right side of it. Though, looking at them, Ella sometimes wondered if anyone admitted to their age any more.

It was a constant source of surprise to Ella that Viv and Angelo also had an allotment. And this, it transpired, was the source of the favour Viv wanted to ask when she rang the doorbell half an hour later.

'Sorry it's so late. Cory said you'd be back. It's just that we're off at the crack of dawn. And I just wondered, Ella love, if you could cast an occasional eye over the allotment for us. Once a week will do, twice at the most.'

'How long are you away for?'

'Only three weeks. Diving in the Isla Mujeres.'

'Where on earth is that?'

'Mexico, I think. Angelo booked it.' Viv and Angelo went on so many holidays even they lost count. Their pastimes always made Ella feel slightly exhausted. Paragliding, hill walking, white-water rafting, cycling round vineyards – there was no end to activities for the fit and adventurous well-heeled retiree.

'And what would I have to do?'

'Just keep it looking tidyish. The allotment police are a nightmare. Keep threatening to banish anyone who doesn't keep their plot looking like Kew Gardens.'

'There aren't really allotment police, are there?' Cory demanded.

'No,' Viv admitted. 'That's what we call the committee. They used to be old boys in braces and straw hats. Now Angelo suspects they're all LGBT.'

'What is LGBT?' Ella asked.

'Mu-um!' Cory corrected, looking mock-offended. 'Lesbian Gay Bisexual Transgender.'

'Good Heavens!' Ella didn't often feel old but she did now. 'Well, that's pretty comprehensive.' In fact it probably said more about Angelo than the allotment holders.

'You just need to do a bit of deadheading, sweep the leaves, look busy. We're always being reminded of what a long waiting list there is – of far more deserving people than we are. Here's the key.'

Viv kissed her three times. 'Oh, and by the way, we've had a burglar alarm fitted next door. Angelo insisted.' She handed Ella a piece of paper. 'Here's the code if it goes off. You've got our keys anyway, haven't you?'

'Yes,' agreed Ella, beginning to feel like an unpaid concierge.

Viv was already down the garden path. 'Off at six. Angelo hates wasting a whole day travelling so we have to get the first flight out.'

'You have to admit,' marvelled Cory, 'they've got a lot of get up and go for oldies.'

'Too bloody much, if you ask me. They're trying to prove there's nothing they're too old for.'

Ella double-locked the door and dragged the bolt across, then began drawing the heavy silk curtains, undoing the fringed tiebacks with their gold gesso moulding. This was a job she especially liked. The old house with its wooden floors and oak panelling always seemed to emanate a sigh of satisfaction and embrace the peacefulness of night-time.

'You know, Mum,' Cory's thoughts broke in, 'you really ought to do the same.'

'What? Deep-sea diving? Or paragliding?'

Cory smiled ruefully, laughing at the unlikely idea of Ella throwing herself out of anything. 'Get a burglar alarm.'

'I hate burglar alarms,' Ella replied. She almost added: 'You can't forestall the unexpected, look at what happened to Dad', but it would have been too cruel. 'You're beginning to sound like your big sister Julia. Come on, time for bed. Do you want a hottie?'

Cory shook her head. 'I think I'll stay up and watch telly for a bit.'

Ella went down to the basement kitchen and made tea, thinking of Laurence. It was the little habits that she missed most, the comforting routines that knit together your couple-dom. And here she was still doing it without him. Now all she had to look forward to was babysitting her neighbours' allot-ment while they swanned off living the life of people thirty years younger. Except that people who were actually thirty years younger couldn't afford to do it.

Ella turned off the light, listening for a moment to the big old house's silence. It had been a wreck when they'd bought it, with a tree growing in the waterlogged basement. She had coaxed the house back to life with love and devotion, steeping herself in the history of the period, studying the other houses in the square so that theirs would be just as lovely.

'Good night, house,' she whispered so that Cory didn't think she'd finally lost it. 'We're all each other has these days. Too much to hope anything exciting is going to happen to me.'

She shook herself metaphorically as she went upstairs to bed. She'd tried so hard to resist self-pity during the dark days after Laurence's death, she was damned if she was going to give in to it now.

Sal stood in the wastes of Eagleton Road hoping a taxi would come past. She shouldn't get a cab, she knew. It was unnecessary and not even something she could charge to expenses, as one could in the heyday of magazines, when staff just charged everything they liked and The Great Provider, aka *Euston Magazine*, paid up without a whimper. Now the publishing landscape was getting as bleak as Siberia.

Sal began walking desultorily towards the tube station, playing one of her favourite games which decreed that if a cab went past before she got there, fate intended her to jump into it, and who could argue with fate? Sal realized she was stacking the odds by walking particularly slowly in her unsuitable high heels. The thing was, these shoes were made for taxi travel and no one, especially their designer, had envisaged a customer schlepping down the uneven pavement of Eagleton Road.

Fate was on her side and a lone cab hove into view with its light on.

Sal hailed it with all the joy and relief of a refugee getting the last berth on a transport ship out of some war-torn hotspot.

'Middlebridge Crescent, please.' They headed off for the rather sleazy enclave in North Kensington, on the borders of upmarket Notting Hill Gate, where Sal had managed to find an unfurnished flat thirty years ago, settling for four somewhat uninviting rooms in an unappealing road in exchange for the nearness of its glamorous big sister.

The truth was, although Sal gave every appearance of being the career woman on top of life, there were aspects of living she was hopeless at: mortgages, pensions, savings plans. None of these had ever caught her imagination like sample sales, freebies to exotic spas, London Fashion Week — these were what made Sal's heart beat faster.

She paid the cab driver, and was touched that he waited till she had safely descended the steps to her front door, in case any marauding mugger should be concealed there. 'Good night, miss,' he called, although he knew and she knew that this description, though technically true, was an entirely generous gesture.

'Good night,' she responded, opening her grey-painted front door. Funny how grey front doors had suddenly become *de rigueur* on brick-fronted houses, and any other colour suddenly seemed strange and somehow wrong. That was how fashion worked, of course. Grey wasn't simply the new black, as far as front doors went; it was the new red, green and blue.

She shivered as she turned her key, grateful for the warm embrace of central heating, which might not be as enticing as a waiting lover, but was a lot cheaper to run and far less temperamental.

October already. Incredible. She smiled at the memory of the photograph of the four of them and then recoiled at the thought of how many years ago it was. She had never imagined that here she would be, more than forty years later, living alone, paying her way, dependent for her standard of living on the whim of Maurice Euston and his daughter Marian, who had just been elevated to Managing Director.

It struck her as she sat down on her aubergine velvet sofa and shucked off her agonizing heels that the all-important Christmas issue would be out by the end of the month. Of course, the whole thing had been put to bed months ago. All those children simpering round the Christmas tree in cute pyjamas had actually been sweating in a heat-wave. All the same, she – Sal – still believed in the fantasy. It didn't matter if they had to cheat a little to make the fantasy work. She had never felt cynical and bored, never wanted to shout: 'Oh for God's sake, I've heard that idea four hundred times before!' at some hapless young journalist.

Sal loved magazines. When she was growing up on her Carlisle council estate, she hadn't been able to afford them and had devoured as many as she could at the hairdresser when her mum had her Tuesday afternoon cheap-rate shampoo and set. They remained a gorgeous parcel of me-time. Gift-wrapped with glossiness and sprinkled with celebrity stardust, they brought pleasure to millions. Well, maybe not quite millions, that was half the problem, but thousands anyway. To Sal, a magazine was still something you held in your hand, savouring the thrill of flicking through the first pages, not something you summoned on your iPad or furtively consulted online during your lunch break. She knew you had to keep up, though, and had worked hard to make sure these options were there, and as inviting as any offered by *Modern Style*'s rivals.

Sal made herself a cup of green tea. She mustn't let the magazine take up her entire waking life. She was no worka-holic. She had other interests and passions.

Didn't she?

Laura parked in the driveway of her solid suburban house. She had been careful only to have two small glasses so that she would be below the limit. Laura preferred driving to taking the bus or tube. Somehow it meant she didn't have to leave the protective cocoon of home, and that was how she liked it. You could argue that the tube was more interesting. All those different nationalities. People reading books, e-readers, free newspapers, playing games on their phones. And the fashions. She liked seeing all the ways young women put their clothes together. But there were also beggars, stringing you some story, the noisy drunks talking out loud to themselves, and the exhausted, worn-out workers who made Laura feel faintly guilty about her easy life.

Tonight, though she knew it was awful, she also felt slightly smug. It was amazing that, out of the four of them, she was the only one who was truly happy with her life. Ella had had that tragedy, so utterly unfair, out of the blue like that; Sal never thought about anyone but Sal, which was why she'd ended up on her own; and Claudia had been married a long time, but she was always moaning about Don's head being in the clouds, and they never seemed to be soulmates. Not like she and Simon were.

It was an object of pride to Laura that Simon loved her and his home as much as he did, that they were perfectly happy in each other's company. Of course she loved her friends, but Simon came first.

And she knew he felt the same about her. In fact, the only source of friction between them was their children. When Bella had become a Goth, Simon was appalled. Laura, on the other hand, rather admired her for it. She knew that she herself was a boringly conservative dresser and partly blamed this for Bella needing to express her individuality by clothing herself like the heroine of a Hammer horror film in a silk top hat, veil and Victorian riding gear. When Bella had dyed her silky blonde hair inky black, Simon had almost cried.

And she knew that their son, Sam, quiet, heavy-metal loving Sam, who loathed all sports, was a disappointment to Simon too. Simon had been so thrilled at having a son that he had plonked him in front of the TV for *Match of the Day* from the moment he was born. And the only result had been that Sam hated football until he was at least twelve.

Even though it could be stressful at times, Laura was still grateful that both her children lived at home. Home and family were the same thing in her book. And, Laura had to admit, their children were especially precious after all the fertility problems they'd had. There had been times when Laura had almost given up. Simon had argued the whole thing was taking too much of a toll on her, though she'd felt that he was referring to himself. He had hated all the rollercoaster of hope and disappointment of assisted conception even more than she had. And then, finally, at forty, to find that she was pregnant with Bella! She would never forget that positive pregnancy test as long as she lived. And to make their world complete, Sam had come along two years later.

Ever since their arrival, she had wanted to be here for them, not out at work, but providing a safe and happy environment. She relished being home when they came back from school and shouted, 'Hi, Mum, I'm back.'

Still hugging herself at how much she loved them she went up to bed. The sight of her bedroom always made her happy. It was so exactly what she'd wanted. Soft carpets, crisp white linen, roses in a vase. The air in the room was cold since Simon, the product of boarding school, liked the window wide open. It was one of the few things besides the children that they argued about. Fortunately, he slept like a corpse so she could get away with closing it as soon as he nodded off. If she remembered, she would guiltily open it a few inches in the morning before he woke.

As she slipped into bed he murmured and turned. She thought perhaps he was feeling amorous and experienced a wave of guilt as he shifted back to the wall, eyes closed.

The sheets had been clean this morning, which always gave her a dilemma. There was something seductive about clean sheets, but, equally, did one want to spoil them with the messiness of making love? Not that they had much of that these days. Simon seemed perfectly affectionate yet rarely pushed for sex. Laura had even wondered about Viagra.

'With my husband we had to wait forever for it to work,' warned Susie, her tennis partner. 'Not to mention me having to wank him like a Thai hooker all the time unless he did it himself. And then, just as you're nodding off, there it'll be, poking into your bum. And once it's up, it's up for hours.'

Laura had giggled, imagining an erotic puppet show with Mr Punch using his willy instead of the usual stick and chanting, 'That's the way to do it!'

On the whole she was glad Simon was sound asleep.

CHAPTER 2

'Hello, Claudia dear, is that you?'

Claudia's mother Olivia had the habit of shouting down the phone as if it were her daughter rather than herself who was slightly deaf. Claudia supposed that at over eighty you were allowed a few foibles. Olivia had plenty.

'Yes, Mum. How are you?'

'My bones ache in the morning. Takes me a good half-hour and a hot bath to get going. Let me give you some advice, darling. Don't grow old.'

'I'll do my best. How's Dad?'

'Not too bad, considering the alternative.' This was the joke her father made every time anyone asked how he was. 'Now look, darling, I'm ringing about Christmas.'

'Of course.' Claudia felt a flash of guilt. Her mother always liked to get Christmas settled early. Usually by Boxing Day the year before. 'Are you coming here as usual?'

'Well actually, darling – not this year.'

'You're not?' Claudia was flabbergasted. They always came. 'Where are you going?'

'We thought Istanbul.'

'Istanbul? Why Istanbul?' Claudia asked incredulously.

'I found this wonderful offer on the Internet. And Dad's fed up with the vicar. Told him we were going to have a Muslim Christmas. Just to annoy him.'

Claudia giggled. She adored her dad. And the vicar was one of those who went on and on about Christingle. 'Do they celebrate Christmas in Istanbul?'

'Apparently there's this lovely little Christian church your father's found right in the middle of the city. He's also got this idea of watching three ships go sailing by on Christmas Day in the morning, like in the nursery rhyme. From the Bosphorus. There are hundreds of ships there, apparently. It's quite a sight.'

'Right.' This did indeed sound like her father, she had to concede. He adored watching ships. 'When do you go? Maybe we should have a pre-Christmas Christmas?'

'That sounds nice.' Claudia could hear the doubt in her mother's voice. 'Though we are rather busy.'

Knowing her mother and father, Claudia knew this was an understatement. Her parents, Olivia and Len, had a social life that was far busier than Claudia's own. Their life seemed to be a whirl of bridge evenings, pub quizzes, and dinner parties. In fact, her parents had time for all the things Claudia would like to do herself but never did. The latest addition was Olivia's passion for Internet offers of cut-price meals, spa days and outings to garden centres which seemed largely to be taken up by silver surfers. Claudia had once accompanied her mother to a three-course lunch with champagne when the entire clientele had white hair and Zimmer frames. The food had been diabolical but Olivia had quipped, entirely without irony, 'I know, dear, but it is half-price.'

'Gaby will be really disappointed if we don't do something Christmassy,' insisted Claudia.

'We're free on Monday the sixteenth in the evening, if that's any good,' offered Olivia generously. 'I'm sure I could find us a Christmas offer.'

'No, no. I'll cook.'

For a moment she wondered if she would still be working by Christmas but she wouldn't worry her mother with that. 'Will you, dear?' Olivia sounded dubious. She had given up cooking altogether since discovering the Internet with all its tempting restaurant deals. 'Are you sure you want to go to the trouble?'

After much negotiation over how long they would stay, all of it due to her parents' busy schedule, they finally agreed their arrangements. It struck Claudia, depressingly, that her mother was probably more Internet-savvy than she was.

'Of course, you could always come here for Christmas, if you wanted a change,' her mother offered. 'The house will be empty. Gaby might like it.'

'Thanks, Mum,' Claudia said, rather too quickly. It wasn't Gaby who'd like it, it was Don. She could just imagine it. He'd become a man on a mission and hang around estate agents' windows.

After they had rung off, Claudia sat at the kitchen table thinking about her mother. There was something strange about Olivia's manner. She couldn't put her finger on it, but her intuition told her something was not quite right. She seemed to be almost gabbling in her eagerness for these offers. There was a breathless enthusiasm, a heightened sense of glittering excitement that was hardly merited by spa outings and trips to the garden centre. She didn't have much time to think about it, since Gaby came back from work pale and distraught because her current boyfriend had suggested they take a break.

'Do you think it's over, Mum?' Gaby raised eyes that were smudged with mascara. Black runnels of misery marked her cheeks, producing an overwhelming tenderness in her mother. The answer was yes, but she would never say that. It was best just to listen.

Gaby had a habit, along with job-changing, of falling for unsuitable older men who seemed wildly exciting but who nearly always ended up breaking her heart. Claudia worried that it was some fault of her upbringing. Nice normal types like her father didn't appeal to Gaby. Only the difficult and unattainable. Maybe, as she was an only child, they had expected her to adapt to an adult world instead of entering into the fun and silliness of the child's. Even when she had been eighteen, Gaby had preferred twenty-five-year-olds to her own age group.

Claudia opened her arms and patted her daughter. First, she'd worried about her mother, now she was worrying about her daughter. The price you paid for being part of the swinging Sixties and delaying childbearing as long as humanly possible was this. You were the sandwich generation who worried about your parents and your children both at exactly the same time.

Ella stood looking out at her garden with its large lawn dominated by a vast cedar of Lebanon. Usually it was a scene she found calming. She remembered her excitement at finding a document in the house stating that the tree had been planted in memory of one Samuel Browne, the house's first owner, and that the said much-loved Samuel was buried beneath it. Ella imagined the person who had effected this unusual burial-site was Samuel's wife and what a struggle it must have been with Church and state to be allowed to do this.

Behind her sat the source of her lack of calm. Her daughter Julia. Julia had taken up a post at the huge kitchen table and was consulting her laptop. 'God, Mum, your WiFi signal is crap here. You really do need to emerge from the eighteenth century!'

Julia was thirty-two and had married young, so that her two sons, Harry and Mark, were already into their teens. To Ella's disapproval they had been sent off to their father's old public school, and though she loved her grandsons, she feared they were fast becoming as pompous and narrow-minded as he was. She knew Julia had opposed Neil at first but she'd been worn down by his endless arguments that their sons' futures would be blighted by going to the local school and that she was being selfish to resist.

Laurence had always lectured Ella about being less disapproving of Neil and giving the boys a chance, they were her grandsons, after all, and Ella did try. It was just that she thought they would be much nicer and more tolerant of other people if they had been sent to a normal school instead of the ludicrously expensive and ultra-traditional boarding establishment which seemed mainly to teach them that they were superior to everyone else on the planet.

The cost of fees for this dire place was so huge that Julia and her husband Neil were permanently looking for ways of paying up. And this house, Ella's beloved home for all her married life, was their perpetual target.

'Look, Mum.' The laptop was open at Zoopla. Julia, it seemed to Ella, was obsessed with house prices – especially the price of this particular house – and seemed to spend half her life on websites which detailed exactly how much every property nearby had gone for. 'Look, that's Number twenty-two.'

Ella studied the house on the screen. It was indeed the house four doors down, where the Lamberts had lived for thirty years. There hadn't been a For Sale sign up and the Lamberts hadn't mentioned anything about moving. But that was what the ludicrous situation with house prices did to people – it made them behave like characters from one of the Molière plays she'd studied at university. In this case *The Miser*. Everyone was terrified that other people would find out how much they'd made. Well, Ella had to concede, property-price websites had put an end to that worry.

'My God, it went for nearly two million!' Julia squawked, too stunned to hide her excitement.

'That's nice for the Lamberts. I expect it's their pension,' Ella conceded.

There was a pause during which Ella had to stop herself grinning, Julia was so transparent. 'What about you?' Julia enquired hopefully. 'Won't you need to downsize too?'

'No. I have a company pension from my time as a lawyer.' She almost added 'Sorry to disappoint you', but thought better of it.

Julia had less sense. 'I mean,' she blundered on, 'this place is far too big for you without Dad. And it's so full of wood that needs endless polishing . . .'

'I love the wood,' Ella said quietly. 'I love the square. I love the garden. I love the tree that makes me think of Dad. I rescued this house and maybe that's why I love it so much.'

'Yes, but think what you could do with two million . . .'

'What *you* could do with two million,' Ella thought but didn't say. She loved both her daughters and of course she loved her grandchildren; she would like to give them a helping hand with money, even though she had never had one herself, but not yet. She would give them a sum to help them buy their own home, but not for school fees to that particularly pig-headed school which seemed to live in a previous century, as did Neil himself. Especially since she suspected Julia was the one who suffered from her sons' absence. And certainly not if it meant giving up this house with all its treasured memories. She might make Cory understand that the house kept Laurence alive in her heart, but Julia would just say that was a bad thing, another reason to sell. 'You should move on, Mum,' would be her instant advice. But Ella thought moving on was over-rated.

If Julia had had any sense she would have stopped there,

but Zoopla had shown her the pot at the end of the rainbow. 'Of course Neil says—'

'You've discussed me moving with Neil?' Ella asked quietly.

'We've got your own good at heart, Mum. We worry about you here all alone.'

'Thank you, darling. And what does Neil say?'

'That giving money away seven years before . . .' Even Julia baulked at saying 'before you die'.

'Julia, darling, I might live for another thirty years.'

'All the more need to plan your financial future.'

'Is that what Neil says too?'

Julia flushed slightly. Clearly Ella and Ella's finances were a popular topic in her daughter's household.

She sat down next to Julia and gently closed up her laptop, then she reached for her daughter's hand. 'Look, darling, I love this house and I'm not moving any time soon. I think it would be better for us all if you and Neil accepted that.'

Her daughter's face took on a mulish look. 'It's just that the school fees are so crippling . . .'

'Then don't send them to that school. They'll only turn out like . . .' Now it was Ella's turn to pause.

'Like their father? That was what you were going to say, wasn't it? Well, I think you're a selfish old woman.'

Ella shrugged. Maybe she was selfish. And then she thought of Laurence and how he would have backed her up although he would also have put it more diplomatically, and it was only because he wasn't here that Julia was saying this. She was damned if she were going to feel guilty.

For now she needed to get outside, to blow away all these thoughts chasing each other round her brain. She would go to the allotment.

'I have to go and change,' she announced, grateful to abandon the subject.

'Out with the coven?' Julia asked acidly. Clearly Don's description of the four of them was catching on.

'Not today. I promised to keep an eye on my neighbours' allotment.'

'You?' Julia laughed. 'Growing vegetables? Neil says it's ridiculous anyway. Grow-it-yourself types are causing potato blight. It would be much better if the land were used for housing.'

'I might agree if I didn't know what kind of housing he means.'

'You've never liked Neil, Mum!' accused Julia.

Ella felt a pang of guilt. 'He has lots of good qualities. Anyway, he's not my husband.'

'No,' Julia replied sullenly. 'He's not. And look at Cory. Thirty and no boyfriend now or ever.'

Ella felt the knife going in. She worried about Cory. That her younger daughter, who had been such a daddy's girl, still hadn't recovered from Laurence's death and that this was an element in her lack of relationship. She had tried to get Cory to go to bereavement counselling but Cory had just replied: 'Julia isn't going to counselling.' But then Julia and Cory were as different as sisters could be.

It was a good day at Sal's office. One of the days when she loved her job, liked the people, adored the buzz of the busy building.

Modern Style, with its rather incongruous name, was based in a tall, thin early Victorian house in Soho. Next door on either side were shops that sold trimmings for costumes, stuffed with row after row of ribbons, sequins and feathers. Sal often wondered how they stayed in business year after year with margins that were infinitesimally small. Maybe a lesson for the magazine world.

Modern Style was owned by Maurice Euston, who had once owned countless strip and porn joints, which explained their location in Soho, but had decided ten years ago to go straight. He was in the process of handing over the reins to his daughter, Marian.

Sal's office was on the second floor. The décor had originally been haute bordello, all plush velvet and deep-pile carpets with crystal chandeliers and more gilding than Versailles. Marian had effected a makeover last year and the entire building was now bone-coloured and minimalist, a victim of Farrow & Ball fascism.

Sal was sitting at her curved glass desk looking through the Christmas edition. This edition sold so much better than any other that they had started bringing it out earlier and earlier so that two editions could be squeezed out of the holiday period. There was always a race between similar magazines to see who could get their Christmas version out earliest.

Sometimes Sal thought it might end up in September.

The phone rang and she picked it up. It was her assistant. 'Great edition,' she congratulated. 'Maurice and Marian want to take you out to lunch. One o'clock at The Ivy.'

This was a good sign. If the two Ms were displeased it would have been the trattoria over the road, the only restaurant in London that had ignored the arrival of modern Italian cuisine and still served stodgy lasagne with pride. Or maybe even sandwiches in the office.

Maurice, short and stocky, with skin that was mottled with dark patches like a bruised apple that had fallen off the tree, sat muffled in a coat and scarf as if the temperature outside were freezing, rather than it being a balmy October day. Marian, dainty in pastel mohair with bows down the front that belied the razor sharpness of her mind, sat next to him, a glass of champagne by her side. She ordered another for Sal.

'Sally, good to see you. Have a seat.'

'I see we're drinking champagne.' Sal beamed. Her contract was due for renewal and she had been worried about the year-on-year sales figures and that the National Readership Survey had shown a small decline in reader reach as well as advertising, but the fizz seemed to belie all that.

'Are we here to talk about the Christmas issue?'

'The Christmas issue is great. What we actually need to address is where we go from here. We have big plans.'

'I hope that means a budget increase?' It amazed Sal that she was expected to produce the magazine for the same page rate as the one she had edited twenty years ago, and had to exploit unpaid interns, streams of hopeful young journalism graduates eager to get their feet in the door, while having zero budget for training anyone.

They ordered their food.

'The thing is, as you know, magazines are changing fast,' Marian announced, ignoring the food on her plate. 'To keep up with the competition we need to extend across all the different platforms.'

Sal hated the obsession with platforms. She saw herself as a magazine editor but increasingly she was expected to be that hideous piece of jargon, a 'platform-neutral content pro-vider', which meant she had to produce endless material for websites, Facebook, Twitter and even appear on everyone else's platforms promoting *Modern Style* whenever she could.

'And the thing is –' Unusually, Marian paused.

At that very moment Sal caught sight of a scene that stunned her. Over Marian's fluffy shoulder sat Simon, Laura's husband, the one she raved about being so happy with, and he was kissing the palm – actually kissing the palm in a restaurant celebrated for its gossipy media types! – of a stunning young woman. Sal studied her in horror. On closer inspection she wasn't as young as she'd seemed at first, probably in her mid- to late thirties, voluptuous, with long red hair and a predatory look.

Oh shit, thought Sal, not hearing what Marian was droning on about, that was the worst possible age. He would be thinking their affair was all about his incredible sexual prowess while she was hearing nothing but the ticking of her biological clock. Poor, poor Laura. Men were so bloody predictable.

'Of course you have been a highly satisfactory editor,' Maurice Euston's voice finally penetrated her consciousness. Sal's radar picked up the past tense and gave them both her full attention. 'But the future is going to be challenging. It requires a digital native, someone who grew up with these platforms, who lives and breathes them.'

'Producing a great magazine is about ideas, not platforms,' Sal scanned their faces for a reaction and found none.

'Certainly, but it's becoming hard to argue that good ideas are enough,' Marian's eyes narrowed, giving her the look of a pink sugar mouse wielding a sub-machine gun, 'which is why, Sally, I'm afraid we won't be renewing your contract.'

At that moment Simon stood up and swept his companion into his arms, kissing her passionately as if there were no one else in the room.

'Bastard!' Sal expostulated, unable to contain herself further at this barefaced betrayal.

Marian stood up. 'I will advise our lawyers of your response. I can't say I'm surprised. I have always found you an intractable employee. You needn't return to the office. We will waive your notice period and have all your things sent round in a cab.'

'Sorry?' Sal asked, recovering her wits. '*What* did you just say?'

'I don't think we need go over it again, Sally.' Marian stood up and waved for the bill even though they were only halfway through the meal. 'I wouldn't pursue unfair dismissal, if I were you. Half the restaurant heard what you called me.'

Marian was struggling into her coat with Maurice Euston helping her. 'Bag up Ms Grainger's meal please,' he asked a passing waiter. 'I can't bear waste.'

Sal stood, uncharacteristically speechless, as a doggy bag of posh shepherd's pie was pressed upon her. What was the point of explaining? Marian was clearly using this as an excuse for something she had already decided on.

Her former employers were halfway across the restaurant when Simon, hiding his shock beneath a front of unconvincing bravado at being caught out by one of his wife's best friends, pretended to greet Sal enthusiastically.

'Sal! This is Suki, a colleague of mine. Fancy meeting you here.'

'Simon, I am a journalist,' Sal replied in what she hoped was a sufficiently withering tone, 'and this is one of the best-known media haunts in London.' She looked his luncheon companion up and down. This sleazebag and his floozy had helped cost her the job she loved. With a sweet smile she handed Simon the greasy brown receptacle. 'Here. Have this doggy bag. Maybe your bitch might enjoy it.'

Laura, entirely unaware of the drama unfolding in town, was happily filling in her diary when she remembered their anniversary was fast approaching. She had been thirty-eight when they married. She could remember the look of amazement mixed with relief on her parents' faces when she'd told them about their wedding plans. 'Going to make an honest woman of you, is he?' her dad had joked. The awful thing was, Laura knew he meant it. He really did see marriage as completely different from living together. That 'piece of paper' was worth its weight in gold to her parents. How stunned they'd be to find their daughter and son-in-law still together twenty-five years on. Of course her parents were both dead now which Laura had to admit was a slight relief as their disapproval of Bella and her Goth propensities would have been stinging.

She was pretty stunned herself. It was quite an achievement in the modern world that she and Simon had lasted so long. She grinned, remembering the day Bella had come to her and said that it was so unfair, nearly everyone in her class had divorced parents. Apparently divorce meant double the presents, no insistence on homework, and the unlimited potential to play off one parent against the other. Bella, with two parents who had stuck together, was apparently a disadvantaged minority.

The question was, what should they do to celebrate it?

Simon didn't really like surprises but Laura loved them. Besides, if she left it to him to arrange something, it would never happen.

So Laura decided to think of a way to mark the last twenty-five years and look forward to the next twenty-five, and which would be a complete secret.

Smiling to herself, she began to make a list. A party? Their oldest friends round to dinner? A romantic weekend away? Laura realized that much as she loved her children, the surprise would work better if it were just her and Simon so she could give him her undivided attention. A weekend away, then. She sat down at the computer and began to browse. The Top Ten romantic locations came up as Venice, Paris, Amsterdam, Rome, Barcelona, Prague, Copenhagen, Budapest, Berlin and – Brighton!

Laura laughed out loud because, amazingly, that was where they had met. It had been a reunion for their year at Sussex University and they'd both gone expecting to have a so-so time, convinced that reunions were for losers.

Instead they'd met each other. Their acquaintance while they were at college had only been slight, but suddenly they'd clicked and couldn't stop talking all night. And then, to crown it all, in what Laura wasn't to know was the only genuinely romantic gesture of Simon's life, he took her hand and led her down to the beach.

Having equipped himself with a bottle of wine, a blanket and a portable CD player, he laid the blanket out under Brighton Pier and played 'Under the Boardwalk', warbling flatly along to the chorus that, under the boardwalk on a blanket with his baby, was where he'd like to be.

Laura had been charmed. And even more so when it turned out that he'd booked them a room in an extravagant Art Deco hotel, just like the ones in the movies in the days when a private detective might barge into the bedroom with a camera to capture infidelity and earn Brighton its reputation as the dirty-weekend capital of Britain.

Laura felt her heart skip with excitement. That was exactly what she'd do again, the same hotel, the beach, under the boardwalk, all of it. And the brilliant thing was she could keep it all secret and pay for it herself. Unlike a weekend in Venice or Amsterdam, a night in Brighton was something she could afford out of her own money.

She hugged the pleasure and anticipation of the venture to her chest. She thought of Ella without Laurence, Sal all alone, and Claudia with her dull Don, and felt like she was the luckiest woman alive.

CHAPTER 3

Ella pulled back the curtains and looked out at the garden, trying to work out how cold it was. Today was the day she was going to seriously tackle Viv and Angelo's allotment. She turned out some old jeans and a holey sweater of Laurence's that she hadn't been able to bring herself to throw away. Unconsciously, she held it up to her nose, checking whether it held any faint aroma of Laurence, that distinctive scent he'd had of shaving foam, citrus cologne and the odd stolen Gauloise, which he thought she didn't know about. There was nothing except maybe mothballs. Certainly no hint of Laurence.

The funny thing was, she'd always wanted an allotment but Laurence had laughed at her. 'You've already got more garden than you can manage!' he'd tease her. But the Moulsford garden had been Laurence's empire – a male preserve of lawn mowed in straight lines and flowerbeds that stood to attention as if on parade. Vegetables had never been part of Laurence's ordered dream. Until now Ella's yearning to reap as she had sowed had been confined to a Gro-bag of tomatoes on the terrace.

Persuading herself that this project was just what she needed, Ella tied up her shoulder-length dark hair with a scrunchy, catching sight of herself in the cheval glass as she did so, surprised that, for a fleeting moment, she looked young, girlish even, provided you didn't stare too closely. Maybe it was because this was the way she used to wear her hair in her teens, or perhaps the action of gathering it also tightened the skin in what Sal naughtily called an Essex facelift. She rifled about in her drawer for heavy walking socks to keep the cold out when she put on her wellies. She was grateful these were made of straightforward green rubber, not some ludicrous Cath Kidston flowery substance which made you look as though you came from Chelsea by way of the Cotswolds.

She shut her sock drawer reflecting that she had a ludicrous amount of storage space for one person. Funny, when the news about Laurence had come she'd thought she would physically collapse but instead she'd gone into the utility room and folded sheets for hours. She'd bought this book on mindfulness, the hip concept of the moment. It told you that the way to avoid being consumed by the past or fearing the future was to make yourself concentrate 100 per cent on the present. And to do this the book instructed you to take a household task and do it 'mindfully'. She had chosen laundry and had spent hours folding sheets perfectly, making herself stay in the moment, feeling the touch of the fabric, smoothing them with the flat of her hand, taking an inordinate pride in the neatness of their appearance as she stacked them in the airing cupboard, folded side outwards, like the spine of a book. After that, she'd just cried but when she stopped, she was sure it had somehow helped get her through that deep dark valley of grief.

She was halfway down the stairs, enjoying the sensation of thick stair carpet underneath heavy woollen socks, when she stopped, suddenly alert. Something seemed unfamiliar. She listened for a moment but there was nothing different about the sounds of the house. She heard the usual faint banging of ancient water pipes, the occasional creak of old wood, but otherwise there was silence. Then she worked it out. There was a strange breeze. The front door, always bolted and double-locked with a mortise key, was wide open. The shock rooted her to the spot. How could the door possibly be open?

And then, on the small half-landing, she noticed a drawer pulled out of the console table. She ran to the nearest bedroom and found the mattress had been pulled up. The same was true in the one next door. Ella ran through the house feeling at first sick and panicked, then spitting with anger. Bastards! She'd been burgled!

The irony was she didn't really have anything to take. A lot of old books, an ancient radio, a TV that no modern-day burglar would want, not even a phone that would merit resale and her computer would probably be more at home in a museum than being hawked about for a cheap bargain in the public bar of the Dog & Duck.

The drawers were also pulled out in the kitchen dresser and here the burglar had had more luck. The jars full of coins she'd collected for charity had gone. Well, good luck to him. He'd have to take them to one of those clanking coin change machines since the bank would never take them and there was probably only a tenner, if that.

The container of keys had been emptied onto the kitchen table and Ella realized with a sinking heart that she'd have to get the locks changed in case he'd taken one. How the hell had he got in? Ella ran downstairs, terrified that she'd left the key in the lock. No, thank heavens, the door had been properly bolted. She rushed through the kitchen and, to her horror, the side door, only used to put out the rubbish, was indeed unlocked. Oh God, what would the girls say? Impending senility at the very least.

Pulling herself together, she rang the police, who sounded

supremely disinterested once she told them how little had been taken. 'Is there any chance the intruder is still present?' asked the woman at the call centre. Ella realized that if she said yes, they would be round quicker. 'I don't know. He might be. I live alone and it's quite a big house.'

As she said this two things struck Ella: that her daughter Julia would be absolutely delighted at Ella's inefficiency and that she had no intention of telling her.

Julia would be delighted not because she was uncaring but because it would be another nail in the coffin of this house. Too big, too impractical, worth too much money and now – unsafe for her mother to live in. Ella could just imagine the song and dance the news would create, her son-in-law Neil shaking his head and saying 'I told you so' in that infuriating pompous way of his, when he hadn't said anything of the sort.

She would get a burglar alarm and keep it to herself.

The police, when they came round several hours later, were impeccably polite and told her she would also be visited by Victim Support and a Scene of Crime officer to take finger-prints. It was all rather exciting, except for her sense of guilt that it was her own fault. She felt as if she were part of *Miss Marple*. Old Moulsford might be under the Heathrow flight path but it had a distinct air of St Mary Mead.

The only thing that scared Ella just a little was that the burglars had been round every room in the house bar hers. What if she had heard them and come out? She could have been attacked or hurt.

Pushing the thought from her mind she made herself and the officer a cup of tea and looked through the *Yellow Pages* for burglar-alarm installers.

She didn't feel up to the allotment today after all. With cup of tea in hand she called Claudia.

'You'll never guess what. I got burgled last night.'

'Ella! How awful!' For once Claudia felt grateful for Don. He might not be the most exciting man on the planet but he would be reassuring in time of break-in. 'What did they take?'

'Virtually nothing. I've got zilch that's worth stealing. I'm probably lucky he didn't shit on my Persian rug in protest.'

'Do burglars really do that?'

'I don't know. Maybe it's an urban myth like discarded lovers sewing kippers in the curtains.'

'Are you all right? I could pop round after school if you like.'

'I'm waiting for the Scene of Crime officer. Or was it the Victim Support people?'

'Golly.'

'By the way, don't breathe a word to Julia whatever you do.'

'I quite understand. You don't want to worry her. But wouldn't she want to be worried?'

'Julia would like nothing more. She's desperate for me to sell up and hand over the dosh so that their pompous little boys can stay at their school and get truly insufferable. This burglary would be another brick in the wall.'

'What about Cory?'

'Cory would panic and move in. Then she'd be more scared than I am. I'm keeping the whole thing quiet and installing an alarm. In fact, they're coming this afternoon. Then I have to remember another bloody PIN code or I'll set the alarm off accidentally. I hope I don't turn into some dithering old lady who can't even remember the date of her own birthday.'

'You're not supposed to use your birthday anyway. Do you know half the population use one two three four?'

'How sweet. You have to love people, don't you?'

'I'm glad you're getting an alarm. We're not as young as we were.'

'I know, only don't tell Sal. Actually, burglars aren't so scary. I just hope I don't get one of those granny rapists. I'd just have to say "Look here, young man, I'm really eighty, I've just got that disease like Brad Pitt in *Benjamin Button*."'

By the end of the day Ella had been given helpful hints by the Scene of Crime officer that she should tack carpet grip on her garden gate which, though it wouldn't stop a burglar, would cut him so badly that they could get good DNA evidence; from the neighbour on one side that she should play a tape of a barking dog; and from the neighbour on the other that she should keep a baseball bat by her bed as did the other half of the population who didn't use one two three four as their PIN code.

The man from Banham's just said she should keep the alarm on at all times, day or night.

Ella ignored them all, put it on only when she went to bed, and mourned the time when you could leave your door unlocked and not wake up to find your plasma screen had disappeared in the night.

'Mum, you've got a burglar alarm,' Cory commented when she came round for supper the next week.

'Yes.'

'Why is that? Are you frightened of living on your own?'

With all the deftness of a computer gamer, Ella assessed the pitfalls in giving the wrong answer. 'No, I'm fine living alone. I thought you girls would worry about me less if I had an alarm.'

'Absolutely. You're very precious, you know, Mum.'

Ella, who since losing Laurence had learned to keep her emotions under strict control in case they overwhelmed her, felt suddenly unbearably moved. 'Come and have a hug.'

Cory smiled tolerantly. 'Mum, you old softie.' But she let herself be hugged all the same.

Unfortunately, the effect was somewhat reduced by the phone going. Cory grabbed it before her mother could.

She held it out to Ella. 'It's someone from the local nick,' she raised a cynical eyebrow, 'about the break-in here the other night, do you need victim support or counselling?'

Sal's alarm woke her at 7.30 as usual, the comforting tones of Radio 4 assuring her that all was familiar with the world. Her bedroom was equally soothing: every shade of grey from wispy-white to smoke, with a luxurious gunmetal velvet bed-spread. Her trademark pale pink roses stood in a large and extravagant-looking bunch on her dressing table, though how much longer would she be able to afford them? She always insisted on a dedicated dressing table where make-up could be applied in the proper light.

Then she remembered that things weren't the same at all. In her entire adult life she had never been without a job for more than a few weeks, a month at the most. OK, sometimes she'd done a bit of freelancing, but that had been to top up an existing salary, to pay for an unexpected minibreak, or maybe a Mulberry handbag which she had reckoned she could buy with two broadsheet articles or a large tabloid one.

She wondered how far the news of her sacking had spread. There was no gossip more relished in the media world than a head rolling at the top. Of course, editors came and went with fairly startling speed. Everyone knew the game and being fired wasn't necessarily the end of the road.

Unless you were over sixty.

There. She'd said it. The 'S' word, one she rarely allowed into her mind, let alone onto her lips. Age had always seemed irrelevant to Sal; she had never considered it a factor even when she was a young writer starting out. Ideas were the thing, being in touch with what interested the readers, noticing what was new in the world, and what people cared about.

Certainly struggling with new technology was an issue.

When she'd first started fresh from college they had used manual typewriters with carbon paper for copies. Her job had been simply to produce ideas and copy. There were plenty of designers, production people and sub-editors to lay it out, check it and send it off to the printers in Glasgow.

Everything was different now; they had to input their own copy, lay it out and sub-edit it themselves using hideously complicated new equipment. She had kept quiet the other day when Claudia recounted how she'd been accused of being out of touch with technology, but it had certainly rung a bell.

Sal slumped back on her cushions. They had been a reader offer in the magazine. She picked one up and threw it at the wall, almost knocking over her roses as she did so.

'Bloody Marian and Maurice!'

In the dim and distant past, when she'd needed a job she'd opened up her Filofax (no one possessed one of these now, yet Sal could remember when everyone had to have one) and contacted all the useful people she could think of. Now it was email, of course. Or tweeting. Or LinkedIn.

Sal buried her head under the pillow. She didn't feel like having to go through all that. She was too old! Too tired!

Reality seeped in through her cloud-grey curtains. Money. How was she going to pay the bills? The downside of refusing to accept that she was sixty was that she hadn't planned for it. She would be entitled to a state pension at some point, but that wouldn't even keep her in white wine! Having grown up in poverty she had a horror of returning there.

Suddenly the topic of pensions, and indeed of ageing at all, which had interested her as much as the football results, felt entirely gripping.

Sal sat up. She felt righteous indignation well up inside her. This was always a good sign. Her best pieces had come out of feelings just like this. Getting a parking ticket from some jobsworth ten seconds after the time limit had expired. Paying for a massage and finding that she was pummelled so hard it was like medieval torture and she had ached for days! Being ignored by a bored and haughty waiter in a restaurant that boasted good service! These had all made excellent rants for which she had been well rewarded. None were about world-changing issues but they had had their impact.

And now she was getting all riled up about something that *did* matter. Still in her grey silk pyjamas, another reader offer, Sal made a quick coffee and sat down at her computer screen.

An hour later she realized that the coffee had gone cold but she had written a stonking article on ageism in the work-place. Older employees everywhere were terrified because they were 'out of touch with technology' and they should be given training to help them adapt. Of course they were bloody out of touch with technology! Admiral Nelson would have been useless with a sub-machine gun! Einstein himself would have struggled with a MacBook Pro!

Sal felt the familiar joy of a good piece, well argued. New technology, which she had just spent the last hour lambasting, now offered her a choice. Should she think about it in a mature way, given her newly precarious position, i.e., joblessness, or just bang it off to some of her contacts in the hope of publi-cation? They would immediately guess that she had been fired, as would the entire journalistic community once they read it. Righteous anger in a journalist was usually the result of outrage at being treated just like an ordinary person.

Sod it! Sal pressed the Send button, feeling better at once. Now she would have a bath and get dressed; maybe she'd go to the little café at the end of the road where she never had time to linger in the mornings and have an over-priced latte.

Life wasn't so bad after all.

An hour later, after she'd drunk her latte and watched all

the yummy mummies crowding into the café with their vast double buggies, moaning on about their children's demanding social lives, regret started to set in.

She was sixty-three, she had no husband to support her like these young women, no children to help her out in old age, no proper pension because she had spent it all on clothes and shoes, and now she had written a piece that trumpeted the fact that she had been fired. Was she terminally self-destructive?

She decided to call someone who would sympathize.

'Hello, Claudia.'

'Sal?' Claudia sounded surprised. Sal never called her in the morning. She was always too busy at work. Claudia was only home because it was half-term.

'Everything all right?'

'Well, no, actually. I've been fired. Or rather, technically my contract will not be renewed.'

'Sal, no! Why?'

'The same reason your deputy head prefers that Dooley bloke. Ageism dressed up as not being tech-savvy. I am insufficiently "platform-neutral", it seems.'

'What does that gobbledegook mean?'

'It means they want some teenager who grew up with the Internet. Producing a mere magazine is not enough. We have to be online. We must tweet. We must have our own TV channel even though the TV channels are becoming more like magazines every day. Do you know you can even buy things direct from the TV now? It's called convergence, according to Marian. And it means I don't have a job.'

'I wonder if there's a message coming through to us all here.'

'There is. It's called Get Thee to a Garden Centre with All the Other Old Folks.'

'Oh, Sal. So you're sitting at home feeling miserable. Tell you what, let's go to The Retreat! A spa day is just what you need to cheer you up; something you can't usually do because you're too busy.' Claudia realized she was beginning to sound like her mother which meant she really was joining the ranks of the retired.

'I haven't been to The Retreat in twenty years. No, make it thirty.'

It was an extravagance, Claudia had to admit, and she would insist on paying while she still could. Anyway, there were moments when friendship mattered more than money. She suddenly thought of her mother's penchant for offers. Maybe one was available at The Retreat.

'They're bound to let us in cheap. Spas are full of wrinklies like my mum these days, all brandishing their half-price vouchers. If Martha Lane Fox hadn't dreamed up Lastminute.com my mother would have done it for her.'

Two hours later, Sal found herself wrapped in a white terry robe, lying on a towel-draped chaise-longue, trying to position herself so that her neck didn't look like a broiling chicken's and hoping her mascara wouldn't run in the steam room.

Claudia was right. All around them were the over-fifties. More sensible over-fifties than Sal. Women with pensions and husbands and houses to fund a little luxury in their retirement. Sal tried to repress a sudden ripple of fear. What the hell was she going to do? She had already borrowed heavily to put in an en-suite bathroom. It had been a great success and she knew it would make the flat more desirable. Except that she didn't want to make her flat desirable to somebody else! The idea of moving to some poky studio with the fridge in the bedroom to save money was hideous in the extreme.

The memory of her parents in their last years came vividly

back to her, eternally economizing, and never putting the heating on unless their breath showed inside the house. But Sal was a working woman, things were supposed to be different for her generation!

'Here.' Claudia handed her one of The Retreat's famous Bellinis. 'They're not bad. Though not as good as Laura's. She uses fresh peach juice.'

Laura! In all the worry and excitement, Sal had forgotten the scene that had preceded, maybe even contributed, to her sacking. 'Claudia, in The Ivy, where my employers thought-fully took me to sack me, I saw Simon. He was with another woman! And the bastard was kissing her, right there in front of the whole restaurant. I mean, doing that in The Ivy, it's like taking an ad out in *The Times*.'

'Simon? You mean Laura's Simon? Oh my God. What was she like?'

'Claudia, she was lethal! Thirtysomething and gorgeous. I could hear her biological clock ticking right across the restaurant!'

'Oh shit, and I've always laughed at Laura's obsession with men leaving their wives. She's convinced it's an epidemic, like buying a Land Rover in Central London.'

'Maybe she had a premonition.'

Claudia shook her head. 'No. That's the worst bit. She's convinced she and Simon are rock solid.'

'Do you think we should tell her? We are her best friends.'

Claudia bit her lip. 'No. Having your friend tell you your husband's being unfaithful makes you feel twice as humiliated. As if you're the last to know. It's bound to come out if he's being that public about it. Stupid bastard.'

'Bloody love.'

'Not bloody love. Bloody men. You'd think after all that time together he'd have some loyalty.' Claudia drained her

Bellini. 'The trouble is men know they can start all over again. Look at Picasso. Women think, Christ, I've got another thirty years, I'd better take up gardening. Men think, I've got another thirty years, I know, time for a new wife and kids.'

'I don't think that's what Simon's thinking. I think the stupid sod believes she's after his body.'

'It doesn't matter what Simon believes, though, does it? If you're right and this woman wants a baby, she won't think twice about breaking up his marriage. I've seen it over and over. Wives are expendable. Simon probably thinks he's entitled to a shiny new family.'

'Oh God, poor Laura.'

'Poor Laura indeed. We'd better be standing by to pick up the pieces.'

Laura hummed to herself, feeling happier than she had for months. Not only did she have this surprise up her sleeve for Simon, but Sam had announced he actually wanted to watch a film with her, and Bella, who had been uncommunicative and surly lately, had suddenly asked if Laura would pick her up at 4 p.m. She would phone before with the address.

Even though it was late afternoon, their slightly unfashionable suburb was bathed in golden light. Sunshine spilled over the black and white mock-Tudor houses, and even the High Street, in decline in the face of stiff competition from the Retail Park, looked attractive, despite one in three of its premises being charity shops. Even the half-timbered McDonald's had an optimistic glow.

Laura hung on to her good mood, only a little concerned that the address Bella had given her turned out to be a tattoo parlour, appropriately entitled Just A Little Prick.

After all, Laura told herself, tattoos were all the thing now, even among her friends' children. Once the exclusive choice of sailors and navvies, they were openly sported by accountants and lawyers. Celtic tattoos were particularly popular with the offspring of the middle class since, she supposed, these conveyed a more cultural message. She had even toyed with a little heart herself.

Laura smiled, grateful she had thought the better of it. What did all those tattoos look like on now-ageing flesh? Grannies with mysterious Chinese symbols above what Bella, ever down-to-earth, referred to as their bum-crack? Crinkled flesh adorned with Day-Glo dragons?

All the same, she did hope that Bella was not here to defile her lovely young flesh too dramatically. A woman walked out of the shop as she approached, her entire arm embellished with brightly coloured tattoos from wrist to armpit. Laura felt slightly sick.

Just A Little Prick turned out to be small and, despite its slightly salacious name, clinically clean and well-lit, with photographs lining the walls of successful illustrations of the tattooist's art. Laura wasn't sure whether to be reassured or not by the sign reading A NEW NEEDLE FOR EVERY CLIENT.

To Laura's intense relief, it wasn't Bella who was seated in the tattooist's chair but a giant of a young man with long black hair and white, white skin which was exposed to the waist of his jeans. Spread around him were the tools of the tattooist's trade: alcohol to clean the skin, green soap for removing surplus ink and blood, plus small containers of different inks. The tattooist, who was wearing a white coat and rubber gloves, reminded Laura of her dentist, although luckily for the young man in the chair, he didn't seem to be in the habit of sticking cotton wool in your mouth before asking you a question. Laura had expected heavy metal but instead there was the oddly reassuring sound of whales calling to each other across the deep.

Along the whole of the giant's shoulder, the tattooist had

drawn the outline of some vast and unidentified creatures.

'Hello, Mum,' Bella greeted her. 'I don't think you've met Nigel.'

The young man in the chair insisted on sitting up and shaking her hand with the formal good manners of a retired general, before submitting once again to the needle.

'He's having a koi carp in a pond of waves that will stretch round his whole body.'

Laura wasn't quite sure how to handle this unexpected social situation. 'Goodness. That sounds painful.'

'He was going to have Wallace and Gromit but Stan here says they're passé. So he's opted for something a bit more New School.'

'Right. I love Wallace and Gromit, but I can see they're a bit babyish.'

'*Babyish?*' Nigel repeated in hurt tones. 'Classic, more like, but Stan says this is more cutting edge.'

'I think I might wait in the car, if you don't mind,' Laura excused herself. 'I'm not that keen on needles.'

'Neither am I,' agreed Nigel cheerfully. 'I have to look away when I'm having a blood test.'

Walking along the street, Laura tried not to think what he might be needing a blood test for, and wondered how her generation had done it. Had their own refusal to accept they were ageing themselves, waiting till they were in their thirties or later to settle down and have a family, meant that they produced offspring who, despite being in their twenties, still seemed like children themselves, needing lifts and wanting cartoon tattoos?

When Bella finally emerged, she was alone, which was a source of considerable relief. Although, Laura was forced to admit, it may have been the arrival of Nigel on the scene that had improved Bella's mood.

'All OK?'

'Yes. He's done the fish and is making a start on the waves. Thanks for the lift.'

'That's fine. Actually, I've got a favour to ask of you in return.'

'Oh?' The sullen tone was making a comeback.

'It's Dad's and my silver wedding anniversary on Saturday.'

'Bloody hell. That sounds a bit dinner-dance.'

'Actually,' Laura couldn't stop herself smiling conspiratorially, 'I've planned a surprise.'

'Ah. Is that a good idea?'

'Of course it is. It's not some big party where we jump out of the broom cupboard. It's just for Dad and me.'

'Just as well. You know Dad hates surprises.'

'Only the embarrassing kind.' Laura was starting to feel irritated. Bella could at least enter into the spirit a bit. 'I've booked us a night away.'

'Oh.' Bella visibly cheered, no doubt planning how she could fill the house with Goths.

'There is one other thing. To make the surprise work, Dad and I need to leave London on Friday afternoon. Could you make an arrangement to meet him for coffee in the Starbucks outside his office? I'll turn up and whisk him off instead.'

'But what am I going to tell him that will make him come?'

'I'm sure you can think of something.'

'I'm sure I can.' Bella grinned.

Laura marvelled, as she often did, at Bella's astonishing competence, so at odds with her outlandish appearance. Bella, she knew, could be trusted to play her part with quiet efficiency.

When the landline phone rang in Ella's house it was increasingly unusual, not because she was a poor, sad, lonely person, but because no one seemed to use landlines any more. Ella herself preferred talking on them, partly because she was convinced it was cheaper but also because the person on the other end didn't start breaking up in an irritating way. But when a friend told her that only Ella and her mother ever called on the landline even Ella considered abandoning it.

So she was doubly surprised to hear Cory pick up the phone and to learn that the caller was her other daughter, Julia.

She was about to rush up and say, 'For God's sake don't mention the burglary', but it was too late.

'Did you hear that Mum got burgled the night before last?' Bugger. 'No, nothing taken. Mum's ancient Nokia was somehow overlooked. Three lots of police came. One of them was quite cool.' She turned to Ella. 'Mum, Jules wants to come straight over.'

Ella picked up her handbag. 'I've got to go out, tell her.'

Her mother's unusual attire of jeans, old sweater and wellies caught Cory's eye at this point. 'What *are* you wearing? You never wear jeans.'

'I'm allotment-sitting. I told you, remember?'

She disappeared before she could be interrogated further. 'The code for the alarm is two eight one zero. Don't forget it or the whole bloody thing will go off and the cool policeman will appear.'

'That's a thought. I'm leaving anyway. Going back to my flat.' She hesitated. 'Unless you need someone to stay with you?'

'Absolutely not.' Ella imagined Julia, with her husband Neil and the boys all moving in to offer her unsolicited masculine protection. 'I'll be fine. I've got Mr Banham.'

'Who the hell is Mr Banham?'

'The burglar alarm.'

'You're not giving the burglar alarm a name?' She gave

her mother a long look. The kind of look daughters give to mothers they suspect of incipient dementia. 'You're sure you didn't leave the key in the door the other night? Mr Banham indeed . . .'

'It's a joke!' Ella ignored Cory's question and moved swiftly on. 'Of course I'm not giving the alarm a name.'

Ella shut the front door, relieved to have headed Cory off, and went to look for the Union Allotments.

In the end she was grateful the allotments had a postcode because they were extremely hard to find. But that only added to their blissful peace, hidden away from concerned daughters and sons-in-law. You could easily walk or drive past without knowing they were there.

They comprised forty narrow strips of land, tucked away between a gasometer and two abandoned kilns. But it was the frontage that was spectacular, running along the Grand Union Canal right bang where it met up with the misty beauty of the River Thames. Ella was amazed they hadn't been winkled out by some developer desperate to transform the site into expensive riverside apartments.

She turned the key Viv had given her in the padlock and slipped in feeling faintly guilty, as if someone would appear and accuse her of being the kind of person who bought all their veg, clean and identikit with no unsightly lumps or bumps, from a wicked supermarket chain. All of which was true. Ella couldn't see the point of wanting potatoes covered in mud when you could buy them ready-washed.

The next thing she noticed about the Union Allotments was how tidy and well-kept they were, especially by contrast to the neighbouring estate, whose gardens were full of over-flowing dustbins, discarded car parts and no-longer-wanted furniture.

Here nature ran its course in ordered discipline. Neat rows

of leeks, carrots and spring onions delighted the eye next to lavish tunnels of runner beans, their flowers finished for the year, and the last few pillar-box-bright tomatoes on their straggling plants. Orange pumpkins and bright green cabbages vied with tawny or green winter squash. Stripy marrows and glossy courgettes filled the raised beds made of old railway sleepers. Tempting russet apples and a few last pears in espaliered trees lined the far wall. The only sign of the unruly intrusion of the non-allotment classes was in the form of an abandoned car, so buried in brambles that it looked like something from *Sleeping Beauty* waiting for a wake-up kiss from Lewis Hamilton.

A faint odour of manure hung in the air, reminding Ella of visits to pongy city farms with the girls when they were small.

'Can I help you?' a gruff voice penetrated her rural reverie.

She turned to find a bearded figure in overalls and gum boots with copious grey hair topped with a bobble hat. 'I was looking for the Taylors' allotment. I'm taking care of it while they're away diving in Mexico.'

The newcomer grunted in what sounded like disapproval though whether it was for her, Viv and Angelo, scuba diving or Mexico it was hard to discern. He didn't look LGBT or whatever the acronym was. More Campaign for Real Ale. She knew if the girls were here they would censor such thoughts, but, hey, they weren't.

'It's this one over here.'

He pointed to a well-kept strip with vegetables one end, then a flowerbed in which a few late roses nodded in the breeze, next to a last hollyhock and some orange and purple blooms. Ella, not much of a plant-spotter, decided they were chrysanthemums. At the far end by the river was an ornate bench made of iron and wood. No doubt this was where Viv and Angelo admired their plot with a glass of wine in hand.

'Isn't it pretty!' Ella exclaimed. 'What glorious chrysanths!'

'Dahlias,' her guide corrected disdainfully. 'We don't hold with flowers here. Allotments are for produce if you ask me. Gardens are for flowers.'

'But what if you don't have a garden?' She held out her hand to make peace. 'I'm Ella by the way.'

He raised a bushy eyebrow. 'Bill. How-de-do.'

Ella wondered if there was a Ben too. There she was back to the LGBT again.

'I'll just do a bit of weeding, then,' Ella offered.

Bill continued to stare at the allotment, disapproval apparent in his every feature. 'We're not sure about your friends, see.'

Oh dear, not reds under the flowerbed, surely? Ella wondered.

'We suspect they may be chemical users.'

Ella tried not to giggle. Angelo looked like an old hippie who might be into nefarious substances.

'Only the ladies next door are seriously organic.'

Ella couldn't wait to see what seriously organic ladies looked like.

She got out the secateurs from her shoulder bag and began her allotted task of deadheading and tidying. This led to a little weeding and watering, and then to gathering the last few windfalls from the espaliered apple and pear trees. It was all surprisingly absorbing and in no time she saw it was getting dark. She must have been here for more than two hours.

'Cheer-o, then,' Bill's bobble hat appeared from behind the fruit canes, followed by the rest of him, festooned in fresh veg and carrying an enormous marrow. 'I'm off now. You'll lock up, will you?'

'Absolutely. I won't be long myself.' In case he thought that sounded like an invitation for him to wait for her, she started to assemble her tools. 'I might as well leave these in the shed.

No point carrying them to and from the allotments every time I visit.'

'That's right. Sound little shed that. Some of them are left in a terrible state, I can tell you. You won't believe it, but he's only got an Italian coffee machine in there.' Bill shook his head at the strangeness of middle-class peculiarities. 'Keeps offering us espresso. What's wrong with tea, I'd like to know?'

Ella nodded sympathetically, thinking she wouldn't mind an espresso herself.

The last rays of the evening sun were dipping into the Grand Union Canal and the interior of the shed was growing darker by the moment. It smelled wonderful, of drying onions and herbs tied up with string, and there was just a hint of the scent she remembered from her childhood of apples being stored over the winter, each wrapped up individually in news-paper.

She was about to put her trowel down on the potting bench when she thought she heard a slight movement and almost screamed. Oh my God, there was an animal in here! A rat, perhaps, or maybe a hedgehog. That was bloody stupid, she told herself; she hadn't seen a hedgehog in London for thirty years.

There it was again. A faint rustling in the darkest corner of the shed, behind the makeshift shelving where Viv and Angelo stored their flowerpots. Now the shelves seemed to be moving, as if someone was pushing them out of the way. This time Ella did scream.

'I am sorry,' said a disembodied voice, clearly foreign, 'I did not mean to frighten you.'

At that moment Ella's hand, which had been scrabbling for the door handle, came across a light switch. Of course, they'd need power here for the espresso machine. Without even knowing she was doing it she switched it on.

In the harsh light of a sixty-watt bulb a young man stood before her. And not just any young man, but the most dazzlingly good-looking young man she had ever laid eyes on. He wore a dark green sweater with holes in it, very like the one of Laurence's which she was wearing herself. He had longish curly dark hair, two or three days' stubble on his chin, and the most extraordinary blue-green eyes which, were they featured on a paint chart, might well be called teal.

Behind him on the floor she noticed a sleeping bag, a backpack with clothes spewing out and a half-drunk bottle of milk. 'You broke in?' she demanded, suddenly angry on behalf of her friends.

'It was not locked.' It was true there were no windows broken or other signs of forcible entry. 'I had been walking along canal. This place look warm and dry.' He grinned ruefully. 'I saw coffee machine.'

'And you thought you'd take it?'

'No, I thought at least here I can sleep and make coffee.'

'But why did you sleep here at all?' She could hear Julia's voice asking a question in her head. *What the hell were you thinking of, making conversation? The man could have robbed you or hurt you.*

'I had quarrel with my girlfriend. She chuck me out. I have not been in London long. I had nowhere to go.'

'Where do you come from?'

'I am Polish. From Warsaw. My name is Wenceslaus.'

Despite Julia's voice, Ella found herself smiling.

The young man smiled back. 'You are thinking of Good King Wenceslaus?'

'Your English is very impressive.'

He grinned. 'No. Everyone say it to me, first thing, so I google it:

Good King Wenceslaus looked out
On the feast of Stephen
When the snow lay round about
Deep and crisp and . . .'

'Even. It rhymes with Stephen,' Ella supplied.

'Of course.'

'Do you have a job? How are you living?'

'I will get building job. It is not so hard, I think.'

Ella thought of all the exhausted East European builders with their big boots and grey faces falling asleep on the tube. This young man didn't seem at all like them. When she was first in London it used to be the Irish, collectively called The Lump, made up of quite old men, who stood waiting in sad little groups at the side of the street to be picked up and taken to work digging roads; they were cheaper than using heavy machinery. A sudden sense of the unfairness of it, the accident of where you were born and how strong your economy was, overwhelmed her. Laurence used to shout at the radio whenever Tory politicians complained about scroungers and layabouts.

'You are smiling. It is good. Like sun coming out.'

'I was thinking about my husband.'

'Then he must be nice man.'

'Was a nice man. Yes. He died three years ago.'

'I am sorry. I did not mean to—'

'I know.' Ella suddenly realized quite how mad this was, having a conversation about Laurence with someone who had broken into her neighbours' shed. 'Look, do you have any money?'

Wenceslaus stiffened, his whole demeanour suddenly rigid. 'If I can sleep here tonight, tomorrow I will get job, no need for money.'

'Have you at least eaten?'

His silence answered her question.

'Look, I passed a greasy spoon down by the towpath. Let's get a bite for you there.'

He hesitated, then shrugged gratefully. 'What is greasy spoon?'

'You'll soon learn, if you're a builder. A cheap café where they fry everything.'

He picked up an old parka from a hook nailed into the wall.

Ella grinned. 'I don't suppose we need to lock up the shed.'

Wenceslaus took the key from her hand and locked it up. 'We do not want other builder moving in.' He laughed again. 'Perhaps they read review on TripAdvisor.'

The café was just closing. A grumpy waitress approached them to point this out, then took one look at Ella's companion and offered a menu instead. 'Better be quick. We're supposed to have closed ten minutes ago.'

Wenceslaus gave the woman a dazzling smile. 'What would you recommend?'

'I'd avoid the lobster and the steak tartare.' She winked. 'How about the bacon sarnie? It's the chef's special.'

'That would be great,' Ella replied on his behalf. 'And one for me, and two teas. You're going to have to learn to drink tea if you're a builder.'

An enormous black and white cat emerged from the passageway that ran back to the kitchen and made a beeline for Wenceslaus. Despite its huge bulk it managed to wrap itself sinuously round his legs, purring noisily.

'I see old Benjy's taken a fancy to you,' commented the waitress as she brought their teas.

'Animals like me.' Wenceslaus shrugged, stroking the blissed-out Benjy.

Ella and the waitress exchanged a speaking look.

It took him so short a time to wolf down the sandwich that Ella gave him half hers.

'I am very grateful. I will return money when I get job.'

'There's no need.' She watched him demolish her half in record time.

'So where were you chucked out of? By your girlfriend?'

'Minka lives in High Street. Above hairdresser. I think she wishes I had stayed in Warsaw. She has new boyfriend. He owns hairdressing shop. I think he is not a very clever man.'

'Why not?'

'He calls salon Split Endz.'

'You may be right.'

Outside the café Ella held out her hand to say goodbye.

'Thank you so much again. You could have called police and I get criminal record. After that no job possible.'

'That's OK. But you'll have to leave tomorrow. If one of the other allotment holders finds you, they certainly will call the police. Especially Bill. Big man in a woolly hat. Don't let him see you. Goodbye and good luck.'

As she walked back towards the tube Ella asked herself if she were completely mad. She'd been burgled only a few nights ago and here she was giving the OK to a complete stranger who'd taken possession of her friends' shed. Maybe he would run off with the lawn mower, but she didn't think so.

And what's more, she was pretty sure Laurence would have done exactly the same thing.

CHAPTER 4

Claudia finished her marking and inputted the results via the hideously complicated software they had to use to assess students' progress. *Bloody hell,* she couldn't help thinking, *this takes twice as long as in the old days.*

Was she just being a whingeing dinosaur? She thought of Peter Dooley and how he loved to show off about how wonderful all this stuff was. Did she want to stay on and fight him? She thought for a moment of Thierry and those heady days in Paris. You wouldn't approve of me throwing in the towel, would you, Thierry? She wondered for a moment what had become of him. She hoped he hadn't become a banker.

Claudia came to a decision. She wasn't going to let Dooley win hands down. Already he'd insinuated himself into her year group. Next it would the French exchange. The next day, as soon as assembly was over, she sought out the deputy head.

'Sonia, could I have a word?'

'Claudia,' the deputy head responded, 'the very person I wanted to see. It's about the French exchange. Mr Dooley has made some exciting suggestions.'

Claudia bristled. 'Our French exchange is the envy of all the schools in the area . . .' she began, trying to keep her hostility under control.

'Indeed it is,' replied Sonia, with an air of indulging a difficult child. 'Which is why Peter has come up with some ideas to make it even better. As I'm sure you'll concede, it takes a while for the shyer pupils to get to know each other.'

'It's a lot better now they all have Facebook.' Claudia was impressed with her savvy in knowing this, though it was actually Gaby who had told her. 'They get into contact long before they go to France.'

'And what about the teachers? Do you go on Facebook to talk to your equivalent at the Lycée?'

'I'm not on Facebook.'

'Well, no matter. Mr Dooley suggests pupils and teachers all get to know each other. Via Skype.'

Claudia said nothing. She'd never Skyped or whatever the bloody verb was.

'You do know what Skype is?' Sonia asked kindly.

'Yes, Sonia, I do know what Skype is.'

'Unfortunately, the Lycée still needs a bit of persuasion. Rather set in their ways, the French. So Mr Dooley is going to Paris this weekend with two of the pupils to set the whole thing up. You know what a techno-whizz he is. Then on Monday morning teachers and pupils can talk to each other face to face. Isn't it exciting?'

'But Sonia,' Claudia asked in a suitably puzzled tone, 'I thought the whole point of Skype was that it saved you the trouble and expense of actually *meeting* the people you were making contact with?'

The deputy head shuffled her papers. 'Yes, well, I'm sure this is a one-off. Can you be in my office at nine on Monday?'

The rest of the week whizzed by as it always seemed to after half-term. Claudia even got Gaby to give her a demo of how to use Skype so that she didn't make a complete idiot of herself.

On Monday morning, Claudia was amazed to find not just

the deputy head, but also Stephen the head teacher and a number of other heads of department gathered to see the famous demo. Tim Miller, Head of Physics, and one of Claudia's mates, caught her eye. 'Ready to witness the future of teaching, are you, Claudia?' he asked in a low voice. He disliked Drooly Dooley as much as she did. 'Soon we won't have to turn up at all.'

With her usual officiousness Sonia decided that she would make contact with Peter Dooley rather than leave it to Claudia.

She clicked on the screen. 'Hello,' she spoke slowly and loudly, just like an old person, thought Claudia with amusement, 'or rather, should I say, *Bonjour*? How are things your end?'

To the surprise of the assembled teachers it wasn't Peter Dooley but one of the pupils who appeared on the screen. 'Hello, Miss Robertson? It's Emma Wilson from Year 13. Not so good, I'm afraid. Mr Dooley's not here.'

'Not there?' the deputy head almost screeched. 'Then where the hell, I mean where on earth, is he?'

Muffled giggles greeted the question. 'He went out all night with the teachers from the Lycée. He *says* he ate a bad oyster.' More giggles in the background. 'But Ben from Mrs Warren's set says you shouldn't mix beer and red wine.'

'Thank you, Emma,' cut in the deputy head. 'Ask him to call me when he's feeling better.'

Emma's face disappeared from the screen.

'Well, that was successful,' commented Tim Miller, catching Claudia's eye. 'I might take my year group to Skype from the Large Hadron Collider.'

When she got home that night, eager to share the description of Drooly Dooley's disgrace, Don was nowhere to be seen. Only the sound of blues music playing on the kitchen radio told her he was home.

A movement from upstairs alerted her that he must be using the computer in Gaby's room. How strange. He normally used his laptop at the kitchen table. She poured them both a glass of wine and took his up as a peace offering.

He jumped when she came into the room.

'I brought you a glass of wine. To say sorry for being so snappish earlier. What's that you're looking at?'

Don was attempting to turn off the computer before she could get a look at what was on the screen. There was a kind of angry defensiveness in the gesture which was unusual for him. Don was usually a sunny-natured dreamer, blessed with a natural, if sometimes infuriating, optimism. *Hopeless*, her mother would occasionally comment. *He'll never get anywhere because he's completely without ambition. Your father was the same.*

At which point Claudia, irritated herself, would find herself 100 per cent behind her husband.

'What on earth are you looking at?' she asked, surprised. He certainly wasn't the type to conceal things from his wife. *Oh God, not Internet porn!* She suddenly panicked. One of the teachers at school had a husband who stayed up all night watching Italian housewives impaling themselves on everything from the plumber to a photogenic Alsatian. It wasn't a joke, the woman had insisted tearfully, in fact, it was wrecking their marriage.

'Nothing,' Don insisted, looking guilty as hell. 'Just checking a work document.'

Claudia knew her husband well enough to tell at once that he was lying.

'No you weren't. You only look at work stuff on your laptop.' His uncomfortable expression endorsed this. If Don was going to start lying he needed to go to evening classes in how to carry it off. 'What was it you were looking at?'

Don shifted unhappily. He wasn't a natural deceiver. In fact, Claudia had often thought, if he was having an affair, she wouldn't need lipstick on his collar or tell-tale Amex statements to find out; he'd probably own up after the first furtive grope.

'If you must know, I was looking at houses. In Surrey.' He turned the screen back on and clicked on the file he'd saved. It was of an idyllic country scene, the kind that could promote Olde Englande anywhere in the globe. 'Minsley Wood. Delightful little place, shop and pub, village green, ten minutes from Minsley station which has a long-stay car park, on the main line into Victoria.'

Claudia was stunned. It was always she who took the practical initiative in their marriage. She made the decisions and Don, smiling vaguely, stepped into line. She wasn't at all sure about this new dynamic Don, especially since he knew her feelings perfectly well. 'My, you have been busy.'

'There's a Victorian cottage for sale, four beds, room for grandchildren, if we ever get any, four hundred and fifty grand. We could sell this place for nine-fifty, according to the agent . . .'

'Excuse me,' Claudia couldn't believe her ears, 'what the hell do you mean, *according to the agent*? Are you telling me you've actually had an agent round without telling me?' This was getting out of hand.

Don looked mutinous, as if he were dealing with a class that had gone too far this time and he was about to put the whole bloody lot of them in detention. 'Don't give me that look. I've hardly sold the place under your feet.'

'Fortunately, you can't, since we own it jointly, but clearly you'd quite like to.'

'I just wanted to know what it was worth, that was all.'

'And he said nine hundred and fifty thousand?' Despite her irritation Claudia was amazed, though she wasn't going to let Don see it. They'd only paid £45,000 for the house when they'd moved here as young marrieds. Admittedly, that was more years ago than she cared to remember. £950,000! No wonder the younger generation couldn't afford to get a foot on the housing ladder.

Claudia glanced round at the home they'd shared all these years. It was nothing special. *She* loved it, of course, but it was a perfectly ordinary Victorian terraced house with a tiled open fireplace, double sitting room (it had been front room and parlour when they moved in but, like all middle-class families, they'd knocked it into what agents loved to call 'a through lounge'), basement kitchen, four bedrooms (they'd turned a box room into the mandatory en-suite bathroom) and a long narrow garden at the back. It was like countless other London houses, all of which had suddenly rendered their owners millionaires simply due to the lack of suitable housing stock and the city's sudden global desirability.

'There is one small fly in the ointment of your Surrey fantasy,' Claudia pointed out acidly. 'As I told you, I don't happen to want to live there!'

It was at that moment, of all moments, that the phone rang. Since it was the landline, neither rushed to answer it. It was probably an irritating call saying they'd won something in a contest they hadn't entered. The phone rang five times then switched to the answering machine.

Her mother's voice, an edge of distress sharpening its already cut-glass pronunciation, rang out through the sitting room. 'Claudia, dear, please call as soon as you can. It's your father. He's had an accident.'

Sal, still stunned by her new condition of unemployment, decided to splurge out on a cappuccino and a croissant in the café at the end of her road. She had a notebook with her and had set her phone to calculator. It was time to face some hard facts.

The figures of her outgoings were so large she had to add them up twice. Rent, lighting and heating seemed ludicrously expensive, especially as she was hardly ever in. People might call things like that the basics but to her the basics were a monthly cut and colour, with nails if possible, wine rather than milk in the fridge, mood-altering handbags, the occasional taxi, a few fashion purchases each season, and going out with her girlfriends. Listening to them drone on about how a child cost you a quarter of a million, she'd always been rather relieved that she didn't have any.

Sitting outside the café, with no job to go to and no prospect of one, Sal felt more than the chill wind of autumn. She felt scared. Actually scared. It was such an unfamiliar emotion that she didn't recognize it at first and thought that maybe she was sickening for something. Then she realized. It was fear that was making her shiver. Fear of not having the strength to go on fighting in the workplace, battling for jobs against women half her age, pretending to be young when actually she felt like admitting her bones ached sometimes, her neck looked like a turkey's and she had started fantasizing about going to bed early.

The truth was she was getting old.

Sixty-three was the kind of age your grandma had always seemed to be, though she had probably been twenty years younger. The kind of age young people couldn't even imagine. And all her icons were even older. Bob Dylan, Paul Simon and Mick Jagger were all still singing for their suppers in their seventies, and lovely Leonard Cohen could probably give them almost a decade, and no one was laughing at them. A thought struck Sal forcibly.

They were all men.

In the past when she'd found herself suddenly unemployed, and in her long career that had happened more than once, she had simply got on the phone and told everyone useful that she was available. It had been her mantra that for every ten calls you made, one might lead to something useful. But at her stage – and let's face it, age – to do that might shriek of desperation.

The answer was a bit of selective targeting. She sent an email to the twenty or so people she knew well enough to approach without losing face and decided to concentrate on them. Over the next few days one or two came back to say that they'd bear her in mind, but from most there was a yawning – and in her view extremely ill-mannered – silence.

One contact had heard of a job in Public Relations she might like to follow up on. The trouble was, Sal had always loathed publicists. Still, sixty-year-old beggars couldn't be choosers. The job, it turned out, was with a luxury holiday company.

Sal smiled. If there was one topic dear to her heart it was luxury holidays, though she had to admit most of the holidays she'd been on were five-star freebies provided by the very kind of company that wanted a PR. Still, surely that would make her doubly suitable? With that in mind she called Oakmore Holidays and Resorts and asked to speak to HR.

The young woman who answered sounded slightly surprised to hear from her and said that the application was being made online.

'Right.' Sal thanked her, realizing how long it had been since she'd actually applied for a job. Certainly before it was done online.

Never mind. She downloaded the application form at once. Bugger, it was one of those box-ticking, multiple-answer efforts which gave you no opportunity to bullshit – sorry, sell yourself – positively.

Sal found she was actually dreading the box marked date

of birth. But of course the anti-discrimination law meant they couldn't ask you that any more. Phew.

Hang on, now it was asking the dates of her education! Surely that was a sneaky way of finding out how old she was?

Strengths and weaknesses? Oh, bloody hell, this was the kind of thing she was used to asking other people, not having to answer herself. *Why Do You Want This Job?* Because I've got bills to pay and I'm desperate!

Why us? I'd like to give something back for all those wonderful freebies you've given me.

If you were stranded on a desert island what two things would you want to take? Oh, for God's sake, that's obvious, my sarong and Ray-Bans. Obviously.

And here it was, in the very last section, pretending to be for monitoring purposes only, they were asking her age!

Surely they couldn't ask that? She was going to have to find out if she had to fill that in. Claudia! Claudia would help, Claudia still had at least one foot in the workplace.

But Claudia sounded deeply stressed and not at all Claudia-like when she answered Sal's call.

'What a nuisance about the job and I'd love to help, but I can't. I've got to go to Surrey. My dad has fallen downstairs and probably fractured his hip. Don is delighted.'

'Why would Don be delighted?' Sal was mystified by this strange assertion about Claudia's nice but dull husband. 'He's such a sweet man.'

'You'd think so, wouldn't you? He turns out to be more devious than Machiavelli. I'll tell you all about it when I see you.' And then, through gritted teeth, 'I'm hoping not to be long. Unless Don has his way. Mafia bosses aren't called Don for nothing, let me tell you.'

Sal listened, flummoxed. What was Claudia on about?

'Sorry, got to rush. I need to get to the hospital. Tell you what, try Ella. Employment was her speciality when she was a lawyer.'

Actually, that was a brilliant idea. Ella was always so modest about her achievements, unlike Sal herself, that you forgot what a powerhouse she'd been.

She would call her straight away.

Ella sat bolt upright in bed, every nerve suddenly alert. What was that noise? Often there would be the strange other-worldly sound, halfway between a howl and a bark, of foxes fighting, a cry so strange that one' guest came to ask if it could be a werewolf. There were also occasional owls calling to each other in the cemetery of Old Moulsford church a quarter of a mile away. But this wasn't a natural sound, more of a crash, like a window breaking. Then she remembered the alarm. If it had been the window, the alarm would have gone off. With another flash of terror she realized that the security lights had gone on in the garden under the huge cedar tree.

It was probably just a neighbour's cat on a midnight assignation.

For God's sake, Ella, pull yourself together! This wasn't like her. When the house had been broken into, she hadn't felt frightened at all and now she was crumbling like a three-year-old on Bonfire Night.

Should she go downstairs? When you heard a noise your first instinct was to investigate, yet surely if there was a burglar that would be the most stupid thing to do when you were alone, as she was?

Really, if she went on like this, her daughter Julia would be right. She was getting too old to stay in her beloved house. With a supreme effort Ella forced herself to put her head under the duvet and to try to go to sleep.

When she woke early the next morning she was relieved

to find there was no sign of a break-in. She made herself a cup of tea and took it back to bed.

An idea had just come to her and she wanted to give it some serious consideration.

She thought about it all the time she was drinking her tea, then during her shower, and while she got dressed and put on her make-up.

By the time she came downstairs she'd made up her mind. Half an hour later she was driving along the High Street.

Split Endz was a smart minimalist-looking shopfront next to an unprepossessing minimarket. A tall blonde Valkyrie, dressed in an eye-popping embellished velvet dress, was opening the shutters.

'You wouldn't be Minka, by any chance?'

'Sure.' The Valkyrie smiled. 'Are you wanting appointment?'

Ella wondered all at once what the hell she did want. 'No, actually, it's about your friend Wenceslaus.'

'He not in trouble?'

'No. Not at all.'

'Good. I surprised if he in trouble. He is very nice boy.'

'But not nice enough to live with you? He told me you had chucked him out.'

Minka laughed, completely without embarrassment. 'Would you like coffee? Shop not opening for fifteen minutes. We talk inside.'

With the supreme confidence of a gorgeous young woman used to getting her own way, Minka held open the salon door.

Inside, despite the fact that Split Endz was at the seedier end of the High Street, the place was both beautifully decorated and immaculate. It could have been one of those big-name Mayfair salons that charged you £200 to get in the front door. Minka took in Ella's admiring glance. 'You should have seen before. Red plastic benches, lino on floor, smell of cat. Clients all – how you say it – OAPs wanting half-price perm on pension day. I bring in Polish builders, bish, bash, bosh, done one weekend. All my own design.'

Ella could see at once what kind of woman Minka was. The type was universal. Underneath the high heels and clingy dress she could have run a multinational company, an NGO or a school governing board.

'You want to talk about Wenceslaus. He is good-looking boy but his taste is too simple for me. I like going out. He like staying in. I like vodka. He prefer Coca-Cola. You see problem.'

'Would you give him a reference?'

'For job?'

'Not exactly.'

'As lover?'

'Definitely not!' Ella found herself blushing like a traffic light stuck on red.

'He is nice boy. Kind. Likes animals. Not interested in money. Not my type.' A gunmetal Porsche drew up and a rather portly, balding middle-aged man dressed in black cashmere got out. Minka grinned and indicated him. 'This my type. I am sure Wenceslaus get you references if you want. One thing,' she grinned suddenly, 'in case you think me hard Polish bitch because I tell Wenceslaus not to come here.' She winked at Ella. 'We keep half-price OAP customers.'

Ella laughed, thinking how much the OAPs would enjoy the improved surroundings. It was impossible not to like Minka, even after five minutes' acquaintance. 'Well, thank you very much. You've been very helpful.'

She was still wondering whether to go ahead with her admittedly bold scheme when she arrived at the allotments. To her horror she found a small crowd had gathered there plus a police car with its light flashing.

'Now see here,' she could hear Bill insisting, his bobble hat nodding up and down in indignation, 'this here illegal immigrant broke into our allotments and made himself at home in one of our member's sheds. He should be bloody deported.'

'Actually, sir,' Wenceslaus was trying to explain, his calm tones infuriating Bill even further, 'not illegal immigrant. I Polish. Poland now part of European Union.'

'I don't care if it's part of bloody Disneyworld, you've no right to break into that shed.'

'As a matter of fact, Bill,' Ella tried to pacify him, 'I said he could. Just for the night.'

'But it's against regulations! No one's allowed to sleep in the sheds. Not even the allotment holders!'

'If it's any help,' the community policewoman interrupted, clearly smitten by Wenceslaus' good looks. 'There's a homeless hostel down the road. If you wanted a lift—'

'Aren't you even going to arrest him?' Bill demanded. 'You should be sending him home. He'll be after my job next.'

'Actually, Bill,' Ella said gently, 'he's got every right to be here. And to work as well.'

'And how do you know so bloody much about it?'

'I'm an employment lawyer.' This was a slight exaggeration as she'd stopped working but Bill wasn't to know that.

Bill looked at her as if she'd pulled an unfair advantage. 'Bloody hell. I don't know. What did we fight a sodding war for?'

'To stop Hitler. And lots of Poles fought with us. On our side.'

Bill seemed much struck by this.

'Everybody happy then?' asked the community officer, a graduate in politics. 'Feel like renegotiating the Treaty of Rome while you're about it?'

Ella laughed.

'What's she on about?' Bill asked.

'Just making a little Euro-joke.'

'There you go,' Bill protested. 'It'll be the British sense of humour that'll go next. They'll probably ban Benny Hill.'

'*Ernie*,' interjected Wenceslaus unexpectedly.

'Come again?' Bill demanded.

'*Ernie*,' Wenceslaus repeated, straight-faced. '*He drove the fastest milk cart in the West*. I see on old TV clips on YouTube.'

Bill's face broke into a broad smile. 'Hey, Les, Stevie,' he called to two of his fellow allotment holders. 'Make this young man a cup of tea. He's only a fan of Benny Hill.'

'Actually,' Ella grabbed Wenceslaus before he was spirited away to discover the joys of builder's tea laced with Carnation, 'I need to have a chat with Wenceslaus myself.'

When she drove home an hour later Ella was surprised to find Julia's pretentious four by four parked in the space she usually parked in herself.

Both her daughters had keys and occasionally dropped round without warning. Cory was the more usual visitor, since she lived alone and sometimes came for a weekend, enjoying the semi-rural feel of Old Moulsford.

She could hear laughter coming from the basement kitchen. How nice to have the girls back. And how unusual that they were both together. Cory and Julia had a spiky relationship that had started in early childhood and persisted into the present time. She knew they loved each other really and would, if the chips were down, drop everything, as they would for her. But when there wasn't a crisis they seemed to inhabit different planets. Even their dress sense was wildly at odds, Julia favouring flowery skirts and pretty cardigans while Cory wore edgy designs in black or grey. The funny thing was, as Cory often pointed out, while Julia festooned herself and her house with flowery prints, she was totally uninterested in nature and had even covered her garden with easy-care decking. Cory, on the other hand, loved the outdoors and often went for long hikes.

Which made it all the odder that they were here together.

'Mum, there you are.' Cory unwound her long legs from the stool at the breakfast bar and jumped down. 'We were beginning to wonder if you'd been kidnapped. The burglar alarm wasn't even on when we came in.'

'Oh God, I forgot.' She'd been so full of her plans this morning it hadn't occurred to her. 'Don't worry, I always put it on at night.'

Was she imagining it, or did this statement elicit an 'I told you so' kind of glance from Julia to her sister?

'The thing is, Mum,' Julia began briskly. 'Cory and I—'

'Less of the Cory, Jules, this is all you and Neil.'

'. . . are really concerned about you after the break-in.'

'Thank you,' Ella decided to be even brisker. 'But there's really no need. As you see, I have the burglar alarm . . .'

'Which you don't even put on,' Julia pointed out.

'Which I always put on at night,' Ella replied firmly, kicking herself for having left it off.

'The thing is, Neil and Cory and I think you should be planning ahead, thinking of the next stage of your life when you might be a bit frailer. You may live for another thirty years . . .'

'I hope I do.' Ella bristled, getting more suspicious by the moment.

'And if you do, you'll probably need care, and to live in a way that suits you, not rattling around in this vast house.'

'I thought we'd get to the house sooner or later. And can I remind you, Julia, how much I love this place, how unique and amazing it is?'

'But the cost of running it—'

'As you know,' interrupted Ella, 'I lost your father, and I got considerable compensation, the one small advantage in what was the most terrible time of my – and all our – lives, so that I could stay on here in the house I loved.'

'But the future, Mum. Neil says the property market's never been higher and besides, it would be so tax-efficient if you made early provision.'

'By which you mean death duties. But that means seven years before I die, darling. I thought you believed I might live another thirty?'

Julia had the sense to look a bit ashamed. 'It wasn't just death duties. We just thought—'

'*You* just thought,' reminded Cory. 'Leave me out of this.'

Julia ignored her. 'You'd be safer somewhere like a flat with a concierge.'

'What about sheltered housing?' Ella suggested sweetly. 'Surely that would be better still?'

'The waiting lists for that are very long. Neil looked.'

'I bet he did,' Cory flashed. 'Mum's only sixty-three, not some old biddy.'

'Or a nice care home?' Ella asked. 'Perhaps Neil thinks that would take too much out of your school-fees fund?'

'Mum, don't be ridiculous.'

'She's got a point. That's what this is all about, isn't it?' Cory intervened. 'Neil sending your boys to his alma bloody mater at twenty thousand pounds a year. Just to turn them into mini-versions of himself.'

'I don't see you offering to move in with Mum and look after her,' Julia snapped.

'This isn't a Victorian novel,' Ella cut in, 'and I don't need to ruin my daughter's life by making her fetch and carry for me. I can fetch and carry for myself.' Ella wondered for a moment if she was being selfish. Were their fears for her genuine and sensible? Was it unfair of her to go on living here when the house was so valuable and they were struggling financially? The thought struck her that she could give them some of the compensation money. It wouldn't be like selling the house, but it would be something and it would be now when they needed it.

But Julia, sensing the fight was being lost, couldn't resist one last argument. 'Neil says it's actually rather irresponsible of you to go on living here alone. After all, if something happened to you, it would be Neil and I who would need to pick up the pieces.'

Before Cory could think of an outraged answer, Ella made up her own mind about the decision she'd been turning over since yesterday. 'As a matter of fact,' she announced quietly but firmly, 'I am not going to be living on my own.'

'Oh my God, Mum,' Cory grinned, 'you haven't met someone?'

'Not in the way you're imagining, no. But I have invited a young Pole called Wenceslaus to move into the spare room upstairs. Instead of rent he will do all the tasks around the house I find so irritating, changing light bulbs, putting the rubbish out, mending things that go wrong. And, the most important thing is – and I am sure you and Neil will find this reassuring – he will give me back a sense of security.'

Even if it didn't work out with Wenceslaus, it was worth it to see the look of stunned horror on her daughter Julia's face. Ella didn't want to be unpleasant but Julia's tendency to encroach on her freedom had to be stopped before it got out of hand.

'But, Mum, what the hell do you know about this man? He could be a con artist. Eastern Europe is bursting with them, Neil says.'

It occurred to Ella that Neil should clearly meet Bill; they'd get on like a house on fire. Though, for Ella's money, she'd prefer Bill. He was an uneducated working man. Neil had been to one of the most expensive public schools in the country, plus university, and ought to know better.

Ella's instinct, on the other hand, was to believe the best in people until proved otherwise. Sometimes in her role as an employment lawyer she had encountered both criminal con artists and legitimate experts making the system work for their personal benefit. Indeed, she'd encountered such people working for the railway operator when Laurence had been killed and had eventually won compensation from them. But most people, she had discovered, wanted to be honest. And Wenceslaus, her gut feeling told her, was one of them.

And if she were wrong, no one would enjoy telling her so more than Julia and Neil.

'Well, I think it's a brilliant idea,' Cory seconded. 'After all, it's all the rage to have male au pairs to look after the kids. Why not a granny au pair for the over-sixties?'

'It would be different if it were someone you knew . . .' began Julia.

'People never know their au pairs. They advertise for them. I was just reading an article about a mother who got two thousand replies when she put an ad for one in a Hungarian newspaper.'

'Is that what you did? Advertise? You never said anything to me.'

'That's because she knew you'd discourage her,' Cory countered.

To Ella's immense relief the doorbell sounded and she remembered it would be Sal who, unusually, was coming round to ask her advice. Which meant she wouldn't have to divulge to either of them the unusual manner in which she had encountered her new lodger.

CHAPTER 5

Sal had been busy in the last few days, applying for every job that was even remotely suitable and quite a few that weren't.

And getting absolutely nowhere. Not even an interview.

'It must be my age,' Sal protested to Ella as they sat in Ella's sunny kitchen. 'There's no other explanation. I'm brilliantly qualified for all these jobs and I haven't had a single interview.'

'Let's have a look at your CV,' Ella suggested, shooing the girls out of the kitchen so they could have some peace.

Sal passed it over, feeling rather proud of all she'd achieved during her considerable career.

'Hmmm,' Ella winced. 'As a professional, I can tell you there is nothing wrong with it. It's very impressive. But between you and me, as a friend, I can tell you it'd scare me shitless. You've done so much!'

'But surely that's a good thing?'

'That depends on the job. Yes, if it's a really big job but not if it makes your potential boss feel you're more qualified than they are!'

'So you're telling me to sound *less* qualified?'

'I think you should streamline it, leave out all but the essential things that make you suitable for each job. Here's another problem: your last salary was way larger than the ones these jobs are offering.'

'So you think I should lie about that too?'

'Maybe just subtract a bit.'

'I'm not sure I'd pay for *your* advice.'

'You wouldn't get it from me officially, but I'm giving it as a friend. Getting a job's got ten times more difficult than when we were young. They really put you through hoops these days.'

At that moment, Sal's phone beeped, making her jump. Ella could see that technology wasn't exactly Sal's thing either, no matter what she claimed. 'I've got an interview! From those holiday people. That's more like it. And without slimming down my CV!'

If anyone had told Sal a few weeks ago that she'd think getting a job interview was almost a miracle, she wouldn't have believed them.

'Let's celebrate,' Ella suggested. 'I've got some cava in the fridge.'

'At midday? No wonder they're worried about the over-sixties drinker!' commented Cory, who'd come back to find her phone.

'Actually, maybe we should wait. Laura's coming round any minute. It's her wedding anniversary today and she's surprising Simon by dragging him off to Brighton to relive their first rapturous seduction. I'm looking after the cat.'

'Oh my God, she's not, is she?' Sal looked aghast.

'Why shouldn't she? I thought it was rather romantic. I'd prefer Budapest to Brighton, if it were me, but Brighton is where they first did the deed, so Brighton it is.'

'And Simon doesn't know anything about it?'

'People don't usually when it's a surprise.'

'Nightmare, more like. The thing is, I saw Simon last week in The Ivy with his tongue down the throat of a nubile work colleague.'

'Oh my God, poor Laura. Obviously, she doesn't know anything about it. What are we going to do?'

'Well, we can hardly tell her the day she's off for this romantic assignation. It'll probably come unstuck without our intervention anyway.'

'Maybe I could ring her up and tell her the cat's sick and she'll have to come home early?'

The doorbell interrupted their deliberations and there stood Laura, wreathed in happy smiles, clutching the kitty carrier.

She had always been a pretty woman, with naturally curly dark hair framing a classic oval face and large round eyes that often shone with engaging childlike enthusiasm. Today, lit up with happiness, she looked wonderful.

'God, Laura,' Sal demanded, 'how come you look about forty while the rest of us are showing every year of our age?'

'Nonsense,' Laura beamed, 'you don't look a day over sixty!'

'Thanks a lot. Remember my new philosophy – age is optional.'

'Not if you are harassed and broke and living on benefits,' Cory commented from behind them, grabbing her bag and heading off with Julia.

'No, well, that's a future I've still got to look forward to.' Sal didn't find the idea as hilariously unlikely as she once had.

'Here's TomTom.' Laura handed over a large ginger cat. 'I'm afraid he's rather randy, so if he disappears, it'll be because there's a lovely lady pussy somewhere in the region.'

'Sounds familiar.' Sal and Ella tried not to catch each other's eye.

'Before you rush, have a glass of cava. How many years is it?'

Laura blushed faintly, making her look even prettier. 'Twenty-five. I was a child bride when we married, obviously.'

'No you weren't,' Sal protested, 'you were—'

'Thirty-eight,' supplied Ella. 'As the divine Sandy Denny put it, "Who knows where the time goes?" Who knew any of us would be celebrating a silver wedding anniversary?'

They clinked their glasses.

A sudden pang overcame Ella. It would have been her thirty-third anniversary in September. The thought of it being snatched away from her made her even angrier with Simon. Why the hell did people squander love? Why couldn't they see how precious it was? Had she even seen it herself? And now here was Laura glowing with excitement when her husband was publicly betraying her. Ella jumped up and hugged her.

'I must dash,' Laura announced, looking surprised. 'Bella has arranged to meet Simon at three and I'm turning up instead.' She kissed them both. 'Wish me luck.'

'Oh, bloody hell,' Ella shook her head as they watched Laura depart, 'she's certainly going to need it. And as for you, you randy ginger tom, if you go looking for pussies you can stay out all night.'

'He's a male. He'll just call in the morning and say he slept at the office,' Sal pointed out.

'Come on, now it's opened we might as well finish that bottle. To your interview!'

They were just draining their glasses when the doorbell rang again. 'I'll go,' Sal offered. 'It's like Piccadilly Circus round here. I thought you said life was quiet since Cory left home.'

'It usually is. This is much more fun.'

Sal opened the door to find an exceptionally handsome young man on the doorstep bearing an enormous pumpkin. 'Good morning.' His manners were as good as his looks. 'Is Mrs Thompson at home?'

'She is indeed. Ella, there's someone to see you.'

'Wenceslaus! Come in.' She looked at the pumpkin.

'Goodness, that's big enough for Cinderella's coach! Is that from the allotments?'

He nodded. 'Is from Bill. Also these.' He delved into his pockets and brought out a handful of weird gnarled-looking things like a very old man's knuckles. 'Are Jerusalem artichokes. I think Bill has taken fancy to you.'

'Has he?' asked Sal. 'And who is Bill? You haven't mentioned a new beau on the scene. I hope he doesn't eat these himself. My dad used to call them fartichokes! I think you can guess why.'

She had a sudden memory of her father digging veg in their tiny garden. He'd never looked happier. It reminded her of the narrowness of her parents' world and how generous they'd been in wanting her to escape.

'I won't need warnings from your dad to keep me away from Bill, thanks all the same.'

'Ah,' Wenceslaus delved into his pockets again, 'here are references. I bring from Poland. They are very happy if you want to telephone. Everyone back home have mobile phone now,' he added with a touch of pride. 'Pumpkin is from allotment belonging to your friends. I see squirrel looking at it with bad intentions so I bring it for safe keeping.'

He waved them goodbye.

'Hmmm,' Sal eyed the departing young man with intentions at least as bad as any squirrel's, 'I wouldn't mind having him for safe keeping.'

'Sal, for goodness' sake! You are sounding like a dirty old woman.'

'There have to be some advantages to power,' Sal murmured, before remembering that she didn't have any since she'd lost her job. 'He has a very nice arse. A bit like a summer squash – or do I mean a swede – I was never very good at recognizing vegetables.'

Ella was busy reading the references. 'More important than his arse to ladies of our years, it says here he is punctual, reliable, honest, practical, good with old people . . .'

'Does it really say that?' Sal queried.

'No, I just put it in to annoy you.'

Not five minutes had passed before Sal, with what seemed indecent speed to Ella, put down her glass and announced she ought to go since she needed to prepare for her job interview.

Ella waved her off. 'And if you see a good-looking young stranger at the bus stop, remember he's young enough to be your grandson.'

Even though her instinct told her loud and clear to trust Wenceslaus, it had always been her policy to speak to referees in person.

Less than an hour later she replaced the phone, beaming. Wenceslaus had ticked all the boxes. Everyone seemed to like him, would recommend him to all their friends, found him completely trustworthy and answered in a strong affirmative to that old chestnut 'Would you hire him again?'

And there was something else he hadn't mentioned and which Ella hadn't asked about.

Wenceslaus, in the eyes of one ex-employer, was a budding Bill Gates who might well make his fortune as a computer whizz. And if this seemed unlikely in someone she'd discovered in Viv and Angelo's shed, she was eager to put him to the test.

Laura navigated her way through the Friday afternoon traffic that inched its way at a snail's pace down Regent Street. The Christmas decorations were already up. How ridiculous. Laura, who was someone who treasured every moment of Christmas, making her own wreaths and decorations, hated this commercialization that tried to string Yuletide right through from the summer holidays to the January sales.

Today she was in such a mood of excitement that she decided to see them as romantically tacky rather than over-commercialized and cheap-looking. Even the Hamleys assistant, dressed as a giant snowman trying to entice customers onto the shop floor, struck her as sweet rather than strident. And she positively beamed at the young man driving a bicycle-rickshaw as he cut her up. Just think, if she'd arrived in one of those to pick Simon up! But she could hardly have got the driver to take them all the way to Brighton, could she?

She was still laughing at the thought when she caught sight of Simon waiting on the pavement talking irritably into his mobile phone.

'Surprise!' She rolled down the window.

'Do you know where Bella's got to?' he asked, not seeming to think it at all odd that his wife should be passing. But then he'd never had much imagination. Laura told herself off for such subversive views.

'She's not coming. I am. Do you know what date it is today?' Simon looked blank.

'Only our anniversary. Our twenty-fifth! Get in the car, for goodness' sake!'

'Twenty-five years?' Simon looked stunned and shaken. There was no apology at having forgotten, she noted.

'Anyway, I have planned a surprise for us. We're going to Brighton.'

'*Brighton?* Whatever for?'

'That's where we met, remember?'

'Oh, right. Yes, yes, of course we did. That would be great, except I have a four o'clock meeting.'

'No, you don't. Elaine rescheduled it.' Simon's assistant Elaine was all in favour of wives. She was one herself. 'We are having dinner and staying the night at a boutique hotel on the seafront.'

There was a long pause when Simon seemed to be struggling with a powerful inner dialogue. 'But I haven't brought any clothes,' he came up with eventually.

'I've packed for both of us.'

After that they drove in silence through the traffic jams of Streatham, with Laura wondering with each moment that passed why she had thought Simon, who hated surprises, might like this one.

Eventually, she put on music to defuse the tension. At first, Laura attempted desultory conversation, then decided that if she left him to sulk he might come out of it on his own.

Brighton, when they finally reached it, was busy with a happy, bustling start-of-the-weekend mood which she hoped would be catching. She'd always loved the place. It had all the sophistication of London, but it just happened to be at the seaside.

Their room was lovely, and just as she had requested it had a sort of sea view.

'Not much of one,' Simon pointed out grumpily.

'Enough,' Laura insisted. 'I booked dinner for nine. It's a glorious evening. Come on, we're going for a walk.'

'I need to make some phone calls.'

'Later.' She picked up the big bag she'd had in the back of the car. 'Come on, let's go and have a drink down by the promenade.'

'It'll be busy.'

'It'll be lovely.'

Brighton's seafront was full of students and skateboarders and people walking their dogs. And lovers. Laura couldn't help noticing how some of them, even the old ones, walked along hand in hand, their steps unconsciously in time, bracketed together against the world. That was what she had hoped for in her own marriage.

The sun was just slipping behind a clear grey sea, misting the horizon with pink reflections. Above them thousands of starlings parabolaed towards their roost like yards of silk thrown into the air. Laura took Simon's hand and pulled him onto the deep swathe of shingle leading to Brighton's famous pier.

'Laura,' he asked, his voice dogged with irritation, 'where the hell are you going?'

Laura was running now, pulling him along as if he were some overgrown and ill-tempered child. 'Under the boardwalk! Don't you remember? The first time we met at that silly reunion? Somehow you got hold of a CD player, and a rug' – she pulled both these items out of her bag – 'and a bottle of terrible white wine. And we sat under the pier and you played me "Under the Boardwalk"? Well, this time I've got champagne instead of terrible white wine. And it's our twenty-fifth anniversary! How amazing is that?'

Simon followed reluctantly and sat down next to her as she opened the champagne. Laura handed him a glass and was about to make a toast.

'Laura,' he stopped her, looking out to the horizon, at the beach, anywhere but at her. 'Just don't say "to the next twenty-five years".'

Laura, who was about to say exactly that, felt as if she had been slapped. Had the last twenty-five been so bad, then?

'Let's get back to the hotel,' Simon suggested as soon as they'd finished their first glass. 'At least it'll be warm there.'

Laura, packing up the stuff, tried not to think of the last time they'd been here, how magical it had been, how romantic and spontaneous and, above all, hopeful.

In their room, the bed had been turned down and a red rose lay across the pillow. She thought for one mad moment it might have been from Simon until she read the message: 'We hope you have a very happy anniversary from all at Grey's

Hotel.' The hotel had made a gesture, no matter how corporate, while her own husband had not.

She had planned the whole thing so minutely. That they would make love before dinner, always the best time – before you had eaten and drunk too much. What was it the famous Lord Chesterfield had said? Never attempt to seduce a married woman straight after dinner, only very young ladies had the stamina after a big meal.

Once she'd had plenty of stamina and so had he.

Suddenly embarrassed, she went to take her dress off in the bathroom. The slip she wore underneath was palest pink silk, chosen with care to be more subtly alluring than black. As she applied a drop of perfume to her neck she noticed Simon's sponge bag had been put in the bathroom by the turndown staff. Laura had just shoved his toothbrush and toothpaste into it when she'd packed. Now she unzipped it and looked inside as if she might find some clue to how the happiness of the last twenty-five years had evaporated without trace.

She found the answer staring at her from a bubble pack of unfamiliar pills.

Viagra.

Laura froze. She and Simon hadn't made love for weeks and yet the pack was half empty. Which meant that whoever his enhanced staying power was intended for, it certainly wasn't for her.

In a blaze of fury she went back into the bedroom and threw the pills at him. 'So this is why you're behaving like a shit! Always distant and aloof, never listening to a word I say, giving me pained looks as if my existence offends you! You're having an affair! You complete bastard! And on our anniversary too!'

Simon looked around the bedroom and shrugged. 'Coming

here wasn't my idea.' He made no attempt to deny her accusations. If anything, he seemed relieved.

'So who is she?'

'A colleague. Her name's Suki Morrison. Look, Laura, we need to talk about this. She wants me to move in with her.'

'*To move in with her*?' Laura repeated, feeling as if she had taken a wrong turn from her own safe and familiar world and wandered into someone else's life. 'How long has it been going on?'

'About six months.'

How could Simon have been having an affair for six months and she not know? There had been the usual evenings when he was working late, of course, client meetings, awaydays spent brainstorming in country hotels, had all those been a cover? She felt suddenly stupid, used, the ever-trusting wife. There she'd been in her make-believe world of silk slips and anniversaries while all the time he'd been screwing someone else.

She should have known when he stopped wanting sex, of course, she thought guiltily. But he'd still been affectionate. And when she'd asked her friends if they were still making love, they'd often replied, 'God, no. Can't remember the last time. Months ago.'

A headline from a magazine article she'd read jumped into her mind: If He Isn't Having Sex With You He's Having It With Someone Else.

In this case, Suki.

Laura felt betrayed, defiled, and then, quite simply, angry. She who never got angry, who saw anger as dangerous and risky, who went to amazing lengths to avoid it, felt a volcanic tide of resentment boiling over.

'How could you do it? Betray me, the kids, our marriage?'

'I didn't mean to. It just happened.'

'That is such a lie. Affairs don't just happen. You make a decision, you pick up a phone, you have a drink, you go for lunch, you kiss. You can turn back at any time.'

He stood before her, granite-faced, ungiving.

'Are you in love with her?'

There was a beat of silence. She realized he wasn't sure. He had risked all this and he wasn't even sure. And suddenly she hated him for not valuing what he had, the years of love, the life she had so painstakingly created for them.

'Well, maybe you'd better go now, then.' Laura was almost shaking but she was damned if she was going to let him see it.

He looked at her, startled, nervous even. 'But what about you? And Bella and Sam?'

'Isn't it a bit late to be thinking about us?'

'Do you want me to go?'

'For Christ's sake, Simon. No, I don't want you to go. I want my family to be a family. But you'd have to give up this woman. And I'd have to believe you had. And that there wasn't going to be another Suki. Have there been any others before?'

The fractional pause before he answered told her everything.

Laura stiffened, wanting to scratch his smug seducer's face. 'I think you'd better leave. I couldn't bear to sit across a table from you. I'll bring your things back tomorrow. You can get them with the rest of your stuff.'

Was that panic in his eyes? Serve him bloody well right! She took the sparkling black dress off the back of the bathroom door where she'd hung it and put in on. 'I'm going down to dinner. It's already paid for, the kind of thing we boring wives care about.'

'Laura . . .'

She wondered if he were going to grovel. But even if he did, how could she ever trust him again?

He didn't even bother, simply accepted her decision.

'We'd better tell Bella and Sam about this together.'

He nodded miserably, but she knew he was feeling sorry for himself, not for the damage he'd done to her or to his children.

The restaurant manager wished her a happy anniversary and poured her a glass of free champagne. He blinked when she said she'd be eating alone, then cleared Simon's place away with a diplomatic smile. No doubt they were used to marital drama in Brighton.

Laura sipped her champagne and thought how it took twenty-five years to build a marriage and minutes to blow it apart. Should she have fought harder to save it?

An hour later, she was back in their empty room. She longed to pack up and go home, but Bella and Sam would be there and she would have to explain why she was back, alone, on the night of the longed-for anniversary. Tomorrow was soon enough.

What she needed was someone to talk to. Someone she could trust who would listen to her misery and help her tell if her marriage were really over.

Claudia was warm and sympathetic but happily married to the lovely Don. Sal would only say Simon had acted like all men do. She would call Ella.

Ella, of all her friends, understood loss.

Ella straightened her back which was beginning to ache. Digging was hard work. But it was also amazingly absorbing. Years ago a friend who'd had a nervous breakdown – which was what they called it in those days – had gone to a trendy hospital where digging was the first thing the patients were encouraged to do. Now Ella could see why. Turning the earth over and over until it broke up into fine soil ready for sowing seeds was deeply satisfying.

It was a perfect day, the kind she liked best, with a bright pale sky with high fluffy clouds, yet there had been a frost in the night and the ground was surprisingly hard. Without even knowing she was doing it, Ella started singing her favourite carol:

> 'In the bleak midwinter, frosty wind made moan,
> Earth stood hard as iron, water like a stone;
> Snow had fallen, snow on snow, snow on snow,
> In the bleak midwinter, long ago.'

Her globetrotting neighbours would be amazed if they saw her up to her ankles in mud. It suddenly struck her that maybe they might not want her coming in and planting stuff of her own. On the other hand, she'd just had a postcard saying they were going on to South America and could she keep it up a bit longer?

She leaned over to the young woman in the next plot, who was brightly dressed in a red jumper and jeans. 'Excuse me, I'm allotment-sitting for Viv and Angelo, and I just wondered, do you think they'd mind if I dug this bed?'

'Angelo hates digging.' The woman smiled back. 'It'd muss up his hairdo. They'll be delighted. Just ask us before you chuck anything away that's growing. Even if it looks like a weed.' She held out her hand. 'I'm Sue, by the way.'

Another young woman, who could almost have been her twin, popped out from behind her. 'Hi, I'm Sharleen!'

Sharleen had an effervescent quality that somehow reminded Ella of Miss Piggy with her habit of unstoppably popping up in everyone else's scenes. 'Pleased to meet you.'

'Cup of tea, ladies?' Bill's mate Stevie had appeared with a tray and three mugs. He handed the first mug, adorned with the slogan I DIG PLANTS, to Sue. Sharleen was awarded GIVE PEAS A CHANCE and Ella got COMPOST HAPPENS.

'Compost Happens, that's really funny.' Ella smiled.

'Is it?' asked Stevie genuinely flummoxed. 'Why?'

Ella looked at him but he was clearly serious. 'Well, you know, it's a pun on shit happens.'

Stevie stared at it then buckled almost in two with laughter. 'Compost happens!' he repeated delightedly. 'Compost happens! I'll go and tell Bill, he'll be tickled to death.'

'Not the sharpest tool in the shed,' whispered Sharleen. 'After all, it's Bill's mug.' She glanced appraisingly at Ella. 'Quite an honour, Bill making a cup of tea. He's never made us one.'

'That's because we're dangerous feminists,' Sue pointed out good-humouredly. 'Bill doesn't approve of feminists.'

'Or benefit scroungers,' added Sharleen, grinning.

'Or social workers.'

'Or foreigners of any hue.' They fell about laughing at the roll call of Bill's dislikes.

The mention of foreigners reminded Ella that she needed to get home. Wenceslaus was coming round at seven and she wanted to make them supper. It would be nice to have a reason to cook. She'd got out of the habit since Cory had left home. It was easier just to chuck fishcakes in the oven and eat them with baked beans out of the tin. 'I must be off. Someone coming to supper.'

'Why don't you take these aubergines?' Sue suggested, handing over a glossy purple handful. 'I've got a terrific recipe for aubergines Mr Barzani from allotment eleven gave me. He used to cook them on his hot coals in Kurdistan. Don't tell Sharleen, though. Our home-grown aubergines are finished. These are imported ones from the greengrocer on the High Street. Against allotment rules.' She grinned at Ella, producing a scrappy piece of paper with grease stains on it.

Ella read it out, suddenly envious of Viv and Angelo mixing

with all these different kinds of people.'"*Take two large aubergines. Slice thinly. Place on kitchen towel and pat till poison comes out.*" Do aubergines have poison in them?' she asked.

'I think he means that bitter juice stuff that comes out rather than actual strychnine.'

'"*Soak in olive oil and garlic. Heat pan till smoking. Cook aubergines three or four minutes. Turn. Squeeze juice half lemon. Sprinkle with fresh coriander. Eat with bread and thick yogurt and thank the Good God for life.*" Anyone got any fresh coriander?'

'Mine's finished but Bill's friend Les up by that green shed may have some, he grows it under glass. He doesn't tell Bill he does, though. Far too fancy. Bill might have him black-balled from the magic circle.'

Bill was at the far end of the allotments doling out advice to Stan, a Jamaican of indeterminate age, who knew nothing about the theory of gardening, yet apparently had amazing results growing everything from sweetcorn to Scotch bonnet chillies, in astonishingly adverse conditions, just by instinct.

'Do you have any coriander I could have, Les?' Ella asked when she'd walked over to the green shed. 'Just a few strands would do.'

Les pulled a small bunch from his herb plot and handed it over as if it were a banned substance. 'Here you are,' he whispered. 'Really good in *omelette fines herbes*.'

'Thanks. I'll remember that.' She waved goodbye to Sue. 'Don't worry, I won't tell Sharleen about the aubergines,' Ella said, laughing.

She really liked Sue and Sharleen.

As the sun began to set behind the misty banks of the River Thames, Ella walked home, glad to be part of this rich world she'd stumbled into without even knowing it was there.

She was also aware of something else, a feeling she was

only dimly conscious of, rather like waking on the morning of a trip you'd been looking forward to when you lay in bed for a moment, eyes still closed, filled with pleasurable anticipation.

With a shock she identified the reason. It was because Wenceslaus was coming.

It would be a hard emotion to convey to anyone but another mother. Sal would ogle and say it was because of his looks. But that wasn't the explanation. Ostensibly he was coming to live in her house to make sure it was safe, to look after her. Yet what she was really looking forward to was looking after him. Not in any clingy or creepy sense, but as a fellow human being, and one who was young enough to have been her son. Since Cory had moved out, the place had felt different. The mellowed wooden boards of the hall and the staircase were beloved and familiar. They still smelled of beeswax and a warm welcome, yet without Laurence and then the girls they had sometimes been empty and echoing.

Now there would be youth and life. Laughter. She thought about the idea of a dog, something she had been considering for a long time. Wenceslaus could help walk it.

'Careful,' warned a voice, '*you're starting to depend on him and he hasn't even moved in yet. Maybe he won't stay. Or maybe he'll want to come and go as he likes and have nothing to do with you.*'

She unlocked the door, switched off the burglar alarm, and started to cook the aubergines with the lemon and coriander, using Mr Barzani's dog-eared recipe.

By the time the doorbell rang the food was ready.

Wenceslaus had only one small bag and a laptop computer.

Ella showed him his room and bathroom at the top of the house. It had a glorious view of the garden.

Wenceslaus stared out at the branches of the cedar which

were right outside his window. 'Lucky to have trees right in middle of city.'

'Yes, we are lucky. Very lucky. There are lots of robins, a jay, two woodpeckers – you know, "Ha-ha ha Haa hah!"' Ella tried to imitate Woody Woodpecker with mixed success. Thank God her daughters weren't here.

'Is very good,' Wenceslaus congratulated. 'I know at once what you mean. I have one question.'

'What's that?'

'Do you have Wi-Fi? I do not mean to be rude, to presume.'

'Wenceslaus,' Ella replied, laughing and remembering her daughter's complaints, 'have you *seen* my phone? We're about as hi-tech here as The Flintstones.'

'And do you want to be? Would you like to learn about modern age? Blogging? Facebook? Twitter? Smartphone? 4G?'

Ella imagined the expression on the faces of Julia and Cory, and even her grandsons Harry and Mark and, best of all, her know-it-all son-in-law, annoying Neil, if Grandma got wired. Or wireless.

'Do you know? I rather think I might. But look, for the moment, come and eat.'

'I should have got wine.' Wenceslaus looked truly apologetic at this lapse in etiquette.

'Don't worry. I'll get some from the cellar. My husband was quite an enthusiast.'

She found a bottle of red that needed drinking anyway or it would go off. As she wiped the bottle she thought of Laurence, and how he had bought it with the thought of sitting in the kitchen enjoying it with her and how bloody unfair life was.

She had a feeling he would have approved of Wenceslaus.

They ate Mr Barzani's aubergines, which were entirely delicious, though next time she'd cook some lamb to go with them.

She raised a glass. 'To our digital relationship!' She hoped that hadn't sounded inappropriately cougar-like, and decided it hadn't. She intended to be entirely straightforward with him and simply ask him to do something whenever she needed it done and not to start agonizing if he'd mind or not.

'I am very grateful you give me room. I will make sure everything runs like house on fire. Maybe that not good way of putting it?'

'That's a perfect way of putting it. Now if you could put the dishes in the dishwasher that would be lovely.' She'd never trained Laurence to do this but she felt she owed it to the next generation to do her bit with Wenceslaus.

She had just sat back, put her feet up to ease her now aching back, when the phone rang.

Before a word was spoken Ella knew from the sobs that it was Laura and that somehow she had found out about Simon's infidelity.

'Where are you now?'

'Still at the hotel in Brighton.'

'And Simon?'

'I asked him to go, so presumably he's gone to her.'

'Oh, darling Laura, I wish I were with you. And on your anniversary too.' She didn't know why that made it so much worse, but it did. 'Bloody men and their bloody predictable stupidity.'

'Not all men. Laurence would never have done this to you.'

'Laura, that's silly. We don't know what Laurence would have done. What are you going to do now?'

'I've chucked him out. He's coming to get his things tomorrow. And we have to tell the children. Oh, God, Ella. What are we going to tell them? They had no idea about any of this. But neither did I. How incredibly blind and stupid was that?'

'Stop that. You trusted him. That's why you managed to

stay married for twenty-five years in the first place. That's quite a record these days. So who is she, this other woman?'

'A colleague. Can you believe it, she's called Suki? He says she's really in love with him and she wants him to live with her.'

From what Sal had said, Ella recognized the type. The type who thought wives were boring and marriage didn't mean anything. Until they got their claws into some poor woman's husband. Then they got him to divorce his wife double quick and married him before he had a chance to miss his family. She'd seen it over and over.

'Oh, Laura, you poor lamb.' The warmth of Ella's sympathy made Laura start crying again. The thought of telling Bella and Sam, who had always felt safe in their parents' marriage, and whose lives would be affected almost as much as hers, was so dreadful she could hardly bear to think about it.

'Promise me you'll come straight round the moment you can,' Ella insisted, 'and I'll administer a big hug and a large glass of Sauvignon.'

'Sounds wonderful.'

'That's what friends are for. To pick you up when you feel like shit. It's in the rulebook.'

Laura smiled despite everything. 'One thing, Ella, don't tell the others. I don't want everyone knowing all the gory details.'

'Of course. I won't breathe a word.' Not that she needed to. Sal had told them all already. But there was no reason for Laura to find that out.

Wenceslaus knocked on the door, interrupting her reverie. 'I go to bed now.' He seemed to notice her preoccupation. 'Everything OK?'

Ella looked at him. He seemed so kind. So nice. And so handsome. Would he behave towards some woman one day the way Simon had to Laura?

'I don't suppose I should ask you this, but why do men leave their wives of twenty-five years?'

Wenceslaus sighed, as if this were a perfectly reasonable question to ask someone you had known only a couple of days. 'Because men are stupid. Because they think grass always greener. And sometimes,' he shrugged apologetically, 'because women let them.'

Was Laura letting him? Should she be fighting tooth and nail to keep him, or was there some part of her that said, if that's what he's like, then let him go?

She remembered that tactless friend who'd told her she was lucky to have her marriage end in death, not divorce, because she still had the memories. She glanced at her wedding photograph, propped up on the mantelpiece. Would you and I have been all right, I wonder, or would we have ended up like Laura and Simon, dragging each other through the divorce courts?

She put her finger to her lips and brushed it across the photograph, missing him more powerfully than she could ever remember.

She brushed away a tear for the lost years they would have had together, then sat and listened to the silence and was glad that its quality had changed. It no longer felt empty but occupied and purposeful.

Tomorrow she would ask Wenceslaus to give her a lesson on the computer.

Sal was feeling more nervous than she had for years as she dressed for her interview at Oakmore Resorts. Since she had left the magazine she had applied for hundreds of jobs and, to her shocked amazement, today's was still her only interview. And this despite taking Ella's advice, which she had rather resented, that she play down her experience and streamline her last salary so that it wasn't higher than the current job was offering. 'No one trusts someone who's prepared to take a drop in salary,' Ella had insisted.

Sal had a bad feeling as soon as she walked through the door of their head office. It wasn't the deep pile of the beige carpet or the fact that the place was so impenetrably silent that unnerved her, it was the staff. From the receptionist to the discreet sales assistants, they were all so *young*. What's more, they were all dressed in neutral colours, just like the walls, in a palate that ran the gamut from ivory all the way to bone.

Sal began to wonder if her Savannah Miller animal-inspired jumpsuit and wedge-heeled trainers had been such a good idea for a job interview in this temple of taupe. The thing was she always felt so good in them. But she could see it might be construed in this environment as weird rather than witty, her favourite fashion attribute. She hoped they knew how much the jumpsuit cost, or would have if she'd paid the full price. At least she had had the sense to leave her beloved black leather biker jacket at home.

'Come on, Sal, old girl, pull yourself together. These are all babies. None of them have your sophistication, your experience, your savvy,' she told herself.

Or your wobbly jowls, added her subconscious meanly.

'Ms Grainger?' the receptionist enquired, a bright smile pinned to her face. 'Would you like to come through here?'

To her horror she saw that the interview panel were all sitting not round a table where she could sit up with a nice straight back but lounging on ludicrously low harem-style couches. This meant, as she took her seat – or couch – that Sal had to lean forward, thus exposing several inches of ageing bosom.

'Perhaps we might start by introducing ourselves. I'm Suzanne Walton, Head of HR, this is Bridget Ripley, Director of Operations, and Angela Harley, our Resorts Co-ordinator, and of course Ben Wilson, from Communications. So, Ms – Grainger – what does Oakmore Resorts say to you as a brand?'

Sal cast her mind back to the press trips she had been on as a guest of Oakmore. 'Understated luxury, unobtrusive service, always there when you want it but not one of those irritating places where they straighten your towel when you go swimming . . . great locations . . .'

Actually, the truth was that Oakmore Resorts were, rather like their offices, the bland leading the bland.

'And what about any negative aspects? Things we might improve?'

The make-up remover pads weren't replenished as generously as Sal might have liked but she thought this might not be what they had in mind.

'Colour,' Sal waded in bravely. 'I would introduce some boldness into the brand, both in your décor and how people see you as a company.'

'And how would you do that?' Ben Wilson asked, nervously eyeing her Savannah Miller print.

'Purple orchids,' Sal announced with a sibyl-like stare. That should give them something to think about. She could expand but decided against it. Let them imagine the orchids were a metaphor.

'I see.'

'And how would you promote Oakmore across the various platforms?'

How she hated bloody platforms, but at least she was ready with an answer. 'You have to be everywhere these days. Social media. Blogging. TripAdvisor. Twitter. Apps. Obviously liaising with websites and magazines for promotions, contests, offers.'

'Tell me, Ms Grainger,' Angela Harley was asking, 'on your

online application you were asked if you were stranded on a desert island what two things you would want to take. Do you recall your answer?'

'My sarong and Ray-Bans,' as I recall.

From the stony faces around her she could see this was not the correct answer.

'Do you not think that a little frivolous?'

'I could have said Google Earth or an iPhone to show my resourcefulness but I thought that might be rather obvious.'

'Can you tell us about your management style? How would you define it?'

Sal almost sighed. She didn't believe questions like this ever got to the truth. Everyone knew the buzzwords. Inclusiveness. Emotional intelligence. Openness. Blah blah blah. Hannibal and Genghis Khan could probably sell themselves as collaborative managers who believed in democratic discussion at the Monday morning meeting.

Suddenly Sal felt that maybe she *was* too old for all this crap. She didn't feel like playing these games which they thought so vitally important. Once you were used to running things maybe you were probably unemployable.

She would just have to freelance.

'Is there anything you'd like to ask us?'

Sal knew this meant the interview was all but over. Suddenly, she recalled one thing that had hit her sharply about the Oakmore Resort she had stayed in on the island of St Lucia.

'Yes, I do have a question. What could you do to reduce the feeling of "them and us", of extreme wealth cheek by jowl with extreme poverty, which can spoil the pleasure of your guests in extremely expensive resorts?'

The panel stared back at her in appalled silence.

Something told Sal she hadn't got the job.

*

Claudia and Don had been driving round the M25 for the last half-hour in complete silence. On Claudia's side this was partly to do with worry about her father, Len. Len was such a lovely man; that was really the only word for him. He always managed to make you laugh even when you didn't want to. Sometimes he did this by telling you a joke – he had an endless supply of terrible jokes which he kept up until his audience finally gave in and got the giggles. Sometimes it was just his natural good humour. He was built on a bear-like scale, with thick white hair that curled in an imperial manner. His taste in clothes matched his jokes, loud and unfashionable to the point of being almost, but not quite, bad taste. And yet it was impossible for anyone to dislike him.

While her mother Olivia had veered towards the snobbish, Len loved everyone. Unfortunately, he also thought everyone he met was equally fascinating, which led to him collecting waifs, strays and bores at a rate that infuriated his wife.

But the quality Claudia had loved most was his ability to reassure. While her mother made her feel as if she were a nuisance, from her earliest childhood it had been her father who'd built up her belief in herself. Lacking a son, he'd turned Claudia into an honorary version. It had been he who had seen that Claudia's skills were practical and organizational and he had encouraged them so that her confidence had blossomed, and had stayed with her all her life.

Now her beloved father was faltering. He had been getting increasingly frail and quiet, cracking only the occasional joke and, much to her mother's annoyance, hanging around the house instead of frequenting pubs, snooker halls and football grounds.

And now the fall.

Don was quiet because he was angry with Claudia. He had never really thought of her as resembling her mother, whom he had christened the memsahib on first meeting her, owing to her bossy and super-efficient manner. But recently he'd started wondering. She had been so bluntly dismissive about his house suggestions, so witheringly disinterested in what *he* might want from the next section of his life, as if it were only her and her friendships that counted.

Olivia was waiting for them at the door.

'Hello, Mum.' Claudia embraced her mother. 'How's Dad?'

'Ah, Claudia, there you are at last!' her mother replied testily. 'I've been waiting all morning to go to the hospital.'

Looking more closely at her mother, Claudia noticed there was something different about her. Her hair. At eighty, her mother's hair was normally a tousled sea of iron-grey waves. Today it was more a grey lagoon, smooth, shiny and expensive-looking. 'Mum, what on earth have you done to your hair?'

Olivia patted her head with a small smile of satisfaction. 'Nice, isn't it?'

Claudia looked again. 'You haven't had one of those Brazilian blow-dries?' she asked, incredulously. This new hairstyling technique was all the rage in London and employed a chemical process that kept the hair straight and shiny for months. It was also unbelievably expensive, which was why Claudia herself had resisted having her own done. How on earth had her mother afforded it? Sal had even run an article about the pros and cons of the technique in *Modern Style*. 'You do know,' Claudia tried not to sound peevish, 'the process is really risky. They use formaldehyde!'

'Oh well,' her mother replied nonchalantly, 'the rest of me is pickled. Why not my hair?'

Claudia felt stunned. Her mother never made jokes. That was her father's department. 'What's the news about Dad? How long will he be in hospital?'

'He's got to have a hip operation.' Olivia could hardly contain her annoyance. 'A stint in hospital and God knows how long to recover. And who'll have to fetch and carry for him? It was really stupid of him trying to take a tray downstairs at his age.'

It was widely acknowledged that her mother Olivia didn't do sympathy. She expected everyone around her to live up to her own standards of brisk efficiency. It never seemed to occur to her that they might not be able to. Poor old Dad.

They were standing in Olivia's spotlessly tidy kitchen. At least they had a cleaning woman, though she, it had to be said, was almost as old as Olivia and Len. 'The thing is,' her mother moaned, 'it's really bad timing. We have so much on at the moment and I really don't want to cancel everything.' Behind her mother's newly coiffed head Claudia noticed a golfer's wall calendar. Her father was a keen golfer, or had been — sometimes, Claudia suspected, to get away from her mother. 'I'll get my coat. I would offer you a coffee but we really ought to get on.'

'I don't know why you had to go on and on about her hair at a time like this,' Don whispered irritably as soon as her mother was out of the room.

Don, being a man, didn't realize quite how extraordinary it was for her mother suddenly to emerge with an £80 Brazilian blow-dry — it was rather like the Queen dropping Norman Hartnell and appearing in Victoria Beckham.

As they waited Claudia studied the calendar with mounting amazement. Her mother had always been busy but this was ridiculous. Tomorrow, she was down for a beginners' bread-making course run by the WI; the day after, a 'massage and body polish' at the posh spa down the road. Next week, there were tango lessons and a thread-vein treatment that Claudia had been rather wishing she could afford herself. Spider-like little strands of red had appeared on her face which she hoped were not attributable to too much white wine. But why was her mother having it?

'Don, look at this. My mother is busier than a minor royal. Bread making. Body polishes. Tango lessons. Look at that – a time management course! She'd need one with all this. *Quad biking!* But she's over eighty!'

'Retired people are supposed to keep active, aren't they?' Don shrugged. 'Maybe people out of London have more interests.' This was another dig, she knew. Well, too bad. She went back to the calendar. 'Teeth whitening! A ten-course Turkish tasting menu! But they hate foreign food! Somewhere in the back of Claudia's mind a faint alarm bell started ringing. Had her parents really been doing all this stuff? And if so, how were they paying for it?

Her mother was back, chic in a belted camel coat. 'I see you're looking at the calendar. That's why your father's timing is so annoying. We're too busy for a hip replacement.'

'I don't suppose he meant to have one. And he is eighty-one. Anyway, what is all this stuff you're doing?'

'Keeping Busy.'

'Yes, I can see that all right. I feel tired looking at it.'

'No. Keeping Busy is a social network. It's wonderful. Everything's seventy per cent off.' Olivia smiled beatifically. 'I'm never at home. Of course, your father doesn't come. Stays here and watches golf on the television, miserable bugger.'

'When did all this start?'

'Ever since I discovered it a couple of months ago. I've got the app on my tablet.'

Claudia wondered if she'd fallen down Alice's rabbit hole. Since when had a tablet been anything more to her mother than something she swallowed when she had a headache?

'You've got a tablet? Don't tell me. Keeping Busy had an offer?'

Her mother nodded. 'It's got eight gigabytes and it's Wi-Fi enabled – all for ninety-nine pounds ninety-nine.'

Claudia thought perhaps she ought to sit down. Her mother really was more tech-savvy than she was. 'I *was* going to book your father and me to see the Northern Lights this week, two nights in Reykjavik for two people staying in an Ice Hotel with flight and tour included, three hundred and thirty-nine pounds per person. Now we can't go, obviously. I don't suppose Gaby would like to come instead? It's all paid for.'

Claudia shook her head. What had her mother been thinking? Her father hated the cold and the only natural phenomenon he was interested in was the hole in one. Claudia couldn't imagine her daughter Gaby wanting to take in the Aurora Borealis unless it was a hip new club in Hoxton, and certainly not with her grandmother, but she let it pass. 'I'll certainly ask her.' She hadn't been invited herself, Claudia noted. Her mother probably thought she'd want to go to bed early and be no fun. No doubt true.

'What about Dad, if you're going gadding?'

'He'll be stuck in hospital. Istanbul will be off too,' her mother added glumly.

'Hadn't we better get to the hospital?' Don reminded them. 'I have an appointment at two-thirty.'

'What?' Olivia demanded rudely. 'At the hospital? You're not sickening too, surely? I don't know. Men. No Stamina.'

'No, not at the hospital. In Minsley.'

He disappeared out to the car before Claudia could say anything, but she hurried after him. 'Don! Have you made an appointment with an estate agent?'

He turned to face her, his expression stony. 'Yes, Claudia. In case you hadn't noticed, there are two people in this marriage and I happen to believe what I want matters as much as your access to your girlfriends.'

They drove silently to the hospital, unfamiliar anger crackling between them, while her mother moaned about Len's irresponsible behaviour in cracking his hip until Claudia wanted to strangle her.

She was totally unprepared for the sight of her father, usually such a larger-than-life figure, in hospital. He seemed reduced, as if he had lost weight to fit into the narrow bed, his beard was unshaven, and his hair stuck out like a scarecrow's.

'Oh, Dad, you poor old lamb. Is it painful?'

'A bit.' Len tried to sit up. 'They're going to put a sliding screw in. I'll be better than a kitchen cabinet and have fun setting off those machines at airports. Here, come and give us a kiss.'

Claudia perched on the side of the bed. 'So how did it happen? Bringing Mum a cup of tea in bed, I bet. You should make her get it.'

Len laughed, sounding a bit more himself. 'Too late for that. I've been doing it for sixty years.'

Sixty years. It was hard to imagine, and yet wonderful that they'd stuck together despite being so different. Her generation would probably have given up. She found herself glancing at Don. Silently she put a hand out to him. He squeezed it, his eyes still on Len.

'You'll be out in no time. Mum's already planning jaunts for you.'

Was that a hunted look she saw in his eye at the mention of her mother's endless outings?

'She's always planning some bloody thing. I think she's getting worse. I hardly see her these days. And now this. Six weeks taking it easy, the doctor says, plus exercises with a physio. Load of bloody nonsense.'

'That would be the end of November.' Her mother, who had been standing outside the ward staring at her phone, came in. She had had the Keeping Busy app on already. 'We could go away. Two nights bed and breakfast on the Yorkshire coast with full English breakfast. Perfect.'

'Except that I don't want to go to Yorkshire. It's two hundred miles away.'

Claudia caught her father's eye. Yes, he definitely looked anxious. Maybe she should have a word with her mother. That would be fun.

'Did you think my mother was more than usually hyper?' she asked Don as they walked back to the car. Olivia, in a rare gesture of sympathy, had opted to stay at the hospital. Probably the Wi-Fi signal was better there.

'She's always hyper. You're just jealous. She has a busier life than you. And more fun.'

'Well,' replied Claudia, nettled, 'I do work.'

'I meant to ask, how did it go with that little prick Dooley?'

Claudia grinned. 'Rather well, actually. For once technology triumphed and made him look a complete tosser.'

'He didn't manage to wrench the French exchange from you, then?'

'Not yet.'

'Throw a paving stone at him when you go.'

'If I go.'

Don looked at her, surprised.

'I'm just not sure it's much fun any more.'

'The French exchange or teaching in general?'

'Both.'

'Let's move here, then. We could both have more fun.'

Claudia wasn't sure she was ready for that.

'So, are you coming to see around the house I like or not?'

'I suppose I'd better. Don't want you buying it without consulting me, do I?'

The cottage, Claudia had to concede, was a very pretty one, standing at the end of a large village. It was a back-to-front house that faced away from the rest of the street, with its entrance and two big windows facing out over a landscape of fields. The previous owner had installed a lacy-edged wooden porch with a bench beneath it and a stone path bordered with lavender, which gave the place a vaguely French air.

To Claudia's eyes the garden looked like a lot of work.

Inside, the rooms were surprisingly colourful; pale pink, pistachio, primrose. It ought not to work but it did. The sugar-almond tones were a welcome break from the epidemic of bone and buttermilk that had engulfed London.

The ceilings were a bit low but the owners had avoided the chintz-and-chocolate-box look of many cottages and kept the lines clean and simple.

There were four bedrooms. A large double, a smaller bedroom, though big enough for a double bed for Gaby, a spare room, and a kind of large box room. The major drawback was that the bathroom was downstairs.

'It could easily go in the box room,' Don said eagerly. 'Not en suite, of course, but you can't have everything.'

It was obvious to Claudia that Don loved it.

He looked out of the window at the garden. 'I could grow vegetables.'

There was a suppressed longing in his voice that took her aback. 'I didn't know you wanted to grow vegetables.'

'There's quite a lot you don't know about me.' It came over as a rather bleak statement of fact.

Could it be true after thirty years together? She had better watch out. Once upon a time people who'd been together a long time stayed together. Not any more. Now the over-fifties were the fastest-divorcing group of all. They even had a name.

Silver splitters. She'd heard it on the radio. Did she want to be one of them?

'So what do you think?' Don asked, his eyes fixed on hers.

'It's a pretty house.'

'But?'

'But you know what I think; I'm not ready to leave London.'

'Or the coven.'

'I wish you wouldn't call them that.' Maybe she should remind him that friendship often lasted longer than marriage.

'OK. Sorry.' His eyes shifted suddenly to the bed. The agent had given them the keys, telling them the owners were abroad for six months and that no one would disturb them. 'Come on, why don't we pretend we're young again. Live dangerously?'

The thought of moving here, spending the rest of her life in this village, making love in a bed like this with Don, closed in on her like a prison sentence.

'We can't,' Claudia lied. 'I said we'd go and pick up my mother.'

They were just locking up when Claudia's mobile rang. She saw that it was the hospital and answered it at once.

'Hello, this is Paul Davies here, Registrar at the North Surrey. Mrs Warren, I'm afraid we've got a bit of a problem here. I wonder if you could come right away.'

Of course. Has there been some development with my father?'

'Not your father, Mrs Warren. He's fine. I'm afraid it's your mother.'

CHAPTER 6

As she made her way home after the disastrous job interview, Sal went through her usual deliberation. Cab or bus? In a cab she could feel temporarily cocooned from reality; on the other hand, she really *really* had to economize.

It had struck her last night that her fridge was more than usually empty. Indeed, it had looked like an aircraft hangar with a tiny two-seater plane, in the form of a two-week-old peach, parked in one corner. And here was a Tesco Express.

Sal had filled half a basket and was queuing to pay when she caught sight of herself in a mirror handily placed in front of the cigarettes and whisky. She looked bloody ridiculous in this jumpsuit. It was one thing wanting to dress the age you felt, but not at the cost of resembling a sixty-year-old toddler.

When the next interview came up she would wear something more age-appropriate – like a ghastly Jaeger suit.

If there ever was a next interview.

A news-stand by the side of the tills had all the day's papers and magazines. Sal glanced at it to see what the usual cast of characters – Katie Price, Liz Hurley, Kerry Katona, the Duchess of Cambridge – were doing in the weekly scandal rags.

Instead her eye was caught by the *Daily Post*, or rather, the enormous strapline across the top of its front page advertising the articles inside. ON THE SCRAPHEAP AT SIXTY, shouted the headline, and there next to it was a large photograph of herself.

My God, the *Post* must have run that piece she'd written without telling her.

'Read it,' advised a woman at her elbow. 'Scare the pants off you. Where the hell are we supposed to work till we can claim our pension? That's if we *have* a pension we can live on, and plenty don't.'

'Scandalous!' agreed the woman in the next queue. 'We'll all be cleaning lavvies till we're ninety!'

Sal bought three copies.

She was hot news in Tesco. That had to count for something. Suddenly, she couldn't face going home. The worst thing about not having a job, apart from the lack of money, status, and something other than QVC to occupy your waking hours, was being stuck at home with no one to gossip with, no chats in the Ladies' Loo about who'd done what to whom.

As she stood at the bus stop, surrounded by a small group of women who varied in age from her own to eighty-plus, including one old lady practically bent double by a nasty case of what used to be called dowager's hump, Sal felt an unfamiliar pride. She had written something honest. It might not get her anywhere but she had made a stand all the same. She was fed up with pretending to be young and vibrant. Sick to death of dieting and Botox. She was going to start acting her age.

Well, if not her exact age, then within a reasonable proximity of it, say twenty years.

When she came downstairs, Ella found that Wenceslaus had clearly been up for some time. The kitchen was spotless and she could hear the whirr of the dishwasher which she'd forgotten to put on last night.

'Would you like toasted bread? People in café eat a lot of toasted bread.'

'I would love some toasted bread. Actually, we call it toast.'

'Like in movie when they say, "You're toast"!'

'Exactly. Only that would mean overdone toast, burnt to a frazzle. By the way, I have a favour to ask you if you have any time.'

'What is favour?'

'To help me learn computer skills. Sometimes I feel like the last computer-illiterate person in a planet full of Facebook fanatics.'

'Of course. I am delighted. But maybe first we should find cat?'

'Why, isn't he in the kitchen?'

Wenceslaus shook his head. 'Disappeared. Like human-rights activist.'

'Oh my God. TomTom! The last thing my friend needs is to lose her wretched cat! Where have you looked?'

'I look all over house, under beds, in clothes-dry cupboard. When I was little kid, cat at home went there to have babies, but this cat not female?'

'No, the clue's in the name. TomTom. A tom means a male. Ginger cats are usually male, in fact.'

'I look in garden. You ask neighbours. If I ask neighbours, they think I am burglar.' Ella didn't think burglars were ever as beautiful as Wenceslaus, but still. 'Cats not faithful like dogs. Go to anyone who feed them.'

That was true. The other thing she asked herself is would TomTom try and go home? After all, in *The Incredible Journey* the cat found its way back hundreds of miles. All this one had to do was get from Old Moulsford to Laura's house three miles away.

As she drew a blank with the neighbours, pictures haunted

her of Laura's cat torn apart by the foxes that barked so eerily at night.

'I have idea,' Wenceslaus suggested brightly. 'We kill two cats with one stone.' Seeing Ella's face he added, 'Sorry, not good joke. We make poster to help find cat and you learn computer at same time. Do you have photograph of cat?' Ella shook her head. 'OK, we get one from Internet that looks similar.'

Twenty minutes later they had created a poster in full colour on Wenceslaus' laptop with a cat that would pass in an identity parade for TomTom. Ella almost forgot her worry she was so proud.

They went out together and fixed the poster to as many lamp posts as they could find. 'Next thing I teach you is Facebook, which is like putting up poster, only bigger.' He smiled reassuringly. 'You see lost cat has useful purpose. To teach you Facebook.'

'I'm sure Laura will appreciate that.'

To Ella's anxious amusement they created a Facebook page for TomTom the cat, announcing that he was lost and giving details of a reward for his return. It was all terribly exciting. Ella felt she had joined the modern age, even if she was disguised as a cat.

The best thing, Wenceslaus explained, would be to spread the word through Twitter. 'You need to get famous person interested in lost cat to re-tweet, who has lots of followers of their own.'

It turned out by a stroke of luck that the lead singer of the cult band The Dogs was actually a cat lover. He tweeted about TomTom's disappearance and TomTom was suddenly the most famous lost cat in West London, possibly the world. But what if Laura saw it? Then she remembered that Laura was probably even less tech-savvy than she was.

'You see how easy it is. World is such a small place through Internet. Now I show you how to blog.'

And it was blogging which Ella found she really took to. Blogging was, it seemed to her, basically a development of the teenage diary, only instead of writing: 'STRICTLY PRIVATE NO ACCESS ON PAIN OF DEATH – AND YES, MUM, THAT MEANS YOU!!!', you basically invited everyone in the world to read what you thought.

This could be fun, Ella realized. I could put down all my thoughts, all those little wasted observations I have no one to tell! And she knew that she wanted to tell the world, candidly and honestly, what it felt like to grow old when you felt young.

What she needed was a catchy title, something that would grab people's attention and that she could also hide behind, because there was no way she was doing this under her own name.

Ella sat and thought about this.

She seriously considered WILL YOU STILL NEED ME, WILL YOU STILL FEED ME? but it was too long. And, surprise, surprise, crowds of other oldie bloggers had bagged WHEN I'M SIXTY-FOUR.

Ella stared at the screen. She wanted something quite sharp because if she did transmit her thoughts, she wanted them to be honest and true. To make people sit up and pay attention. To agree or disagree. To generate discussion through blogs of her own.

And then it came to her. MOAN FART DIE. It was so wonderfully rude and unromantic. So utterly unladylike. And it was just right to tell the unvarnished truth about what getting old was really like. The more she looked at it the more she liked it.

And the best thing of all was that no one need know it was her.

She thanked Wenceslaus and shut off her PC.

She'd just settled down on the sofa with a glass of wine, so taken up with blogging that she'd forgotten about the cat, when the phone rang. It was Laura's daughter, Bella, and she was in a panic.

Poor kid, had she heard about her father leaving already?

'Oh my God, I had to call,' Bella explained, distraught. 'The lost cat on Twitter, tell me that's not our TomTom? Only Sam's had him since he was six and he'd be heartbroken if anything happened to him.'

'Don't worry,' Ella's heart started thumping. 'I was just learning to tweet and I used TomTom to practise. When does your mum get back?'

'She's on her way now. She and Dad have asked me and Sam to stay in later. You don't know what it's about, do you?'

Oh God, poor kids. Their nice safe suburban world was about to be blown apart. And one thing they could do without was losing their cat. Ella put down her glass and started another search. Where was that wretched bloody animal?'

Laura drove back from Brighton in a blur of pain and uncertainty. Had she over-reacted? For the sake of her twenty-five-year-old marriage should she be giving Simon a second chance to explain things? Telling Sam and Bella was so final and it would hurt them so much. She could always invent some excuse for his absence while they thought about their future. He was away often enough.

Then the voices of her friends came into her head like a kind of Greek chorus: Ella always so reasonable, Sal intolerant of men generally, Claudia realistic and down-to-earth. *Get real, Laura. He doesn't care about you. If he cared, he would have put up a fight.*

And, of course, they were right. This wasn't just some affair.

The woman wanted him to live with her and he had gone, just like that, on their anniversary, of all days. Admittedly, it had been she who had told him to go but he hadn't shown any real regret or appreciation of the pain he was causing and it struck her that there had always been callousness in Simon. He probably called it focus, the capacity to concentrate on his goal. And this Suki was his goal now, not she and the children. The painful realization came to Laura that, in fact, she had offered him the chance to stay if he gave the woman up and he hadn't even replied.

She'd had no option.

Besides, Bella would guess that something disastrous had happened. She was like a litmus test where emotion was concerned and she had been involved in planning the surprise, so she would know instantly that something was wrong when Laura returned alone. If she lied to Bella, her daughter would work it out and be furiously angry that they had tried to conceal the truth. They would be better off telling her the real situation because Bella would guess it anyway.

The tape machine in her car clicked to the end and switched itself over. Simon had often laughed at her for having a car old enough to still have a tape machine. But Laura liked things that were serviceable rather than flashy. Perhaps she had always thought her marriage fell into that bracket. How wrong she'd been.

All at once the car was full of the one song she didn't want to hear: 'Under the Boardwalk'. She pressed eject, pulled it out and unravelled it before flinging it out of the window, watching the tape unwind like silly string in her rear-view mirror. The sign for a petrol station came up and she pulled into its car park, a sense of loss finally engulfing her. And as the tears blurred her vision and her chest hurt so much she could hardly breathe, a random thought came into her mind: By Bexleyheath Services I Sat Down and Wept.

Life was not grand and dramatic, it was small and ordinary, predictable and repetitive. People got married. They fell out of love, they were unfaithful, they got divorced. She looked around at all the normal, everyday people going about their business. Half of them, maybe more, if the statistics were right, must have been through what she was experiencing. It wasn't *Anna Karenina*. She wouldn't jump in front of a train.

And yet, what the hell was she supposed to do with her anger? She had always tried to be a good wife and a good mother. Now it seemed that being a good mother would mean hiding her feelings of betrayal and resentment. She would have to pretend to be reasonable when what she really felt was *I hope you both die in a plane crash!*

She began to see why discarded wives went around cutting the arms out of their husbands' suits or scrawling *Adulterer* on their office wall. It was because they felt so powerless and humiliated.

She cleaned up her mascara-stained face with a wet wipe, conscious that she was the kind of woman who kept wet wipes in her glove compartment even though she no longer had small children; good old competent down-to-earth Laura. She drove on round the perimeter of London, taken with the fantasy that as the motorway was circular she could keep driving round and round and never get to her destination.

Except that there was her turn-off. The road home. Where everything would be changed forever.

And now she was actually in her own road.

She parked in the driveway. Bella, as she had often done as a child, heard the car and immediately opened the front door, her pale face against its black Goth hair lit by a sweet and welcoming smile.

At least we produced you and Sam, so our marriage can't be a complete waste.

'Hey, Mum,' Bella greeted her, skipping down the steps of the porch, 'how was the big romantic surprise?'

'Not quite what I expected.' Laura had to fight not to break down.

'Well, you know Dad. He only likes surprises if he organizes them. Where is he, by the way?'

'He's coming later. Where's Sam?'

'Where would you expect? Playing World of Warcraft. I said to him, "Don't you think you're a bit old for that?" and he said the average age of gamers is thirty-five. God, do men *never* grow up?' She put her arm protectively round Laura, all the sullenness of previous days forgotten. 'So what's this big-deal announcement anyway? You're not getting divorced?' She laughed at her own joke, skipping back up the steps so that she didn't see the anguish on her mother's face.

'I'll just take my bag upstairs and unpack.'

'Want a cup of tea?'

'No thanks. I may have a relaxing bath.' At least in the bathroom she could lock herself in and be alone.

On the way up she pushed open the door of the sitting room. 'Hello, darling!' she called to Sam.

'Hi, Mum,' he replied, raising a hand in salute, and went back to his game. Laura's mother, a stickler for good manners, said Sam was offhand, but Laura attributed his lack of social graces to a sense of security, something she herself had never had as a child and had been determined to give him. He didn't feel the need to curry favour. What would happen to that now?

With so much emotional upheaval it seemed strange that the exterior of her life was so unchanged. Her bedroom was just as she'd left it, the bed made, the cushions straight, flowers on her bedside table. She liked to leave a room perfectly tidy, already imagining how she'd feel when she walked back into it. Was that weird and anal? Did this Suki live in a whirlwind of clothes thrown everywhere, nothing planned, everything exciting and spontaneous, including the sex?

Well, that wouldn't last. Laura sat down on the bed. That was almost what depressed her the most. Simon would go and live with this woman and their life would become more like his life with Laura. That was the way of commitment; it was shaped by habit and routine. In a good marriage that could be comfortable and reassuring. The routine could hold you up like scaffolding when you felt shaky until you felt strong again.

Habits could be good. She thought of the cup of tea they drank in bed together every morning. It was companionable. You chatted about the day, the children, your worries. It was more important than it seemed. It glued the edifice together. Sex at the end of the day helped too, but of course that was the bit that got forgotten first. It struck her that lately Simon had taken to doing the crossword or even checking his emails on his phone when they used to talk. Maybe she should have noticed the signs. A broken pole in the scaffolding.

She noticed the photograph she always kept on her bedside table. It was of them both looking incredibly happy, on some holiday or other, laughing. She threw it across the room, grateful that the distant boom of World of Warcraft muffled the sound of broken glass. The depressing truth was that there was nothing really wrong with their marriage. It was a perfectly good marriage, solid and serviceable like the tape machine in her car. And yet it hadn't been enough for Simon.

And then she remembered how much he'd hated her tape machine.

The sound of steps on the gravel of their driveway penetrated her thoughts. Simon must have come early. For a brief moment her spirits lifted. If he walked in, ashen-faced, abject with apology, insisting it was all a terrible mistake, would she take him back? Yes, she probably would.

She quickly picked up the broken glass, shoved the picture frame in a drawer and went downstairs.

Simon was in the kitchen with Bella. He was neither ashen-faced nor abject. Just a little jumpy. 'Where's Sam?' he asked.

'Where do you think?' Bella shrugged. 'Sa-am!' she bellowed in the direction of the sitting room.

'Why don't we all sit down,' suggested Simon as Sam appeared, as if it were the beginning of a board meeting.

They sat round their familiar pine table, the one they'd sat round for supper every night for so many years, with its familiar bunch of daisies and fruit bowl in the middle. Sam and Bella exchanged bewildered glances.

'The thing is . . .' Simon hesitated, then went back to the speech he'd presumably prepared. 'I know you're all going to hate me, as I'm the villain of the piece; I'm a shit, I accept that, but the thing is—'

'You said that,' Bella interjected rudely.

'The thing is, I've fallen in love with somebody else and I'm going to live with her.'

Bella and Sam stared, not quite understanding fully what he was telling them.

Bella was the first to recover. 'So this is all about you, then, is it?' You're not going to bother with all the "your mother and I really love you and this isn't your fault" stuff?'

'No. Although obviously that's also true.'

'You mean you're leaving Mum?' Sam asked, beginning to push his chair back, 'and us as well?'

'You're not children any more. I know this is hard. It's hard for me too.'

Sam stood up. He was as tall as Simon. 'And you think it's OK if you say, "I know I'm a shit",' Sam's voice, on the edge of tears, nevertheless shook with anger, 'well, you're right. You *are* a shit and I'm glad you're going. I couldn't live with someone I'd thought I could respect who behaved like you. We're the kids here but you're the one who should BLOODY GROW UP!' He ran from the room before they could see his tears.

'So how old is this woman you've fallen for?' demanded Bella.

'I don't really see how that matters.'

'How old?'

'Thirty-six. And her name's Suki.'

'I bet you're her boss.'

Simon looked embarrassed.

Unlike her mother, Bella had no problem with anger. She couldn't believe that her parents could betray her and Sam as well as each other like this. Despite her outlandish appearance she had a powerful sense of morality, and this to her was a simple breach of loyalty. Forget the divorce statistics. Her parents had made a promise to each other and, implicitly, to their children and they were breaking it. 'You do realize what a walking cliché you are?' she accused Simon furiously. She suddenly turned towards Laura. 'And what about Mum? Don't you care how much you'll hurt her?'

'Yes, obviously I do.'

'But not enough to give up this . . . Suki. What kind of a stupid name is that anyway?'

At that moment the phone he had left on the table began to vibrate.

Bella grabbed it. 'It's her, isn't it? Making sure you don't change your mind and start behaving like a decent human being!'

A sudden inspiration came to Bella. 'I bet she's outside!' She threw the phone down and ran out of the front door into the night. It had started raining but the night was clear with a hint of mist over the new moon. At the end of the road a car flashed its lights. She'd been right.

Bella ran down the road, her black Victorian skirt, with its lace fishtail, dragging in the puddles.

A young woman sat in the driving seat watching Bella's approach with growing apprehension. Bella wrenched open the door just as the woman turned on the ignition to try and drive off.

'I'm sure this is all down to my father, but I wanted you to know that I blame you too!' Bella screamed at her. And then she spat. She hadn't meant to or planned to. It just happened.

Which is when the red-haired home-wrecker in her father's Audi turned on the car alarm.

Everywhere along the street curtains twitched as the neighbours, all hoping it wasn't their own car, witnessed Bella burst into tears, while Simon and Laura shouted at each other that all this was the other's fault.

Ella decided there was a small chance that the delinquent cat might somehow have got into her car and come with her to the allotment. It was definitely a long shot but she was getting desperate. She couldn't lose Laura's cat. Not ever. But especially not when the rest of her friend's life was disintegrating around her.

If it had been a hamster or a goldfish she could have just replaced it, but ginger toms were different and TomTom had a distinct personality. He was probably hanging around some restaurant being fed by the owners like bloody Top Cat.

At least at the allotment there were plenty of willing helpers when she explained her predicament. They searched the rows of runner bean canes, their crop long dead, behind the manure heap and in the water tanks, as well as in all the sheds that were open, but there was no cat to be found.

'Pity it wasn't a dog,' Stevie opined. 'Dogs are easy. Someone takes it to the pound. But cats do what they fancy. We had one disappear for months then wander back in as if it had never been away. We'd all but given away his cat bowl.'

'If I were you, I'd go and buy some tasty fish and leave it at the back door and watch out for it like Bill does with dog food for hedgehogs,' Les suggested.

'Do you get hedgehogs here?' Ella couldn't help being fascinated. 'Right under the flight path to Heathrow? I thought they were such shy creatures.'

Since there was no sign of TomTom at the allotment she decided to follow Les's advice and get some fish. She had just bought half a pound of haddock when her phone rang. It was Laura.

Ella knew at once that it was serious. Laura could hardly speak. 'Can you come round? I don't think I can bear being alone. I'm worried about Bella, and Sam's barricaded himself into his room and won't let me in.'

'I'll just nip home, then come at once.'

'Ella?'

'Yes?'

'Bring a bottle of wine.'

'White or red?'

'I don't care as long as it's alcohol.'

Ella rushed up her front steps, unlocked the door and turned off the burglar alarm. She was about to put the fish outside the back door when she felt something wrap itself round her legs, almost knocking her over.

'TomTom!' she squealed with relief. The bloody animal had been at home all the time. 'Come here, you stupid sodding animal. You don't even know how you've made me suffer! I bloody hate you!' He purred furiously in her ear. 'You like being insulted, hey? TomTom the ginger masochist. Where the hell did you get to?' She picked him up and stroked him.

TomTom stretched in her arms and yawned happily. He was a beautiful specimen, the glowing picture of unthinking masculinity. 'Your mistress would have been heartbroken. She's had one man ruining her life, she doesn't need to be abandoned by another.' With ruthless efficiency she forced the still-purring cat into his cat carrier. 'You're a cat. You can at least plead that you're following your natural instincts. And don't tell me it's the same for Simon or I'll drop you in the Grand Union Canal.'

Laura fell into Ella's arms the moment she opened the front door. Ella hardly even had time to put down the cat carrier.

'Oh, God, it's all been so horrible,' Laura blurted. 'I wanted to yell at Simon, call him a selfish bastard, demand how he could do this to us, but I couldn't, I had to try and make it civilized for Sam and Bella. And then Bella does it instead. Calls him everything she can think of, while poor Sam runs out of the room. It's almost worse for Sam because he's close to his dad, he needs to respect him, and now he finds he can't. He has to face the fact that he isn't as important as this stupid Suki. You can see how awful that must be.'

'Yes. Yes, I do.'

'And then she rings him. Of course he's got the phone on vibrate so it doesn't actually ring, but Bella grabs it and works out that she's only outside in the car, come to fetch him. So Bella goes out there and has a go at her.'

'Good for Bella.' Ella had always admired Laura's spirited daughter. Despite her outrageous appearance Bella had always struck her as far more sensible and down-to-earth than either of her own daughters.

Laura smiled sadly. 'Yes, I think it probably helped her deal with it all. I would have loved to do it myself. And then the car alarm goes off and all our neighbours are watching! And Bella spat at her!'

Ella couldn't suppress a giggle. 'Sorry. C'm here.' She opened her arms to her friend and hugged her.

Laura couldn't help laughing through her tears. 'Yes, it was quite funny, I suppose. If it wasn't so bloody sad.'

'And I haven't even told you about the cat yet.'

'TomTom! Is he still in his basket? Poor old thing.'

'He can stay there as far as I'm concerned. Let's get you a drink.'

'I'll just take him up to Sam. He won't open the door to me but he might to the cat.'

Laura knocked softly on her son's door. There was no reply but then she hadn't expected one. 'I've brought TomTom up. He's outside your door.'

She then retreated to the far end of the landing and hid. Five minutes passed and she was about to go downstairs when the door opened and Sam picked up the cat carrier and took it into his room.

Thank God for that.

Downstairs Ella had lit the fire and poured them both a large glass of wine.

'Bella won't come back. She'll stay with the tattooed boyfriend.'

'She'll be all right. She's a fighter, that one.'

'Oh, God, Ella. Bloody life. It's not what you expect, is it?'

'No, indeed,' agreed Ella, thinking of Laurence catching that train to Birmingham. 'You can say that again.'

CHAPTER 7

'Did the doctor say what the problem was?'

'No.' Claudia struggled to keep calm. 'That was what was so odd. He didn't mention anything about a fall or a heart attack or anything like that. Just asked me to come in.'

'Come on, then, that's good,' Don reassured. 'If it were really serious, he would have mentioned it.'

'I suppose so.'

They found a parking space in the street behind the hospital. Don's phone rang and Claudia guessed it was the estate agent. Diplomatically, he didn't answer it.

It took a long time to track down Dr Davies. While they were waiting Claudia asked Don to go and see her father. 'Don't worry him with questions about Mum. Just ask him how he is. He'll tell you if he knows anything.'

She could see he was about to flash back at her that he was sensitive enough to work that out, but stopped himself, which brought it home to Claudia what a kind and thoughtful person he was. She should remember that.

'Don't worry. I'm sure it's nothing we can't handle. I'll go and see your dad now.'

'Don . . .'

'Yes?'

She smiled at him wanly. 'Thanks. It's much easier with you here.'

'Good.' He smiled back. 'Sometimes I wonder.'

A few seconds later, Dr Davies appeared. 'Mrs Warren? Come this way.' He led her into a small room crowded with medical supplies. 'I just wondered if your mother had been behaving differently at all?'

'What kind of thing do you mean?' Claudia asked, bemused.

'Does she talk faster than usual? Experience restlessness or have an unusual amount of energy?'

'My mother's always been like that.'

'Do you ever get the sense that your mother feels only she sees the world as it really is?'

Claudia almost laughed out loud. The truth was, Olivia had always believed herself to be in the right and that most of her fellow human beings, Claudia and her father included, were somewhat paltry beings who lacked her understanding of the universe.

'You could say that, yes.'

'How old is she?'

'Eighty-one. What exactly is the issue here, doctor?'

'Your mother has been going round the wards persuading people to sign up for highly unsuitable activities. She talked one of our patients with a broken leg into booking a course of paragliding. His wife was really quite upset.'

If it hadn't been so serious, Claudia would have smiled. 'Oh dear, I'm sure she means well. She's got a mania for these Internet vouchers where you get things cheaply. She's become quite evangelical. She probably thought it would cheer the poor thing up.'

'Your use of language is very interesting, Mrs Warren. Mania and evangelical seem particularly apt. Has she become more evangelical lately, would you say?'

Claudia considered this. She remembered the slight look of anxiety in her father's eyes at the idea of being dragged to

Reykjavik and other proposed jaunts. 'Now that you mention it, I think she has gone a bit crazy over these offers. I just put it down to discovering the Internet.'

'I think it may be more than that. Has she experienced other mood swings, becoming down and depressed or such?'

'Not that I've detected.' She wished Don were here, to see what he thought.

'We think you should keep quite a close eye on her for a while. These can be signs of bi-polar disorder. Has she taken on any serious financial commitments, do you know?'

'Financial commitments? At eighty-one?'

'It's very common in the manic phase. People take out loans, splurge on unnecessary items. It's part of the hyper condition. It could calm down. Possibly it's anxiety at your father's fall. And if it continues, there is therapy or medication. We aren't talking about Alzheimer's or anything degenerative but it can lead to quite erratic behaviour. I do think you should take her home for now, and try to keep an eye on her. Keep her calm, try and get her to sleep properly.'

'I see. The thing is I live in London.'

'And do you have any other relatives nearby?'

Claudia shook her head. 'Where is my mother at the moment?'

'I'll ask someone to take you to her.' He pressed a buzzer on his desk and a young woman's head popped round the door.

'Can you take Mrs Warren to find her mother?'

'The older lady with the lovely hair?'

That would be her mother with her new Brazilian blow-dry. Suddenly it didn't seem so funny.

Claudia went to look for her mother, wondering what to make of the interview with Dr Davies. Keeping an eye on her mother would be no mean feat, and her father being laid up made it even harder.

Eventually they found her in the patient's day room. In fact, they could hear her all down the corridor.

'But you'll love the hotel,' Olivia boomed with all the insistence of a timeshare saleswoman about to hit her bonus, 'it's only ninety-nine pounds for two nights in an "area of outstanding natural beauty" just near the Devil's Punchbowl. That's fifty-six per cent off the usual price.'

'But I don't think Bill's really well enough,' pleaded a mousy-looking middle-aged woman who was clearly no match for Claudia's mother.

'How about two tickets for "a taste of Christmas with lovely Jamie Oliver", then? You'd get to ride on the Docklands Light Railway.'

'Mum,' Claudia tried to intervene, 'I don't think—'

'Or this great golf package?' Olivia was brandishing the offer at them on her iPhone. Sixty balls per person for only twenty-nine pounds! You'd be saving seventy-one pounds!'

'Mum . . . Mum!' Claudia put her arm round her mother.

Olivia turned round at last and smiled at her brightly. 'Hello, dear. Maybe you and Don would like the golf package?'

She and Don both loathed golf and her mother knew it. Oh God, the doctor was right, this was more than a mild eccentricity. It had become such a crazy obsession that she didn't even notice the effect it was having on other people. In fact, other people didn't seem to exist.

Tenderness and concern for her mother suddenly overwhelmed Claudia. 'Come on, Mum, Don's waiting to take us home.' She gently eased the iPhone out of her mother's hand. 'He's just been to visit Dad.'

'I'll just get my coat.'

Don was outside holding a cup of Costa coffee for her. 'Your dad is fine, but he didn't mention your mum, so I didn't bring up the subject. What's the news?'

'We need to take her home. She's been going round the wards signing up patients for endless unsuitable activities. Their families are really upset. Oh, God, Don, they think it's some kind of mania, that Mum's really quite ill.'

'But she's always had mad enthusiasms as long as I've known her.'

'Yes, but it's got worse lately. To be honest, I was beginning to worry about it, and I think Dad is too. They want me to keep an eye on her and try and calm her down.'

His raised eyebrow said it all. Trying to keep Olivia calm would be like persuading Joan Collins to act her age.

'Right. Will you stay down for a bit, then?'

'Yes. But only till Tuesday. After that I'd have to put in for leave. I wonder how sympathetic Stephen, the head, would be?'

'Do you want to keep the car? I can go back by train.'

'Don't worry, I can use theirs. Don –' Claudia hesitated, knowing that once she said the words, there was probably no going back. 'Why don't you call the estate agent? See if that house is still available.'

She saw a sudden light in his eyes, like the first gleam of dawn. 'You really mean that?'

'I'm beginning to think God's on your side.'

He put his arm round her. 'God wouldn't give your mother manic depression just to move us down to Minsley.'

'I'd be letting Drooly Dooley win.'

'He'll burn out by forty. Some younger whizz kid will suggest the French exchange is replaced by video conferencing.'

'I love you, Don.'

'Well, that's all right, then.'

Sal sat in her flat with a rug over her knees trying not to freeze. She was a hothouse flower, accustomed to steamy spas, thick-pile carpets, centrally heated cabs and a mean temperature of 24°C at all times. The word economize had not hitherto been in her vocabulary. She was now learning fast that a lifetime of telling herself she would be eternally youthful, not paying into a private or a company pension plan, living up to her income if not beyond it, and renting rather than buying had not been the pattern for a contented old age. And because the reality was now looming over *her* rather than sad-looking old folks in ads for Age Concern, she was quite extraordinarily angry.

Her anger was not helped by having to write up an interview with a half-witted anorexic celebrity who'd risen without trace from a TV reality show, but she needed the money and was grateful for the commission.

Deep down, Sal knew she had no one but herself to blame. And there was no more irritating position to be in than that. Besides, she had made a good living out of blaming other people and she was damned if she was going to stop now.

She started to wonder who was responsible for the fact that she was sixty-three, single, jobless and alone. Had she sacrificed home and family for the sake of her brilliant career? She was certainly served right if she had. But Sal knew it hadn't been like that.

The truth was she had always done what she wanted. She had never married but she had had plenty of lovers. It was just that they usually turned out to be married to someone else. And in those days men didn't leave their wives like stupid Simon had just left Laura. Why was that, Sal wondered? Back then society condemned them and now society couldn't give a stuff. Leave your wife and children and have another set? Good plan! And another set again. Why not?

That was one thing she vaguely prided herself on. She'd never broken up a marriage. She had been happy as a mistress, convinced she got the best deal, the nice restaurants, the flash hotels when she went along on business trips, the flowers, the sexy underwear. A bit shallow and meaningless? Sal hadn't thought so. Yes, there had been lonely Christmases, but she'd always made a point of getting a freebie and writing it up. Christmas in Thailand. Christmas in the Seychelles. Even, one particularly adventurous year, Christmas up Mount Kilimanjaro. Now that had been a mistake.

Besides, she hadn't wanted to marry any of them. She was no tragic figure pining in the wings. She had grabbed life and enjoyed it. She had only been truly in love once. She'd been so young. Had she really known him? If they had stayed together, if he had not left her so painfully in the lurch at Oslo airport, could they have made a solid life together, been a Claudia and Don or an Ella and Laurence?

It was a door she hadn't opened for years, and now the emotions came rushing in like freezing water into a lock. She had been on a ski-trip to Norway just after leaving school and, in a cliché to end all clichés, had fallen in love with her ski instructor, a philosophy student called Erik. The irony was, being a working-class girl from the North, no one had warned her about these Lotharios of the leisure industry. She thought Erik actually loved her. Until she got pregnant and gave him the good news. Sal could remember his face now, blank and cold as a glacier, blue eyes bright with dislike that she could have so misunderstood the rules, and all these years later she shivered involuntarily.

Erik had promptly left her when she refused to have an abortion. Would he have stayed if she had? Instead, she had found a job as an au pair and kept quiet about her pregnancy. Her condition hadn't shown that much, given that she was so tall and slim. Luckily it was the era of baggy vintage clothes so, like an eighteenth-century servant girl who knew she'd lose her job, she'd kept the pregnancy to herself until it became blindingly obvious and she'd had to move into a hostel. And then, without fuss, she'd given birth alone in a charity hospital, handed the baby girl over, caught a plane and come home. Another life. Nothing to do with her. Sometimes she even forgot she'd lived in Norway and told people she'd never visited.

She went home without breathing a word to her family. It might have been the Sixties, but liberal morality hadn't hit her small hometown. She took up her place at university and, afterwards, down in London, she'd got her first break almost at once — a junior job on *Yes*, a teenage magazine, where she'd written the problem page and always advised young women who got pregnant to go for termination or adoption, but never keep the baby. This trend became so fixed that her editor had called her in and said, 'There must be *some* circumstances where girls should hang on to it', but Sal always shook her head and said no, 'Not fair to either of you.'

God, how many years ago was that?

She felt nothing but relief when the phone rang, rescuing her from all this useless reminiscence. Sal was one to look forward not back, although even she was finding that a challenge now.

'Hello, is that Sally Grainger?'

Sal agreed that it was.

'Good. Michael Williams here. MD of *New Grey* magazine.'

New Grey was a publication dedicated to the over-fifties. It had a vast circulation and was a big success story, yet was viewed with jokey disdain and secret envy by the rest of the media.

'We really liked your piece in the *Post* about feeling on the scrapheap at sixty.'

Oh God, Sal could just imagine what was going to come next. They would ask her to write some gruesome diatribe about sex for the over-sixties or why every sexagenarian should take up skiing.

'Actually, I'm calling about a job. Our editor is going on leave and we need someone to step in for six months. We're talking to a number of people about taking over as Acting Editor and we'd like you to be one of them. We'd like it if you came in. Would that be agreeable? Say the day after to-morrow at three?'

Sal could have jumped for joy. A few months ago she would have died rather than have anything to do with *New Grey*. Now she was feeling distinctly third-agey herself; not to mention the fact that it would pay the rent. She might even be able to start a pension.

God clearly *was* an old man with a beard. He probably read *New Grey*. Maybe he was even a subscriber.

'Sam,' Laura knocked on her son's bedroom door, 'I've brought you a cup of tea.' It was hardly a wake-up cup in that it was now after two in the afternoon but she'd wanted to let him sleep today at least.

She knew she had to watch him, that, left alone, Sam would become entirely nocturnal, like a badger or a mole, and sleep all day, only getting up to play computer games at night or to go out. Ever since he'd left university he'd been trying to find a job, but found himself caught up in the Catch-22 common to so many young people: no job without experience, yet you couldn't get experience unless you had a job.

She took the tea into the darkened still-teenage-smelling room, almost tripping over his laptop charging on the floor.

'Sam?'

A grunt from under the duvet signified that he was at least semi-awake. Laura sat on the bed. 'Come on, darling, wake up. It'll be getting dark soon.'

Suddenly he emerged like a whale rising from the deep, bringing the duvet up with him. His face was pale and anguished.

'I just don't get why he's doing it.' Sam took the tea and sipped noisily. 'I mean he's so *old*. What's the point? Why doesn't he just stay with you?'

Laura decided to ignore the unflattering implication of this comment. He didn't mean to hurt her, she knew. It was just the insensitivity of youth.

Sex.

That was the blindingly obvious explanation for Simon's behaviour but clearly Sam was still too innocent to imagine this could be his father's motive. Age, or rather fear of ageing, was Laura's second theory. She wasn't even prepared to entertain a possible third. Love.

'I suppose he doesn't feel that old,' Laura suggested.

'Well, he is. He's a stupid old man. And you know what'll happen now, don't you? I've seen it over and over with my friends. He'll want to get divorced and we'll have to sell the house. Billy had to leave that fantastic place with a swimming pool we all used to go to, and Ben moved to a flat where he didn't even have a bedroom. Joe's about the only one of my friends with two parents.'

Laura's heart shrivelled at his words. She'd been so caught up with the moment that she hadn't even imagined the future, losing the house she loved, a future alone when Sam and Bella left, which would be soon now, filled with nothing but a yawning emptiness.

They both heard the front door open and the sound of two people coming in, talking to each other. Bella and Nigel.

Bella ran up the stairs and burst into the room, her face still streaked with tramlines of pain and mascara. She threw herself onto the bed and hugged her brother.

'God, I hate him! How can he be so selfish? He's ruined our life. And what about trust? Does he think I'll ever trust a man again? Or marriage. All this time he must have been pretending to be happy when our whole childhood was a sham.'

'That's not true.' Laura was disputing this version as much for her own sake as for theirs. 'We were happy. Your childhood wasn't a sham. He just met this woman and things changed.' The truth was Laura would have loved to join in slagging Simon off. Nothing would have given her more delight than to call him every name she could think of. But not to their children. She'd have to save the truth for her girlfriends.

'Don't be so saintly, Mum,' flashed Bella. 'You must hate the bitch too.'

'Yes,' conceded Laura. 'I probably do. But I have to admit that even if she did deliberately seduce Dad—'

'Euch! She must be blind as well as totally lacking in taste or judgement!' Bella shuddered.

'. . . Dad had to agree. But I know he loves you and feels totally terrible about the pain he's causing.'

'Come on, Mum,' Bella retorted angrily, 'let him hire his own violins.'

Laura crumbled. 'OK, I think your dad is a selfish shit and I hope he will be deeply unhappy and regret leaving me and, if he has any children, I hope they will cry all night and turn out to be drop-outs and delinquents!' Hardly had the words come out, and she saw the effect the reference to other children had on Sam, than she longed to unsay them.

'He wouldn't have another family though, would he?' Sam's voice begged for reassurance. 'Not at his age.'

It's *her* age that matters, Laura wanted to shout.

Of course he'd have another family.

*

Ella sat at the computer to write the very first instalment of MOAN FART DIE.

What was going to be the point of it? To try and tell some truths that she couldn't tell any other way, with the kind of honesty that would be impossible if anyone knew it was her.

She thought of Laura and the pain she was going through in being abandoned by her husband after so long together and she tapped out:

*WHY DO MEN LEAVE THEIR WIVES
AFTER TWENTY-FIVE YEARS?*

A quarter of an hour later she allowed herself a deep sigh of satisfaction.

She'd written her first blog!

It was only when Sal sat down in The Grecian Grove, the tatty wine bar that had somehow become their unofficial clubroom, that she realized how long it had been since her four best friends had actually physically been together, and how much had happened since they had.

Ella, always the reliable one, had organized the occasion and had arrived first. She and Sal had ordered the first bottle when Claudia arrived.

'Is Laura coming?' she asked them anxiously. 'Maybe it's too soon after the break-up?'

'No it certainly is not!'

They turned to find Laura, thinner but as pretty as ever, wrapped up in fake fur against the chill winter night.

'You look glamorous!' Sal embraced her, surprised at the change of style direction. Laura usually went for ultra conservative.

'In my Marks and Spencer fake leopard? I needed something

to make me feel brave.' She peered at the hideous mural of satyrs chasing tarty-looking nymphs. 'Is it just me or does that hairy lech look a bit like my husband?'

They all laughed from relief that Laura could crack jokes.

'God, I hate men sometimes,' Sal announced.

'Isn't that a bit sweeping?' asked Ella, laughing.

'No,' was Sal's serious reply. 'I honestly don't think it is.'

'What about nice Don?' Laura reminded them, raising her glass to Claudia.

'As a matter of fact,' Claudia informed them, 'nice Don has been driving me to distraction. He's had a bee in his bonnet for months about us downsizing and moving to Surrey.'

'He should meet my daughter Julia. They'd get on like peaches and cream,' Ella commented.

'Poor Don,' Sal shook her head in sympathy, 'doesn't he know you're the most urban woman on the planet? More than twenty minutes from John Lewis and you start needing oxygen.'

'I know,' Claudia sighed. 'Dr Johnson had it on the nose. If you're tired of London, you're tired of life. All the same, believe it or not, I've agreed. We saw a house down there last Saturday. I'm about to put ours on the market.'

The silence was so profound that Claudia could have just announced she'd murdered someone.

'Claudia, you can't! What about your job?'

'I'm putting in for retirement. I think they'll agree because they want to get rid of me.'

'Claudia!' Sal blocked her ears. 'Don't use words like that in front of me!'

'You're not old enough. Look at you!'

Claudia grinned. In her oversized sweater and jeans tucked into boots, her brown hair shining and fashionably cut, she could pass for forty-five on a good day.

'Well, sometimes I feel old. But once Drooly Dooley had

made such an arse of himself I felt I could leave with my head held high.'

'But you loathe Surrey!' Ella protested. 'You always say it's pure gin and Jaguar!'

'How will we get to see you?' demanded Sal.

'Well, actually,' Claudia reassured them, 'one of its saving graces is that it's only half an hour from Victoria.'

'But why are you going at all?' Laura was still mystified.

'Life, my darlings, has caught up with me. Funny, I'd been rather jealous of my parents. They're the ones who're in their eighties and they seemed to have a better time than me. Then my father had a fall and I got called in by the doctors because they wanted to warn me about my mother.'

'Your *mother*?'

'They think she's suffering from some form of bi-polar.'

'Like Catherine Zeta-Jones,' Sal could never resist a celebrity reference.

'So both my parents, hale and hearty five minutes ago, suddenly need looking after and Don's desperate to downsize . . .'

'So it's Hi-ho, hi-ho, off to Surrey you go.'

'You poor thing.'

'How dreadful.'

'For God's sake,' Ella pointed out, 'it's only Surrey, not the Outer Hebrides.'

Sal picked up her knife and plinked the bottle of Greek wine. 'Since we all need cheering up, I've actually got some *good* news. A job interview!'

'What for?'

'Well, that's the best bit. *New Grey*, you know, the magazine for oldies, so I won't even have to try and pretend to be young any more! I can chuck out my Spanx and my hellish high heels and start wearing elasticated waists and shoes from Clarks! And now that I've got you all here, let's have some ideas about what I can do with the magazine. I'll need them at the interview!'

The only trouble with this scheme was that none of them had actually read *New Grey*.

'I'd be ashamed to be seen reading it,' Laura confessed. 'What does that say about me?'

'It says more about the magazine,' Sal snapped, a messianic look appearing in her eye.

'Why don't you do an article on men leaving their wives for younger women when they should have more sense and dignity!' suggested Laura.

Ella jumped guiltily. Had Laura read her blog? But surely she couldn't have? No one even knew about it yet.

'Yes,' agreed Claudia, 'I once read a really sweet quote from Paul Newman that he would never leave his wife because it would be disrespectful and rude.'

'Unfortunately,' Sal pointed out, 'he seems to have been about the only man on the planet who thinks so. And he's dead,' she added glumly. She turned to Laura. 'So how are the kids coping?'

'The way they do about everything. Bella's angry and Sam's withdrawn. I could have kicked myself when I said this bloody Suki would probably want more children. How could I have been so stupid and tactless? That was what upset Sam more than anything.'

'I'm sure you're doing the right thing, though,' Sal reassured her. 'I recognized the type. They treat some poor old saddo like Simon as if he's Brad Pitt, when all they want is his sperm. She'll be pregnant before you can say maternity leave.'

Laura put down her glass. 'What do you mean, you recognized the type? You've never even met the woman.'

An ominous silence filled The Grecian Grove. Even the nymphs and satyrs seemed to be suddenly watchful.

'Well, actually,' Sal confessed, 'I did see Simon out with a woman at The Ivy.'

'The Ivy!' Laura repeated incredulously. 'How did you know it wasn't just a meeting?'

'They weren't behaving as if it were a meeting.'

'Meaning?'

Sal was determined to spare her friend the gorier details. 'They were holding hands.'

'You saw my husband out with another woman, holding hands in The Ivy, and you didn't tell me?'

Sal looked miserable. 'It might not have meant anything. I didn't want to hurt you.'

'You sound like Simon.' Laura stood up and grabbed her coat and handbag. 'I thought when marriage let you down you could at least rely on friendship. It looks like I was wrong about that too.'

She ran out of the wine bar, pushing aside startled diners as they tucked into their platters of meze.

'I'll go.' Ella got up. 'She's really raw about how Bella and Sam are taking it. Good luck with the job interview.'

'Oh God,' Sal dropped her head onto Claudia's shoulder, 'I really screwed that up!'

'It feels tough to be the last to know.' Claudia patted her.

'That's why I didn't tell her! Would you have wanted me to tell *you*? Of course, with Don, that's a stupid question.'

'Yes. No. I don't know. Don't beat yourself up. She'll come round and realize you were actually trying to protect her.'

'Will she? At the moment I just feel I've made things worse.'

'Maybe she just needs someone to be angry with. Simon's the obvious candidate but she can't lose it with him because she thinks it'll hurt the kids. Laura's a very decent human being.'

'Unlike me, you mean? Sorry, I didn't mean to be touchy. You're very wise, Claudia.'

'Thank you. I don't feel it. I feel helpless. I didn't realize how much I relied on my parents somehow looking after *me*. Now I suddenly have to look after them, I'm not sure I'm up to the task.'

'Of course you are!'

'We're getting old, Sal. I never thought I'd say it but we are.'

'Look, we can afford a glass of this terrible wine and we've still got our marbles. Anyway, look at you, moving to leafy Surrey. Next time I see you you'll be deep in seed catalogues and joining the WI.'

'That's just what I'm afraid of.'

Claudia sighed. She gestured at the nymphs and satyrs. 'God, I'm going to miss all this.'

'Don't worry. We'll just have to meet earlier, that's all.'

'So I can get back to Surrey for my cocoa?'

CHAPTER 8

Ella had just had a wicked but very enjoyable idea for her next blog when there was a loud rap of the big brass knocker on her front door. She opened the door to find Julia on the doorstep. Unlike her usual outdoor style of practical parka and man's tweed cap, presumably borrowed from Neil, she was wearing a rather fetching navy-blue velvet confection, vaguely Edwardian in design, which gave her face an unusual softness, plus a pretty coat in lavender and purple tweed which Ella had never seen before. She seemed remarkably dressed up for a soggy winter Tuesday.

'What a fabulous hat!' Ella embraced her.

'Yes, and it's waterproof!' How like Julia to point out the hat's practicality. She was so different from her dreamier sister Cory, whom Julia regularly accused of being too fanciful for her own good. Cory would have chosen the hat because she'd imagine herself as a character from Henry James or one of the ladies from *Downton Abbey*.

'Such a beautiful day,' Julia enthused. 'I thought we might go for a walk and then come back for a coffee.' She plonked down a packet of biscuits on the polished dining table. Ella hoped this wasn't a ruse to spy on Wenceslaus and make sure he wasn't abusing her generosity by making unauthorized phone calls to Poland or putting the heating on in the middle of the day.

'Moore's Walnut Crunch! I love these. Where did you find them? I thought you could only get them in Dorset.'

'I have my suppliers!' Julia smiled, and her face lost its usual buttoned-up expression. She hadn't been buttoned-up as child, Ella mused, quite a free spirit in fact, always off on her own adventures.

'Do you remember that time when we were on holiday in Dorset and you ran off with the milkman? To help him with his rounds? You were gone for so long we were about to call the police!'

'God, imagine going off with the milkman nowadays? We were all so trusting. I really wanted to *be* a milkman in those days, or a barmaid or a shop assistant. Cory was the ambitious one who wanted to be a vet or a doctor.'

Ella tried not to feel slightly sad that these ambitions had reflected what had actually happened to them. Julia had been young when she'd married Neil – she mustn't call him Nasty Neil, as Laurence had done secretly – and Cory had gone on to a successful career. To be fair to them both, Julia had had two sons and had devoted herself to them, though quite what she did with herself when they were away at boarding school was a mystery to Ella, while Cory hadn't yet found a man she really liked enough to settle down with.

'Don't you miss the boys when they're away?' she asked her daughter, knowing she was treading on dangerous ground and breaking the prohibition against grandparents daring to interfere.

'Mum, of course I do. I really didn't want them to go at first, but it mattered so much to Neil, and he made me see I was just being selfish.'

'Selfish to whom? Surely it isn't selfish to want your children around and to watch them growing up like I did?'

'Actually, Mum,' Julia replied tartly, 'you were always at work. The nanny was the person who was there for us.'

'Is that how you remember it?' Ella asked, stung. In that case maybe she had no right to question Julia's decision not to work.

'Let's leave it, Mum.'

Ella tried to put away her hurt feelings, but Julia's criticism of her mothering had really hurt.

'Down to the river or through the park?'

'The river for me every time,' Ella replied. They headed off across the square. A left turn took them through the narrow winding lane that led to the High Street with its old-fashioned grocers and vegetable shops. It always amazed Ella how unchanged the place felt, despite cars and the arrival of a discreet Starbucks.

The road down to the river was bordered by walls made of ancient brick, seven feet high, and lit by early Victorian lamp posts. Ella always half expected to see a lamplighter with his taper, in the company of the bellman shouting out the cry everyone would have recognized in centuries past:

> *Maids in your smocks*
> *Look to your locks*
> *Your fire and your light*
> *And God give you Good Night*
> *At one o'clock!*

They walked along the river bank, watching the far side still wreathed in mist. 'Look,' Ella pointed out, 'a swan's nest! There's the cob swimming up and down. Did you know they mate for life? I don't know why I should find that touching.'

A moment's silence fell between them which they both felt the need to bridge. 'Do you still miss Dad?' Julia asked unexpectedly.

Such a question was so unusual from matter-of-fact Julia

that Ella stopped. 'Yes. Yes, I do. Not every day, but sometimes it ambushes me when I'm least expecting it.'

'Have you never thought of looking for someone else? On the Internet maybe?'

'I'm not sure the Internet's the answer to everything. A weekly shop, perhaps, but not a husband.'

'Lots of people do.'

'I can imagine. And if Cox's apples aren't available you end up with Braeburn instead, just like you do at Waitrose. I'd rather just remember the Cox's.'

'So how's it working out with the handsome Pole?'

'He is charming and extremely helpful. I feel a lot safer with him there.'

'You're not falling for him or anything, are you?'

'For pity's sake! He's not much older than Harry!' Harry was Julia's oldest.

'Ten years older. Harry's fifteen.'

'Do you still resent me for inviting him?'

Julia stiffened. Clearly she did. Ella wondered if Cory shared her resentment. To them it must seem a strange gesture to ask a stranger to come and live with you, but to Ella it made perfect sense. 'We just thought maybe it was a bit self-centred of you not to consider moving somewhere smaller. A lot of people your age do.'

'Including my friend Claudia. Entirely unwillingly.'

'God. Your friends. They're so selfish. Most parents are happy to downsize and give their kids something instead of handing out free board to foreigners.'

'Julia, you're beginning to sound like Neil. And my friends aren't selfish. They have lives of their own and don't live through their children. I could be skiing.'

'You don't know how.'

'Skiing – Spending Your Kids' Inheritance. Besides, it isn't free board. Wenceslaus is very helpful in exchange for his lodging. And he makes me feel safe.'

'Well, I hope he's not taking you for a ride, that's all.'

The sun went in suddenly and it felt very cold. Ella suggested they head home for a cup of tea.

One of the things Ella most liked about her new guest was his extraordinary intuition. It was as if he sensed her mood. Sometimes when she opened the front door she liked to hear nothing but silence, and feel the place still belonged just to her. At others she felt the need for companionship and miraculously the aroma of coffee would drift up from the basement or she would hear the muffled sound of a distant radio. Occasionally Wenceslaus himself would appear, once in a frilled pinny which made her roar with laughter, and tell her he was making Polish *pierogi*, dumplings filled with potato, cheese and onions or spicy Kielbasa sausage with pickled cabbage.

Today she and Julia had hardly taken off their coats when he appeared in the hall, teal eyes flashing with good humour, a lock of black hair escaping that a woman of any age would have wanted to tuck neatly back behind his ear. 'It is cold outside. Almost like Poland except in Poland it cut you like stalagmite – or do I mean stalactite?'

'Maybe you mean icicle.'

'Icicle.' Wenceslaus repeated the word with pleasure. 'Icicle. Today we celebrating.' He produced a big bottle of cherry vodka. 'Because today I get job.'

'That's great. Where?'

'I am going to be barista!' he announced with all the pride of a toreador waving his cloak at the bull.

Ella smiled, yet couldn't help experiencing a prick of middle-class guilt at the plight of the immigrant settling for a job like this when he was capable of so much more.

He poured a tiny glass. 'To excellent and most generous lady El-la.' Julia noticed how he put the emphasis on the last not the first syllable. 'Others at allotment wanted to call police when they found I had spent night in your friends' shed. But El-la trust me. She decide to give me chance. Now I hope I repay belief in me.'

'Mum,' hissed Julia like an angry swan when Wenceslaus had left the room, 'you said you advertised for him, not that you'd found him in a shed! Are you completely mad?'

Ella giggled. Partly it was Julia's outrage, partly the idea itself. 'You make him sound like a garden gnome. Besides, I didn't tell you I advertised for him. As a matter of fact, I didn't tell you how I met him at all. Mainly because I knew how you'd respond when you found out. And I do wish you'd stop treating me like a cross between a recalcitrant child and a feeble wrinkly!'

Wenceslaus came back in with the vodka bottle to top up their drinks. Julia refused by putting her hand over the glass in a particularly irritating holier-than-thou gesture. What a pity, thought her mother, it would do her good. She'd thought for a moment on their walk that Julia was unbending and becoming a free spirit again, safely away from the influence of Neil, but obviously she'd been mistaken.

'Anyway,' Julia enquired nastily, 'isn't it a bit early in the day for spirits?'

Wenceslaus' answer, delivered with another flash of the devastating blue eyes, was engaging if unfortunate. 'In Poland never too early for vodka.' He held up his glass and winked. '*Na zdrowie!*'

Ella raised her glass in response. '*Na zdrowie!*'

Oh Julia, Ella wanted to say, *stop looking like that. You were so much nicer before.* But Julia was already getting her coat.

'I'll see myself out,' she announced.

'Oh dear,' Ella sighed, wishing Julia had stayed to join them instead of rushing off. 'She's forgotten her walnut biscuits. You and I will have to eat them.'

'Julia your daughter very pretty lady.'

'Yes, but always so disapproving.'

'Is simple. Not get enough love from husband.'

'You may be right. But it isn't simple at all. In fact, I think it's rather sad.'

Once the decision was made to sell the house, Claudia found things starting to move with the speed of a rollercoaster.

Don had bowled in, grinning like a gargoyle, the day she got back to London. 'Great news! The owners of the cottage have accepted our offer. If the survey's OK, it should be all smooth sailing.'

'We have to sell this place first,' Claudia reminded him.

'Shouldn't be difficult.' He put his arm round her, gesturing round the kitchen. Her kitchen. The room she had created out of love and warmth, making biscuits round the table with Gaby when she was little, the place where they'd eaten endless family meals, the heart of their home.

Some people moved constantly, seeing one house as simply a step to the next larger or grander one. Others saw them as investments, taking the property experts' advice that to maximize the profit you should move every four years.

To a lot of people, 47 Manton Avenue might have seemed a perfectly ordinary house. Just one in an Edwardian terrace like thousands of others, but to Claudia it had been the centre of her life for almost thirty years. She knew it through every season, where the sun came up, how it set in the distance, pink and glowing over the distant landmarks. Even the wildlife in the garden, the squirrels and jays, robins and rooks, the occasional fox, all seemed familiar.

She began to understand how Ella felt about her house and why she had stayed on there even after Laurence's death, maybe because of it, even when people told her to move on and start again.

Was it a female thing? An extreme form of nesting, that made women invest so much of themselves in the place in which they lived?

The doorbell buzzed, interrupting her reverie with the arrival of the estate agent and another hopeful couple.

As she unlocked the front door Claudia could hear them discussing her house on the doorstep. 'So which one's this?' asked the wife.

'The small one, only four beds, but room in the garden for a big extension,' replied an irritated male voice. 'You've got to stop seeing houses as they are now and imagine the potential.'

'I'm not sure this one's got much potential.'

Claudia hated them already. How *dare* they talk about her beloved home like that?

'Shall we start at the top?' Claudia disguised her dislike under a bright smile. 'Spare bedroom. A bit cold because we don't use it much. My husband's study.' She saw them glance at the rows and rows of books and the poster saying DON'T MAKE ME USE VIOLENCE.

'My husband's a teacher,' Claudia explained as the wife raised an eyebrow. 'Daughter's bedroom. She's moved out but you wouldn't think so. These are just the clothes she's left behind.'

Silence.

'Our bedroom.' If they didn't like this she'd spit at them. 'En-suite bathroom through there.'

She caught sight of the view she loved, over the rooves of the leafy suburb to the square tower of a distant church. 'I always think we have the best of both worlds here. It's still in London but feels like the country. Look, you can even see a steeple.'

But the prospective buyers weren't listening. 'If you knocked down the wall behind the bed you could have a dressing area going through to the en suite,' the husband intoned.

'Yes,' the wife complained, 'but it'd still be tiny compared to the one we've got already.'

'I think you're going to love the kitchen/diner,' the estate agent enthused as he led them back downstairs. 'It really is the heart of the home.'

'No point looking really,' the husband pooh-poohed. 'We're planning to demolish and build a glass extension.'

Claudia almost wished them luck. The owner of the house directly opposite had a habit of walking around naked. That should give them something to look at over breakfast.

'Can we see the cellar?' the husband requested. 'We were wondering if you could dig it out.'

'It's a bit full,' Claudia replied, doubtfully. The truth was her cellar was so chock-a-block there were things in there she hadn't seen for a decade.

The husband surveyed the Aladdin's cave of cardboard packaging, old toasters, skateboards, computer paraphernalia, Christmas decorations, Gaby's school exercise books, some-what worm-eaten, and old paint tins. She could tell he was a tidy cellar man. He probably knew where every last screw and light bulb was kept.

The pièce de résistance were the dear little plastic trays of rat poison placed to deter a once-glimpsed rodent that had popped out of the understairs cupboard and nearly given Claudia a heart attack.

'My God,' the husband murmured, loud enough for Claudia to hear, 'you'd think if you were selling your house you'd make a bit of an effort. Bet they'll leave all this rubbish for the next people to clear out.'

'Well, it won't be us!' his wife replied.

Claudia smiled as she waved them off, feeling a little glow of satisfaction that they wouldn't be back.

But wasn't that somewhat self-sabotaging? Maybe the agent had better take the next lot round on his own.

'Laura, we need to talk.' Simon's voice had been stressed and anxious. Under other circumstances she might even have felt sympathetic, but all she'd thought when he called was *Good. I hope you're in hell*. 'Could we meet for a coffee, or a drink? Somewhere other than the house? This afternoon about four?'

Laura had stared at the phone, her stomach churning. Why was Simon in such a rush? There were so many questions she hadn't even confronted yet. It had all come at her like a plane crash, Simon's revelation about the other woman, her fury at discovering the affair and chucking him out, the awful confrontation with the children.

She supposed he was going to ask for a divorce. God, she was such an innocent. She didn't even know the grounds! Thank God for the Internet, at least she could find something out from that.

To Laura's horror, the moment she had typed in 'Divorce' the sites started appearing – Quickie Divorce . . . DIY Divorce – sites offering a decree absolute in less than six months if the divorce was uncontested.

She'd clicked on 'Grounds for Divorce'. As far as she could tell, she could divorce Simon as a result of his adultery with Suki as soon as she liked. But what if she didn't want a divorce? Would Simon and Suki have to wait five years? And what about the house? Was Sam right about him being able to sell it whether she liked it or not?

The reason Laura knew for certain that she didn't want Simon back was because she'd made absolutely no effort with her appearance before their meeting. This might seem a frivolous and shallow indicator, but, as every woman knows, it is the most truly honest. Had she wanted a reconciliation she would have pulled out all the stops, blow-dried hair, perfect make-up, smart but understated clothes. Laura noted with interest that she did none of these things.

Simon hated women crying. Whenever she'd cried during a fight he had looked entirely unmoved or faintly bored. So, even if she'd wanted to, even if she'd felt desperate, Laura would not have cried.

Her hair was clean, that was important. It was impossible to feel strong and morally determined with dirty hair. She put on jeans, a simple shirt, boots. Looking in the hall mirror as she left, she saw she looked younger than usual. Normally that might have given her a moment's pleasure. Today, what did it matter how old she was?

Before she left she knocked on Sam's door. Silence. As usual he was still in bed. His nocturnal habits had got out of hand since Simon had left.

'I'm just going out for a bit,' she told the lump under the duvet. It didn't move or even register her presence. Today there was too much else to face to take on this too. 'I'll see you later, darling. I love you.'

Simon had chosen a coffee shop in the busy High Street which was crowded with yummy mummies. As a stay-at-home mother herself, Laura found herself resenting these confident young women, with their au pairs and their Babyccinos. No doubt they all thought marriage was a good career choice. Ha!

Simon was sitting at a table for two right at the back nursing a large black coffee. He stood up awkwardly when she arrived as if it were a date and he needed to make an impression. It was because he was nervous, Laura realized. At first this didn't strike her as suspicious.

'How are you?' he asked.

'All right. I've been better, but that's only to be expected.' She kept her tone brisk, avoiding his glance.

'And the kids?'

'Bella's largely absent. Sam never gets out of bed. Next?'

'Don't be hard, Laura.'

Laura resisted the temptation to throw her coffee over him. 'I'm not being hard. I'm surviving. Now what was it you wanted to talk about?'

'I wanted to say I'm still paying money into the joint account for the moment, so don't worry about that.'

'Thanks.' OK, no mention of divorce or selling the house. 'Well, if that's it, I'll be off. I'd appreciate it if you kept in touch with Bella and Sam, even if they don't agree to see you yet. For their sake I'm trying not to make this any harder than it has to be, even if personally I'd like to slap your selfish face.'

Simon winced as if she had. 'Laura . . .'

Laura had stood up and was reaching for her shoulder bag.

'It's Suki. She's three months pregnant.'

Laura sat down again. Sal had been right.

'I'm sorry about this. It wasn't deliberate, I assure you. At least Sam and Bella aren't children any more, they'll understand in time. But I can't pay the mortgage forever. We both need to go and see a solicitor and sort this out.'

It took all Laura's strength of character not to cry. She was trying so hard to hold on to her emotions for the children's sake, but the cost to her was that she felt powerless.

Even if it was the last thing she felt like doing she needed to find out what rights she did have. Probably not many. Unless you could afford to take your husband to court like the fur-coated millionaires' wives in the gossip columns, most discarded spouses seemed to go quietly.

Would she be one of them?

To say that the location of *New Grey* magazine wasn't exactly flashy was like saying the Queen was only a bit posh.

To be precise, it was in Kensal Green, an area of North-west London Sal had never even visited before. In fact, the only reason she'd ever *heard* of Kensal Green was because of the famous cemetery there and the equally famous poem by G. K. Chesterton about going to paradise 'by way of Kensal Green'.

At least, Sal noted, it was near a tube station and a very large Sainsbury's. The cemetery she would rather forget.

Unlike for her last interview, this time Sal had been doing her homework. She knew the magazine's circulation, that it was owned by a famously eccentric family business, and that it had a reputation for being rather old-fashioned, an image which its owner prized and which the current managing director was desperate to dump. This might make the editor's job a poisoned chalice, but Sal was so desperate for this job she'd swallow weed killer and ask for a refill.

The exterior of the building put Sal in mind of a workhouse, all forbidding red brick blackened by soot, but once inside it was a revelation. That any offices could conceivably be cosy was a minor miracle, but somehow *New Grey*'s were.

Clearly the eccentric owner had raided her own home for the décor. There were chandeliers, Turkish rugs, nests of tables with lights on them, bookcases stuffed with what looked like wonderful old books. In fact, the look that immediately came to Sal's mind was the Orient Express, for which she'd once blagged a freebie from London to Venice.

The only touch of modernity was in the gleaming laptops on every desk.

As she waited, the previous candidate emerged. It was the successful editor of a rival magazine, renowned for being sharp and clever, and who was at least twenty years younger than Sal. They nodded warily.

As soon as she was ushered into the managing director's office the difference in style between owner and MD became even more obvious. It was like stepping from the nineteenth century into the twenty-first. Here all was pale and minimalist with sisal flooring, wheat-coloured sofas and, no doubt, state-of-the art software. A man in his mid-forties sat behind an enormous metal desk shaped like an ammonite. He stood to shake hands. 'Michael Williams, MD, welcome to *New Grey*. You know Rose McGill, I'm sure.'

A flamboyant octogenarian in an orange fitted suit waved regally at Sal.

'Actually,' Sal held out her hand, 'we've never been officially introduced. I know you by reputation, of course.'

'That I'm a cantankerous old cow, no doubt.'

'That you invented the magazine market for older people.'

'Older people!' Rose McGill huffed. 'God, I hate that expression. It's like calling people mildly obese. They're not mildly obese, they're fat! Do you know I visited a friend in hospital and the man in the next bed weighed twenty-six stone? They carried him in with ten paramedics and had to have a specially reinforced bed. That's what comes of calling people mildly obese. We're not "older" we're old and we should be old and proud of it!'

Sal could see this was going to be a challenge. 'But the thing is people aren't proud of it. None of my generation – the baby boomers—'

'And there's another bloody stupid expression,' interrupted

Rose McGill. 'It makes me think of infants flying through the air like rocks from catapults.'

'Rose,' interrupted Michael Williams with barely concealed irritation, 'please let Ms Grainger explain.'

'My generation just don't see themselves as old,' Sal continued. 'They may be sixty plus but I call them the "Young-Old".'

'Sounds like a mountain in Switzerland.'

'You notice them everywhere. They're an entirely new phenomenon. Fit, energetic, well-dressed people who've decided that age is irrelevant.'

'Like you,' pointed out Rose McGill. 'But then, when you look more closely at their jeans and their Lycra and their short skirts, you see they're old after all.'

Sal, in a sensible jersey wrap dress, was doubly grateful she'd decided against the animal-print jumpsuit. She had to admit Rose's observation was true. Once or twice she'd seen someone she assumed from behind to be thirty and they turned out to be seventy. 'But they're your market,' she insisted. 'And what they want to read about is the things that interest them – gardens, auctions, clothes, even rock concerts by people their own age like Leonard Cohen and the Rolling Stones. Take cars: women over fifty are supposed to be lovers of safe little hatchbacks, but have you noticed how many sports car drivers have grey hair? *New Grey* should ask Jilly Cooper or P. D. James to test-drive cabriolets. Why leave all the fun to blokey blokes like Jeremy Clarkson?'

Rose McGill was quiet for a change and Michael Williams took over.

'What circulation should a magazine like *New Grey* achieve, in your view, given the competition?'

'Your ABC is what – half a million?' Thank God she'd done her homework.

Michael Williams nodded. 'Give or take fifty thousand. But the readership surveys tell us it's read by a million.'

'I'd aim to add twenty thousand.'

'You'll be lucky when everyone else is losing out to their rivals online.'

Sal had wondered when they'd get to platforms. But she was blowed if she was going to mention the word. Rose McGill would say platforms were where trains came in, and Sal agreed with her. 'Online is where you'll pick up more readers. Plus social networking sites. Reader events. Roadshows. Maybe even speed-dating for the over-sixties. It all helps the circulation.'

'And costs a bomb, as well as shooting ourselves in the foot.' Rose McGill was not a huge Internet fan, clearly. 'Online is expensive and it still isn't replacing circulation. I'm not sure I believe you can put on twenty thousand.'

'Neither am I,' Sal admitted, 'so why don't you pay me by results?'

It was a risky strategy in an industry that was in decline, but she needed a bold stroke.

Rose McGill and Michael Williams exchanged a startled glance.

'I'm assuming,' Sal decided to press the advantage while she had it, 'that my own age is not going to be a factor.' Sal had never before admitted her age in a job interview, indeed, as Ella had advised, she'd often taken twenty years off. 'I'm sixty-two.'

'Sixty-three,' corrected Rose McGill, enjoying Sal's stunned expression. 'I looked you up. I'm eighty-one, so I think we can discount age discrimination in this company. You are only as old as your ideas, in my view. You will be hearing from us, Ms Grainger.' She held out her hand, suddenly reminding Sal of Barbara Cartland dictating her five hundredth novel from her sofa. They shared the same terrifying energy. 'It shouldn't take long. Old age has made me value the need to act swiftly.' She smiled faintly. 'While there's still time.'

On the walk back to Kensal Green tube station Sal called Ella. 'Well, I have no bloody idea how that went!' she admitted. 'But what an extraordinary woman Rose McGill is. I couldn't decide if I liked or loathed her but I tell you one thing, she makes you wonder what the hell it means to be old. The woman is over eighty and one of the sharpest people I've ever met. I hope to God I'm like that.'

But Ella had stopped listening. Thanks to her friend she had just decided on the title of her latest blog and couldn't wait to get off the phone and start it.

HOW THE HELL DO YOU KNOW
WHEN YOU'RE OLD?

CHAPTER 9

It might have been the shock of Simon's revelation, or the fact that it put a brutal end to any fantasies of happy reunions, but Laura felt overwhelmed by quite astonishing pain. She had, she saw now, been living in a kind of suspended animation, sheltering herself from the worst as she tried to protect her children. And now that protection had been brutally stripped away.

Simon was going to have a baby with somebody else.

The other dream that had been lost forever was one she hadn't even been conscious of having – growing old together. By the time you got to sixty and you were, or thought you were, reasonably happy, you expected it to be permanent. By that time, you had already navigated the choppy waters of child-rearing, and even the Scylla and Charybdis of extramarital affairs and mid-life crises. The days of wine and roses might be over but you could at least look forward to the nights of cocoa and hot-water bottles.

Laura found herself, for the first time since Simon had told her about his affair, dissolving into sobs of self-pity. And what was wrong with bloody self-pity when you had something worthy of feeling sorry for yourself about?

Outside it was beginning to get dark. Laura lay on their bed and looked out at the sky, feeling bleaker than she had ever felt before. The familiarity of the room she'd loved no longer brought her comfort.

Beside her, on the bedside table, her phone rang.

'Laura?' Claudia knew at once that something was very wrong. 'Laura, you sound strange. Are you all right?'

'As a matter of fact, I'm not,' Laura admitted, hardly able to rise out of the depths of her misery. 'I had a bit of a shock this afternoon. Simon wanted to meet up . . .'

'And? He's not demanding a divorce already?'

'No. He wanted to tell me that the woman he left us for is three months pregnant.'

'Oh my God, Laura, the stupid shit! Come to think of it, he probably can't believe it either – Laura? Laura?'

But Laura had dropped the phone. In the corner of the room, just as she unburdened herself to Claudia, she had noticed the shadow of someone opening the door and coming in.

It was Sam.

Just as quickly he disappeared.

'Sam, darling! Stop!' In her stockinged feet Laura ran downstairs in pursuit of her son. 'Sam!' she kept yelling. 'I'm coming. Wait just a minute.'

But she wasn't fast enough. By the time she got to the middle landing the front door banged shut and Sam had run out into the darkness of his private pain and misery.

Ella sat at her screen and thought about the blog Sal's comment had prompted. While her first attempt had been inspired by anger at how Simon was treating Laura, this time she thought she'd have a go at something lighter.

TEN TIPS TO SPOT YOU'RE OLD

1. *Forget what you went into a room to get?*
   Don't worry, it happens to us all.

2. *Reading obituaries*
   Once upon a time you skipped over these. Now you read them with a sense of deep gratitude at still being alive.
3. *Deciding the tunic is an acceptable fashion item*
   No more needs to be said.
4. *Saying goodbye to modesty*
   Who needs a changing room? Just try it on here.
5. *Deciding you quite fancy David Attenborough*
   Go on, admit it!
6. *Forgetting your mobile number*
   Especially in moments of stress.
7. *Needing to pee*
   At least three times a night.
8. *Loathing technology*
   Not all of us are silver surfers.
9. *Talking about illness*
   Every conversation now starts with an organ recital.
10. *Wearing popsox without shame*

And send posts of all of yours!!!

Ella laughed and sent it off into the blogosphere. She was really enjoying writing these, even if no one else on the planet got to read them.

'Is good to see you smiling,' Wenceslaus commented when she went down to the sitting room.

'I've just done another blog!' Ella informed him. 'I'm finding it great fun. Like writing a diary.'

'But now you should learn to tweet. Then you can tweet about blog and more people read it.'

'*Read it?*' Somehow the idea seemed almost bizarre to Ella. She was just enjoying the fun of writing her posts.

'But surely that is idea?' Wenceslaus asked, puzzled. 'People read blog all over world and leave post of what they think. Is global conversation. But first you need to buy new phone.'

'Hang on, Wenceslaus, I'm perfectly happy with my old phone.'

'Yes, but old phone is for children and very old. Now you are Internet expert you need better one.'

'Me? Internet expert?'

'Yes, El-la. Today blog, maybe tomorrow own website.'

'No, no, Wenceslaus. The thing is, I don't want anyone to know who I am!'

A rap on the French window of the basement startled her until she saw that it was Julia.

'Hello, Mum, I've brought you some more of those biscuits you liked.' Julia was proffering two more packets of Walnut Crunch.

It was freezing outside, yet Julia was wearing a rather pretty flowered dress that reminded Ella of the 1940s fashions her mother wore. The look suited Julia's dark hair and pale skin. There was something else different about her. Ella tried to put her finger on it.

Then she worked it out. For the first time in about five years, Julia was wearing eye make-up.

'Thank you, darling,' Ella took the biscuits, glancing across rather nervously at Wenceslaus, 'but we've haven't even finished the last lot yet.'

*

'Hello, love, good news.' Don paused a beat. 'At least, I'm hoping you'll think it's good news. We've had an offer on the house.'

Claudia, who had been sitting at her father's bedside when her mobile phone rang, felt a jolt of shock. She had only just decided to move. But then, she had to be realistic. If neither of her parents were well and both needed her, how could she balance that with working in London? There would be hospital visits, not to mention ferrying them both about and making sure their house was clean, their shopping done and bills paid. She would end up having a nervous breakdown. And she knew the school wanted her to go.

'I hope it wasn't the people who were going to build the glass extension.'

'Thankfully not. The thing is, and if you're not up for this I'll understand, but they want to move by Christmas.'

'Christmas!' Claudia realized just how far she'd had her head in the sand. 'But it's November already.'

'Yes.'

'Was that Don on the phone?' her dad asked. 'You seem a bit thrown by it.'

Claudia looked across lovingly at her father. He had moved out of the bed to a chair and there seemed a little colour in his cheeks instead of the awful hospital pallor.

'I didn't tell you this, Dad, because it seemed rather a long way off and things could still go wrong . . .'

'What's that?'

'Don and I are moving to Surrey. We've found a place we like in Little Minsley. That was Don saying someone's offered for our London house. So it looks as if it's really happening. Maybe even by Christmas.'

'That's wonderful.' She could hear the uncertainty in her

father's tone. 'But is it what you really want? You seem to like London so much. This isn't because of my hip, I hope?'

Claudia got up and gave him a big hug. Being near him would make the whole thing worth it. 'Don's been wanting to downsize for decades. He's a Surrey man through and through. Always thought Londoners were a namby-pamby lot. Couldn't wait to get back to green fields and real ale.'

'He'll be pushed to find either of them these days. Surrey's all commuter belt now.'

'Well, don't tell Don that. He thinks you all sing folk songs and do Morris dancing.'

The door opened to reveal Olivia carrying a walking frame. 'Come on, Leonard dear, time for your amble down the corridors.'

'Olivia, have you heard Claudia's wonderful news? She and Don are coming to live in Little Minsley.'

'Are you now?' Her mother turned gimlet eyes in Claudia's direction. 'First I've heard of it. Nothing to do with me or the stupid questions that doctor was asking?'

'No, no, nothing at all.'

'Good, because if it is, you can go straight back to London.'

Claudia felt her spirits, already drooping, droop further. She would be giving up the job she loved. And keeping an eye on her parents was going to be no picnic.

When Sal saw the email in her Inbox from *New Grey*, she took a deep breath before opening it. If this didn't work out, she might as well get a job stacking shelves – if there were any jobs left.

'Dear Ms Grainger,' read the email. 'We would like to offer you the position of Acting Editor at *New Grey*, subject to terms mutually agreeable to both parties. This is a six-month position with no guarantee of further employment after that period.'

Fair enough. She'd always known it was a fixed term. She'd just have to wow them so much during her six months that they couldn't go on without her.

How utterly amazing! Champagne was definitely called for. She'd love to gather the girls together but Laura wasn't speaking to her and Claudia was stuck in deepest Surrey looking after her parents.

Ella, on the other hand, was delighted with the news and instantly agreed to come and celebrate.

'Sal, that's fantastic!' She hugged her friend as she sat down opposite her in the bar of the Fitzrovia Hotel. Sal had always loved this place. It wasn't as hip as some media haunts or as busy and bustling as others but a firm favourite with the more mature media type, mainly because the prices were more reasonable, the glasses large and the acoustics such that you could actually hear a conversation without shouting 'What?' at embarrassingly frequent intervals.

'When do you start?'

'Pretty soon. Their current editor is having a sabbatical so it's only for six months. I'm going in tomorrow to sign the contract. As Scott Fitzgerald said, "Happiness is the relief after extreme tension" and my God, am I relieved! I've spent so long trying to hide my age. Now I feel like a nudist who can finally take their clothes off and live!'

'Steady on.' Ella raised her champagne glass. 'My advice is once you've turned forty it's wiser to keep your clothes *on*!'

'I just can't wait to get my teeth into the magazine. I've got so many good ideas I'm itching to try out. And what I want most of all is really fresh new voices, people who can talk about getting older and be really funny and true.'

'I know just what you mean,' Ella agreed, flushed and vivacious after two glasses of Veuve Cliquot, 'just this afternoon, I finished my second—' She halted suddenly, spluttering into her drink. What the hell was she up to? She'd almost blurted to Sal about her blogs when the whole point of them was that her identity needed to be secret.

'Second what?' asked Sal.

'Row of broad beans. I told you I was looking after my neighbour's allotment. Allotments are full of wrinklies. You should definitely do something on them.'

'Really?' Sal's eyes had glazed. 'I'm not sure allotments really grab me. Not unless romance blossoms among the red-currants and the radicchio?'

Ella thought about Bill and his ardent artichokes. Actually, it might make quite a funny blog. 'So,' she changed the subject skilfully, 'have you heard from Laura or does she still think you should have told her about seeing Simon at The Ivy?'

'Zero communication. I wondered if I should try and apologize.'

'I should leave it for now. You were right, which won't make it any easier. Simon's just broken the news to her that the stupid girl's pregnant.'

'Oh, no, poor Laura!' Sal sympathized. 'It's completely ridiculous. I don't know what the woman sees in Simon anyway.'

'His sperm, stupid. When you've got the baby bug those little bastards are more alluring than millions or a Maserati. Simon might think it's his looks and charm but it was his semen she was after all along.'

'The scheming sperm-digger! Funny thing, fertility. Up till thirty-five you spend your life desperate *not* to get pregnant, then suddenly you can't wait to be up the spout.'

'Even by Simon.'

*

When Ella got home she was surprised to find the lights still on. It was Wenceslaus' first week at work and he'd been going to bed early. As a newcomer he'd been landed with the really early shift and had to be busy behind the coffee bar by seven to catch the morning rush hour.

She looked around the kitchen and the ground floor but there was no sign of him.

Just as she was turning off the lights she caught sight of a parcel wrapped in pink tissue paper. She undid the wrapping to find a brand new iPhone with a message that read: 'Thank you, Ella. Tomorrow we tweet!'

Ella felt herself welling up. It was such a surprise and so characteristically generous, that Wenceslaus, who had so little, had spent most of his first month's wages on buying her this phone. She only hoped she'd be able to work it.

Laura was beginning to feel frantic. She'd tried Sam's mobile a dozen times, rung his best friends to ask if they'd seen him, and still drawn a complete blank. She'd even driven around the streets in case he was wandering around somewhere.

Then in desperation she'd called Simon at 2 a.m.

'He's twenty-two, for God's sake, Laura,' Simon had replied angrily. 'Old enough to deal with his own problems. He's probably at a friend's or gone to an all-night showing of Fellini or fallen asleep on a bus.'

Fellini! That showed how completely out of touch Simon was with his own son. Laura slammed the phone down and went straight round to look for Bella at her boyfriend's flat.

After a long wait, a whey-faced Bella answered the door, her hair straggling in rats' tails, wearing a black Iron Maiden T-shirt and tiny briefs with BITE HERE embroidered on them. 'God, Mum, why didn't you call first? This time of night when the doorbell rings the house is on fire or it's a drug bust.'

Laura decided to ignore the worrying implication of this statement. 'It's Sam. He rushed out of the house this morning and I can't get hold of him on his phone. The thing is, he was really upset about something and I'm so worried about him.'

Behind Bella the enormous half-naked figure of Nigel loomed, his koi carp tattoos even more terrifying in their scale, or rather scales, without clothes to cover them.

'What was he upset about?'

Laura couldn't face the revelation on the doorstep at 2 a.m.

'We'll go and look for him, Mrs Minchin,' Nigel offered instantly. 'He probably just wanted to be on his own for a bit.'

Laura looked at Nigel in amazement. It struck her that this was only about the second time she'd heard him speak.

'I'd be so grateful. I'll go and wait at home in case he comes back.'

Laura stayed downstairs in the sitting room for the rest of the night with the throw from the sofa wrapped round her, waiting for news, hopping from channel to channel watching endless out-of-sequence episodes of *Friends*. In some of them Chandler had long hair and in some short. Monica was both fat and thin and so was Chandler. Laura had no idea which of the episodes came first but it didn't seem to matter. They were still oddly comforting. Like the rest of the population of the planet Laura saw the flatmates as her best friends too.

At around 6 a.m. a car drew up and she heard voices. She ran to the door to find Nigel and Bella on either side of Sam, who was exhausted and fighting back humiliating tears.

Speechlessly, Laura held him. 'Come on, up to bed. I'll bring you a hottie. You must be perished in this cold.'

Sam allowed himself to be led unresistingly away, too tired to raise an argument.

'Nigel found him in the cemetery down by the river, the

funny little one that isn't attached to the church.' She smiled up at the silent giant. 'He used to go there himself sometimes.'

'You can hear the river,' Nigel added. 'There are ducks and seagulls. An owl or two. It isn't frightening or anything.'

Laura could imagine no circumstances in which spending most of the night in a graveyard could be peaceful but she was so glad to have Sam back. 'Thank you, Nigel. I'm so grateful to you.'

'You're watching the one when Rachel finds out Ross has got engaged,' Nigel pointed out. 'That's one of my favourites.'

A Goth giant who was a secret *Friends* fan. It could be worse.

'Do you mind if we stay here?' Bella asked. 'We're too knackered to go back to Nige's.'

Bella took his hand and they went upstairs to bed, looking like escapees from the Addams family.

Finally, exhausted herself, she followed them with TomTom, who had been enjoying Laura's unexpected late-night companionship, trailing behind.

Sal put a frozen pizza in the middle shelf of the oven, and Norah Jones on the CD player. She hadn't been exaggerating. She really was excited about this job. She had edited so many magazines over the years, thought up a thousand ideas for features, forever trying to make the familiar sound fresh and to put a new twist on things and not be cynical when young journalists came up with a suggestion that had been done a million times already. Her ex-colleagues would probably laugh at *New Grey*, apart from its circulation figures, but to Sal it seemed like a novelty, something she'd never ever done before.

She just had time for a quick bath before the pizza was ready and then – what heaven! – she'd have it in her dressing gown while watching a favourite box set.

While the bath was running she lit some candles and had a check through her wardrobe. She was going to need some new clothes for the job. Mature not boring, grown-up yet subtly stylish. Oh, and no leopard skin. This had been a parting shot from Ella. It was true she did have a weakness for leopard skin. 'Leave the leopard to Jackie Collins and Bet Lynch,' Ella had counselled.

As it happened she already had a few suitable outfits. A new dress in gunmetal grey with a high neck (no ageing tits!) and clever asymmetrical folds which looked both appropriate and flattering; a beloved ISSA wrap dress (the frock that never dates despite what fashionistas claim) and a gorgeous silk blouse in leaf green.

Sal smiled to herself, breathing in the exotic scent of patchouli in the bath gel. Finally, after weeks staring into the unemployment abyss, things were looking good. She'd have six months at *New Grey* to make herself indispensable.

She'd have to use it wisely.

She slipped into the warm enticing water, submerging herself in its fragrant embrace.

In a gesture of sudden joy she raised her arms above her head, launching into a shaky version of 'It's a Wonderful World' and began to soap her breasts.

For a moment she enjoyed the luxurious feel of soap on skin. Then she stopped, the song dying on her lips.

She had found a lump as distinct and hard as a marble in the side of her left breast.

CHAPTER 10

Sal's first instinct was to pick up the phone to Ella.

She wanted to hear Ella's sensible, undramatic tones giving her advice. 'Keep calm. You don't know for sure. Just get down to your doctor first thing tomorrow.'

And of course that was what she would do.

Fear fought with anger as she tried not to panic. *It was so bloody unfair!*

She only had this job for six months. How could she go and tell them she had a lump in her breast?

Maybe the lump was benign.

Funny, that word. You hardly heard it in modern life except in relation to cancer. And its opposite, 'malignant'. The word made the tumour sound like a Shakespearean villain, a deliberately evil character with a chilling and lethal intention.

Sal rushed to her laptop and googled 'How to tell if you've got breast cancer'.

'Only you know your breasts best . . .' In Sal's case that was particularly true; she admitted it with wry bitterness, since no man had been near them for years. The truth was she'd never been one for self-examination. In fact, she remembered guiltily that she'd cancelled her last mammogram because it clashed with a sudden meeting. Maybe the Almighty had an irrational prejudice against career women.

Did she have inverted nipples? Dimpling or redness of the

skin? Sal rushed to the bathroom mirror, relieved to find she had neither.

Suddenly she smelled burning pizza and rushed to the oven. Inside was a blackened and inedible mess.

It didn't seem a good omen.

It was after ten o'clock next morning and Laura was still in her dressing gown when Bella came into the kitchen bearing brioche from the café down the road. She must have got up early to go and get it. 'For you and the runaway. His favourite.'

'Thank you, darling.' She was touched and relieved that Bella seemed to be coping so well.

Exactly how Bella made a living in the strange nether world of Goths was always a mystery to her mother, and a source of fury to her now absent father. Despite having a perfectly good degree she freelanced here and there, worked in shops for a stint, cooked food at weird festivals, ran up spidery fashions on her sewing machine and sold them in pubs with names like The Bat Cave or The Hobgoblin.

In fact, what sometimes upset Laura most was how very competent Bella was and how successful she would have been if she had chosen a more conventional way of life.

'Mum!' Bella took in the fact that Laura was still in a dressing gown and slippers. 'You're not dressed yet. Aren't you feeling well?'

Laura turned away, not wanting her daughter to see that she had been crying.

'I realize how awful it must be for you, the way Dad's been behaving.'

'I'm just so worried about Sam, and you as well.'

'Don't worry about me. You really don't need to. I'm twenty-four, I'll be OK. If Dad wants to go off with someone half his age and have babies, I just feel sorry for the babies.'

'You know about this woman' – Laura couldn't bring herself to name her – 'being pregnant, then?'

'Sam told me. I think he minds more than me. He's closer to Dad. All that staying up playing World of Warcraft together. Sam's given it up for Call of Duty in protest.'

'That *is* serious.' Laura couldn't repress a small sob.

Bella came and put her arms round her mother. 'We'll be all right, Mum. Bloody angry and a bit hurt, but OK. It's you I'm worried about. Look, I've been online and found this great course you should sign up for. It's called Relationship Recovery.'

'Sounds like roadside assistance. Will they come and tow me off to the scrap yard for discarded spouses? Maybe I can be recycled into a hopeful single.'

'Woah. That might be asking a bit much, but, it's kosher, honestly. I read all the reviews.'

My God, Laura wondered, is there anything that doesn't get graded on the Internet any more? Great funerals? Top ten car accidents?

Bella pressed a piece of paper into Laura's hand. 'There's one starting next week. In town, just near that art gallery you like, so you can go and look at paintings afterwards.'

Reluctantly, Laura read the flyer.

RELATIONSHIP RECOVERY

Relationship Recovery will help you to recover from marriage or relationship breakdown in only six sessions.

Getting through marriage or relationship breakdown is enormously painful. It's one of the most common reasons people come to counselling. Whether you stay stuck in self-pity or learn to move on will determine your future happiness. Seek help now from our experienced counsellors.

St Alphage's Church Hall
Montague Street
Tuesdays 11 a.m.–1 p.m.

Booking in advance only. Max 10 people in group.

Laura was about to throw it in the bin when the cloud of pain and misery descended again. It was almost physical how much it hurt. And the worst thing of all was the loneliness. Laura knew she was luckier than some, her children were not being taken from her, she wasn't out on the streets or fearing for her safety from a vengeful partner. But she was alone. Alone in her sense of loss. Alone in her sense of failure.

In fact, just alone. For twenty-five years every aspect of her life had been woven together with Simon's from the moment she woke up, knowing he was next to her, to the moment when they switched off the light. There had been times over the years when she'd resented him, when he'd irritated the hell out of her, as well as when she'd loved him and enjoyed his physical closeness. But she had never pictured life without him. And she had never imagined this aching, yawning, painful void.

She hadn't got anything to lose. If she hated it, she didn't have to go again.

Before she could change her mind she dialled the number at the bottom of the sheet and booked herself in.

Now she'd better go and get dressed before Sam came down and started worrying about her as well.

Much to her surprise, Ella was having great fun with her new phone, signing up for all sorts of apps and even taking the occasional photo.

Of course it helped having technical support on tap in the

form of Wenceslaus. Otherwise she would be endlessly bothering those poor people at the call centre in Bangalore asking them for the nineteenth time: 'Sorry, *which* button did you say I needed to press?'

She was especially delighted with the GPS app because, although she hadn't admitted this to her daughters, she did get lost quite a lot while driving. Whatever synapse there was in your brain which informed you how to get from A to B had got disconnected in hers and she had to think quite hard about even familiar routes. She hadn't mentioned it as Cory and Julia would start thinking *Oh my God, Mum's got Alzheimer's* and start deciding she wasn't safe to go out unaccompanied, whereas she was perfectly fine in every other way.

For the moment she was enjoying following the GPS as she walked down the familiar streets of Old Moulsford on her way to the allotments. Viv and Angelo had decided to stay away for even longer and the allotment would be hers for as long as she wanted. How nice to be so well off and free of ties that you could just extend your holiday semi-permanently.

The red cabbages were almost ready and Wenceslaus had let it fall that it was his birthday at the weekend. She knew he liked red cabbage and intended to cook him some with roast pork. When she'd asked him if there was anything he'd like to do to celebrate, the surprising answer had been 'Go hunting for wild mushrooms!'

Ella, who could write all she knew about mushrooms on a Sainsbury's till receipt, was surprised to learn this was such a popular hobby.

As it happened his shift on Saturday didn't begin till ten, so now, much to her surprise, Ella had been signed up to go foraging in Moulsford Woods, starting at six tomorrow. No one could say her life as a sexagenarian was without its excitement.

Wenceslaus, she had discovered, was very much a country lover. Last week he had suddenly insisted on taking her carp fishing. Which was how Ella had found herself, dressed in khaki, sitting on the bank of a sunlit pond, surrounded by herons, moorhens, coot, and Canada geese. To her delight there had even been the electric-blue flash of a kingfisher.

'Ssssh!' Wenceslaus had whispered. 'Not to frighten birds. If birds moving tells fish we here. Frighten birds and you frighten fish.'

They had sat silently listening to a wren sing, only slightly muffled by the sound of passing jumbo jets. Ella had watched fascinated as Wenceslaus cast off after scattering a handful of hemp seeds into the water. 'Sometimes,' he'd grinned at Ella, 'I use dog biscuits. Fish not know they are dog food so OK. You like to hold rod?'

Ella had tried not to react as Wenceslaus steadied her arm, but she had to repress a slight shiver of pleasure at finding his strong young arms round her after so long without any kind of masculine encounter.

Really, Ella, she'd told herself sternly, *you're turning into a cougar like Sal. Pull yourself together! He's forty years younger than you!*

Why, she found herself wondering, did the poor old cougar become the symbol of predatory older women? But then were coot queer or newts pissed?

'So what *do* you do if you catch a fish?' she'd asked him, to bring everything back to normal. 'Are you allowed to take it and eat it?'

'At home yes, not here. There was row in paper, Minka tell me, Polish fishermen accused of eating all British carp. Here, you catch, weigh, take photograph, throw back in pond.'

'Isn't that a bit pointless?' Ella had asked, though to be honest the point of most sports passed her by.

'My grandfather once spend whole summer and not catch one fish. He wait night and day, twenty-four hours. Catch nothing. He says is like game of chess – and fish is Grand Master!'

There had been a tug on Ella's line and excitedly she'd seen the float bob up and down on the surface.

'Pull fish in now, gently, gently, hold steady.'

She'd thought he might strengthen her grip again with his arms, but he'd just watched, smiling, as she gradually pulled in the fish.

It was a big one. Ella, despite her un-sporty nature, found her breath coming faster as she fought the fish and a pure stream of excitement flooding through her as she reeled him in. Suddenly the tackle had run out and there he was, threshing with his tail in the water at her feet. A big yellow carp with brown markings. Wenceslaus had caught him in the net.

'He's huge!' Ella had exclaimed, nervous that such a big fish could be swimming below the surface of this peaceful pond.

'Is baby, maybe twelve pounds. Big one is forty.' He carefully released the hook from the fish's mouth.

'Does it hurt them?'

'Fish not feel, mouth hard.' Wenceslaus had thrown him back in. 'Bye bye, fish. Tell your grandfather we are looking for him!' He turned to Ella. 'Did you enjoy?'

She'd nodded. It was true.

'Fishing bring you close to nature. In harmony with surroundings. At end of day you feel more complete person.'

Ella had nodded. None of her children ever took the time to talk to her like this. She wondered if they ever even thought in such a philosophical way. He really was rather an exceptional young man.

The allotments were busy today. Sharleen was packing apples away in brown paper for the winter; Stevie was cleaning his tools in a bowl of water, and Bill appeared to be having a clear-out of his shed.

'Anyone want any pumpkin seeds?' he called out.

'Put them in the seed-swap box with the other three million,' Sharleen suggested.

'How's your illegal immigrant getting on?' Stevie asked. 'Got a council house yet?'

'Stevie!' Sharleen rolled her eyes.

'He's living with me, actually. Doing odd jobs to pay his way.'

'I wish *I* could have got a free house for putting a few shelves up,' Stevie moaned.

'Not unless you're on top of Apple, Twitter, Google and Facebook,' Ella smiled.

'What's she on about?'

'Platforms.' Sharleen grinned. 'Are you not online, Stevie?'

'I'll stick to celeriac and swede,' Stevie insisted firmly. 'You know where you are with a celeriac.'

'Stevie Norman speaks,' Sharleen teased. 'They'll be asking you to do a TED talk next.'

Getting an appointment with Sal's family doctor was marginally harder than applying for tickets for the Men's Final at Wimbledon. The phone line opened at 8.30. If you called at 8.29 you got a recorded message saying the practice was closed. If you called at 8.31 the line was busy and stayed so continually until you finally got through to find all the emergency appointments had already gone.

It took all Sal's powers of cajoling, charm and finally losing her temper and yelling that she might bloody well have breast cancer before she was grudgingly given a slot later that morning.

The doctor turned out to be a young woman, but then all

the doctors these days were young women. What had happened to all the young men, Sal idly asked herself, trying to take her mind off her situation. Had the men decided if medicine was increasingly female it was somehow downgraded? Or were the women just cleverer? It would make a good piece.

'What can I do for you today?' the doctor asked brightly.

Sal sat down. She was never ill, mainly because her mother had never believed in illness and not even an aspirin had been administered in their hardy household. In fact, as far as she could recall she'd only been to see the GP about once before.

'I've found a lump in my breast.'

'Fine.' The young woman nodded.

Fine? Of course it wasn't fine!

'Could you take your top off and pop up on the examining table?'

Sal did as she was asked.

'Left or right?'

'Left. At the side.'

The doctor gently examined her. 'Yes. Yes, I can feel it. Now I don't want you to worry. There are lots of explanations for lumps and bumps in the breast that have nothing to do with cancer. The vast majority of breast lumps are absolutely nothing to worry about.'

That meant that there were still quite a lot of breast lumps that *were* something to worry about, Sal concluded.

'When did you last have a mammogram?'

'I'm afraid I had to miss the last one. Pressure of work.'

'I see.' The doctor raised an eyebrow. 'Well, let's get one done now.'

'When?'

'Today.' She printed a form out and signed it. 'The thinking now is that you should go straight to a specialist breast clinic where they can do all the treatment in one place. All much more efficient than the old days.' Sal supposed she should be grateful for this improvement. 'I'm going to send you to the Princess Lily, their clinic is excellent. I'd send my own mother there.'

Sal smiled wryly as she got up and thanked her, the voice in her head repeating the mantra, *Don't worry. This is only a routine procedure.*

Outside on the pavement she thought again about calling Ella and stopped herself. Ella would say, 'Great, I'm coming with you.' This was ridiculous, it might well be nothing. Her mother's voice replaced Ella's in her head: *Stop making so much fuss, Sally. You always did cry at the smallest scratch. Grow up, for goodness' sake.* Could you still grow up at sixty-three? Besides, her mother was long dead. Sal replaced both the voices with the previous comforting mantra: *Don't worry. This is only a routine procedure.*

'Come on, Mum, you can't possibly want to hang on to that!' Claudia's daughter Gaby was holding up the misshapen pottery vase she'd made at infant school aged four-and-three-quarters.

'To be honest,' Claudia admitted, 'the teacher insisted you'd made it yourself, but I was a tad sceptical when I saw all the other identical pots they gave the other mothers.'

'That's because the pottery teacher made them all and forged our names on the bottom. It's hideous anyway!'

'Not to a doting mother, it isn't.' Claudia had been so dreading clearing the house that she'd enlisted her daughter's help.

'Right,' Gaby announced, revealing a whip-cracking sternness that would have impressed Rosa Klebb. 'Three Piles: OXFAM. KEEP. THROW. I've got two hours before I have to meet my friend. Let's go for it!'

Claudia proceeded to drive her daughter mad by putting

something in the THROW pile then immediately swapping it back to KEEP.

'Come on, Mum, you can't be emotionally attached to an old toaster.'

'But it was a wedding present!'

'Along with about ten others. Anyway, you're hopeless with toasters, you get through a new one every six months.'

'That's because no one makes them to last.'

'Well, that one's definitely popped its last slice.' Gaby threw it firmly onto the THROW pile.

'We can't chuck away those Sylvanian families!' Claudia almost misted over at the memory of Gaby, aged eight, playing with the tiny figures of bears, foxes and badgers all dressed up in tiny suits and dresses.

'Look, Mum, if you're thinking of grandchildren, stop right now. There's no one I even fancy and if I did the thought of you hoarding Sylvanian families for our future children would have him hopping onto the next bus.'

Claudia conceded, looking at her daughter out of the corner of her eye. Gaby was bright and pretty but rarely seemed to have a boyfriend. Claudia wondered if any of her friends did or if they just went out together, just girls. When Claudia was growing up, a boyfriend – *any* boyfriend – was an essential. Nowadays girls seemed to dispense with boys altogether.

'OK, the Sylvanian families can go as long as it's to Oxfam so they find another home.'

Soon the THROW pile was resembling a curious bonfire made of incomplete board games, a moth-eaten fur coat which even Oxfam would decline, soleless trainers, a tennis racket with broken strings, a pile of empty video cases, and a very smelly black plastic bag which neither Claudia nor Gaby wanted to check inside. 'I think it might be the duvet you were sick on when you had gastric flu and missed your school trip that time.'

'But that was about ten years ago,' Gaby pointed out in horror.

Claudia wrinkled her nose. 'More like twelve.'

'Mum-um!'

'Well, Dad wouldn't touch it, so I just picked it up with tongs and bundled it into a bin liner.'

After the allotted two hours the cellar was almost clear.

'It's quite big, isn't it?' Claudia remarked. 'Maybe I should call that couple who wanted to turn it into a basement.' She hugged her daughter. 'Thank you, darling. You were fantastic. You could have a great future as a decluttering specialist.'

'No I couldn't. I'd go mad dealing with all those bumbling old dears who want to hang on to their baby's first nappy.'

'Like me, you mean?' Claudia produced a battered one-eyed teddy from behind her back. 'I quite agree. We shouldn't hang on to useless objects for ridiculous sentimental reasons, should we? I'll just put this on the THROW pile, shall I?'

'Edward Bear! Where did you find him?' Gaby clutched her long-lost bed companion to her chest.

'In that corner. Behind the un-used rowing machine.'

'OK, I take it all back. He can wait for me in my new bedroom.'

'Now who's the soppy sentimentalist?'

'What are you talking about, Mum? Edward Bear is a real person. By the way, when is D-Day?'

'Next week. Unless there are any hitches, the removal van comes on Wednesday.'

Claudia could hardly believe it herself. The head teacher had been suspiciously understanding about her announcement and was obviously going to reorganize her job. Peter Dooley had been smug. Some of her pupils had been regretful and produced little French-inspired presents. But the thing that had touched her most was a mini Eiffel Tower with a note attached from one of her pupils' mothers, whom she had taught as well. It read:

Dear Mrs Warren,
    Thank you for teaching me and Becky French. I will always remember the tapes. They really helped me with the oral. *Merci* and *Bonne chance* with your retirement.

That word. Retirement. It brought to mind superannuated greyhounds or horses sent to the knacker's yard. Surely there should be a better word? Refocusing? Re-engaging with life? Rediscovering? How about Rebalancing? That wasn't too bad. '*I am not retiring. I am rebalancing my life.*'

'Come on, Mum,' Gaby gee-ed her up. 'It's so exciting! A whole new chapter starting.'

'Yes, Dad's over the moon. He's already planning the garden shed he's always dreamed of. I may have to stop him installing a TV or I'll never see him again.'

Gaby hugged her. 'I'll be down for some country air practically every weekend.'

'Mind you do and bring as many friends as you want. I won't know a soul in the village.'

'Mum. You're going to make friends really easily.'

'Not unless I take up bell ringing or peasant shooting.'

'Don't you mean pheasant shooting?'

'It's all the same thing in the country.'

'Mum, Surrey is not Siberia. They have a Gap in Guildford and I hear they even run to a Whistles in Weybridge. Besides, there's the Internet.'

'So I'm leaving London and all my friends to spend the rest of my life at a screen!' Even Claudia was beginning to feel she'd gone far enough down this road and was boring herself. 'You're right! Of course you're right! I'll make tons of new friends.' And couldn't stop herself adding, 'They just won't be like my old friends, that's all.'

Feeling suddenly selfish, she put an arm round Gaby. 'Thank you for helping me. It's always fun doing things together.' She realized she'd probably miss Gaby much more than Gaby would miss her, which was of course quite right and proper. 'You'll be all right without us?'

'Mum,' Gaby shook her head, 'I'm a big girl now. Of course it'd be nice if I met somebody tall, dark and glamorous.'

'I'm sure you will.'

'It's so much harder now than it was for you.'

Claudia was at a loss to understand why the young thought it so much harder to meet the opposite sex now. Surely it was easier with women sharing the workplace and standing on so much more equal terms? Equality couldn't have made it harder, could it?

'Why is that?' she asked.

'Boys won't commit. They want to keep their options open.'

Claudia wondered how many generations of women had had the same complaint. Maybe some things never changed. Probably even Adam wouldn't say 'I do'.

'I'm sure you'll meet someone soon.'

'Yeah. Obviously I will. By the time I'm forty and too old to care.'

Sal sat down in the reception area of the Princess Lily's imaging department and was given a bleeper which would sound when it was time for her to be seen. With quite astounding efficiency this happened about five minutes later.

She was asked to go into a cubbyhole, lock the door, remove her top and put on a robe. The far door then led straight into the imaging area, where a vast, humming machine, which at first sight made Sal think of a salami slicer, dominated the room.

'If you could just place your breast *here*,' the radiographer requested brightly.

Sal attempted to get her small breast onto the machine's flat plate. She'd been right about the salami slicer.

'Do you have breast implants?' enquired the helpful young woman.

'Have you *seen* my breasts?' Sal demanded. 'Two fried eggs on a plate.'

'It's a routine question.'

'Why?' Sal had a sudden vision of silicon-splattered staff starring in *The Texas Breast Implant Massacre*. 'Do they explode all over all the consulting room?'

'They can spread internally if punctured, yes.'

'Thank God that's one procedure I resisted.'

The radiographer pressed the machine down hard on her breast. Sal was convinced it was deliberate. 'Ouch!'

'It can be uncomfortable. Only a few seconds, though. We need two images of each breast.' She released fried egg number 1 and inserted number 2.

'Thank you, you can put your clothes back on now.'

'Everything OK? Can I have a look?'

'I'm just going to quickly consult.' Was that a note of concern she could detect in the young woman's voice? They were *Sal*'s breasts, after all. 'If you could wait here just a minute.'

Five minutes later, she returned with someone who seemed to be a junior doctor. 'Hello, Ms Grainger, we'd like to send you up for a core biopsy, if that's OK.'

'What is a core biopsy?'

'We insert a needle into the breast and remove some cells to examine under the microscope.'

Sal felt her world begin to unpick at the edges. 'There is something to worry about, then?'

'There is a mass of tissue that we'd like to take a further look at, yes.' He pointed to her mammogram on the screen. There was a patch in the top left-hand side of her breast that was thicker and darker than the rest. 'If you'd like to follow me?' The young doctor smiled encouragingly, remembering his bedside manner.

Despite his smile, Sal was convinced he wasn't looking her in the eye.

She sat in the waiting area trying not to panic. Once in the consulting room she avoided looking at the size of the needle in a sort of gun thing laid out and ready.

'Don't worry,' the doctor reassured, 'we'll numb your breast up first. I'm told it doesn't hurt.'

Sal bit back the quip 'I bet you say that to all the girls'. She must stop cracking jokes. Especially ones as bad as that.

She lay back while they numbed her breast, still in her hospital gown, with a screen to her left. It made her think of all those happy pictures of young mothers going for their first baby scan. Strange that the same piece of technology could bring such good or bad news.

The ultrasound wand hovered over the darkened mass in her breast and the doctor attached the needle to what looked, on closer inspection, like a pair of scissors rather than a gun. Sal closed her eyes and heard a click, and then another.

'Good,' congratulated the young doctor a shade too heartily. 'That's all done now. Just lie there a moment. We're taking a look at your lymph nodes at the same time.'

'How long till we get the results?'

'I'm afraid the lab needs a week before they report.'

Sal felt like screaming. All this modern technology and it still took a week!

She put her on her clothes, trying to think about what the tests might discover.

There was a coffee shop in the foyer. The aroma reminded her that she hadn't had any food for hours and that she was starving, so she treated herself to a large cappuccino and a toffee muffin.

The whole of the next table was taken up by a group of medical staff wearing light-blue scrubs and discussing their mortgage payments. Surely they shouldn't be out here gathering bacteria while discussing variable interest rates? Sal decided to listen in. If she wasn't going to find out whether she had breast cancer, maybe she'd at least hear of a cheap mortgage deal.

And then, halfway through her muffin, she burst into tears.

CHAPTER 11

'First of all, hello, everybody, my name is Suzanne and my colleague here is Stephen. We're going to be assisting you in your relationship recovery.'

St Alphage's Church Hall was a large, chilly building which the local playgroup had clearly tried to cheer up with colourful collages stuck on with cotton wool. One entire screen was covered in children's paintings of an assortment of ghosts and ghoulies from Halloween and another with the shepherds and the three kings in an early nod to Christmas. A small convection heater attempted to bring warmth to the twelve chairs set around one end.

'We'd like to start by acknowledging your pain,' continued Suzanne, who was clearly wrapped up in three layers of warm lamb's wool. 'You have been through one of the most distressing and agonizing experiences of your life. I think we should all be silent and take a moment to recognize that.'

Everyone closed their eyes and looked down, as if it were the minute's silence on Remembrance Sunday. Laura, despite acknowledging her pain, felt the temptation to giggle.

'Why don't we all begin by introducing ourselves before you start on your own personal relationship recovery?'

Laura felt herself flinch. Somehow, every time she heard the words 'relationship recovery', she imagined a TM for 'trademark' on the end.

The group of ten consisted of seven women of varying ages, from one in her twenties to the oldest who, Laura guessed, had to be well over seventy. Clearly you were never too old to divorce. Most of the women were in their late thirties or early forties. One, she discovered, was even here for the second time.

Somewhat to Laura's surprise there were also three men.

Each stated their name and a simple sentence on what had happened to make their relationship disintegrate. It was the usual pattern so familiar to fans of TV soap operas: infidelity, unreasonable behaviour, arguments over money, fights over children. There were also one or two new notes.

'I'm Louise,' the white-haired lady Laura had spotted earlier was speaking, 'and as you can see, I'm nearly eighty. My marriage came to an end because, frankly, I just stopped trying to make it work.'

'Ouch,' murmured one group member to another, acknowledging how many marriages would crumble if more women did the same.

When it came to Laura's turn she stood up, just as the others had done. 'Hello, I'm Laura. My husband Simon left me for a younger woman. On our twenty-fifth wedding anniversary.'

A murmur of shocked sympathy ricocheted round the group, which Laura took in with a certain guilty pleasure.

In a way, the men were the most interesting. The oldest, Gerald, reminded her a little of Simon. He had the bemused yet angry look of a cornered bull. 'My wife went off, not with another man, just went off. She said if she was going to live another thirty years, she wasn't living it with me.'

One or two of the women exchanged glances of immediate understanding. Maybe they had felt the same.

Ricky, in his thirties, was clearly something of a Jack-the-lad, faithless but charming enough to carry it off – at least for a while. 'My missus said I was addicted to other women and she'd had enough.'

Laura was surprised that someone like him had bothered to come, but maybe underneath all the smart talk he'd had enough of a jolt to end up here.

The last, Calum, was probably in his late fifties, more prosperous-looking than the others in his khaki-coloured shirt, with black T-shirt underneath, with his well-cut grey hair and dark wool coat. 'To be honest,' he shrugged with what seemed to be likeable honesty, 'I'm not sure why my wife left me. She said it was because we never saw each other but I think there was a lot more to it. That's what I'm hoping to find out.'

'Good,' congratulated Suzanne. 'That leads me neatly back to our session. Today we're going to ask ourselves one question: What was our own role in the break-up of our relationship?'

One or two people in the group, especially Gerald, looked unhappy at even admitting they had a role.

'What if it wasn't our fault at all?' he demanded.

'That's not really the point, Gerald. This isn't about fault. I want you to look at it differently. All of us have a part in what happens to us. It may have been the initial choice we made, or the reasons we chose that person, which were more to do with us than with them. Perhaps there are patterns – avoiding conflict, assigning blame – which we follow in all our relationships.'

Laura thought about her marriage to Simon. How had she not known her husband was having a six-month affair? The truth was she'd been a bit relieved that he hadn't wanted sex much; it meant she could read her book in peace. Hadn't she been somewhat complacent about the time he spent away from home? And beyond that, was there not a part of her that didn't really like him any more? Perhaps Simon had sensed that and it had been part of why he sought out Suki's arms instead.

Suzanne went round the circle eliciting from each member an admission that they all had some input into the demise of their relationships.

'In my case, quite a lot,' Calum, the last to speak, admitted. 'I think my wife put up with a lot from me before she left. I used work as an excuse not to play as much a part with our children as I should have. When they were little, I found them a bit dull and when they were older, they didn't like me much.' He shrugged as if he could quite see their point. 'It's better now. They seem to have been able to get on with their lives. So has my ex-wife. Funnily enough, I'm the one who's stalled.'

'Right, time's up, I'm afraid,' Suzanne announced with the brisk sympathy which seemed the hallmark of her trade. 'That's an excellent start. Next time we'll be looking at the reasons why you are better off without the other person – even if you can't see that yet. Goodbye, and thank you all for coming. You have taken the first step towards relationship recovery.'

Again Laura heard that hidden echo of branding and smiled.

'Is breaking up not that hard for you to do?' a voice asked. She found Calum behind her. 'I was quoting the song,' he explained, 'not trying to pry, by the way.'

'Actually, I wasn't thinking about my marriage.'

'That has to be a good thing.'

'Yes.'

He held out a hand. It was reassuringly firm. 'I'm Calum. See you next week.'

As she walked towards the tube, Laura felt the shadow of her pain lessen a little. Bella had been right. Just talking about it with people you didn't know but who shared your situation was helpful. She had wanted to shelter her kids from the pain by not saying what she really felt and her friends just wanted to defend her. But here she would have to decide if being defended would really help her.

Sal sat at her screen and tried to make a list of ideas for *New Grey*. Not surprisingly, the recurring theme seemed to be about breast cancer: Angelina's double mastectomy; post-surgery swimwear; the importance of breast screening. One figure she'd gleaned from her researches really hit her. She and all her friends might think they were still young but you were ten times more likely to get breast cancer at sixty than at forty.

Come on, Sal, stop all this.

At least she'd had lots to do preparing for the new job to take her mind off waiting to hear from the hospital.

She went back to her ideas list. Given the long lead times on magazines, by the time she joined *New Grey* they would already be working on the Easter issue.

Sal loved spring. It meant new beginnings, longer days, the promise of summer. The readers of *New Grey* had time on their hands, limited resources and a huge thirst for knowledge. What about a travel piece on Easter in different places from Seville to St Petersburg to Rio? They could do a tie-in contest with one of the intelligent travel companies who provided really knowledgeable local guides.

Sal thumbed through her pile of copies of the magazine. She had been studying these along with the *New Grey* website. What they really needed, Sal decided, were some new columnists, especially an entertaining one. The usual practice would be to sign up a well-known celebrity with a talent in wisecracking humour. The only problem with this was the budget. Celebs expected celebrity fees. And they were often a nightmare to deal with.

Sal began to browse the web again. When she'd raised the

question with Rose McGill, Rose had said she'd stumbled across a funny blog while looking for a discussion of sex for the over-sixties. 'You should read it. It's got a wonderful title – a pun on EAT PRAY LOVE – but blow me if I can remember it. I'll let you know when it comes to me.' Rose McGill had laughed loudly. 'I warn you, it'll probably be in the middle of the night.'

As Sal sat here, hand on her chin, staring into space, trying not to think about cancer, three words leapt suddenly onto the screen of her phone: MOAN FART DIE.

It was a message from Rose McGill. 'Just remembered the name of the funny blog. Enjoy. Rose.'

A moment later Sal was reading it and laughing uproari-ously. The writer of this was certainly someone with an uncom-promising sense of humour. No sentiment wasted here.

With a tickle of excitement she read through the blog. Maybe the writer could be her new discovery!

To her disappointment there were no details given about the blogger. No picture. No self-serving descriptions of the individual's previous career. And, so far, only three posts.

The first was entitled: WHY DO MEN LEAVE THEIR WIVES AFTER TWENTY-FIVE YEARS?

Sal read it at once, grinning and squirming in equal measure. This was great stuff. Biting. Witty. Outrageous in its black humour. This must surely be written by someone whose own husband of twenty-five years had recently left them. Yikes. Poor guy. He was being slowly skewered on the turnspit of his ex's merciless wit.

Should she show Laura this? No, maybe she was still too raw. The next blog was a very funny quiz to find out if you were old yet. The final post was probably the one that had caught Rose's eye: STILL SEXY AT SIXTY. But do the over-sixties actually *want* more sex?

What followed was a hilarious demolition job on every

famous person from Jane Fonda to Joan Collins who claimed that sex had never been better, and the writer's own submission that after sixty, sex – no matter how erotically it was offered – couldn't touch a glass of wine and an old movie.

Yes, thought Sal, even keener now, if I could get the writer of *this* to do a column for *New Grey*, it would be really new and original.

When the doorbell rang she didn't even take it in, so caught up was she with her new discovery. It turned out to be her upstairs neighbour, clutching a letter which had been put in her post box by accident.

Sal saw at once it was from the Princess Lily Hospital.

Sensing her neighbour's interest in this development she resisted the temptation to tear it open there and then, thanked her, and shut the door.

Once inside, Sal ripped open the envelope and pulled out the letter, tearing it as she did.

The letter gave no information, but merely called her back for her follow-up appointment. Sal panicked and looked at her watch to check the date. She hadn't missed it. It was in two days' time.

A fine mist still hung in the trees, lit from behind by veiled pink sunlight, giving Moulsford Woods a peculiar and delicate magic even at the ungodly hour of 6 a.m.

Wenceslaus had gone ahead, his nose wrinkled like a truffle hound's.

'Look, El-la!' he called excitedly. 'Is chanterelle. See there, buried under big tree!'

At her feet Ella spotted a shiny ochre-yellow fungus the size of her hand, buried under leaves and mud.

She knelt down and started to scrape the mud off. A small snail fell out and Ella shuddered.

'Snail likes chanterelle too.'

'Careful, Mum, let's make sure it really is a chanterelle!'

Ella repressed the annoyance she was feeling at Julia, both for being her usual bossy self, and also for being here at all, especially clutching a mushroom-picker's handbook. Neither Ella nor Wenceslaus had invited her and yet she had turned up at 5.30 a.m. armed with coffee, croissants and the guidebook to spotting the different fungi. God knows where she'd even found a café that was open.

Still, it was too glorious a morning to be resentful. The sun was rising now, burnishing the tops of the trees with gold, and it felt as though they might be the only people awake in the world, or in London anyway, witnessing all this beauty.

'It says here there's something called a false chanterelle which looks the same but isn't edible.' Julia pointed to the collection in Wenceslaus' basket. 'That one's an oyster mushroom, that's definitely edible. And those are just normal field mushrooms like the ones you buy at the greengrocer's.'

Ella realized Julia was slipping into head-girl mode, Ella's least favourite Julia mood.

'That's a penny bun.'

'Can you actually eat that?' Ella asked, poking the large mushroom with a tawny pink top, which did indeed look a bit like those old-fashioned loaves.

'Absolutely,' decreed Julia. 'Apparently, it's delicious with pine nuts and lemon. Oh my God, what is that smell?'

From behind his back Wenceslaus, a wicked look in his eye, produced a six-inch fungus with a slimy green cap on top shaped exactly like a penis.

'What the hell is that?' demanded Ella.

Julia's gaze stayed fixed on Wenceslaus and the penis.

In the end, Ella grabbed the book. 'I think it must be a Stinkhorn. *Phallus impudicus.* Well, it certainly looks *impudicus* to me, not to mention positively *erectus*. Insects eat the green slime, it says here, and spread the mushroom's spores that way.'

Eventually Julia managed to drag her eyes away from Wenceslaus and his phallus, but only after an indecently long time. 'Look, Mum! There's a puffball.' Quite a small one but I bet it'll taste good! Let's all go back and have it for breakfast.'

'And this is edible? Are you sure?'

'Yes, Mum,' Julia was back to being head girl now, 'I am absolutely one hundred per cent sure.' Just as they were leaving Julia spotted a small pink-capped mushroom and slipped it in with the others. 'We can look that one up at home.'

Half an hour later, they were sitting round the kitchen table, tucking into fresh-picked mushrooms on toast, cooked by Julia in lashings of butter, and tasting like food straight from Heaven.

Ella noticed that Julia was giving all the best mushrooms to Wenceslaus, and hoped it was only because it was his birthday.

An impatient knock on the door heralded the arrival of Neil, even angrier than usual, to collect Julia for a visit to their sons. 'We're supposed to have left half an hour ago!' he informed Julia, casting a hostile glance round the table, especially at Wenceslaus. 'I'm glad you were happy to cook his breakfast rather than mine.'

'You didn't get up at dawn to pick the mushrooms.'

'And why weren't you answering your damn phone?'

'I forgot it.'

He glanced at the phone on the table. 'What's that, then?'

'That's an iPhone,' Julia pointed out. 'It's Mum's.'

'You mean your mother has an iPhone?' he asked incredulously.

'Wenceslaus bought it for her.'

'Well, I hope it was with his money, not hers.'

Wenceslaus said nothing, refusing to take the bait.

'What a particularly unpleasant thing to say, Neil,' Ella replied.

'We must get on the road. The boys will be waiting. Naturally, their grandmother doesn't want to come and visit her grandsons,' he added.

'Their grandmother doesn't think they should even be at boarding school,' Ella replied affably. 'But as she feels it's entirely your decision, she stays well out of it.'

Wenceslaus, clearly wishing to remove himself from the miasma of disapproval Neil had brought into the room, began to clear the table.

After Julia and her husband had left, Ella tackled the frying pan. The basket of mushrooms next to the oven was empty. 'Gosh, we got through the whole lot.' Behind her she heard the sound of Wenceslaus violently retching. With great presence of mind he made for the downstairs loo.

Ella remembered that Julia had slipped an extra mushroom in with the others, intending to identify it later. Half of it was still on the floor. Ella picked it up and opened the book. Its name spoke for itself. *Russula nobilis*. It was closely related to the *Russula emetica*, the Beechwood Sickener.

'Come on, laddie,' Ella ordered him with a presence of mind equal to his own, 'get in the car. I'm taking you to hospital.' She handed him a bowl to have on his knee. 'Just throw up in there.'

Laura saw the letter the moment she walked in the door.

There were others on the mat but there was something about this one that gave off trouble like the glow of lethal radiation. The stationery was cream vellum and the paper was thick and superior. Laura picked it up and examined it. In the corner was a franked stamp with the words Merlin & Whittle, Solicitors.

The tiny stream of relief and self-confidence that had started to flow in her was instantly dammed.

She made herself a cup of mint tea and stared at it. Whatever was in it, she guessed it would not be good. She knew Simon. He would only resort to expensive lawyers if it were something he didn't dare say to Laura face to face.

She was right.

The letter stated pompously that since the marriage between herself and Mr Simon Minchin had suffered irretrievable breakdown, Mrs Minchin might like to prepare a draft divorce petition citing Mr Minchin and appoint legal advisors of her own.

Laura found that she was shaking. Simon wanted a divorce and the easiest way to get it was if she accused him of adultery.

She knew that in these days of so-called No Fault divorce the law didn't care who was to blame when a marriage collapsed. But what if she didn't want to go and see a lawyer, what if she didn't want a divorce at all?

Laura found herself turning, as she often did, to Ella.

She tried the landline first, then Ella's mobile, but there was no answer. She was about to put down the phone when Ella finally came on the line.

'You'll never guess where I am. In A and E.'

'Oh my God, what's happened?'

'It's all right. Crisis over, I hope. I went mushroom picking with Wenceslaus, and Julia my know-it-all daughter managed to feed him something called a Beechwood Sickener.'

'Is it poisonous? Some of these mushrooms are absolutely lethal.'

'Fortunately, this one just makes you very, very sick. I don't think mushrooms will be on his menu for a very long time. What did you want, by the way?'

'I've just had a letter from Simon's lawyers. He wants me to start divorce proceedings.'

'Bloody barefaced cheek! We need to get together and discuss this.' Ella saw Julia getting out of a taxi and running towards them.

'Got to go. Here comes my penitent daughter. I'd better make the most of her being in the wrong for once.'

Laura put the phone down and turned round. Sam was standing two feet away, his face as blank as a polished slate. 'I told you Dad would want a divorce,' he muttered bleakly. 'Now we'll have to move, you'll see!'

'Have you talked to Dad since it all happened?' Laura asked gently.

'He's left messages. Obviously, in this age of limited communication, he's found it hard to connect.' The bitter irony in Sam's voice made her long to hug away the hurt. In recent years he had been much closer to his father. While most boys grew away from their fathers in their teenage years, Sam had been the opposite. Until now. How could Simon simply tell himself Sam was an adult now and could deal with a break-up? She suspected the truth was that seeing Sam face to face would make him feel too guilty. He might tell himself that marriages come and go, but he knew he'd let Sam and Bella down badly and just didn't want to face them.

How cowardly was that?

'I'm going out. To Joe's. At least they still have some kind of family life!'

Laura bit back the tears as she looked around the house she had nurtured and loved over the twenty-five years of their marriage. It had always felt like a real home. Laura knew she had the knack of making places warm and welcoming. It was something about the atmosphere, the comfort of the place. Sofas to sink into. A real fire. A mantelpiece with objects collected carefully and all imbued with meaning. The smell of polish from the oak boards. Flowers in vases. Framed photos. The warmth of the kitchen. It had always been a house that enveloped you and held you safe. But that, as it turned out, had all been an illusion.

Julia rushed up to her mother in A & E, looking pale and distraught with no sign of her usual calm self-righteousness. 'Oh, my God, Mum, is he OK?'

'They think so. They're keeping him under observation for a while just to be on the safe side.'

'Can I see him?'

'As long as you don't feed him any mushrooms.' Julia gave her a sour look. 'Come on, I'll show you.'

Wenceslaus was in the end bed in what seemed to be a ward full of people with smoker's coughs.

Julia rushed up to him and, without any warning, kneeled down by the side of his bed and took his hands in hers. 'Wenceslaus, I am *so* sorry. This was all my fault. The poisonous mushroom must have got mixed in with the others. I only brought it back to look it up. Are you really all right?'

There was a desperate edge to her voice that startled Ella. This was more than just friendly concern or even worry that it might be her doing. Julia's eyes were fixed on Wenceslaus as if he were Michelangelo's David.

Wenceslaus, for his part, was behaving entirely normally. Either he was so used to female worship that he took it for granted or he was so genuinely modest he hadn't even noticed.

Ella almost wished that she hadn't caught sight of that desperate worshipping glance. She suspected her daughter's marriage wasn't particularly happy but Julia had never said anything to her about it. She'd assumed, like countless other women, Julia loved her children and had decided to put up with a rather mediocre relationship rather than rock the boat.

Ella wondered if it was her maternal duty tactfully to warn her daughter about falling for Wenceslaus, even if Julia didn't intend to act on her feelings. Ella decided she wasn't up to it. Julia was so difficult anyway. Besides, she might be exaggerating the problem. A little crush on Wenceslaus would probably light up a dull life. Ella was also aware of something else – surely it couldn't be possessiveness on her part?

'Come on, Julia, let's give the boy some peace.' Ella realized she'd unconsciously stressed the age difference between them. 'Wenceslaus, call me when they say you can go home.'

'No,' insisted Julia fiercely, 'call me. It's the least I can do since I caused the problem.'

'Two ladies fighting over me,' Wenceslaus produced a cheeky grin that made him look about six, 'I must eat more often the poisoned mushrooms.'

Ella did up her coat. If Wenceslaus' joke about them competing for his attention was even a little justified, it would be highly undignified and more than a little embarrassing.

Claudia was waiting for the removal van and telling herself she wasn't going to cry. This might be the end of a major chapter in her life, but it was also the beginning of a new one.

During the day of packing up, Don had been in his element, jotting down on the outside of each box a list of all the objects inside to make it easier at the other end, making cups of tea, telling the post office their new address to forward things to.

'You're so efficient you could start a business,' Claudia told him. 'Don Does Moving.'

'Is that a compliment or an insult?' Don asked, looking faintly guilty that it was he who had wanted so desperately to go.

'A compliment, of course.' Claudia ruffled his still-abundant grey hair.

'Are you OK?' he replied. 'Do you want to go round the house and say goodbye?'

'I think that would make it worse. Best just to go, I think.'

An ancient little Fiat pulled in the drive and Gaby jumped out, wearing an enormous baggy old coat. 'Phew! Thought I'd missed you.'

'Just off, as a matter of fact.' Don put his arm round her. 'Your mother's feeling a bit weepy at saying goodbye.'

'I thought that might be the case so I've got you a little surprise to soften the blow.' Gaby delved inside the voluminous coat and produced what at first appeared to be a fur ruff.

Until it moved.

'Oh my God, it's a puppy!'

'He's the cutest dog on the entire planet. Everyone on the street stops and asks about him, and my flatmates really, really didn't want me to take him away.'

Gaby handed him over. He was long-haired, with ears in a lighter-coloured fur, and vast, soulful eyes. 'I've never seen anything like him. What is he?'

'A cross between a cocker spaniel and a Bolognese.'

'You're making that up!' Claudia shook her head. 'I've never heard of a breed called Bolognese!'

Don tickled the little dog's ears. 'Sounds very saucy.'

'They're Italian. From Bologna. They're usually white but I thought that was a bit impractical so I found a black one! You have to have a dog if you live in the country. Everyone does. He'll help you meet people.'

'Does he have a name?'

'One of my flatmates calls him Vito – the Dogfather!'

'Vito it is.'

Vito, who had clearly been to charm classes in a previous

life, was already looking blissfully comfortable in Claudia's arms. 'We haven't got a dog bed,' she suddenly remembered, 'or any dog food.'

'Both in my car. I'd better say goodbye to you. The removal men look eager to go. I'll call later. Goodbye, Dad. Goodbye, Mum. Goodbye, Vito. See you all in Surrey.'

And Claudia, who had never particularly wanted a dog, now saw how clever and thoughtful Gaby had been. Vito provided a small, fluffy, big-eyed distraction.

'God knows what they'll make of a Bolognese in Minsley.' Claudia leaned down to settle the little dog on the carpet next to her feet. 'They'd probably eat you on spaghetti.'

By the time she had successfully installed Vito in the space by her feet they were at the end of the road and her home, her *old* home, was already out of sight. Claudia decided she wouldn't drive past it when she next came to town. Houses belonged to the people who lived in them and hers would now be in Little Minsley.

They reached Minsley an hour and a half later after ages stuck on the M25. The van was already waiting for them. Claudia was grateful that the sun was shining and she could even detect the last faint scent of lavender as the removal men brushed past the flowerbed carrying their endless packing cases up the front path.

Don took charge with obvious relish, leaving Claudia to unpack her treasures and Vito to play in the discarded newspaper and hide in the empty cardboard boxes.

Four hours later, the sitting room, kitchen and their bedroom were unpacked and the boxes flattened into a neat pile. Claudia made everyone tea and found that Don had even put 'Chocolate Digestives' on the list of contents in a packing case destined for the kitchen. He was wasted as a teacher.

They didn't need to unpack everything as the rest of the boxes wouldn't be collected for a couple of days.

'Let's go and eat in the pub later,' Don suggested. 'Introduce ourselves to the most important place in the village.'

Claudia heard the sound of the front gate being opened and looked out. Her father Len was hopping up the garden path on crutches carrying a large bunch of dahlias.

'Dad!' Claudia ran up the path. 'When did you get out of hospital?'

'Three days ago. Not a moment too soon. I was going crazy in there. Would have shot them all with a tommy gun if I'd had one.'

'Just as well you didn't, then.' It was so wonderful to see him back to his old impish self.

He handed over the magnificent red flowers. 'There you go. Last of the season. Our neighbour Ted grows them, sells them from a jug at the bottom of his garden, a pound the lot.'

Claudia remembered from her childhood how many old men did exactly this, growing and selling flowers and the surplus produce from their cottage gardens, and she was delighted it still happened. She would make a point of buying as much from them as she could next year.

'Where's Mum, by the way?' It had just struck her as odd that her mother hadn't come too.

'Oh, she's never around. Always off on some jaunt.' He sighed, looking momentarily troubled. 'Hardly see her these days.'

Claudia sighed inwardly. Still, that was part of the reason she'd come, she'd face up to that tomorrow.

'Dad,' Claudia suddenly cheered up, 'come and see what Gaby's given me.' She led the way into the sitting room.

Vito raced towards them and launched himself at Len's tweedy trouser legs.

'So what's that when it's at home?'

Claudia couldn't face telling everyone in Minsley her dog was called a Bolognese. 'He's cocker spaniel mixed with some kind of Italian breed. That's why we call him Vito. Like the Godfather.'

'Italian, is he? We'll have to teach him to chase English rabbits. Here, boy.' Len slumped down into an armchair and the little dog instantly leapt into his lap. 'It's the country for you now, lad. No more *dolce vita* in London.'

It warmed her heart to see her father's face take on its old jovial lines, and it struck her how long it had been since she'd seen the larger-than-life father she was used to. A hip fracture was bad enough at his age, and the loss of independence that went with it, but she suspected the real cause lay with her mother. Tomorrow she would ask her father directly, but she knew his protectiveness of Olivia, as well as his reliance on her, would mean that he didn't tell the whole truth. She needed to see for herself. If only she could pin her mother down in this whirlwind of activity she wrapped herself in.

'Tell you what, Dad, why don't I drive you home? I can walk back. Vito needs the exercise.'

Claudia helped her father swing his still-painful hip into the car and tucked the little dog by his feet. She waited a moment till he was comfortable.

'So, how's Mum been?'

His face took on a strained quality. 'Claudia, I worry about her. She's never admitted to her age, always been such a live wire, but she's like one of those spinning tops that go careering all over the place. I'm afraid one of these days she'll spin right off the edge.'

They were approaching her parents' house.

'Dad.' Claudia pulled the car in for a moment.

'Why are we stopping here?'

'Because there's something we need to talk about.'

Her lovely father, always full of jokes, the life and soul of the golf course, looked almost fearful, as if whatever it was she had to say, he wasn't sure that he wanted to hear it.

'When you were in hospital, the doctor called me in. They were worried about Mum. They thought her behaviour was odd.'

'Odd? Why?'

'She was going around the beds in the wards signing people up to all sorts of unsuitable activities.'

'She's always doing that. She wanted me to do tenpin bowling – and I can't even walk.'

'Exactly. The doctor thought she might be driven by some kind of mania.'

'Mania?'

'Yes, as in what they used to call manic depression.'

'But your mother's never depressed. Far from it.' He looked as if a little depression might come as a peaceful change.

'Not yet. They wanted Don and me to keep a bit of an eye on her.' She reached over and took his hand. 'That's partly why we've come to live nearby. Though for goodness' sake don't tell Mum that.'

'I did wonder. It was all so sudden.'

'Don's in seventh heaven moving here.'

'Manic depression! That sounds so serious.'

'There are degrees of it, apparently. It can respond well to therapy and they have very good medication nowadays.'

Len shook his head. 'Therapy! Can you imagine your mother having therapy? She's always despised that kind of thing. And she'd never take medicine, your mum. She won't even take pills for her rheumatism.'

'Then we may have to persuade her. The tricky bit will be getting her to see she needs to.'

'You're telling me,' her father underlined the job ahead of them. 'I'm glad it's you rather than me.'

Claudia repressed a sigh. Still, wasn't this the reason she'd left London and moved to Little Minsley?

The phone in her bag rang and Claudia jumped. They'd been here such a short time she wasn't expecting any calls.

'Claudia, Ella here. We need an urgent meeting. Simon the Shit wants Laura to divorce him and I think we should all be there for her to discuss it. Any chance you could make it up to town next Tuesday?'

Claudia felt as if Ella had offered her some cool spring water after a long walk to a destination she didn't want to reach anyway. 'London! Ella, I'd love to!'

'Seven-thirty at The Grove, then?'

'I'll be there. Don't worry.'

Ella then rang Sal to make sure she could come as well.

'Ella,' Sal hesitated, not at all convinced she could carry off an evening with her best friends and keep her news to herself, 'I'm not sure I can come . . .'

'Sally Grainger!' Ella commanded. 'How often do I issue a three-line whip? Laura needs us.'

Sal bit her lip. If only her friends knew how much she might need their support as well. But she had come to the decision she could only get through this if she kept it to herself, and there was no way she could weaken so soon. Besides, the doctor might be summoning her in for good news. The worrying mass of tissue might not be cancer at all.

'Of course I'll be there. Seven-thirty at The Grecian Grove?'

As she watched her daughter helping Wenceslaus out of the car Ella could guess the explanation for her behaviour. Julia was the kind of person who wanted, needed even, to look after people. Her sons had been sent off to boarding school and her husband required very little from her except clean shirts and his meals on the table.

It struck Ella what a curious mix her daughter was. Strong, forceful even, in some ways and yet frighteningly fragile in others. Julia, she was sure, had been furious when Wenceslaus moved in, seeing him as a cuckoo in the family nest, devouring advantages which should be hers. But then she'd got to know him. As well as his extraordinary looks, Wenceslaus had an innocent charm and an open and appealing nature. To Julia's horror she'd clearly found he evoked her sympathy. But sympathy had metamorphosed into attraction and now, Ella feared, even obsession.

'Are you all right?' Julia fussed, trying to help him up the garden path.

'I fine. Thank you.' Wenceslaus disentangled himself from her grip.

Ella caught the bereft look on Julia's face.

Oh dear God, this wasn't good news. What the hell should she do?

'So, Julia,' Ella asked brightly, knowing her question sounded like something from the 1950s and would be deeply unpopular, but wanting to bring Julia back to reality, 'what are you giving Neil for supper?'

Julia shot her a look of deep irritation. 'I don't really care. Something from the freezer will do.'

'But you're such a good cook.'

'I could put deep-fried rubber tyre in front of Neil and he'd still eat it.'

Wenceslaus started to laugh at what he clearly found a very witty joke from Julia.

Well, that reminder of her domestic duties had been a success.

'How about you, Wenceslaus,' Julia enquired solicitously, 'are you feeling hungry enough to eat?'

'Don't worry about that,' Ella said firmly. 'I'll cook something plain later for us both. Why don't you get off home and defrost that rubber tyre?'

'Claudia, it's so good to see you!' Ella folded her old friend in a bear hug of an embrace as she arrived in The Grecian Grove. 'You look different already!'

'Don't be daft, I've only been gone a few days.'

'No, I'm sure you're all apple-cheeked and rural.'

'That's running for the bus, not moving to Surrey! Anyway, where's Sal?'

It seemed strange that there would only be three of them meeting up but Ella had decreed that if Laura needed their help they would be better deciding what to do without her.

'There's she is!' What on earth has she got with her?' Sal seemed to be struggling with an oversized brown package. 'And what's more, what is she wearing?'

Amongst the drab suburban early evening drinkers Sal, in her black leather studded jacket, chiffon handkerchief skirt and black leggings, stood out like a punk rocker in a group of postulants. 'Sal! Sal! Over here! What have you got there? It looks like a pull-along coffin.'

To their surprise Sal flinched, then shook her head as if to rid herself of an unwelcome image. 'It's for you.' She placed the enormous parcel in Claudia's arms.

Intrigued, Claudia tore open the paper. Inside was a large shopping trolley in an eye-catching zebra-skin fabric.

'I never gave you a goodbye present,' Sal explained. 'In the country everyone has a shopping trolley.'

'Yes,' agreed Ella, 'you'll blend in at once. Especially if you stop in the middle of a pedestrian crossing.'

'Like in Abbey Road,' Sal agreed.

In fact, most people in Minsley, Claudia had discovered, carried their shopping in either baskets or occasionally even trugs, but tactfully she kept this to herself.

'Thank you, Sally. No one will ever guess I've moved from London now.'

'So how is it?'

'Don loves it.'

'I didn't ask about Don.'

'The dog loves it.'

'*Claudia!*'

'I expect I'll get used to it. It's just such a huge jolt. Resigning from teaching—'

'Are you coping with that OK?' Ella interrupted. 'It must be such a change for you.'

'Actually,' Claudia admitted, 'I'm missing it like hell. The backbiting in the staffroom, being shafted by Drooly Dooley, patronized by the deputy head for my lack of techno skills . . .'

'Yes,' Ella laughed, 'I can see it must be nice to leave all that behind.'

'No, I mean it!' Claudia grinned. 'I really do miss that stuff. And, of course, the pupils.'

'You could probably do some teaching in the country. Volunteer in a school or something?'

'I know. Anyway, there's lots to take my mind off it. My father's fractured hip. My mother's manic depression.'

'Oh my God, I suppose this is the future for us all.'

'But your mother's such a powerhouse.'

'I know, but it's all got out of hand. She's had the manic bit for months, now we're waiting for the depression. It's going to be hard for her to accept it. How about you two?'

Sal bit her lip. She longed to tell them about the biopsy she'd just had but she couldn't face the sympathy she'd see in their eyes. If she told her friends, then she'd have to tell the magazine. The only way she could hold all this together was to keep silent. Besides, it might all be nothing. 'I'm still looking for ideas for the new magazine. And a new columnist. As a matter of fact, I found a blog I love and I'm trying to track down the writer.'

'And have you found them?'

That's just it. The blog's anonymous. It's so infuriating. The writer has the most wonderfully black sense of humour; I'm itching to sign them up.'

'Oh yes,' Ella sipped her wine, her interest piqued, 'what's the blog called?'

'It's a pun on that silly *Eat Pray Love* book. Moan Fart Die. Isn't that terrific? So brilliantly unsentimental.'

Ella choked on her white wine.

'Good title,' Claudia agreed. 'Probably some crusty old gent.'

'No, it's definitely a woman.'

Ella quietly panicked. If she confessed to being the author she would lose the freedom she revelled in. Besides, it would mean admitting that she'd drawn on their private lives as well as on her own. Especially Laura's.

'Anyway,' she changed the subject abruptly, 'I thought today was about Laura and Simon. First he admits to having an affair on their silver wedding anniversary, then he tells her the bloody woman's pregnant. Now he wants Laura to divorce him so he can marry the Sperm-digger before the baby arrives.'

'Oh my God, that's dreadful. Why are men never satisfied? Laura's been the perfect wife.'

'Not perfect enough. She committed the unforgivable sin of growing older.'

'It's so unfair!' Sal insisted. 'She's been a better homemaker than any of us. She cooks brilliantly, looks amazing, the house is like a page out of *Interiors*! She doesn't even have a demanding job to distract her from looking after Simon. If Laura isn't safe, no one is. What's the matter with men? It's like that song by the Eagles. You know, the one about having lots of fine things laid upon your ta-a-ble and only wanting the ones you can't have.'

'Oh my God, she means "Desperado"!' teased Claudia. 'Sally Grainger discovers The Eagles' Guide to Life!'

'You could learn a bit from them yourself!' Sal flashed back. It might be the stress of waiting for her diagnosis that was making her impatient, but really Claudia was always moaning on about having to move to Surrey as if it were the Siberian salt mines.

'Now, now, girls,' said Ella. 'We won't be any help to Laura if we quarrel amongst ourselves.'

'You're absolutely right.' Claudia held out a hand to Sal. 'Shake, pardner?'

'Is that another "Desperado" dig?' Sal asked suspiciously.

'No, no, I mean it. Poor Laura. This is all so shitty. How's she taking it?'

'She's gutted. And frightened about the future. God, it's so unfair. I mean, you'd think after twenty-five years you could at least look forward to sharing your old age together, sitting on the sofa with a TV supper watching David Attenborough. Here we all are, looking ten times better than our mothers, and our husbands still run off with younger women!'

'Simon would never have sat on a sofa watching David Attenborough,' Ella speculated. 'He's much more the type to join the gym and get a Maserati.'

'If she's not careful he probably won't even leave her a sofa to watch television *on*!' insisted Sal. 'She doesn't need David Attenborough, she needs a shit-hot divorce lawyer!'

'And do you know what?' Ella smiled, remembering one

of her fellow law students from university days and realizing that she could be useful. 'I think I know one. Rowley Robinson.'

'He sounds like a firm, not a person.'

'There's only one of Rowley. Erring husbands quake at the mention of him. From Russian oligarchs to Persian property tycoons, no one wants Rowley on the other side.'

'But isn't he incredibly expensive? Laura hasn't been earning for years.'

'Maybe she's saved up the housekeeping; besides, I'll get Rowley to do it at mates' rates.'

'Stupid Simon.'

'Let's drink to that. To Stupid Simon – may his nights be broken and the baby's nappies smelly!'

Sal raised her glass and silently added: 'And to me not having bloody cancer!'

CHAPTER 12

Laura looked up at the grand and forbidding exterior of Rowley Robinson's office in Lincoln's Inn Fields and wondered how much this visit was going to cost her. The last thing she could afford was to start paying an expensive divorce lawyer, yet Ella kept insisting this was exactly what she had to do or she would be royally stitched up.

Once she'd got past the equally forbidding receptionist, Rowley himself was a pleasant surprise. With his curly black hair, horn-rimmed specs and bow-tie he was less Rottweiler, more standard poodle.

'Hello, Mrs Minchin, delighted to meet you. Any friend of Ella's is immediately welcome here, though I'm sorry about the circumstances. Coffee?'

He signalled to the young man sitting at a desk outside his office. 'Two coffees, Ben, thanks.'

How refreshing, a male assistant; this boded well.

Rowley's office had none of the panelled and intimidating air of an old-fashioned lawyer's chambers. It was light, airy and functional. Laura sat down on one of the pale blue sofas and decided she would get through this as quickly as possible. She hadn't had the nerve yet to ask about fees.

'Now, Mrs Minchin, can I call you Laura?'

'Please do.'

'Just give me a brief outline of what has happened with your husband.'

'We have been married twenty-five years. In fact, it was on our anniversary that it all came out, that my husband Simon was having an affair with a much younger work colleague, and that she wanted him to leave me and go and live with her.'

'And how did you respond?'

'I told him to go.' Laura closed her eyes for a moment. 'Maybe I shouldn't have been so violent in my reaction but I was so hurt. I'd planned this romantic night away and that was when it happened.'

Rowley Robinson smiled gently. 'Don't beat yourself up. In my experience, when a couple are deciding to break up, they act in their own interest irrespective of the other person's response. Your husband had probably already made up his mind what he wanted to do. The timing simply made it more painful for you.'

Laura felt a burden of guilt being lifted from her. If he was right, then losing her temper with Simon hadn't been so bad after all.

'He moved out immediately?'

'He went that night and came back the next day for his things. He just simply said he knew he was behaving badly, that he was the villain of the piece and we'd all hate him but that was the way it was.'

'Unusually candid,' Rowley remarked. 'Most husbands like to blame the wife.'

'It didn't endear him to our daughter. She guessed the other woman would be waiting for him in his car and ran out and confronted her.'

'Are there other children?'

'A son. He's twenty-two, he's just left university. Our daughter is twenty-four.'

'And what about yourself? Have you worked during the marriage?'

Laura's chin went up defensively. She hated this question. 'No. The thing is, I had a very unsettled childhood myself, with parents I never saw who eventually ended up divorcing. I wanted something different for my own children.' A small sob escaped before she could repress it. 'I haven't done a very good job.'

'Marriage is a contract. It involves two people. If one party breaks the agreement it is hard to repair sometimes.' Rowley gave her a small smile. 'And since then?'

'The woman he left me for is now pregnant and Simon wants me to bring a petition for divorce.'

'Citing adultery? Unreasonable behaviour is also an option.'

'But isn't that harder to prove? Wouldn't Simon have had to have beaten me or got drunk every night?'

'These days it can be something quite trivial – such as telling you you're fat or the fact that he didn't listen to your opinions. There was even a case the other day of a wife claiming unreasonable behaviour because her husband criticized her map reading.'

'Sounds as if the law's trying to help people get a divorce as easily as possible.'

'Yes, well, the law isn't trying to make it hard, certainly, or point the finger at either party. Some couples prefer unreasonable behaviour because they don't like using adultery. For the children's sake sometimes.'

'Not much of an issue in our case since my daughter spat at my husband's mistress and called her a selfish cow.'

'Big question now. Are you happy to go ahead with proceedings or do you have hopes for reconciliation?'

Laura laughed hollowly. 'I have no hopes for a reconciliation.'

Rowley thought for a moment. 'You're aware I have a certain reputation? People come to me if they want to play dirty and screw the maximum from their ex. In fact, I expect that's why Ella thought of me, but, as it happens, I'm going to give you the advice I give my friends rather than my clients.'

'And what's that?'

'Don't be vengeful. Anyone with children has a future tied to each other. There will be weddings. Maybe grandchildren. Be generous. Be delightful. Be accommodating. Even if you'd actually like to strangle him. Don't give him any grounds for feeling justified in leaving you. We will go for a clean break and the best financial settlement we can. What's crucial is, do it quickly while he is still feeling at least a morsel of guilt.'

'I'm not sure he is. Hannibal Lecter feels more guilt than my husband.'

'You'd be surprised. If you have, as you say, had a reasonably happy marriage and he's not blaming you for the break-up, he will be feeling guilty, I assure you, but it won't last long. The other party will poison him against you and probably plead her pregnancy to speed things up. Our window is very small. Shall we go for it?'

'Yes.' Laura felt as if she was standing in an unknown sea and didn't know if the tide was going out or coming in. Her only chance of survival, according to Rowley, was to swim with the current.

'One question. What will happen to the house?'

Rowley shrugged sympathetically. 'The house is always an issue. It will depend on what other capital your husband has. It's possible, if you forgo a claim to half his pension, that you may be able to keep it, but you would have to maintain it and pay any mortgage. And it would very much depend how much other capital he has.'

'Thank you.' Laura stood up. She didn't want the meeting, which, no doubt, was costing the earth, to go on any longer than it had to.

Rowley Robinson stood up too. 'Perhaps you're disappointed? A lot of my clients want to nail the bastard. How dare he be unfaithful and abandon me? They want him publicly condemned, turned into a social pariah. But the truth is, I'm afraid, adultery is commonplace; it doesn't even raise an eyebrow. Wives think crucifying him will give them satisfaction. And do you know what? The opposite is true. Because the only power they have is through using the children and that wrecks their own lives and it screws up the children. Don't be one of them.' He held out his hand. 'And don't tell anyone I'm giving this kind of advice.' He smiled ruefully. 'If it got out, my career could be over.'

Laura stumbled out into the brightness of Lincoln's Inn Fields. Life all seemed so normal. The shouts of children playing. The thwack of tennis balls. Old men sitting on benches. Someone strumming a guitar. Office workers eating their sandwiches in the cold winter sunshine. While all around the big law firms crowded together deciding everyone's future, including hers.

She got out her phone and called Ella.

'He says I should be nice as pie to Simon and go for a clean break. No point expecting a court or anyone else to disapprove of him and Suki. Adultery is commonplace now and doesn't even raise an eyebrow.'

'Oh doesn't it?' Ella was starting to feel very annoyed on behalf of her friend. She could feel another blog coming on, though she'd have to be careful if Sal was reading them. 'Well, I hope Rowley's right. He usually is. Why don't you come over and share a glass?'

Laura sighed, feeling a tiny lifting of her black mood. 'That sounds absolutely lovely.'

On her way to Ella's she dropped some shopping off. Milk. Teabags. Pizzas for Sam. She knew she should probably make him cater for himself but doing his washing and making him the odd meal gave her something to think about outside her own misery and that helped her. She kept on nagging about finding work and she knew he was trying and that he'd applied online for dozens of jobs. He'd at least got some paid work walking the neighbours' dogs.

In fact, she discovered not Sam at home, but Bella.

'How did you get on? Sam says you've been to see some Jaws of a divorce lawyer.'

Bella, Laura noted, had acquired another tattoo, a delicate spider's web, across one of her hands. Laura tried not to shudder. 'Yes. He's advised me to go for a clean break and not play dirty.'

'*Not* play dirty?' Bella's pale Goth face actually went red with fury. 'You mean let Dad off the hook so he can go and play geriatric mummies and daddies with that home breaker?'

Laura paused, her mind in a whirl. Part of her sympathized with Bella's black-and-white view of life and especially of Simon, but Rowley Robinson's words about trying to preserve some kind of family life for the future had had a powerful effect.

Bella might need to hate her father, Laura understood that, but it would be a mistake, even for Bella's own sake, to act on it.

'The thing is, Bella love, whatever he's done he's still your father and you only have one father. Don't cut him out of your life completely.'

'God, Mum! You're hopeless! You're going to let him walk all over you, aren't you? You'll lose the house and he'll have little Fruit of the New Womb to dandle on his knee. He won't even want *us* any more. We'll be his *ex*-family, and his *ex*-kids!' She slammed out, leaving Laura close to tears. She knew it was Bella's anger and hurt that were speaking but her daughter could be so undermining.

Half an hour ago she was feeling positive, clear that she was making the sane, rational choice, the best thing for her children. And now here was Bella yelling at her that she should be fighting to the death.

Come on, Laura, pull yourself together, she told herself sternly, *you're the adult here.* She needed that drink. She shouted to Bella that she would see her later but Bella had disappeared upstairs.

As if by some sixth sense of friendship, Ella was standing under the lovely Queen Anne portico of her lovely Queen Anne house waiting with her arms wide open.

'Come on, I've lit the fire in the sitting room. Let's sink into the sofa and open the Sauvignon. Come and tell me everything Rowley said.'

As she stood outside the Princess Lily Hospital, Sal asked herself again why she hadn't told her friends what was happening. Any of them would have been happy to come with her today.

Partly it was pride. Sal had always had this feeling, encouraged by her stoical, unsympathetic mother, that illness was somehow weak, something that should be resisted. Besides, if the news was bad, she didn't want to suddenly be 'Sal-with-cancer'. She didn't want people to adopt that special cancer voice when they asked 'How *are* you?' She didn't want anyone to tell her stories of other people's cancer.

In fact, she deeply resented the thought of having cancer at all and not admitting to even the idea seemed to make it less real. It was much easier to treat the possibility of cancer as a massive inconvenience than to acknowledge its true seriousness.

In the waiting room for the breast clinic, Sal discreetly studied the other patients. There was a fashion-conscious woman in orange leggings and matching Converse trainers, wearing an Orla Kiely top Sal had envied when they'd featured it in *Modern Style*. She had two young women with her, perhaps in their early twenties, who must be her daughters. They were chatting ten to the dozen to take her mind off where she was. Occasionally, they swapped anxious glances. How old was she? Fifty? Certainly not as old as Sal.

Opposite sat an older woman with a dramatic-looking companion whose bright red lips and dark eyebrows grabbed one's attention. She seemed too old to be a daughter. A work colleague accompanying the patient to hold her hand, perhaps? Sal could hardly believe it when a name was called and it turned out to be the younger woman who got up.

Finally, it was Sal's turn.

'Ms Grainger? Hello, I'm Pam, your Breast Care Nurse. I'll be your contact at the hospital.' Sal found herself confronting a plump, blonde Australian who radiated confidence. She pressed a card into Sal's hand. Sal's stomach lurched. If she was going to have a permanent contact, the news must be bad. 'Mr Richards is ready for you now.'

'Right, Ms Grainger, come in.' This was a new tone. Authoritative and brisk. She could do business with this tone. Its owner was tall and suave and surprisingly young. 'You've met Pam already?'

Sal nodded. Was it significant that she was seeing both of them at once? The women before her in the queue had only seen him, she was sure.

'We have the results of your core biopsy. There was an

indication from your mammogram that we ought to look further. I'm afraid the pathology report confirms it.'

'I have cancer then.' It was a statement rather than a question.

'You have a tumour, yes. It is quite large, and palpable to the touch.'

'Is that bad?'

'Palpable would indicate a tumour is cancerous.'

Sal took a deep breath, trying to keep calm. 'Can I just say,' she wanted to get things clear from the outset, 'I'd rather you were completely honest with me. I am sixty-three, unmarried, used to looking after myself, and I have no dependants. What I do have, which is worrying me no end at the moment, is a terrific new job editing a magazine which I am due to start imminently.'

'I see, yes. Well, I'm afraid breast-conserving surgery is not suitable in your case. The problem is not so much the dimensions of the tumour, although it is quite large, but the relationship to your breast size.'

Sal almost felt the temptation to laugh. She'd always had this crazy notion that one positive about being flat as a pancake was that she wouldn't end up with breast cancer.

'Your lymph nodes are also infected, which indicates the advisability of a mastectomy.'

Shockwaves reverberated through Sal. Somehow she had known all along the news would be bad. The lump was too big and too hard to be trivial. But a mastectomy!

On the other hand, if she had to have it, there was no point delaying. 'Can I have the operation immediately? The thing is, I can't afford to delay. Given my age, this job was pretty hard to find and I really don't want to lose it.'

Mr Richards looked at her over his glasses, penetrating light-blue eyes boring into hers. 'I'm afraid not. You will need neoadjuvant chemotherapy first. We need to reduce the size of the tumour before we operate and there are other factors that tip the balance towards waiting.'

Sal knew there must be a hundred questions she ought to be asking. It was just that she couldn't think of any of them.

Instead she said simply: 'Am I going to die?'

Mr Richards leaned back in his seat. 'With a mastectomy, plus five years of Anastrozole, the prognosis is excellent. It may not seem it at the moment but you have one of the best cancers. But I think we should start the chemotherapy as soon as possible.'

Sal realized that she had started to cry and hated herself. It was the thought of losing her hair.

'Your Breast Care Nurse will talk you through the process further and will always be on hand for your appointments.' He shook her hand.

Pam led her to a smaller consulting room and handed over a small carrier bag.

It was much like the goody bag she got at glitzy press launches, but instead of designer samples and free body lotion this one contained helpful booklets on coping with hair loss, a catalogue for post-surgery bras and a leaflet explaining different drug regimens. Welcome to cancerworld!

'Read the leaflets and look on the Internet, everyone does, and then please come back to me with any questions you want to ask. Any time. My number's on the card I gave you.'

It struck Sal, as she made her way out of the hospital, that everyone else had someone with them. White-haired Asian grannies had their daughters-in-law, and some had their tiny grandchildren there too, who doubled as translators; grumpy men on crutches had wives trailing behind them; anxious middle-aged sons pushed frail-looking old men in wheelchairs; even a drunk had a fellow drunk.

Of course, given the statistics of how many people live

alone, she couldn't possibly be the only one who was un-accompanied. Besides, it was her own stupid, stubborn fault.

She bought herself a consoling Twix and made her way home to wait to hear how soon it would be before the poison would be pumped into her veins.

The time had come, Claudia decided, when she had to have a proper talk with her mother. Since Olivia was never at home, the only way to do this was to join her mother on one of her endless jaunts. Today it was a furniture-painting workshop in a local art gallery.

'I'm so thrilled you're coming!' Olivia did indeed sound delighted. 'I know you'll love it. Think, you take some hideous unloved old table and turn it into something beautiful. What could be more rewarding?'

An unexpected wave of guilt washed over Claudia. Maybe her mother signed up for all this stuff not because she was manic, but because she was lonely. Claudia had never been one of those daughters who did everything with her mother. In fact, she rarely did much beyond the occasional duty visit. Perhaps the doctor was exaggerating?

Then she remembered the crazy round of skiing lessons, colonic irrigation, tequila tasting and laser eyebrow treatment Olivia had been signing people up for. Not to mention the £99 teeth-whitening treatment for an ancient neighbour who had dentures.

'The thing is,' Olivia was busily telling her daughter, 'you never were a joiner. As you get older you have to start joining in, dear, or you'll end up being miserable. Too many old people are stuck at home in front of the TV. You don't want to become like them, do you? In fact, your father's becoming one, now that I mention it.'

'Mum, he has fractured his hip.'

'That was weeks ago. He used to be such a live wire.' Olivia started enthusiastically stripping old paint off a small table with coarse-grained sandpaper. 'Now he never does anything. He's turning into an old man.'

Claudia knew it was no good reminding her mother that he actually *was* an old man.

'Very good, Mrs Williamson,' the course organizer congratulated her mother. 'Come on, Claudia, is it? Chop chop, look how well Olivia's doing!'

Claudia took out some sandpaper and began on the wooden chest she'd brought.

'Excellent.' The organizer smiled. 'Now use the coarser sandpaper to give it a key for your paint. Then go and choose your paint colours from over on the table. Did you bring the brushes I suggested?'

Claudia shook her head. She was beginning to feel like the dunce of the class.

'Never mind,' Olivia offered generously, 'you can share mine.'

By lunchtime, Olivia's side tables and the wooden chest Claudia was working on were sanded, primed and ready for the next stage.

'What design are you going for?' Olivia enquired. 'I'm doing fruit and flowers on mine, a sort of autumn cornucopia.' She began busily painting her base colour.

Claudia decided on a starry sky for hers, consisting of silver stars on a midnight-blue background. At least that couldn't be too artistically challenging. The process was surprisingly absorbing and somehow the afternoon flew past without any kind of proper talk with Olivia.

It was actually dark outside when the workshop organizer did a final tour of all their efforts. She picked two out for special commendation. A geometric design with a hint of

Braque about it, and Claudia's starry sky. Claudia, who had rarely won anything, felt absurdly pleased. It was only as they were packing up their stuff that she remembered the purpose of today was supposed to be less creative and more a way of finding out how her mother was.

On today's evidence, Claudia had to admit, she seemed absolutely fine. 'Why don't we have a cup of tea on the way home?'

'Let's go to Igden Manor,' Olivia suggested enthusiastically. 'They have an offer on there. Three-for-two afternoon teas.'

OK, maybe not so fine. How did her mother even know all this stuff about offers?

'Since there are only two of us, let's ask Caroline who's running the course if she'd like to come too.' Olivia was about to bustle off and ask her.

'No. No, nicer with just us,' Claudia insisted.

They were just in time for tea at the hotel, which turned out to be one of those country houses, all log fires and wood panelling. The afternoon tea consisted of enough sandwiches, scones and cakes to feed an army. Surreptitiously her mother emptied most of it into her handbag, wrapped up in one of the hotel's white linen napkins. 'That'll do for your father's tea. I'll be out tonight. I've signed up for a course in digital photography.'

'But, Mum, you don't even have a digital camera!'

'You're always so negative, Claudia.'

'Look, Mum, we need to talk. I'm worried about you. You're always rushing, rushing, rushing – signing up for all these weird and wonderful things. How do you even pay for them?'

'They're mostly seventy per cent off.'

'Even so, you have to pay something. It must mount up.'

Olivia beamed. 'I put them on the credit card.'

'Does Dad know?'

'I don't know what your father knows. He's such a sad old stay-at-home these days.'

'He's worried about you. So am I. Mum,' Olivia was staring into space, refusing to acknowledge the concern, 'so is the doctor at the hospital.'

'Worried about Dad, you mean.'

'No, *you*. He called me up specially. He thinks you may be suffering from manic depression.'

'I've never heard anything so ludicrous in my life! Can't someone be busy and enthusiastic without being landed with some ridiculous label!'

'All right, Mum, let's leave it for now.'

'I should bloody well think so!' Her mother's voice was almost a shout, making the other guests turn round. And then, just as suddenly, she was back to normal. 'Do you want that last cucumber sandwich? If not, I'll take it home for Dad.'

She went off to argue with the management that if there was a 3-for-2 offer, there ought to be some reduction pro rata of 2 for 1.

'Got a fiver off!' she announced on her return. 'You don't need to worry about me and money.'

But Claudia wasn't reassured. The next day she called the credit card company and asked to discuss her mother's situation. They were deeply unhelpful. It was bad enough that they refused to talk to her because of 'data protection', but they didn't need to sound positively gleeful about it.

There was only one thing for it. She'd have to enlist her father's help. As soon as she knew her mother was out at yet another activity, she went straight round.

'Look, Dad, we really are going to have to do something about this. She must be spending a fortune. Where does Mum keep her bank and credit card statements?'

Len was unhappy about going behind his wife's back, but finally agreed after much persuasion.

'Goodness knows. But she stuffs all the things she doesn't like the look of into that bureau over there.' He indicated a battered old piece of furniture in the corner of the sitting room.

Claudia opened it up. It was the old-fashioned type where the lid lowered into a desk top revealing rows of small drawers and cubby holes. There was nothing of any financial interest in these, or in the top two larger drawers. The bottom drawer was more hopeful. It was chock-a-block full of papers and letters. Claudia got them out and sorted them into piles, feeling more and more sick as she did so.

Her mother had signed up for countless cut-price courses, outings, hotels and products. She had even paid for hotel stays she had not taken. Claudia sat down with a calculator and went through every bank and credit card statement.

Since April that year her mother had spent over four thousand pounds, only paying off the minimum she'd had to each month. And, what was more, Claudia was pretty certain it was four thousand pounds they couldn't afford and probably didn't even have.

Ella sat at her computer screen and began to tap out an indignant post. She knew she probably shouldn't but felt that this was something she had to get off her chest.

ADULTERY IS NOW SO COMMONPLACE IT DOESN'T RAISE AN EYEBROW

This is the statement made to a friend of mine by her divorce lawyer, Ella typed furiously, releasing all her indignation, *and I think it is one we should all be angry about. We are lucky to live in a fairly liberal society, and that is a precious thing.*

I am not about to advocate stoning when a husband or wife strays from their marital vows, but not even raising an eyebrow, and viewing adultery as commonplace? That seems equally wrong to me. Adultery is a breach of the marriage contract, and, worse than that, it is deeply disrespectful to your partner. Sometimes in a very unhappy marriage it may be unavoidable, but to accept adultery as a minor social breach like using the wrong knife and fork means there is something wrong with that society.

If adultery is considered so trivial, there is nothing to stop any of us being unfaithful whenever we feel like it. And if we do that, the whole idea of marriage becomes pointless.

ADULTERY SHOULD NOT BE CONSIDERED COMMONPLACE BUT A HURTFUL BREACH OF CON-TRACTUAL RULES FREELY SIGNED UP TO BY BOTH PARTIES. IT IS ALSO A BREACH OF THE MUTUAL RESPECT THAT UNDERPINS MARRIAGE.

IF WE CONSIDER MARRIAGE AN INSTITUTION WORTH HAVING WE SHOULD ALWAYS RAISE AN EYEBROW.

Eyebrow-raisers of the world unite!

Ella pinged her blog into cyberspace and logged off.

She had some dry cleaning to pick up from the High Street. She'd do a shop while she was there and cook something nice for tonight.

By the time she'd been to the fishmonger, greengrocer and dry cleaner she realized it was time for Wenceslaus' shift in the café to end and she might as well offer him a lift home.

When she saw him behind the bar, now a fully qualified barista, no doubt greatly adding to the customer base with his soulful good looks, she felt a wave of almost maternal pride. There was no doubt that he was an asset to the place. To your average Moulsford teenager it would be like discovering Robert Pattinson serving you a flat white.

She was about to wave to him when she saw the painful evidence of her last thought. A young woman sat at one of the tables nursing an empty coffee cup and watching Wenceslaus.

But it wasn't a lovesick teenager who would languish and then recover.

It was her daughter Julia.

Ella caught Wenceslaus' eye and could tell he was well aware of Julia's presence.

Steeling herself for a scene which she knew would make her deeply unpopular, Ella decided to take action. 'Hello, Julia, love!' Julia jumped, looking guilty. 'I'm just driving home. Fancy a lift? I thought I'd offer Wenceslaus one, but it seems he's got to work later.' She glanced towards Wenceslaus and saw that though he was pretending to clean the counter and tidy up the stack of biscotti, he was also listening. Fortunately, although he had said nothing, he had enough intuition to understand what lay behind this conversation.

'Oh,' Julia eyed her mother suspiciously. 'All right, then. As long as you don't ask me what I'm "giving" Neil for supper, as if I were there to anticipate his every need. He's out anyway, like he is most nights, at a business dinner.'

'Right.' This information explained a lot. Julia's main problem, it seemed to her mother, was neglect by her husband. 'Do you fancy having supper with me? Just some roast fish, nothing special?' Julia could have the portion she'd been going to cook for Wenceslaus.

Julia paused, sensing a trap. But clearly an evening out, even with her mother, was preferable to another at home alone. That in itself spoke volumes.

Ella decided not to say anything until they were sitting at the kitchen table, sharing a glass of wine and even then she would have to tread carefully.

The sun was setting over the river as they parked, filtering through the leafless branches of the trees in the square. The people next door, Ella noted, had already put up their Christmas wreath. They were always the first, kicking off a wild competitive streak in everyone else to adorn their own front door with even greater luxury or originality. Ella was planning to make hers with produce from the allotment.

She put the fish on a hot roasting tray and quickly sorted out new potatoes and some spring greens before opening some wine.

They sat looking out into the now-dark garden, lit up by the faintest afterglow from the sunset. As they watched, a noise startled them. There was a shed at the bottom of the garden, half hidden from view, surrounded by a small veranda with a lacy wooden edge, and it was this edging that must have fallen off. 'I must ask Wenceslaus to mend that before it comes down and hurts someone,' Ella announced, almost forgetting Julia was there.

'You could almost live in that little shed,' Julia commented wistfully.

Ella detected the danger signs that Julia, like Viola in *Twelfth Night*, was fantasizing about building a willow cabin to be near the object of her love.

'Except that you have a perfectly nice home of your own,' Ella pointed out briskly.

Julia looked so deflated that Ella softened her tone. 'Don't you remember, you practically did live there when you were little? You had a café and Dad and I were your customers. You were a very stern proprietor.'

'It is amazing here, I must admit.' Julia looked around the large garden. 'You'd hardly know you were in London.'

Ella wanted to say *Ah-ha, then you can see why I don't want to leave*, but she made herself come up with a less provocative reply. 'Yes, those early weavers knew a thing or two when they built this square right down near their piers and docks. They could watch their bales of silk being loaded from the comfort of their own sitting rooms.'

'You know we only wanted you to move because we were worried about you living in this great big house alone,' Julia suddenly volunteered.

'I'm not alone now, though, am I?' The matter of Wenceslaus rose up again between them. 'Julia . . .' Ella began carefully.

As if sensing what might be coming next, Julia ploughed on. 'Of course, it was also about the value of the house and how much tax you'll have to pay.'

'When I die.'

'The truth is, Mum, we're really short. That's where Neil is all these evenings. Visiting clients trying to bump up his bonus.'

'Just for the school fees?'

'They're twenty grand a year and they're about to go up.' Ella tried not to look shocked.

She knew what she was going to say would make her un-popular. Grandparents these days were expected to keep their mouths shut, but she couldn't bear watching her daughter's unhappiness.

She sat down and took one of Julia's hands in hers, noting the strained look on her pretty face. 'The thing is, money aside, wouldn't you be happier if the boys were at a day school? Cluttering up the hall with their football boots and their washing?' She thought of Julia's clinical, too-tidy house. 'It seemed to me, when you and Cory were growing up, that parents who sent their kids away missed so much fun. Children are young for so short a time. It's like that folk song about how much your children grow up each time they turn around. The boys'll be eighteen and off to university in the wink of an eye and I know how much you love them.'

'Mum, please . . .' Julia was avoiding her glance.

'And then maybe you'd be too busy to have a crush on handsome young Poles.' There, it was out! Ella could hardly believe she'd finally said it.

'Mum! What the hell are you talking about?' The anger in Julia's tone crackled between them.

'I think you know what I mean.'

'I do *not* know what you mean. This is completely bloody ridiculous.' She stood up and grabbed her bag, knocking over a glass of wine as she did so.

'You need more in your life, darling. Especially with Neil out all the time.'

'In case I chase the help?'

'Wenceslaus isn't the help.'

'He lives here rent-free, doesn't he? Putting up the occasional shelf? Stopping you selling and letting the rest of the family share in your security!'

'Julia, that's not fair. Even without Wenceslaus here I wouldn't move. I love this house and I intend to go on living here. At least until I get dementia and have to sell to fund my care.'

She'd intended this as a joke but Julia pounced. 'Neil thinks you're getting it already. You completely missed a meeting with him last week.'

'That's because I forgot to put it in my diary.' The truth was, she hadn't wanted to go anyway. Neil wanted her to come and meet a tax lawyer and Ella knew the subject of avoiding death duties would come up again.

'Hello, El-la,' they turned to find that Wenceslaus was back. 'You leave keys in front door.'

The look of satisfaction on her daughter's face made Ella's palm itch.

And yet, if Ella had known her daughter's true state of mind, she might have been surprised. As she drove home, Julia had to admit that she was feeling lonelier than she'd ever felt in her life. Neil was perpetually out and hardly seemed to talk to her if he was in. She sometimes wondered whether he'd notice if a robot served him dinner. And that was exactly how she felt – worse, because robots didn't have feelings.

And she missed her boys desperately. Occasionally she found herself in their rooms, just standing there with no purpose. Once she'd picked up a T-shirt and held it against her cheek, breathing in Mark's scruffy teenager smell. Each time she saw them they were a little more grown-up and a little more distant. Harry had even stopped butting into her accidentally-on-purpose which, ever since he was a small boy, had been his special way of being physically affectionate.

Laura was about to drop Sam off for a dental appointment when she heard the wild scrunch of tyres on gravel. There was only one person who would drive that fast and that angrily.

Simon let himself in. Of course he still had a key and Laura would never have thought of having the locks changed. He came storming into the kitchen, his face red and angry, his eyes narrow chips of fury.

'So this is how you respond to my generosity!' he accused.

Sam looked on sullenly while Laura tried to work out what the hell he meant.

'I offer you the chance to start a divorce petition against me, which I was even intending to pay for, poor schmuck that I am, and you only go to the most notorious divorce lawyer in London! If you're intending to take me to the cleaners,

Laura, you'd better bloody watch out. You'll end up with nothing but what you can carry in a suitcase.'

'Nice touch, Dad.' Sam's irony was biting. 'I didn't know you were so poetic.'

'And you can get a bloody job and start paying your way!' Simon rounded on his son. 'Do you good.' Then it was Laura's turn. 'Twenty-five years I've been married to you, Laura, and you haven't done a day's work. Time you worked for a living. You'll need it to pay for your lawyer.'

Laura wanted to shout that she had worked as hard as he had making a home for them, but Rowley's words came back to her. Be nice. Be accommodating. Not that they'd worked so far. 'I refuse to be provoked by you, Simon. Rowley Robinson is a friend of Ella's, that's why I went to see him. He did not advise me to take you for all you've got, but to go for a quick settlement and a clean break. For the sake of our children.'

For a moment Simon looked faintly abashed.

'To think I used to quite like you, Dad,' Sam muttered.

'Maybe I went a bit far.'

'Apology accepted.' Laura picked up her bag and keys. 'And believe me, if I could find a suitable job, I would take it like a shot. It might distract me from the rest of my life. I'm afraid we have to go. Sam's got a dental appointment.'

After Sam had been seen by the dentist, Laura assumed he was coming home with her but he had other plans. 'Billy's down from Oxford and we thought we'd go to the cinema.'

'Fine. Will you eat out?'

He nodded. Laura masked her disappointment. Maybe Simon had been right when he'd accused her once before of depending too much on her children for companionship. 'I'm sorry about that row with Dad. He does love you, you know.'

'Oh, really? Strange way of showing it.'

'It'll pass. He's stressed out by the divorce as much as I am.'

'Stop making excuses for him, Mum. He's behaving like an arsehole.'

A chink of mischief invaded Laura's misery. 'Yeah, but he's still our arsehole.'

She watched as Sam strode off angrily into the night. Some people might wait till their children were grown-up before getting divorced, but it didn't seem to Laura that there was any good time to break up your family. But then, the kind of people who put up with a bad marriage out of consideration for their children would bear very little relationship to Simon. Simon only ever seemed to think of himself.

Rowley Robinson's words that it takes two for a marriage to go wrong invaded her mind. But, to be quite frank, she didn't feel like blaming herself at the moment.

Instead, she went home and ran herself a hot scented bath and sat in the candlelight thinking through all the nasty things she'd like to do to Simon. This made her feel so peaceful that she actually fell asleep and woke to find the bath cold and the phone in the bedroom ringing insistently.

She leapt out, grabbed a towel, and padded towards it just as the phone stopped. Dialling 1471 told her that it had been Simon. What the hell was he doing ringing at 11 p.m.? She was just contemplating whether she felt like finding out when it started to ring again.

'Hello, Simon,' she began.

'You bloody bitch! You pretend your lawyer says you should be all sweetness and light and then you come and slash the tyres on my Audi! Do you know how much they cost? Two hundred and seventy-five pounds each!'

Laura had been about to deny furiously any such accusation

when it struck her that she had a good idea as to who might have done it. It wouldn't have been hard for him to get Simon's new address out of his secretary.

'Calm down, Simon,' she tried to mask her panic, 'I've been at home all evening. It's probably an envy attack. Expensive cars are always getting scratched or done over with brake fluid. Maybe your next car should have cheaper tyres.'

'Very funny.' He slammed down the phone.

Laura waited a moment then rang Billy's home. Amazingly, she still had the number, dating from primary school days.

'Hello,' she asked the sleepy male voice that answered, presumably Billy's dad. 'I'm so sorry to disturb you, but could I speak to Billy?'

'Billy!' the voice repeated, sounding increasingly pissed off. 'Billy's still in Oxford.'

Laura dressed quickly and got into her car. She needed to find Sam before he did anything else.

She circled what seemed like the whole of W4, far down the high road, past the burger bars, and the scabby local disco which desperate teenagers liked to pretend was as smart as anything in the West End. Nothing. Sam wasn't answering his phone either.

Then she saw Bella's boyfriend, the silent and tattooed Nigel, emerge from a pub and remembered that he'd tracked down Sam before. 'Nigel!' she yelled, stopping him in his tracks halfway across the main road.

'Mrs Minchin! Are you OK?'

'Sam and his dad had a fight earlier this evening, Sam's feeling pretty sore about the break-up.'

'You should see Bella. I'd get a hard hat, if I were him.'

'Someone slashed his tyres tonight.'

'Bella will be thrilled. In her view he'd be lucky it's only his tyres.'

'It couldn't have been . . . ?'

'Bella? Not her style.' He smiled a tender, mysterious little smile which made him look sweet and engaging, like an elephant in a tutu. 'She's at home. Taking it easy.'

'She's not ill?'

'Nah. Just putting her feet up. I tucked her up with a hottie and a DVD.'

This glimpse of their domestic life wasn't at all what Laura would have expected of a pair of edgy Goths, yet it was oddly appealing. 'Give her my love.'

'Do you want me to come and help you look?'

'Thanks, that'd be a big relief. Where would you go after you'd slashed your dad's tyres?'

Nigel gave this proposition some serious consideration. 'Confession?'

Laura stared at him.

'Joke, Mrs Minchin. Probably go and get rat-arsed.'

'Yes, but *where* would you get rat-arsed, I mean drunk?'

'Southforks. The beer's piss but it's very cheap. And they let kids in without ID.' He pointed to a basement entrance, surrounded by teenagers, some of whom were leaning over the railings to vomit.

'Can we go and have a look?'

Once inside, Laura, in her pale pastel sweatshirt and smartly ironed jeans, felt like a nun in a betting shop. She could hardly make out anything in the gloom. The music blared, there was a horrible smell of urine and spilt beer, but no sign of Sam.

'Thanks for trying.'

Nigel, with an unerring instinct for masculine angst, especially when stoked up by four pints of Rocket Booster lager, disappeared into the Gents. Moments later he hove back into sight, his trunk-like arm supporting an extremely drunk Sam.

'Let's get him out of here.'

They half carried the slender figure, which stopped occasionally to throw up, back towards the car.

Just as Nigel opened the back door Sam opened a bleary, anxious eye. 'Sorry, Mum,' he half sobbed before collapsing, catatonic, across the seat.

Laura wanted to sob herself. She was furious at Sam for his act of vandalism but she also knew how much pain he must be in to behave so out of character.

'Shall I come and help you get him in?' Nigel offered.

'Would you?'

'He'll be all right in the morning.'

'Yes, but will his father? I'm just wondering what he's going to do if he works it out.'

The answer arrived around eleven the following day when a squad car from the local police station turned up, sirens blaring.

'We've had a report of criminal damage to an Audi motor vehicle,' announced the uniformed officer.

'Indeed?' Laura asked briskly. 'And why should that have anything to do with us?'

'The vehicle's owner, a Mr Simon Minchin, believed it might be the work of a Mr Sam Minchin.'

Laura asked if the officer could wait a moment and moved to the end of the drive where her mobile signal was good. 'Simon!' she hissed with deadly venom when he answered the phone. 'Get right down here now or I'm tweeting that you have not only left your wife for a younger woman but shopped your son to the police!'

'It's for his own good. He can't go around doing illegal acts like that.'

'Just as you can't go around doing immoral ones. I mean it, Simon. Come round here now, this minute, and get the police off his back. Or I'll tell Rowley Robinson I want to play dirty after all.'

'You complete shit,' Laura murmured when the police had finally left. 'Shopping your own son when you know perfectly well he'd never do a thing like this unless you'd really hurt him.'

'So it's my fault my son's a psycho, is it?'

'He's not a psycho,' Laura challenged, livid. 'He's been badly hurt, that's all.'

'I bet you put him up to it.'

'Simon,' Laura looked at the man she had lived with and loved for twenty-five years and thought she had known almost as well as she knew herself, 'stop this. This is me, Laura. Not some castrating ex-wife from hell. And this is Sam who you held in your arms as a baby, who you kicked a ball about with, helped choose a university. Even when you have a new baby, he will still be your son.'

'It's more than a grand, Laura.'

Laura felt like yelling, *What price do you put on losing the father you loved?*

CHAPTER 13

'Four thousand pounds?' Claudia's father Len looked as if he'd felt a ghost walk across his grave. 'But she can't have spent four thousand pounds on ice skating and eyebrow threading and whatever these stupid spa things are which she keeps going on about! I mean there have been a couple of hotel jaunts, but to Cornwall, not the Caribbean!'

'She hasn't just been buying them for herself but for lots of other people too.'

'Oh dear God.' Len sat down shakily. 'We don't have that kind of money. We're over eighty, living on a pension.'

'I think the first thing we need to do is talk to Mum. Then take her credit card away. And her iPhone. I think I'd better get her an old Nokia – in fact, she can have mine, it's Gaby's old one. God, we may even have to stop her going on the computer.' Claudia had been trawling through her mother's PC. 'She's paid for some things she's never even taken up.'

'It really is a mania, then.'

'Yes. I'll have to see if we can plead medical reasons and get out of some of it.'

Olivia chose that moment to breeze into the sitting room, back from yet another activity. 'Oh, Claudia, hello, dear. Has anyone seen my wrap?'

Claudia jumped. She'd thought her mother was safely out.

'Where are you going now?' Claudia took in her mother's smart grey evening frock. She always was a stylish dresser.

'Just back for my wrap. Anyway, darling, I'm sure I told you. A cocktail-mixing course at the Cross Keys in Shenford. It's all sponsored by Bombay Sapphire and they provide all the gin. By Christmas I'll be a qualified mixologist.'

Claudia almost despaired.

'Sorry, Mum,' she shut the door to the sitting room firmly, 'you can't go. This has got to stop. You've spent thousands of pounds on these courses.'

'Don't be silly, dear,' Olivia clucked at her daughter's obvious ignorance. 'They're all seventy per cent off. I told you.'

'Even with seventy per cent off you've still spent four grand.'

Olivia looked genuinely puzzled. 'But how could I have? We don't have that kind of money.'

'All you've been doing is making the minimum payment on your card.'

'Oh dear,' Olivia looked as if finally the truth were filtering like dim sunlight through the canopy of her obsession. But the hope was short-lived. 'I'm sure you're making too much of this,' her tone took on an edge of aggression. 'You can be such a killjoy. I sometimes feel quite sorry for poor Don.'

'I'm not being a killjoy, Mum. You're ill and you've got to stop all this signing up for things. Now.'

'You mean I can't go tonight?' The disappointment in her mother's tone was almost funny.

Claudia shook her head. 'Do you remember the doctor said all this stuff was a mania?'

'But it's such fun,' Olivia replied mulishly. 'It's what keeps me going. Otherwise I'd just be an old person sitting around at home.'

'But you can't pay for it, Mum.'

Olivia sat down on the arm of the sofa, her face set in angry lines. 'But what will I do with myself?'

'Tell you what. Why don't you go and change. We'll make a cake together like we used to. You'll show me how to. Just like you did when I was little. We'll have a nice fire and have tea and cake in front of it.'

'What about scones?' asked her father, trying to join in the forced jollity. 'Your mother's scones are second to none.'

'We'll make scones too,' promised Claudia.

Olivia went up to change.

Twenty minutes later she still hadn't returned.

'I wonder where Mum's got to,' Claudia thought aloud. 'I'd better go up and see.'

Olivia was sitting on the end of the bed, still wearing her grey dress, staring into space.

'Mum, are you all right?'

Olivia looked up. Her eyes had taken on the odd opaque look of a very old person. 'No, dear, I don't think I am.'

Claudia sat down next to her, taken aback at the transformation. Her bossy, energetic mother looked vulnerable and frail as if some inner life force had been quenched.

Claudia felt a stab of guilt that this had been because of her. She had turned up and confronted her mother in the hope that she would see sense. Instead, the argument seemed to have brought on a dramatic and abrupt change of mood. It was as if her mother had no choice but to be either restless, hyper-energetic, ceaselessly planning or silent as a block of stone.

'Maybe there is something wrong with me after all.' Olivia turned to her daughter. 'I'm frightened, Claudia, I don't always feel like me.'

Claudia took her hand. 'You're not alone, Mum. You have Dad. And me and Don. And Gaby. And all your friends and neighbours. It's a well-known condition. There are treatments which will help.'

'You mean I'm loopy.' It was a statement not a question.

'Not at all. There is therapy and also pills which are really effective.'

'Pills!' She almost spat the word out. 'I've never had any time for pills.'

'You'll get better, Mum. I promise.'

And for the first time since her move from London, Claudia was glad to be here in Minsley, near her mother, where she might be able to help.

Laura found after only a few sessions she was actually looking forward to Relationship Recovery.

The thing was, she didn't even want to share with her best friends how shittily Simon was behaving. At Relationship Recovery she could come clean about how she was really feeling and no one would be shocked.

The memory of the slashed tyres and the police visit came vividly back to her and she started to feel sick. Not that she was a brilliant role model. When Simon had first called to tell her about his car she had felt a distinct wave of satisfaction. Until the police arrived.

'Hello, everyone,' Suzanne greeted them brightly as the group arrived in the church hall and began to seat themselves in the circle. She reminded Laura more of her old hockey teacher than a marriage guidance counsellor. *'What you girls need is fresh air and exercise!'* Come to think of it, that seemed to be pretty much what the current medical establishment recommended nowadays for everything from diabetes to heart-break or depression.

'How have you all been doing?'

'Pretty well,' Laura found herself saying. 'My son slashed

my husband's tyres and my husband decided to call the police.'

'That must have been hard,' Stephen, the co-counsellor remarked, his tone all practised sympathy. But even practised sympathy made Laura want to cry. 'And you're feeling angry?'

Laura nodded. 'And powerless. My lawyer told me to be reasonable and not to lose my temper. But when my son slashed the tyres I felt delighted.'

'That's perfectly understandable,' Suzanne soothed. 'But perhaps not very useful for your recovery.'

'I was over the moon when my kids wouldn't go to their dad's wedding,' confessed another group member.

'When my daughter refused to even *talk* to her father, I thought, Yes! Serves you right, you bastard!'

'Today,' Suzanne steered the discussion deliberately away, 'the session is about discovering the reasons – admittedly hard at this stage – why you are actually better off without your ex-partner.'

There was a silence as deep as the Continental Shelf.

'He snored. At least I can get a good night's sleep.'

'She undermined me constantly. I'm lonelier but I don't feel got at.'

'He wanted to control me. In fact, he still tries even though we're separated.'

'He spent every penny in the betting shop.'

'Actually,' Laura admitted when it was her turn, 'until I found out he was having an affair I quite liked my husband.' Nine pairs of eyes swivelled disapprovingly in her direction. 'Of course I didn't realize what he was really like.' The terrible moment came back to her when Simon had simply announced that he knew he was the shit and the villain and that they'd all hate him and that he was leaving, end of story, as if by admitting his fault he could somehow get away from the consequences.

Had he really even been sorry?

Laura closed her eyes, then stared ahead as if she'd seen Moses and the burning bush. 'I really am better off without him,' she announced in a tone almost of wonder.

To her intense embarrassment she found the rest of the group were clapping.

Laughing, Laura stood up and took a bow.

As they filed out Calum came up to her. 'That was quite a moment.'

'To be honest, it smacked a bit of casting out demons. I wasn't that comfortable with it.'

'Don't knock it. You actually look a lot happier.'

Laura smiled and shook her head. 'For the moment. Till I get home and find my son's being sent to a young offenders' institution.'

'Actually, I was wondering if . . .'

'Yes?' she asked as his question petered out.

'Oh nothing. Just a thought. See you next time. Hang on to that happiness! It's a rare enough commodity around here.'

Laura watched him walk down the street, convinced he had been going to ask her for a coffee or something. Would she have wanted to go? She could just imagine Bella's reaction. 'Oh, yeah, that's a good place to meet a new man, at a group full of desperate divorce victims on the rebound! Good choice, Mum!' But there was something attractive about Calum, she had to admit.

When she got home she was surprised to find Bella there again. Maybe she'd come to give Sam moral support. Bella, dressed like a Jack the Ripper victim in a black bustier over a long Victorian skirt with laced-up ankle boots, was lying on the sofa. She and Sam were eating pizza and watching television. The wonderful normality of the scene made Laura want to shout with joy. She was delighted she didn't even have to nag him about job applications.

'Where have you been?' Bella asked, grabbing her hand and giving it a big-sisterly squeeze. The break-up had meant that, even more than before, she treated her mother as if she were the wayward child who needed looking after. It infuriated the hell out of Laura.

'To the Relationship Recovery group you signed me up for.'

'Is it useful? I hope it gives you the chance to say what a shit you think Dad is instead of ludicrously protecting him like you do to us!' This was so blisteringly accurate that Laura had to smile. 'Have some pizza. It's Meat Feast. Sam was telling me about the police coming.'

Laura remembered her maternal responsibilities. 'It was quite wrong of Sam to slash Dad's tyres.'

'Yeah, Sam, dumb idea.'

Laura found herself relieved she had Bella's backing.

'I mean, a car's just a piece of machinery. Wait till he finds out what I've got to tell him.'

'What do you mean?' Laura demanded, a sense of foreboding beginning to envelop her.

'I'm going to have a baby too, Mum,' Bella announced, a diabolical smile lighting up her pretty features. 'And I'm not going to let Dad anywhere near it!'

Laura sat down and closed her eyes. Bella was going to have a child with a tattooed giant who could hardly string a sentence together and who had no visible means of support.

And then the full impact struck her. She was going to be grandmother to a baby that might have been conceived as a grudge to get back at Simon for leaving them.

The night before her treatment started Sal stood at the mirror and surveyed her body.

All these years she'd prided herself on defying age and doing whatever she wanted. Now she was probably going to lose a breast and quite probably all her hair into the bargain.

Almost defiantly, she got out the jumpsuit she had considered embarrassingly youthful and laid it out to wear. Even if the chemo knocked her for six she would simply have to go ahead at *New Grey* in spite of the tiredness and pain. She would work nine to five and say no to anything extra so she could spend the rest of her time recovering. Willpower would have to carry her through.

And if the chemotherapy didn't go well? There was no point even thinking about that since everything, her entire life, would then be up for grabs. It wasn't a scenario she was prepared to face.

A thought struck her. She might not want fuss and sympathy but how on earth was she going to explain to her friends what was happening to her?

Next morning, when the cab she'd ordered arrived, Sal was feeling particularly pathetic.

'Where to, love?' the minicab driver enquired.

'The Princess Lily Hospital.' He gave her a quick double take and to her great relief didn't ask what she was going in for, engage her in proto-racist banter or even put on a loud football channel.

'Lovely day,' was his only comment.

Sal looked out of the window. He was right. The sky was a bright blue and the pale winter sunshine softened the edges of the office blocks and rows of shops, making Sal think of that Joni Mitchell song about the sun coming in through yellow curtains and making rainbows on the wall. God, Joni Mitchell. She must be seventy and still singing. Good for you, Joni. There's life in us old birds yet.

They passed the life-size crib outside the Catholic church on the hill and it made Sal feel suddenly alone. She'd been brought up a Catholic but had abandoned her faith along with her

Northern accent the moment she'd arrived in London. Would it have helped her now? Christmas was coming and here she was having her first ever cycle of cancer treatment. Unlike her friends she didn't even have children to hold her hand like that mother and two lovely daughters she'd seen. For a moment she found herself back in Norway all those years ago. No, she wouldn't think about that. Not now. Too late. All too late.

And then they were at the hospital.

'Righto,' said the driver, 'nine pounds, please. I won't say have a nice day.'

It suddenly struck her that she'd need a cab home too and she'd liked this driver's restful silence. 'Can I have a card, please? What's your name, by the way?'

'Ricky. They call me Ricky Reliable.'

'Thank you, Mr Reliable,' she laughed at her own feeble joke. 'I'll ask for you when I need to go home.' A mad idea suddenly struck Sal. 'I don't suppose you could come in with me? For an extra fiver?' Suddenly, madly, she felt the need for moral support. Even from a stranger.

'Dear lady,' he climbed out of the cab and bowed with all the insouciant gallantry of a Walter Raleigh throwing down his cape for Queen Elizabeth I, 'if I can find a parking space I'll do it for nothing!'

He let her out and promised to follow her up if parking permitted.

Sal took the lift to the chemo suite on the tenth floor, feeling silly at her sudden weakness.

She reported to reception.

'One of Mr Richards's breast lumps,' the receptionist informed the chemotherapy nurse, indicating Sal.

'Poor man,' Sal was about to flash angrily back, 'how many breast lumps does he have?' when Aussie Pam, suddenly annoyed on her behalf, intervened.

'Lucy, for crying out loud! Ms Grainger is a patient, not a breast lump. I do apologize.' Pam shook her head. 'You can't get the staff!'

'Now, I have to tell you,' Pam explained as she led her through the suite, 'this may take a while, maybe even all day. In fact, it can drive some of our patients wild. You need your blood done to make sure your count's not low, then you get checked over, see the pharmacist, hang around a bit, then they'll put you in one of these nice chairs.' She pointed to a row of large squashy seats facing out towards the London skyline, each attached to a stand to which a delivery unit was fixed and various monitors and infusion pumps.

'Oh, no,' Sal said in her best Monty Python tones, 'not the comfy chairs!'

Pam looked bewildered. 'Would you rather sit somewhere else?'

'The Ritz bar?' suggested Sal. 'These will be fine.'

'Then they'll put in your cannula and off you go! The one compensation is the chemotherapy nurses. Everybody loves the chemotherapy nurses!'

Pam handed her over to a smiling middle-aged Irish woman who fitted Sal's head into a freezing ice pack in the hope of saving her hair. Sal hoped it bloody worked. At the moment having a cross between a long-distance swimming cap and a jockey's headgear full of frozen gel felt like the final indignity.

Once she'd sat in her cold cap for forty minutes she was finally ready for the first drug onslaught.

'Your arm, please. Wonderful,' the chemo nurse congratulated. 'Virgin veins!'

'That sounds ominous. Are they usually so hard to find?'

'It's a lot easier to get a line in at the beginning when your veins stand out nicely like yours do.'

Sal decided to take this as a compliment. The journalist in her was intrigued. 'How do heroin addicts manage to find a vein, then?'

'In their bums, earlobes, toes, elbows, you'd be amazed. Mind you, heroin isn't as bad for your veins as this stuff.'

As the line was fitted into her arm through a cannula, a surge of sickness swept through her.

'It's the impact of the drugs,' the nurse told her. 'You're on FEC – Fluorouracil, Epirubicin and Cyclophosphamide.'

'What's the red stuff?' Warily, she eyed the contents of the injection going into her arm.

'That's the Epirubicin.'

There was no sign of Ricky. Sal was beginning to feel relieved. What the hell had she been thinking of, appealing to a total stranger like that?

Suddenly, he materialized on the other side of the room carrying a copy of *Grazia*, a large bottle of Lucozade and the rug she'd noticed on the back shelf of his cab. He waved to her cheerily.

'Here's your husband,' the chemo nurse informed her with a smile. 'And he's brought lots of goodies.'

He proceeded to wrap her in the tartan rug.

'It's the air con,' he explained. 'Cold enough to freeze your tits off.'

He looked stricken at this outbreak of tactlessness and by way of apology produced a bottle of massage oil out of his parka pocket. He sat down next to her chair and began to massage her feet. Taken aback by having her feet grabbed by a strange minicab driver, Sal almost protested, then suddenly grinned and relaxed. What the hell, she had cancer!

She surrendered to the delicious luxury of the fragrant oil. What did it matter if he was an almost total stranger? As far as she knew he could be the angel Gabriel.

'Where on earth did you find massage oil? Don't tell me you carry it to lubricate your sumps?'

'Chemist across the road. My other wife gets migraine. Massaging her feet is the only thing that helps.'

'You're a better actor than Kenneth Bloody Branagh,' murmured Sal, almost forgetting the fear, panic and nausea. 'And twice as good at foot massage.'

'Me and my other wife are keen on amateur dramatics.'

'What a lovely husband,' murmured the chemo nurse admiringly to Lucy, the receptionist.

'Funny,' Lucy whispered back, 'only I could have sworn I've seen that man down the Arndale Centre with another woman.'

'Oh no, not another one!' The nurse quickly revised her opinion of poor Ricky. 'How can men do it? The wife gets cancer and he has to stick it to someone else.' She shot a disdainful look at Ricky. 'And he looks so harmless too.'

Unaware of this assassination of his character, Ricky took himself off with instructions that Sal should call when her chemo was finished and, even if it meant a few white lies, he would try and come and collect her.

Three hours later he was as good as his word. He wouldn't even accept the tenner she tried to press on him. 'My mum got the big C when I was working abroad. I always felt guilty.' He opened the car door for her. 'Are you going to be all right, love? When you get home, I mean.'

'Ricky, dear, I've lived on my own for sixty-three years. I will be absolutely bloody fine. If you could just stop outside this LateExpress while I pick up some supplies, that'd be quite enough help for one day.'

As he waited outside Sal filled her basket with cereal, bread, paracetamol, a lasagne ready meal, a bottle of red wine and a Crunchie. At the last minute she added sausages and mash, another ready meal for tomorrow, bread and butter pudding, plus a bottle of cava. She hadn't actually asked the doctor about alcohol, but that was because life had taught her that if you intended to do something anyway it was more sensible not to enquire.

As she was going out she noticed a sign saying the store was looking for staff on a part- or full-time basis. If she didn't get better in time for the new job, that might be her future. If she was lucky.

Once inside the flat, the flashing on her answering machine told her there were eight messages but suddenly she felt too exhausted to talk to anyone. Not even bothering to put the lasagne in the oven she crawled into bed and fell asleep.

Ella opened the fridge and was amazed to see that it was almost empty. She would have to do another shop.

Wenceslaus came into the kitchen and she remembered the favour she'd meant to ask him. 'How are your woodworking skills?'

Wenceslaus grinned. 'I am demon with power drill.' He adopted a James Bond-holding-a-Black & Decker pose. 'Even Minka admit this. Where is job you like me to do?'

'The shed at the bottom of the garden. A bit of wood fell off the porch. Could you have a look at it?'

'It would be pleasure.' He bowed as if he were asking her to dance. Ella laughed at this old-fashioned courtesy.

'Good to see you laugh. Where is power drill?'

'In the cupboard under the stairs. Nails and screws are in there too.'

'It will be right as rain by time you are back from super-market.'

Ella hummed as she manoeuvred the car out of its parking

space. How nice it was to have a competent man about the place.

She rather enjoyed supermarket shops. Of course, there was the nagging guilt that if she wanted them to stay in business she ought to be supporting the butcher, the baker and the candlestick maker (actually, look what had happened to the candlestick maker), but she rather loved shopping in giant chains. There was the fun of finding some unexpected piece of cheap jewellery, or pillowcases on special offer, pretty notebooks, tights, and, once, a pair of pewter herons which now graced her hall table. And, of course, the groceries.

The only drawback was the parking. It was too far to the nearest retail mall so Ella had to negotiate the dreaded multistorey, a fiendish environment whose entrance ramp had tighter turns than the hairpin bends on Mont Blanc and pillars purposely placed to trap the slightly incompetent parker, among whose number Ella counted herself.

Aha, a space in the middle, furthest away from the dreaded pillars. Brilliant.

Ella spent a happy hour in the aisles filling her trolley with essentials, plus a bunch of roses imported from Kenya (guilt again!), Christmas crackers, rather a lot of wine, and a bumper pack of fizzy water.

She even came across a remarkably pretty scarf in the shade Julia especially liked, with small pansies all over it. She was feeling a little guilty about their recent confrontation and bought it as a small peace offering. Smiling, she texted Julia that she would drop it round.

Five minutes later, Julia texted her back. 'Are you in Sainsbury's?' She knew her mother well. 'Neil's office is next door. He could collect at 1 p.m. on lunch break.'

'Brilliant,' Ella texted back. 'Am in car park will look out for him.'

But when she went back to put her shopping in the car she was panicked to find it wasn't there.

She was absolutely certain of where she had left it, middle floor, pillar B. Yet it had vanished. She trundled her trolley back to the lift, and searched the floor above. No sign. And then back to the lift and down to the floor below, even though she was convinced it wasn't there. She was right.

By now her heart was beginning to race. It must have been stolen. BMWs were in demand and though hers was old, it was quite a desirable model; in fact, her son-in-law, Neil, had often suggested she sell it for something more suitable, which had made Ella want to hang on to it until it fell to pieces.

Her phone rang and made her jump. It was Wenceslaus saying he had finished and was now at work at the coffee shop. He immediately picked up her panic. 'Are you all right, El-la?'

'Fine. It's just that I seem to have lost my car. I'm in the car park near Sainsbury's and I could have sworn I left it here on the top floor but it's not here.'

'Is there someone who works there who could help perhaps?'

After ten minutes' searching she found a car park attendant who spoke no English and appeared to think she was accusing him of being responsible for her car's disappearance.

Eventually, her hips beginning to ache from walking around again, she called 999 and asked for the local police.

She was in luck, they had a car not far off, and since it was a quiet day in Old Moulsford it was only twenty minutes before she heard the siren and saw the flashing blue light.

Two young officers, a man and a woman, stepped out. 'How can we be of assistance, madam?'

'This lady say her car stole,' announced the attendant.

'You are sure this is where you left it?' The two officers shared a knowing smile. Ella was not the first lady shopper to have her car stolen, then discover she'd left it at home all along.

'One hundred per cent. I wrote it down.' She produced the notebook she always carried. 'Middle floor, pillar B.'

At that point another car arrived in the car park. To Ella's horror she recognized Neil's four by four.

Ella didn't know whether to weep or curse as her son-in-law Neil walked officiously towards them. There was something about Neil's demeanour that had always irritated Ella. He was fond of telling people that he didn't suffer fools gladly, and to Neil everyone bar himself seemed to fall into that category.

'Everything all right, Ella?' He eyed the officers in astonishment.

'The lady believes her car has been stolen, sir.'

'What's the betting it's on another floor?'

'I had thought of that, Neil,' Ella informed him tartly. 'I've been to the other floors. Besides, I know it was middle floor, pillar B.'

A smile of sudden satisfaction lit up Neil's face. 'You know you're in the east car park, don't you?'

The stress was beginning to get to Ella. Her certainty started ebbing away. Had she come to the wrong bloody place altogether?

'I'll go and look in the other section,' Neil announced.

Five minutes later, Ella could tell from his walk, quick and cocky, almost falling over himself in his eagerness to get back to them, that he'd found it.

'In the west car park. Sorry to waste your time, officers. My mother-in-law's getting a bit forgetful.'

Ella would have loved to have kicked him, and herself. How could she have muddled the car parks?

'Easily done,' replied the young officer. 'You'd be surprised how common it is.' He didn't add, 'Among the doddery old', but the glance he exchanged with Neil said it all. Ella would have liked to have made a scene and shouted that she hadn't lost her marbles, thank you very much, but being arrested for affray would hardly be a useful outcome.

The lift doors opened and Wenceslaus appeared, dishevelled and out of breath from running. He must have rushed straight round from the café.

'Are you all right, El-la?' he enquired anxiously, seeing the police car.

'I made a silly mistake and parked my car in the west instead of the east car park and when I couldn't find it I thought it was stolen.'

'Do you want I go and get it for you?' he asked solicitously.

She handed him the car key. Suddenly, she was shaking, partly from shock but also embarrassment and anger at herself.

'We'll be off, then.' The officers got back in their car with a cheery wave.

If Neil hadn't been there, she might even have thought it was funny, a good story for the girls.

Meanwhile, Neil was watching Wenceslaus' departing back, his disapproval almost comic in its obviousness. 'You mean you let that character drive your car, yet you call the police because you think it's been stolen from the car park? How do you know he won't just take it back to Romania or wherever he's from?'

'Wenceslaus is from Poland. Because I happen to trust him.'

'Well, maybe you trust him too bloody much.'

Neil was a narrow man at the best of times but the venom in his tone made Ella wonder if he suspected Julia's feelings.

They waited another five minutes, a hostile silence hanging between them, until Wenceslaus reappeared with the car and started to help her pack the boot.

'Try not to forget where you park it next time.'

'Neil, whatever you think, I am not a stupid, senile old woman.'

Before he could say anything, Wenceslaus backed her up.

'El-la not stupid. El-la is bright spark.'

Neil regarded him with dislike. 'Well, make sure this bright spark doesn't burn the bloody house down or we'll be holding you responsible, matey.' He turned to Ella. 'Julia said you had something for her?'

Ella delved into one of the shopping bags. 'Just a silly little thing. A pretty scarf I thought Julia might like.' She handed it over and Neil stumped off back to his car.

'Why is this Neil so angry with everyone?' Wenceslaus asked when Ella got in the car. 'With you? With me? With wife?'

'I really don't know. I wonder if he knows himself.'

'Is time he learn. I finish shed, by the way.'

Ella had forgotten about the shed in all the excitement and panic.

'Is amazing place. Big enough to live in.'

Ella grinned. 'I'd forgotten your fondness for sheds. When my husband was alive we used to have barbecues down there. It's quite hidden away, isn't it?'

'Like other world entirely.' He stared into space for a moment, his blue eyes fixed on some distant point, and she wondered if he were thinking of his home. Life for migrants, she suspected, was a lot harder than people like Neil ever imagined.

CHAPTER 14

'Bella, darling, are you really sure about this baby?'

It might seem a cruel or tactless question but Laura couldn't bear it if the baby had been conceived to serve Simon right. Bella's face, lit up by that fiendish little smile of triumph, had haunted her mother all night. 'I mean, it wouldn't be fair on you or the baby if you were doing it, even a little bit, to get back at Dad.'

'Then it's just as well I'm not, isn't it? I think the timing's quite funny, admittedly, and I will take a certain delight in telling him, but actually it happened by accident.'

Laura was sitting on the sofa in Nigel's incredibly untidy flat. She glanced around her. The place had come furnished with odds and ends no one wanted and Nigel had supplemented this with pieces he'd found abandoned or in skips. There was a single light bulb lighting up Sleepy Hollow posters and a vampire bared his blood-soaked teeth from the other wall. Laura found herself wondering what baby Goths wore and had to shake herself back to reality.

'Going ahead with it is different, though.' She reached for Bella's hand but Bella snatched it away.

'Look, Mum, I know you've come to try and talk me out of it. I don't earn enough, blah. This place is a dump, blah. Nige isn't exactly an investment banker, blah. But I know all that, Mum; I'm twenty-four, not some pregnant schoolgirl

267

wanting a free council flat. And the answer is yes, I do want this baby.'

Laura couldn't help feeling a free council flat wouldn't be that bad a thing.

'But how are you going to support a baby?'

'Nigel's found a job.'

Laura found herself wondering what that might be. Bouncer at a Hell's Angels convention? Body double for the Incredible Hulk?

'He's going to do supply teaching.'

'Don't you need training for that?' Laura could remember all the horror stories Claudia's Don told them about supply teaching. How they were given the worst pupils in the worst classes at the worst schools and even then the pupils traded mercilessly on their unfamiliarity with the place. Poor Nigel. Though maybe pupils would be less likely to try it on with a giant Goth.

'Well, actually, he is trained.' There was a hint of pride in Bella's voice.

'What as?' The words slipped out before Laura had thought them through. 'A football coach?'

'An RE teacher. He studied theology at uni.'

Laura was lost for words.

'OK, Mum,' Bella's tone took on a sudden intensity, 'You obviously think this is a disaster, that I should be getting on the career ladder, making money and all that, but I really want this baby. Life's made so much more sense since I found I was pregnant. I'm going to keep it safe and protect it! Always.'

Her fierce determination cut Laura to the quick, for implicit in her words was the fact that Laura herself had not succeeded in protecting Bella always.

'Another thing, Mum.' Bella reached out a hand covered

in its new spider's web tattoo. 'I'll really be needing your help. There's no way I'll be able to cope without it.'

In spite of her misgivings, Laura felt unbearably moved. 'And of course I'll be there in any way I can.'

If Bella was going to go ahead, there were practical issues to be sorted. 'When is the baby due?'

'In June.'

'*June?* Then you must be . . .'

'Nearly four months pregnant. I must have been pregnant long before Dad left, I just didn't know. So, you see, no one can accuse me of doing it to get at him.'

Joyous relief flooded through Laura.

'What a lovely month to have a baby.'

'Yes,' Bella agreed. 'All those roses out and Wimbledon on the telly. Maybe we'll call her Venus or Serena.'

'Or might it have to be an Andy or a Roger? Or do you know already?'

Bella shook her head. 'God, can't male tennis players have more exciting names?'

'I suppose there's always Jo-Wilfried.' Laura opened up her arms and Bella slipped into them. 'I'm really happy that you're so happy.'

'I am, Mum, I really, really am.'

Laura felt a huge wave of relief that at least something good was coming out of all this pain. Even if the relationship with Nigel didn't last and Bella failed to protect this baby and keep it safe forever and always, the baby was being born out of love, not revenge, and that at least had to be a better beginning.

Ella decided that after the stress of quarrelling with Julia and being dismissed as a demented old bat by Neil, she needed the peace of the allotment. Viv and Angelo were extending their globe-trotting still further, one destination seemed to be segueing into the next with all the blithe insouciance of New Age Travellers. Except that they were Old Age Travellers. Now they had emailed Ella to suggest she just keep digging until somebody made a fuss.

How very pleasant for them to feel that all they needed was each other.

Ella felt a pang of sudden loss. Would she and Laurence have wandered the world, free as two kids, as Viv and Angelo were doing? She didn't think of him quite so often these days and wasn't unhappy with her life, and yet now and then there was a yawning sense of what might have been if he had only lived . . .

To restore her sense of calm she would choose a task she'd been looking forward to: making her wreath out of veg. But when she arrived at Grand Union she could tell there was something unusual in the air.

'It's Stevie and Les,' said Sue from the next-door allotment. 'Les has accused him of nicking his January king cabbages.'

Stevie and Les, usually as inseparable as Morecambe and Wise, stood in Les's neat allotment staring at the leaves from which his cabbages had been removed.

'There were three there yesterday, plain as the nose on my face, all beauties.'

'And you think I've had 'em, do you?'

'And two winter caulis.'

'And *why* would I want your bloody brassicas when I've got spring greens and Savoy cabbages of my own?'

'Quality,' announced Les. 'Your greens have been ruined by root fly so you helped yourself to mine.'

'Now, now, lads,' intervened Bill, as solemn as Solomon, 'it's probably a fox or even a badger. Mr Barzani says he's heard both of them down here at night time.'

'A badger? Round here?'

'There's a sett in Kew Gardens. You can sign up to see it,' offered Stevie.

'Well, it must have been a bloody brilliant badger,' Les exploded, pointing at the neatly cut leaves, 'or a fox with a Swiss army knife.'

Everyone needed cheering up, Ella decided, or she'd never get her peaceful wreath-making done. Fortunately, she had the ingredients to achieve if not world peace, then at least a degree of harmony. 'Come on, one and all, back to my shed for a whisky Mac to warm you up!'

Once she'd poured them all the seasonal mix of Scotch and ginger wine she sought their advice on what would work in her wreath.

'You're making a wreath for your front door out of vegetables?' Ella thought Bill's eyebrows might nest in his bobble hat. 'What's wrong with pine cones and slices of dried lemon?'

'And cinnamon sticks,' added Les.

'Don't forget holly berries,' Stevie reminded.

He and Les glanced at each other, enmity forgotten, reunited and restored in condemning the middle-class madness that led to wreaths made out of garden vegetables.

Ella ignored both of them and began happily to adorn her moss-filled wire base with plaits of garlic and shallots she'd been keeping in her cellar. She took some wire and attached a few carrots which she'd specially lifted and stored in sand. Then she added red radicchio de Treviso and dark green Tuscan kale. It was really beginning to look rather festive.

Deciding it needed something more Christmassy, she tied on a few bright red Scotch bonnet chillies, admittedly bought in the greengrocer's and imported from some distant part.

A Jane Packer flower arranging course she'd once done advised you to add everything in threes, so she added three lots of Brussels sprouts.

'That won't half pong if the weather warms up,' Les commented.

'Then let's hope it stays cold.' Standing back to admire her handiwork, Ella saw what was missing: it needed a bow. The only thing was she didn't have anything suitable. Never mind, there was bound to be something at home. All the same, it was irritating. Ella hated leaving a job unfinished.

'Do you know what, Les lad,' Stevie admitted magnanimously, 'it don't look half bad!'

'It'd look better with a bow,' Ella replied. 'I don't suppose any of you boys have red ribbon hidden about your persons?'

They shook their heads.

'Oh well. Have another whisky Mac,' Ella offered generously.

'Is that invitation open to anyone?' enquired a familiar female voice.

Ella turned to find Laura, resembling a very pretty Eskimo, in a fur-trimmed parka standing behind her.

'Laura! How lovely you look! Though more Gstaad than Grand Union Allotments! Where did you materialize from?'

Laura accepted the warming drink. 'Good God, a whisky Mac! I haven't had one of these since I was sixteen and Jeffrey Niven from the second-year sixth was trying to get me drunk so that he could have his end away. All his dad had in his cocktail cabinet was whisky Mac – the pre-mixed stuff which is truly and genuinely disgusting!'

'And did Jeffrey Niven succeed in his seduction?' Ella asked.

Les and Stevie were listening intently for the answer, but after a sharp look from Ella they dispersed. 'Of course not. Far too uncouth. Now if it'd been Paul Mills . . .' She noticed Ella's wreath. 'Gosh, that's really stunning. Who would have thought the humble carrot and shallot could look so stylish? I might make one for our door. It'd make a change from all the fake wreaths we get in our road.'

'So, what brings you here?' Ella asked as Laura started to select some vegetables to make a wreath of her own. 'Not a hitherto-submerged desire to grow spring greens and kohlrabi, I'm assuming.'

'Er, no. It's Bella.' She put down the plait of garlic she was holding. 'Ella, first it's Sam slashing Simon's tyres, now Bella's only got herself pregnant.'

'Oh my God, Laura, not with whatshisname, the Goth Giant Haystacks?'

'The very one.' She sat down on the decorative garden bench. 'Bloody hell, Ella, I'm going to be grandmother! To a baby Goth!'

'Maybe it'll be a chrysalis – no, that's a moth, not a Goth. Sorry.' She sat down next to Laura. 'Is this going to be a Jerry Springer special – "I had a baby to punish my dad and his new underage girlfriend"?'

'Suki isn't underage; she's not even under thirty! But I get what you mean. Actually, I wondered that myself, but Bella says she got pregnant before Simon even told us. It was an accident but now she's over the moon. And Giant Haystacks turns out to be a theology graduate who's got himself a teaching job.'

'That all sounds very normal and encouraging. Maybe she'll give up the scary black lips and skin the colour of a frozen corpse and go all wholesome. Look at Peaches Geldof: apart from the tattoos, she'd blend in at Mothercare any day. There's hope yet.'

'I'm glad to hear it. I don't want to be stuck knitting baby shawls out of black spiders' webs.'

'I didn't know you could knit.'

'I can't. I'd get the lady in the dry cleaner's to do it. And I couldn't stand it if all the other babies wore fluffy suits with bear ears and my grandchild was dressed as Dracula.'

Ella could detect the edge of anxiety behind the joking. 'Are you all right with this, Laura?'

'What can I do about it anyway? It isn't my life. Bella's strong, stronger than me, probably. It was just that when she said she was going to protect the baby forever, I knew I hadn't done that for her.' Laura turned her face away and brushed the tears from her cheek with a jerky gesture. 'Somehow it's worse when you see how your own disasters affect your children.'

Ella put her arms round her friend. 'It's called Life. You did your best. It wasn't you who walked out from under the board-walk in Brighton.'

'Yes, but maybe that was all a load of nonsense. Why didn't I notice what was going on instead of enacting teenage fanta-sies at sixty-bloody-three?'

'We all need a bit of romance in our lives, Laura.'

Laura attempted a smile. 'So it seems.'

Bill, wearing his usual bobble hat, was standing behind Ella. 'I thought you might make use of this for your wreath.' He held out a skein of bright red raffia. 'Only I usually use it to tie my CDs to the redcurrant bushes to keep the birds off.'

Ella took the raffia and fashioned it into a large bow.

'Bill, you're brilliant. That is absolutely perfect. My wreath will be the star of Moulsford Square.'

'Right then.' He slipped shyly away, then, at the last minute, turned. 'I might pop round one of these days. See how the raffia's getting on. If it breaks I can always get some more from the Flower and Vegetable Supplies.'

'Thanks, Bill.' Ella avoided her friend's eye or she knew she would break down in giggles. 'Why don't you do that?'

Sal was deeply thankful that after her initial onslaught of the revolting FEC she had had a gap before the next cycle, which she spent mostly lying on the sofa.

Now it was time for her second. At least she knew what to expect and didn't have to drag poor Ricky in.

'Are you in for chemo too?'

Sal looked round to find that a startlingly young woman wearing an equally startling purple wig was talking to her from across the waiting room in the chemotherapy suite.

'Yes,' Sal replied. 'It's my second time.'

'Lucky you, and you've gathered that despite the cosy chairs it isn't exactly a day at the spa?' She glanced round to see if Sal was accompanied. 'On your own, are you?' She gestured to the other patients who all seemed, as usual, to have friends or relatives with them. 'Me too. I've been doing this so long I've worn all my lot out. My name's Rachel, by the way.'

'Sally Grainger. Everyone calls me Sal.'

'Hello, Sal.'

'Have you had a lot of chemo?' Sal enquired.

'Oh yes. Hello, my old friends nausea, exhaustion, head-aches, aching bones, mouth ulcers . . .'

'As bad as that?'

'I was editing out the stomach aches, depression, and being a shit to your nearest and dearest. Didn't want to scare you at this early stage.'

They both laughed.

'What kind of . . .' Sal began then stopped, wondering if the etiquette of the chemo suite meant you didn't actually ask.

'Cancer have I got?' Rachel shrugged. 'What haven't I got? It all started with breast, then we had a little bit of lymphoma, then lots of tiny little buggers of tumours. The consultant was actually quite upbeat about those, thought he could zap them like some sort of video game. Wrongly, as it turned out. All I have now is bones, stomach – oh, and ovaries.'

Sal, ever the indiscreet chatterbox, was temporarily lost for words.

'Don't worry. At least I won't have to buy any Christmas presents. Fizzy water? Amazingly enough it's free.'

Sal took a paper cup, still feeling gobsmacked in the face of this amazing girl. How old could she be? Twenty-five? Twenty-six?

'Twenty-five,' stated Rachel, reading her thoughts. 'Bummer, isn't it? Anyway, what do you want to know about cancer treatment? You might as well make use of the resource. I can't leave it to posterity. Fire away. You may even get the truth from me.'

'What's the worst thing about it all?'

'Frustration. No one knows anything so they don't tell you anything. They think it's gone and it comes back. Then you go into meltdown. Total fucking despair. Next?'

'Does everyone lose their hair?'

'Most people. And then it grows back afterwards all curly like pubic hair. You end up with a Hollywood on your head! Now here I have a helpful hint. Get yourself a wig while you still have hair. If you get it now it's fun. Wait till your hair's gone and you feel like a bald loser. Tell you what, I'll come and help you choose.'

Sal looked at Rachel's purple bob. 'I'm not sure I'm quite as adventurous as you.'

'I'm sure they have blue-rinsed ones as well.'

'Thanks a lot! You're on. It'd be fun.'

'I know a really good place. They even make syrups that look realistic. You should see the NHS ones. Like Matt Lucas with a bird on his head.'

Rachel got out the diary on her phone. 'What about the day after tomorrow? Leave it much longer and it might be hello hospice for me.'

'Wednesday it is,' Sal agreed. 'Give me something to look forward to.' If this amazing girl could be cheerful, so the hell could she. She was just going to suggest they had a glass of fizz afterwards when she remembered drinking was probably banned. No one could say cancer didn't give you a whole new lifestyle.

The nurse was back, this time with a paper cup of water. 'You may find you get a sore mouth, I'm afraid, that and digestive problems are our most usual complaints.'

'Not losing your hair?' Sal found she was touching hers. Funny how utterly fundamental to your sense of self your hair was. It was the one thing she truly dreaded. Every time she'd seen another woman with the cancer hairstyle, short and fuzzy, she'd thought *Thank God that's not me.* 'I can take the pain, it's going bald I could do without. Any other nice surprises I've got to look forward to?'

'Your arm may bruise where the cannula was introduced; possible nausea, tiredness, diarrhoea or constipation, and occasional tingling in your hands or feet. But you may be glad to know, sex should be perfectly normal.'

'I'll look forward to it.'

As she dressed and started to walk towards the lift, Rachel hissed at her.

'How was it?'

'Not as bad as I expected.'

'Did they tell you about the MCI? Aka Mild Cognitive Impairment, aka chemo brain. Look out for it. You'll probably forget what day of the week it is.'

Great. Sal began to doubt the impossibility of what she was trying to achieve. Getting cancer. Keeping it a secret. Starting a new job. It was total fucking madness.

On the other hand, so were most things she set herself in life. And what was the alternative? Turning down the job and meekly accepting an impoverished retirement? No way.

'See you Wednesday. I've made an appointment at Wigs For You in Frith Street. About four o'clock?'

If Rachel at twenty-five could keep up that defiant humour and utter lack of self-pity, then Sal could cope with a few challenges.

For now she'd better get back to the flat, open up her laptop and start on some pre-joining work for *New Grey*.

Before the chemo brain set in.

'It's so frustrating!' Claudia attempted to get Don's attention. 'I'm trying to get Mum along to see the GP for some medication, but she absolutely won't go. Don. *Don!*'

Finally Don looked up from the crossword. 'Nineteen down: "Fabulous supporter of royal arms". Seven letters. Any thoughts?'

Since they'd moved to Minsley five weeks ago Don had begun every day, regular as clockwork, with the *Guardian* crossword. He even sat in the same chair to do it. While he claimed it was to keep his brain sharp, it was driving Claudia mad that he was often still sitting there in his pyjamas at eleven o'clock.

She knew he was trying to give some structure to a life that was suddenly without its familiar boundaries since he'd given up teaching, that was something she was struggling with herself. After all, they were both used to dividing their lives into lesson-sized chunks, so that suddenly having limitless open-ended time was extra hard.

She was missing work herself. Not the stress or the endless deadlines, but feeling part of something beyond yourself. The cottage was lovely but they'd already settled in – it had been remarkably quick – and now Claudia knew that she'd have to find something useful to do with her considerable energy. She hadn't thrown paving stones in Paris to settle down to a life that held nothing but gardening and golf.

Already Don seemed to be looking to her to organize their life here. She could see that if she wasn't careful he might develop a marked and deeply irritating dependence on her to provide the diversions.

'What do you want to do today?' he had taken to asking, expecting her to have a programme planned out like some rural tour guide. When she suggested he come up with some ideas he had drawn up a chart, more than vaguely reminiscent of a school timetable, the high point of which was the weekly visit – with lunch in the cafeteria – to their local Tesco superstore.

It was driving her crazy.

'Don, did you hear? I need you to drive me to the doctor when I take Mum tomorrow so I can sit in the back and keep her calm. It's going to be a battle royal to get her there.'

'But tomorrow's Tuesday. Our Tesco day.'

The look she shot him silenced future supermarket-based protest.

'All right. If we must.' He went back to the crossword. 'How about "Frank, ensnared in sex scandal, reveals all". Eight letters?'

'No bloody idea.' She was so cross she had to get out of the house. She knew part of the problem was that she felt cut off here from her usual pattern of life and, more than anything, from her friends. Was it weird, at her age, to value friendship so much? 'Here, Vito,' she dangled his lead enticingly, 'let's go out for a walk, shall we?'

Vito was a wonderfully cheerful little dog who relished a walk, long or short. Thank heavens at least someone was contented with his new life.

They were just crossing the street outside the cottage when a mobility scooter sped round the corner and, if Claudia hadn't acted fast, Vito would have been roadkill.

'Watch out!' Claudia shouted.

The scooter ground to a halt just ahead of them. A very

old lady wearing a man's cap leaned over her shoulder and shouted back, 'It's you who should keep that dog under control. What kind of dog is it, anyway? Never seen anything like it in my life.'

Claudia approached the scooter with Vito safely under her arm. No way was she telling this old bat about Vito's canine antecedents.

'No actual breed, just a bit of this and a bit of that. He's a rescue dog,' Claudia lied.

Vito barked in protest.

'Should have left him to moulder. Better still, have him put down. Too many mongrels roaming the streets.'

Claudia bristled. This was exactly the kind of intolerant, narrow-minded country-dweller's attitude she'd expected to find here. Any minute now the newcomer would start on undesirables and immigrants and condemn them to a similar fate.

'Here, give him to me,' the old lady commanded unexpectedly. 'He can have a ride with me and Henry.' It took Claudia a moment to work out that Henry was the scooter. The old lady put him in the basket at the front. Vito obligingly stood up with his front paws resting on the wire, looking just like a miniature figurehead on a ship's prow. 'Dogs always like riding there. My old border, Ginger, never travelled any other way. The name's Betty, by the way. Betty Wilshaw. You're Olivia's girl, aren't you?'

Claudia almost laughed out loud at being called a girl.

'I'm glad you're here, by the way. We were all getting worried about Olivia. We used to see her at everything: church, yoga, bell ringing even. Now she's always off chasing her tail on these mad exploits. Do you know what she invited me to?'

Claudia dreaded to think. Belly dancing? Advanced Zumba?

'Stretch-mark erasing at some posh beauty parlour! I'm eighty! I had my children sixty years ago. I haven't seen my stomach for some time now. What would I want with stretch-mark erasing?'

'My mother gets a bit carried away sometimes.' Did she dare tell Betty the truth? She was beginning to revise her initial snap judgement, maybe she was the intolerant one. Vito was certainly looking as if he would never leave her side – or, at least, her basket. No, she wouldn't tell Betty the truth about Olivia's condition. Her mother was, underneath her boldly confident façade, an intensely proud and private person who would hate the idea of being talked about, and, even worse, pitied.

'How are you finding it here? Bit of a shock after London, eh? Now that you're here you should get involved. The Village Hall committee is always looking for volunteers. Then there's the church cleaning rota. And every month there's a senior citizens' lunch. Despite the name they're quite fun.'

Horrified, Claudia realized Betty wasn't asking her to come as a volunteer but as a fully paid-up over-sixty!

'Come on, you've got to join something. That's what village life's all about, otherwise you might as well stay in London and never speak to your neighbours. I know,' Betty persisted, 'why don't you join the choir? Our choir's top notch. We beat the Great Minsley Chorus in Sing For England last year. They were furious.' In fact, Claudia had been thinking of joining a choir for some time. Everyone said it was good for the soul. 'The choir master's very forward-looking. None of your old fuddy duddy stuff. He had us doing *Les Mis* in the autumn.'

'Maybe I will,' Claudia replied. Betty was right. She needed to get involved. 'What day do you meet?'

'Tuesdays at eight. We go to the pub afterwards.'

That clinched it. She would definitely think seriously about joining. 'Right. I think I'd better take my dog out of your basket.'

'Nice little chap. Looks to me like a cross between a cocker spaniel and a Bolognese, by the way. Give my regards to your mother.'

'Sam,' Laura asked her horizontal son, who was lying on the sofa, under a rug, playing yet another computer game, 'would you mind if I tried to find a job?'

'Why should I mind?'

'I suppose because you're used to me being at home.'

'Mum. I'm twenty-two. A grown adult and a graduate. I'll probably move out soon, anyway – that's if I can find a job myself.'

Of course it was natural that he should move out. It would probably be very good for him not to have everything done for him. But even so, it gave Laura a painful jolt. Instead of the future she'd imagined with Simon, their children off their hands, free to travel, go for long walks, stay in bed in the mornings if they felt like it, almost be young again, her future seemed empty and rather bleak. She was so used to thinking of her husband and her children before herself, Laura had forgotten what it was *she* wanted. And now she was finding that all the things she did want were somehow tied up with them.

Come on, Laura, get a grip. She still had a home, at least for the moment, Bella and Sam, friendship – and the prospect of a first grandchild. She was healthy and not bad-looking for her age. Besides, there were all the little things in life that were always there for you: sunsets and sudden smiles at strangers; frosty mornings; warm duvets; silly films; morning tea, even though each cup reminded her of the ones she'd shared with Simon; girls' nights out; flowers from the garden.

I need to get out of here, Laura suddenly thought, *I need to build a life again. On my own.*

She was going to stick to that thought about getting a job, even a little job, however menial it might have to be; something to open the door to a world where people were ordinary and friendly and cheerful.

Sal had been looking for a job and had even found one. Maybe she would have some advice.

Laura reached for her phone and then remembered how angry she was with Sal for not telling her about Simon. Somehow it all seemed rather a long time ago and she missed Sal's outrageous humour and instinctive defiance. Sal might well have some good advice.

Laura dialled Sal's mobile and was surprised when it went to voicemail. Sal always answered her phone: her nature was too inquisitive to let any opportunity pass. Disappointed, Laura left a message that she had finally decided to get a job.

She was just sitting down in the kitchen, trying to shake off the thoughts of how empty her life seemed, when Sal called back.

'Great to hear from you. I've been really busy for the last few days.'

'Anything fun?' Laura asked.

'Oh, you know, work stuff. Getting ready for the new job. But hey, what's this about you deciding to join the world of work? Won't that make it harder to fleece the old ex?'

'Don't *you* start!' Laura exploded. 'Sorry, it's just that I'm not trying to fleece him.'

'Pity. He deserves it.'

'I just need to get out there. I need structure. Some kind of job. Any kind of job. The trouble is, I haven't worked for twenty-five years. Quite a gap in my CV.'

Sal had a sudden inspiration but hesitated to suggest it.

Laura might be insulted after all, at such a lowly occupation. Still, beggars with twenty-five-year holes in their CV would find any job hard to find. 'The thing is . . .'

'Spit it out. It can't be that bad. Sexagenarian pole dancer? Lunchtime Lollipop Lady? Junk Mail distributor?'

'Well, actually, I noticed they were looking for shop assistants at LateExpress.'

'The supermarket?' Laura sounded dubious.

'I know, I know. Not exactly what you had in mind. There is one advantage, though.'

'And that is?'

'It's right bang opposite Simon's office. Think of the potential for total embarrassment.'

Laura didn't hesitate. The idea of Simon's colleagues coming in to buy a chicken Caesar wrap and discovering the boss's dumped spouse stacking shelves was too delicious to pass up.

'I'll pop in there later and take a look. At least it'd show a divorce judge I'm not a total parasite.'

'Laura, they wouldn't need convincing. Your kids would tell them how it was you who held that whole family together.'

'Yes, but I don't want the kids involved at all, if I can help it.'

'Simon didn't deserve you.'

Laura grinned, feeling better already, thrilled she was actually taking control of her life, however minutely, and glad that she and Sal were talking again. 'You're too right he didn't.'

When the phone rang again a few minutes later, she thought it might be Sal with another job idea. But it wasn't. It was Bella.

'Hi, Mum. The thing is, I've got an ante-natal appointment tomorrow and I wondered if you might like to come with me? You know me, I'm hopeless at hospitals.' It was true. Bella had always loathed the places ever since she'd had her knee stitched in A & E at the age of six and howled so loudly that they had to turn up the TV. But Laura knew it wasn't really that. Bella was deliberately trying to involve her.

'Of course I'd love to. If you're really sure.'

'I'm sure. I really want you to be involved with this baby, Mum. It may have pretty dodgy parents, but if it's got you as a grandmother it'll be OK.'

Ella had to confess, she was worried.

Ever since the incident in the car park she'd been watching herself closely. The truth was, she was getting quite forgetful. She tried to remember what she'd watched on TV last night and found she couldn't. People's names, even people she knew quite well, eluded her so often that she left everyone to introduce themselves at parties. She couldn't even remember quite simple words at times. The other day she'd had to go on Google to retrieve the word 'chicken'. And losing things! She spent part of each day trying to find her glasses, wallet, phone or lipstick. Yesterday it had been a piece of paper with a phone number on it. She had been absolutely certain she'd put it in her wallet, yet there had been no sign of it.

Sal had told her there was nothing to worry about. She was simply having a CRAFT moment.

'What the hell is a CRAFT moment?' Ella had asked.

'It's an acronym: Can't Remember a Fucking Thing. Don't worry, it happens to everyone.'

Worst of all was finding her way from A to B. Once this had been completely instinctive, now she had to sit in the car and mentally visualize the route. And it was quite a struggle.

To someone who prided themselves on being well-organized, efficient and still young it was all deeply irritating.

She had even thought of going to see her GP about it, but a few hours browsing on the Internet convinced her it was pretty common and probably more to do with ageing than Alzheimer's.

Instead, she sat at her computer screen and started blogging. The time zipped by as she recounted to her unknown audience the story of losing her car, calling the police and the car being discovered exactly where she had left it, but in the adjacent car park, by her smug son-in-law; then there was her little problem with leaving her keys in the door; forgetting the name of her next-door neighbour whom she had known for twenty years, and having to look up the word for chicken.

This time she rang the changes by ending with an appeal:

> *AM I GOING GAGA OR ARE THERE SOME OF YOU*
> *OUT THERE WHO DO THE SAME???*

To Ella's astonishment she had barely posted her query before the replies started to appear.

Dozens of confessions flooded in from people her own age, and sometimes even younger, who had not only forgotten where their cars were parked, but had also left the key in the ignition overnight, locked it in the boot, forgotten their phone numbers or the name of their best friends and, in the case of one shamefaced Londoner, parked their car in a car park and gone home on the tube, only to panic the next morning wondering who had nicked it. Best of all was the reply from a geriatric psychiatrist who told her that forgetting stuff was quite common. She was simply suffering from Benign Senile Forgetfulness. Well, that was okay then!

Ella realized what fun it was to talk to total strangers and hear their reassuring tales of amnesia. The Internet was a wonderful place. Anonymous and friendly at the same time.

She was laughing out loud when a new response arrived that made her freeze and panic.

YOU ARE WONDERFUL, it read, WHAT IS YOUR NAME AND WILL YOU COME AND WRITE FOR *NEW GREY* MAGAZINE?

It was signed by one Sally Grainger.

Mr Ahluwalia, the manager of the W4 branch of LateExpress supermarket, universally known by staff and customers as Mr A, wasn't accustomed to job applicants like Laura.

Most of the ladies who came to seek work were from the council estate over the road, had few educational attainments, wore unsuitable clothing, and often failed to turn up for the start of their shifts. So he was somewhat taken aback to be handed a CV which featured glowing examination results and a university degree.

On the other hand, Laura's manner was, in Mr A's view, very much a recommendation. She seemed friendly, down-to-earth, and reliable. Unlike some of his staff who wore ridiculous stilettos to work, Laura favoured smart trousers, a jumper with a shirt underneath, and sensible, flat shoes. He felt his wife would greatly approve of this lady, a definite advantage as she was prone to come and inspect the staff at random intervals in case, as she put it, any slag or Jezebel had insinuated herself into her husband's employ and, since they lived above the shop, this could happen at any time without any warning.

Even better, Laura seemed happy to work the early morning shift starting at 7 a.m., which few of his ladies wanted to do, since they were trying to get their idle children out of bed, shovel unsuitable foodstuffs down them, and try – often unsuccessfully – to deliver them to school.

All the same, Mr A decided he must rein back his enthusiasm and conduct an on-the-spot interview. His wife, he knew, would question him on this matter.

'Do you have any experience of working in a shop at all?'

'Yes, I do. When I was a teenager I worked as a Saturday girl in Boots the Chemist.'

'Ah,' Mr A was impressed at the name of a nationwide chain. 'But what is a Saturday girl?'

'When I was growing up nearly every teenager who needed money worked on Saturdays in a shop or café, hence "Saturday girl".' Laura gave him the benefit of one of her most whole-some smiles and hoped he wouldn't work out that her stint in Boots had been more than forty years ago. 'My mother said it was a good way of bridging the world of school and the world of work. It's a great pity it's died out, in my view.'

'Indeed, yes. Now teenagers spend Saturday hanging round shopping centre. What is it they call them? Mall rats. Some shopkeepers even have device to make noise like angry mos-quito and get them to go away. My wife would like me to purchase one. What did you do at Boots the Chemist?'

'Everything from stocktaking and stickering to serving behind the counter. But I liked being on the till best.'

'How many shifts would you like to work?' enquired Mr A.

Laura thought about this. She wasn't looking for a full-time job, just a way of earning a bit and keeping herself sane. Of course she could try for something more socially acceptable but it was the fact that working here was of its nature tem-porary and anonymous that appealed to her. She saw it as doing a few shifts rather than having a real job, which suited her injured state of mind.

'Maybe three days a week?'

Mr A nodded in satisfaction. That happened to suit him well at the moment. Even so he dared not make an offer without first discussing the matter with Mrs A. 'You leave me mobile number and I ring you back tomorrow.'

With her usual intuition Laura swiftly followed his thinking. 'Would you like me to come in and meet anyone else first?'

Mr A stood on his dignity. He did not want to incur his wife's wrath but he was not going to ask her permission. 'Thank you but not necessary.'

'May I ask the pay for the job?'

'Six pounds fifty an hour.'

Laura gulped. She'd paid her cleaner more than that. When she'd had one.

He started to walk her towards the door, indicating that the interview was over. 'Very nice meeting you. I call tomorrow and let you know.'

CHAPTER 15

'Good morning, group.' Suzanne's determined cheeriness evoked the usual mumbled response of 'Good morning, Suzanne. Good morning, Stephen.'

My God, Laura couldn't help thinking, *how old does she think we are?*

'And now, just to vary the format, today we're going to have a little quiz.'

Laura caught Calum's eye and they both grinned.

'In this session,' Suzanne looked encouragingly at each member of the group in turn, 'we want you to move to the third stage of our programme. At our earlier meetings we acknowledged our own role in what happened to our relationship. We've also looked for reasons why we are actually better off without the other person. This week it's the Big One: have we actually accepted the relationship is over? Are you ready?'

Some people responded enthusiastically, though others were clearly less evolved in their own personal route to relationship recovery.

Stephen began to hand out sheets of paper and pencils to the people sitting round in a circle. 'Be honest now!'

1. HOW MANY TIMES A DAY DO YOU THINK ABOUT
   YOUR EX?

2. DO YOU CHECK PHONE OR EMAIL TO SEE IF THEY
   HAVE CALLED?
3. DO YOU BLAME THE PERSON WHO BROKE UP
   YOUR MARRIAGE RATHER THAN YOUR PARTNER?
4. DO YOU EVER FANTASIZE ABOUT A REUNION?
5. DO YOU THINK OF THE FUTURE WITHOUT THEM?
6. ARE YOU HAPPY OCCASIONALLY?

'Surely they won't announce who's recovered the most?' Laura whispered to Calum. 'Half the group will want to kill themselves.'

'Or kill the person who's most recovered.' Calum grinned.

In fact, the group leaders simply marked the quiz and gave it back.

On Laura's page they had written: 'Congratulations, Laura, you are well on the way to relationship recovery.' Despite the silly jargon Laura felt a definite lift of the heart. She didn't know if it was impending grandmotherhood, no matter how unsuitable, or the possibility of a job, even a lowly supermarket job, or just being able to see a life beyond her present misery, but things were looking up.

A deep sigh coming from beside her told her that things weren't going so well for Calum. 'I have to try harder to move on, apparently.'

Laura felt a wave of sympathy. He was a good man, she was sure of it. 'Why don't we go for a coffee one of these days?' she found herself suggesting. 'We could promise we'll neither of us mention our ex-partners.'

When he smiled, the deep lines etched either side of his mouth seemed suddenly rather attractive.

Watch it, warned an inner voice which sounded like a combination of Bella and Suzanne, *you don't want to risk where you've got to.*

But Laura just smiled to herself. She reckoned she could manage a cup of coffee without imagining it would lead to another relationship fiasco.

'I'd really like that,' Calum replied softly, hoping the others hadn't heard, which was rather naïve of both of them.

When Laura got home she found a phone message from Mr A asking if she could start the day after tomorrow.

Laura found herself doing a little skip round the kitchen. If you'd told her six months ago that an offer of working in a supermarket would make her happy, she would have laughed.

But the funny thing was, it did.

In the end Claudia took her mother to the doctor on her own because Don came down with a nasty dose of man flu.

In a way she was glad. It meant she got to spend a little time alone with Olivia in the strange confessional-box atmosphere of the car. She had noticed with Gaby, especially if her daughter happened to be sitting in the back in the dark while Claudia drove, that her daughter would tell her things on the way home from school or a party that she would never have told her under other circumstances.

The same was true today with Olivia.

'How have you been, Mum?'

There was a long silence.

'Mum?'

Olivia was staring out the window. She turned an anguished face towards her daughter. 'Not so good, Claudie.'

The childhood name, so rarely used in recent years, pierced Claudia's grumpiness with Don and his flu symptoms.

'I can't sleep. My mind races and keeps me awake. I don't have any of my old energy.' She reached out and touched Claudia's arm as she drove. 'There's something the matter with me, isn't there? Maybe the doctor's right.'

In the waiting room Olivia sat quietly by her side looking ahead. Once she would have struck up a conversation with a fellow patient or at least found something to complain about in the running of the surgery. Claudia, used to being embarrassed by her mother's urge to interfere, felt a sudden wave of protectiveness.

In the consulting room it was almost as if Olivia wasn't present. Claudia found herself answering the questions for her, explaining the racing thoughts, the impulsiveness coupled with overconfidence, and the chronic lack of sleep that characterized her mother's personality.

The doctor nodded. 'Relatives often find the manic phase very disturbing, yet the sufferers themselves can't see it. They just feel positive and can't see the problem. Often they get angry with anyone who criticizes them. It's only when the depressive phase sets in that the sufferer tends to seek help.'

Claudia nodded, her gaze fixed on the silent Olivia. It did seem true of her mother that only now was she more open to being helped.

'Mrs Williamson, may I call you Olivia? You need to take things quietly, take care of yourself, avoid agitation, try and sleep a lot. This will definitely help.' The doctor wrote out a prescription. 'As will these. Perhaps you could come back in a few weeks?'

On the way home they stopped at the chemist and Claudia went in to get the prescription filled. She had never thought she would miss her bossy, managing, bulldozing mother. But she did.

When she got home, Don was up, standing looking out of the sitting-room window waiting for her to get back.

'How was she?'

Claudia longed to share her worry over her mother, but something stopped her. In London, Don had been a quiet tower of strength. When she was blue, he would produce an impish face, do some silly clowning, make her laugh, yet she sensed a change in him, as if it were he who was missing their old life even more than she was.

Men, she suspected, drew even more of their sense of self from work than women did.

'Are you OK, love?' she forced herself to ask him. 'With living here, as well as having the flu?'

Don nodded, making an effort. 'Fine. It's just been more of a shock than I was expecting.'

'Why don't you go up to town and have a night out with your friends like I do?'

Don nodded. 'Maybe I will. I'm sorry, Claudia, dragging you here and then going all pathetic on you.'

Claudia touched his cheek, softening. 'The good thing about marriage is you can take turns to be pathetic. It'll probably be me next.'

The sight of a mountain of cardboard boxes from their move, piled in the corner, caught her attention and gave her an idea. She'd always enjoyed going to the dump in London. There was something pleasurable about recycling. Even sorting things out into cardboard, plastic and wood gave you a sense of order. Maybe just what Don needed.

'Why don't you do me a favour and take that lot to the dump?' she asked. 'Meanwhile, I'll sort out some lunch.'

As she bustled in the kitchen the thought came to her of an old saying of her mother-in-law's: *For better, for worse, but not for lunch.* She hoped her mother-in-law didn't have a point.

The doorbell rang, just as she started wondering what delightful activities her friends would be getting up to in London. Christmas shopping in Liberty's? A coffee in Pret? Maybe a visit to the Wallace Collection or a glass of fizz in Covent Garden?

Claudia shook herself and answered the door. It would be Don forgetting his key as usual.

As it happened, Claudia would have felt shocked and sobered had she known what Sal was actually up to.

Wigs For You was in a small street in Soho, midway between Leicester Square and Oxford Circus. On a mad whim, and partly because she was late for her appointment with Rachel, Sal decided to travel the final bit by taxi rickshaw. She felt self-conscious at first, like a tourist being – literally – taken for a ride, then she began to relax and enjoy herself and the journey began to seem entirely magical.

Dusk was falling and all the Christmas lights on the Oxford Street store fronts twinkled and shone. In Bond Street the expensive shops vied to outdo each other with glitter and giant bows. Fortnum's window, always a highlight, boasted a tableau of 'I saw three ships a-sailing'. Gorgeously robed medieval figures watched three galleons loaded down with gifts, rocking gently up and down on mechanical cardboard waves. Outside little children pointed and laughed.

Sal was instantly back in her childhood, reliving the magic and wonder of Christmas morning. A sudden backwash of sadness engulfed her that her life had not turned out as she might have expected it to. No husband to bring her morning tea. No children to jump on the bed clutching their stockings to show her the tangerine and puzzles and chocolate money.

A brief image of snowy Oslo and the baby who had been so briefly in her arms came back to haunt her.

'Frith Street,' announced the rickshaw driver.

And there was Rachel, standing outside Wigs For You wearing a hairband with bobbly reindeer on it, and she had to laugh out loud. Despite all the worry, at this moment, life seemed suddenly precious and good.

'Right, what are we waiting for?' Sal greeted Rachel. 'Let's get wiggy.'

Inside, there was a delicious aroma of mulled wine. There was even a non-alcoholic version since a lot of the shop's clients were cancer patients.

'Maybe we could get a girl band together,' Rachel suggested, trying on a Diana Ross curly version. 'We could call ourselves The Survivors — as long as you didn't ask me to join.'

Sal felt the urge to hug her but resisted. Rachel's extraordinary self-mocking bravery discouraged easy sentimentality.

The assistant tied up Sal's hair and flattened it against her head with kirby grips. 'I like this look. Ena Sharples by night.'

The assistant selected various wigs. Short, red and bobbed. 'Ooh, Mary Portas!' Sal cooed. Then dark and long. Sal put her finger in her mouth. 'Very Nigella.' And, finally, a shoulder-length layered wig with russet highlights.

'That's the one!' Rachel insisted. 'No one would ever know it isn't your own hair.'

On the assistant's advice Sal bought a block to put it on when it wasn't in use. 'Then you can wash and blow dry it yourself, just like the hairdresser does.'

'Think of all the money you'll save on salon bills,' pointed out the irrepressible Rachel. 'And don't forget a roll of double-sided tape. You stick one side to the wig and the other to your baldy head. No more red faces when your syrup decides to blow off in the wind — and you end up like Telly Savalas in a frock and leggings!'

Just as they were leaving, Rachel grabbed a pink nylon wig from a display model. 'I'm going to have to get this!' she insisted. 'It's only twenty quid.' She plonked it on her head.

The amazing thing was, it looked great.

'Tell you what,' Rachel giggled, 'let's go for that drink. Eat, drink and be merry, for tomorrow we – no, let's forget that bit, shall we?'

Sal led the way to the Paramount, right at the top of Centrepoint at the far end of Oxford Street, where they took the Express lift to the thirty-second floor. There they stood in the bar, crowded with pre-Christmas revellers, looking down on frosty light-bedecked London laid out beneath them.

Sal ordered two glasses of champagne. She wanted to forget the bloody cost, or whether they should be drinking at all.

'To friendship old and new.' For a brief second they held each other's glance, then looked beyond at the dazzling lights of the city far below where people were getting on with the serious business of living and loving, and hoped fervently it would go on including them.

Laura set off for her new job, feeling pleasantly excited.

She knew this was a shockingly un-PC response, but she'd always loved playing shops as a child, weighing out potatoes and carrots on her mother's kitchen scales, wrapping them in brown paper bags which she twirled over and twisted like the professionals she'd seen in the greengrocer's. She was sensible enough to know that shifts in LateExpress would be a far cry from her mother's kitchen and the challenges would be mind-numbing boredom, zero social status and possible RSI from swiping endless items through the till. But the truth was, she didn't yet feel strong enough for a job which required decision-making or great responsibility. She was rather looking forward to just taking a few small steps.

Mr A turned out to be friendly and chatty and soon she had his family history: coming to Britain with nothing but his shopkeeping skills and slowly building up his business from one small corner shop to three outlets in West London. 'And do you know how we did it, Mrs Minchin? By working all hours God gave and now Tesco Metro does the same!'

His greatest object of both pride and heartache was that none of his three sons were prepared to follow him into the business. 'Too educated to work in shop. All want to be bloody bankers!'

Laura's first task was indeed shelf-stacking. One of the other assistants showed her around the storeroom which was filled from floor to ceiling with cardboard boxes, each with the front torn off to reveal the contents. She was then shown how to use the price gun and given a list of prices to sticker onto each product.

The morning passed quietly enough with a few late office workers buying biscuits and cigarettes, and old ladies popping in for a pint of milk, until about midday when the school round the corner broke for lunch. An enormous rowdy queue formed outside owing to Mr A's insistence on only two pupils coming into the shop at a time.

'Keep an eye out, Mrs Minchin,' Mr A had warned. 'They are like Tartar hordes, carry everything away in their school-bags. Keep special eye on crisps and Coca-Cola.'

Then came the sandwich rush. Despite the modesty of much of his stock, it seemed that Mr A's sandwiches were famous and that this was down to Mrs A, who came up with the recipes for unusual fillings.

'Cheese and pickle still number one,' Mr A confided to Laura, 'but chicken fajita, hoisin duck, and falafel in pitta all sell pretty good. Also many onion bhaji butty.'

'Onion bhaji butty?' Laura echoed.

'Fish and chip shop sell chip butty, why not onion bhaji butty?'

Just before one, Laura was taking her turn on the till when she noticed Simon's long-time assistant, Elaine, musing in front of the sandwiches. Eventually, she selected a chicken Caesar wrap and a bottle of Evian, which she brought to the counter.

Laura swiped the sandwiches and water. 'Thanks, that'll be two pounds eighty. Would you like a bag for those?'

Elaine counted out the money and began to hand it over.

'*Laura!*' she blurted out, stunned. 'I mean Mrs Minchin! What on earth are you doing here?'

'Hello, Elaine,' Laura replied, greatly enjoying herself. 'I'm working here. Since Simon and I split I needed a job and, as you can imagine, there's not a lot out there for a housewife who's been at home for twenty-five years.'

'Twenty-five years?' echoed Elaine, who had only been married for three and was finding that hard going. 'You were together for twenty-five *years*?'

'We split up on our silver wedding anniversary. Good timing, eh? Can I pick that up for you?'

Elaine had let the bottle of Evian slither through her fingers in stunned amazement. Laura nipped round from behind the till and handed it back to her. 'Sorry, better get on. Enjoy your lunch.'

A queue of irritable sandwich purchasers, in which Laura gleefully recognized the HR director from Simon's office and another of the senior partners, had formed behind Elaine. Their expressions, when they recognized Laura, were price-less, as if they'd discovered the Duchess of Cambridge serving in KFC.

After the lunchtime rush, Mr A told her to choose a sand-wich for herself, as it was her first day, and to take it off to eat somewhere peaceful on her break. She chose to sit on a cardboard box in the stock room and munched her onion bhaji butty, which turned out to be absolutely delicious, wondering how long it would take Simon to hear the good news of her gainful employment.

Not long at all, as it happened.

Mr A had asked her to sort through the stand of birthday cards at the front of the shop when her soon-to-be ex-husband, white with fury, burst into the shop.

'What the hell do you think you're up to?' Simon demanded, taking in her admittedly not very stylish nylon overalls emblazoned with LateExpress on her left breast.

A very old lady who was browsing nearby jumped violently. 'Hunting for a card for my sister. She's going to be ninety.'

'Not you!' barked Simon.

'As a matter of fact,' Laura replied in a pleasant tone guaranteed to drive him berserk, 'I'm taking your advice.'

'What are you talking about?'

'You accused me of being a leech, as I recall.'

'Well, I never, how rude,' commented the old lady.

Simon studiously ignored her.

'You said I had sat on my arse for the twenty-five years of our marriage,' Laura continued, straightening up the cards, 'and that I should, I think your exact words were, get a bloody job.'

Simon looked as if he might pull the rack down on top of her in his fury.

'I was angry. Anyway, I didn't mean a menial job like this, which you have chosen deliberately next to my office for maximum embarrassment.'

'Actually, I think you'll find paid jobs, menial or not, are pretty thin on the ground. This is part time, which suits me since Sam needs me at the moment, and as you so kindly pointed out, sitting on one's arse for twenty-five years doesn't look too good on a CV. Although,' she stooped to retrieve an envelope, 'a judge might consider I was at least making an effort.'

Simon looked as if he'd like to throttle her.

'Or he might consider that deliberately taking a job to embarrass me in front of my colleagues constituted unreasonable behaviour!' he snapped back.

'I think you're doing that perfectly well without my help.' She indicated two young women from his office who were surreptitiously pointing at him and giggling.

'You'll be hearing from me, Laura. How I put up with you for twenty-five years God alone knows.'

He turned on his heel.

'Oh, my dear,' sympathized the ancient card-buyer, 'what a horrid temper. It makes me quite glad I never married. You're much better off without him.'

Laura smiled back at her. She realized she was beginning to agree.

Claudia hated herself for being so grumpy. It was just that, here in Little Minsley, without her friends or her job, and with Don becoming so suddenly dependent on her, she was going quietly mad. Her mother was right, of course, that she'd never been a joiner. Maybe it was time she joined something now. She would start with the choir. After that she'd volunteer for something more substantial. Not church cleaning or bell ringing but something that might make her feel useful and involved. Volunteers, she'd read in a survey somewhere, were much happier people than the rest of society, and it was true she'd stopped being such a pain and was starting to be positive.

The Minsley Choral Society didn't sound exactly like a hotbed of thrills and excitement, but, on the other hand, taking on *Les Misérables* would have been no mean feat, and everyone said singing was good for the soul.

Claudia decided to go down to the school where they met and to check it out. The only thing was, she was pretty convinced she couldn't sing. What if you had to audition?

Hideous memories flooded back to her of being the only girl in her class who'd been banned from joining the school choir owing to her inability to hold a note. Did she really want the humiliation all over again?

Outside the school there was a large board displaying parish notices, including one for the choir.

'Interested?' a voice enquired.

Claudia turned to face someone who appeared as much a refugee from the big city as she was. Unlike the usual tweedy or bejeaned males she'd encountered in Minsley, he was wearing a sweater in green cashmere and a tartan scarf under a soft and expensive-looking navy coat with the collar turned up. It gave him a faint look of José Mourinho. He even had the same faint scowl.

'I might be,' Claudia answered cautiously. 'It depends if I have to audition.'

'Scared, eh?' The newcomer laughed. She had to admit his smile transformed his whole demeanour from stern to mischievous, which was a step forward. Without even realizing it, she found herself smiling back. 'No auditions for our choir. All we ask for is commitment. Once you sign up, we have you for life.'

'Like the Jesuits?'

'Exactly like the Jesuits. Or the Scientologists. Daniel Forrest, by the way, I'm the choir master.'

He held out his hand. Claudia took it, wondering if his handshake would be limp and fishy like Peter Dooley's or firm and friendly. It was almost vicelike. Claudia, who had a theory about the meaning of handshakes, felt a faint blush colour her cheeks.

'It's me who'll be getting you to sign in blood,' Daniel continued, a quizzical look taking in her confusion. 'Have you sung before?'

'Only at school. Plus hymns and all that.'

They had started walking towards the village centre. 'So why do you want to join? Sorry, I don't mean this to be the Spanish Inquisition.'

'I've just moved down here.' For reasons she wouldn't like to examine too closely she almost forgot to mention Don. 'My husband and I used to live in Chiswick.'

'Aha. Chasing the rural rainbow?' She got the distinct impression this Daniel Forrest was putting a label on her and she didn't like it one bit.

'To be honest, I had to be dragged from London kicking and screaming. For a start I loved my job.' She found she wanted him to take her seriously, and not dismiss her as a housewife.

'What did you do?'

'I was a teacher. French.'

'Interesting. I run a charity for disadvantaged kids. Maybe I could interest you in that?'

'I think I've had enough to do with education for the moment.'

'Kids had enough of your dark sarcasm?' She caught his impish smile as he recalled the Pink Floyd song and found herself suddenly thinking of Thierry and the Paris paving stones. Funny, he'd be about Daniel Forrest's age now.

'Sorry, did I sound disillusioned?' Claudia apologized.

'Just a little.'

Claudia couldn't help smiling at his wry tone. 'The real reason I came is because of my parents. They live here and they are starting to need looking after. So here we are in Little Minsley. I bumped into Betty Wilshaw and she suggested I join the choir.'

'Glorious Betty! You know she used to be a chorus girl?'

Claudia thought about the white-haired old lady on the mobility scooter; she certainly had plenty of personality.

'A Bluebell Girl at the Paris Lido, no less.'

Claudia blinked, trying to imagine the lively octogenarian in feathers and sequins at some of Paris's most famous cabarets.

'Our Betty high-kicked with the best of them. Called herself Betty Blue. She was quite an attraction, I'm told.' They stopped by the zebra crossing outside the village shop. 'So, will you be coming to choir next Tuesday?'

'I'll think about it,' Claudia replied, not wanting to be roped into something she'd regret.

'Are you always this impetuous?' Claudia had the distinct impression Daniel Forrest was laughing at her.

'No,' she replied tartly. 'Often I make up my mind on the spot. Especially about people.'

'I have to pray I've made a good impression, then. See you Tuesday, I hope.'

Ella sat in her warm oak-panelled kitchen, looking out at the garden birds. A couple of tits were fighting a robin over the breadcrumbs she'd put out and naturally the robin won. Funny that such a fierce little bird had become the symbol of peace and love just because of the colour of its breast. She could hear the sudden laugh of a woodpecker on the wing. A flash of colour like a leaf in the air told her it was a green one.

This fascination with birds, Ella recognized, was one of the things she could have put on her How To Spot If You're Old list, like reading obituaries or starting to go deaf. There came a time in life when telly bored you and yet you could watch wildlife on a bird table for hours. Her daughters saw this as a sign of incipient decrepitude, and maybe it was. Perhaps, the shorter the road you saw ahead of you, the more you appreciated the wonder of the natural world around you.

The thought of her list reminded Ella of her other problem: Sal's email. Should she confess to being the author of MOAN

FART DIE? If she did, she would lose the glorious anonymity which made her enjoy writing it so much and which she thought was the wonder of the Internet. She smiled, remembering a New Yorker cartoon card someone had sent her of a dog sitting at a computer confessing to its canine friend: 'On the Internet no one knows you're a dog.' Well, she liked no one knowing she was a dog.

The other issue was about what she'd said already, especially about Laura's marriage.

No, despite the appeal of getting a tiny bit famous, if she accepted Sal's offer, she'd prefer to keep her secret.

Sal had to admit, she was feeling truly terrible.

She had arrived at *New Grey* two days ago and had been allocated a nice desk over by a big window which caught the morning light. Admittedly, it looked out over a goods yard but it was still a wide-open space which had to be good for the soul. But it wasn't her soul that was the problem, it was her body. Although the two cycles of chemo had gone well she had been completely floored by the after-effects. Painful ulcers had appeared on the roof of her mouth, and she was feeling cold, sick and dizzy by turns.

She was supposed to be preparing for the meeting, yet all she could do was stare out at the departing goods train and ask herself if she could conceivably carry this off. It had all seemed perfectly reasonable in theory. She was a determined person, and though she had sometimes taken the easy route in life, she knew she had steel within. It was all a question of self-control, she had insisted to Rachel, when she'd told her new friend about starting at the magazine. Rachel had said nothing. Merely raised an eyebrow and made a face that said, 'You wait'.

On the other hand, what was the alternative? That she go

and tell her new bosses that she'd taken the job under false pretences, that she had cancer, and go home to her empty flat, with no money, virtually no pension, and an equally empty life?

Instead, she used the last few minutes before the meeting to nip to the loo, where she retched into the sink.

Oh well, Sal's graveyard humour came to her rescue, *if anyone comes in I can always tell them I'm pregnant.*

The worst of the sickness passed and she was able to drink a glass of water, take some more anti-nausea pills and go back to her desk.

The meeting, as it turned out, was lively and productive. All the staff, young as well as middle-aged, responded to Sal's proposal that the magazine should focus not on age, but on the issues and interests that affected their readers, and all of it in an upbeat tone.

'Our readers are a new breed. I call them the Young-Old. They aren't interested in Bingo and knitting patterns. They want to travel. They want adventure. They like to look good. And they want to stay healthy so they can enjoy the time ahead. So just remember that when you're thinking up ideas for *New Grey*.'

'But what about something really new to mark out the Sally Grainger era?' asked Rose McGill. 'What is it that makes it so different about ageing now?'

Sal thought about it. 'Learning to be in charge of your life. Look at what's happening out there. There are more single women than ever – the divorce rate among the over-sixties rose four per cent in the last two years. And it's often women who start divorce proceedings. They realize they might live another thirty years and they want to live them on their own terms. In fact, I'm looking for someone outspoken and fresh to be our star writer, who'll reflect all that, set the tone of the revamped *New Grey*.'

'Any idea who it might be?' Rose McGill pressed.

Sal didn't want to admit that she hadn't yet managed to track down the mystery blogger.

'I'm keeping it under wraps for the moment,' Sal lied.

'How exciting. We'll all be waiting with baited breath.'

Sal gathered up her stuff and stood up. 'Right, everyone, repeat, "Sixty is the new forty".'

Everyone round the table laughed and repeated Sal's mantra.

If only she felt it herself.

Wednesday was one of the days when Laura didn't work. She lay in bed late, relishing it as a new and unfamiliar luxury, ran a long bath, made a cup of tea for herself and for Sam, and hummed to herself as she picked up the post.

Today she was going with Bella to the ante-natal clinic.

'I'm going to be a grandmother,' she repeated to herself. 'I'm actually going to be a grandmother.'

She stopped as she noticed what was on the mat. Another letter from those damn solicitors of Simon's. She tore it open, hardly able to believe what she was reading.

Simon had done exactly what he had threatened. He was starting divorce proceedings against her on the grounds of her unreasonable behaviour. Her job at LateExpress, he alleged, was entirely unsuited to someone of her education and experience, and had been designed maliciously and unreasonably to cause her husband embarrassment and distress.

The bastard!

She found her phone and called Rowley Robinson. To her surprise, he answered it himself.

'Don't worry, Laura. To be honest, I'm not surprised. What do you want to do?'

'I want to defend it. The whole idea that it's unreasonable of me to get a job near his office is ridiculous,' Laura raged, ignoring the fact that actually there had been a teeny weeny bit of truth in Simon's allegation.

'Of course this may well be at the instigation of the new partner,' Rowley soothed. 'She may want him to move ahead more quickly with the divorce so they've come up with this.'

'But it isn't *right*! He's the one who's behaved unreasonably, the one who had an affair and dumped me on our anniversary.'

'I'm sorry, Laura, but the actual grounds for divorce are just a device. Quite a lot of people actually prefer unreasonable behaviour because there's less stigma. No one bothers to challenge a divorce any more unless they're an oligarch with bottomless pockets. To be honest, it doesn't really matter what the grounds are, the divorce will go through anyway.'

'What if it matters to me?'

'Defend it, then. But I really wouldn't advise it. It'll cost a fortune, take twice as long and you'll all end up hating each other.'

Laura put down the phone. How could the law have ended up being so bloody unfair?

Suddenly Laura realized the time. She would have to run or she'd be late for Bella. Screw Simon, she was going to concentrate on the good things in her life.

Half an hour later, Bella was waiting for her outside the Princess Lily Hospital. It was one of those vast places that covered every department. Bella had moderated her dress from Ripper Victim to Victorian Governess and even forsaken her usual black lipstick. She was also hopping from one foot to the other like a lace-clad parrot.

'Are you all right?'

'I need to pee but I'm not allowed to till after the scan.'

Laura hid her smile. It was usually she who needed to pee all the time, another of the joys of ageing. Sometimes, as she got up for the third time in the night, she wondered if it would be easier to resort to incontinence pads. 'We'd better get on, then. Is Nigel coming?'

'He's got a job interview. He's going to get here as soon as he can.' She put her arm through her mother's. 'But, anyway, I've you.'

The ultrasound department was on the second floor.

It was so long since she'd had her children that Laura had forgotten the unique atmosphere in the ante-natal unit. Maybe it was that everyone was here because they were pregnant rather than ill and that made it so different from ordinary wards. Here you were, surrounded by fecundity, by pod-like bellies, and the happy smiles of impending motherhood. There were exceptions, obviously, the reluctant mums who already had too many children at home; the young girls who looked like children themselves, pregnant women who had had news of some problem with the baby, or were just utterly knackered, but mostly the mood was of rare cheerfulness.

Places like this were all about giving life, about the future, about mother love. She glanced at Bella, wondering if she had any real idea of how this baby was going to change her life, that this one single act of having a child would be the most significant decision she had ever made.

Bella, as if reading her thoughts, smiled. 'It's going to be OK, Mum. You can't plan everything. Look at you and Dad. You were expecting to get old and grey together and now you're on your own and you're coping amazingly. I'm really proud of you and so is Sam.'

Bella, it struck her mother again, was an extraordinary young woman, possessed of all the strength Laura herself had never felt she had.

'Look at you,' Bella insisted, 'you're getting out, you've got a job.'

'In a supermarket.'

'Yes, but a supermarket that's causing Dad total embarrassment. Don't let's forget that.'

She squeezed Bella's hand. 'When are you going to tell Dad about the baby?'

Bella grinned. 'When I can think of an occasion that is truly and deeply inappropriate.'

'Isabella Minchin?' enquired the ultrasound operator.

They followed the young woman into the consulting room. Bella changed into a gown, looking suddenly childlike without all her Gothic finery, and lay down on the bed. The operator applied jelly to the slight swell of Bella's belly and began to run a probe across it. 'This is what we call the anomaly scan,' she explained.

'Anomaly?' Bella's voice had lost a little of its shiny confidence. 'You mean as in defect?'

'We just like to look at the size of the baby to confirm exactly how many weeks pregnant you are, examine the placenta and where it's sitting, and take a good look at the baby's head and spine.' She pointed at the screen. 'Do you see the baby's heartbeat?'

They both stared at the screen.

'There's the head.' She pointed at what seemed to Laura an indecipherable mass of grey lines. Then the probe shifted and the lines solidified like a 3D cartoon into the distinct shape of a tiny head and shoulders. As they watched the mouth opened and the baby yawned.

'Bella, did you see that?' Laura clutched her daughter's arm.

'Yep. Bored already, this baby's definitely mine.'

Behind them the door opened and the huge frame of Nigel almost filled the tiny room.

'Hey, Nige,' Bella greeted him, 'come and say hello to Junior here. He's having an existential crisis.'

Nigel took her hand and stared at the screen, entranced. 'He's probably wondering *Am I still an embryo or have I graduated to being a foetus yet?*'

Bella laughed.

Laura decided he would make a good RE teacher if he thought like that.

'Actually,' she smiled at the pair of them, 'I think maybe he's gone beyond all that. This one's definitely a baby.'

'Would you like a photograph?' the young woman asked. 'Three pounds fifty each or five pounds for two.'

'Make it two,' Laura reached for her wallet.

'Or maybe three.' Bella grinned. 'I might turn one into a Christmas card and send it to Dad.'

When Claudia got home she found that Don had gone out.

Claudia celebrated joining the choir by opening a bottle of wine far too early and attacking her emails. She was used to getting hundreds: the head, the deputy head, her head of department, the governing body, the canteen – all when half of them could have popped a head round the door, but emails were simpler. Now she only had one from Laura telling her about the new job, another from Gaby sounding a bit low, she must get back to her at once, a couple of updates on orders from Amazon, an invitation to take part in the RSPB's Big Birdwatch – one for Ella more than her – and the rest were all uninvited offers from the various shops she patronized.

Except one.

Her most recent communication, sent only ten minutes ago, was from the Little Minsley Choral Society with an application form attached. There was no mention of Daniel Forrest, but it had to be from him.

The funny thing was, she hadn't given him her email address. Claudia sipped her wine thoughtfully. It would be silly to read too much into it, but he must have gone to some lengths to get it from her mother.

Claudia smiled to herself. Maybe the Choral Society was desperate for mezzo-sopranos. Or maybe Daniel Forrest just really believed in spreading the word about music.

Laura had had a peaceful morning doing some stocktaking. This was done mostly via the till but Mr A liked all the herbs and spices to be dusted and wiped, and anything past its sell-by date to be reduced or thrown away, depending on date.

Coming from a privileged family home – or, rather, privileged until recently – it always made Laura feel guilty to see how many people made a beeline for the reduced section. Quite a few pensioners and single mums never bought anything from anywhere else, and would even wait in line till 5 p.m. when that day's reductions were usually made.

Apart from meeting deprivation face to face, Laura enjoyed working in LateExpress much more than she'd expected. She loved getting to know all the customers and being granted a brief glimpse into their lives; the cheeky kids were usually entertaining rather than a problem; and the other staff were always friendly.

Even Mrs A added the spice of drama by her sudden swoops from the flat above. She seemed eager to discover Mr A in the act of some lustful congress with an underage schoolgirl or over-sexed customer and was positively disappointed at his good behaviour. 'That man has no balls!' she once pronounced before helping herself to a packet of Tunnock's Caramel wafer biscuits and disappearing back to her self-imposed exile upstairs.

Laura was hidden behind the cereals stickering packets of All-Bran when Simon blustered in angrily. 'I thought after my solicitor's letter you might have had the decency to hand in your notice,' he insisted.

'And I thought you might have the decency not to divorce me on the grounds that I got a job.' Laura tried to keep her voice calm.

The argument might have got increasingly bitter had they not been silenced by the familiar voice of Elaine, Simon's secretary, from behind the other side of the shelving unit; she clearly had no idea they were present.

'Bloody Suki Morrison. Who does she think she is anyway?' Elaine demanded loudly of her friend. 'Only four months gone and she's forever running out of meetings to sit down and claiming endless doctor's visits, then coming back with her hair blow-dried.'

'You know Simon isn't the first she's had in her sights to be the Daddy,' replied a second voice.

'No!' The whispers grew softer but were still audible.

'She went after Mark Baker first, big affair, leaves his wife just like Simon, then she discovers he doesn't want kids and she sends him packing!'

'She didn't!'

'Next cab off the rank was Martin Steeples, but he wasn't a partner so she threw him back in the sea. Now there's Simon and he's finally done the deed.'

'Poor old Simon.'

'He'll be earning till he's ninety!'

Simon stood next to her, rooted to the spot, torn between hiding from the girls and bursting out in fury to confront them.

He avoided Laura's eye but she knew from the angry tautness of his body that he'd heard every word. She almost felt sorry for him.

Almost but not quite.

CHAPTER 16

OK, Ella said to herself, *I really am going senile.*

Her daughter Cory had come to stay for the night and she wanted to show her the photo she'd taken of a fox sleeping in the sun on their garden bench but couldn't find her camera anywhere. She'd just spent the last hour looking for it. The wildly irritating thing was she'd only had it for a month and it had been quite expensive.

Anyway, it was lovely having Cory here. She worried about Cory. There was something rare and special about her younger daughter, but like a precious stone that was found under deep layers of rock, she suspected it had to be mined for and not many people had ever reached it. She was sure that one day someone would, but until then Cory's life almost seemed suspended, waiting.

'How's the job?' Ella knew this was safer territory than asking about relationships.

'Fine.'

'And the flat?'

'That's fine too. In fact, I'm fine altogether.'

Ella took the hint and decided to ask no more questions.

'Anyway, no one uses a camera any more. I thought your lodger gave you an iPhone? Use that instead.'

But Ella didn't want to use her iPhone. She was used to a camera, she liked taking photos, having them developed in the conventional way, then putting them in frames or albums. To Ella, photographs weren't just something to show off with on Facebook and then forget, they were an important part of life. If she hadn't taken so many photos over the years she would have had even less of Laurence to hold on to. As it was, his face smiled at her from shelves and side tables and especially her dressing table. Though she wouldn't admit this to Cory or Julia, she occasionally talked to him and kept him up to speed with their lives.

Now where was that damn camera? The last time she could actually remember having it in her hand was when they went mushroom picking. Could she have given it to Julia to put in her parka pocket?

The thought of ringing Julia and asking her made Ella droop. Losing a camera would be added to the growing Signs of Senility she suspected Julia and Neil were mentally drawing up.

The sight of a large and pretentious car arriving outside her front door settled the argument. It was her daughter and son-in-law arriving to drop off her Christmas present. Julia was one of those women who bought presents throughout the year and had them all wrapped and tagged by about July. Another sign, in Ella's view, that she didn't have enough to do in her life.

'Julia! Neil!' She opened the front door and stood with a smile that was all the more welcoming because she was putting on a bit of an act. Being natural with Neil was too difficult; she just ended up wanting to kill the man. So she put on her Delighted Mother-in-Law face instead. It was somehow easier all round. 'Come in.' She looked at the enormous package, wrapped in purple foil and festooned with a bow. 'Gosh, how exciting.'

'Don't get too carried away,' dampened Neil. 'It's only a

shopping trolley. Julia thought it might be useful for you so you don't need to take the car out all the time.'

This, she knew, was a disguised dig at the car park incident, and she couldn't help wishing her daughter had got her a present without a hidden agenda.

'How lovely and useful.' She wondered if it would be leopard skin like the one Sal had got Claudia to take to the country, but doubted it. Julia, sadly, wasn't the type for witty presents. This one would be a tasteful tartan, probably in dark green or blue, something suitable for old ladies.

'Cup of coffee?'

'Actually,' Neil commented pointedly, 'we're on our way to the bank manager. He wants to discuss our overdraft.'

If he was hoping for Ella to reach for her chequebook, he was going about it the wrong way. She even began to wonder if the early arrival of the Christmas present might be a tactic in their guilt-tripping war of attrition. If so, then a tartan shopping trolley was hardly much of an inducement.

Ella glanced out of the kitchen window at Neil's ludicrous car and it was on the tip of her tongue to quip, 'Of course, you could sell the four by four.'

'By the way, Julia, you haven't by any chance seen my camera?'

Neil rolled his eyes, mentally adding this memory lapse to the others in his collection, while Julia made a big show of searching in her handbag.

'Sorry,' she shrugged eventually, 'not guilty.'

'It's so irritating,' Ella persisted. 'It's nearly new and I hadn't downloaded the photographs from it yet.'

'That was silly,' pointed out Neil, who was the kind of man who had back-ups of everything on his key-ring.

'You're sure you haven't seen it?'

Julia shook her head.

'Funny. The last time I had it was when we went to the woods with Wenceslaus. Before he got ill.'

Julia stared out of the window as if some especially fascinating event was happening there.

'Why don't you ask him?' Neil suggested. 'Maybe he's sold it.'

'Neil!' flashed Julia with sudden spirit, 'don't be bloody ridiculous. That isn't even funny.'

'I didn't mean it to be,' Neil replied coldly. 'There's something I don't like about that chap. I mean, what does he actually *do* for his free rent? He's never even here, as far as I can see.'

'That's because he's found himself a job.'

'Bet he doesn't pay any taxes. None of these people do. They come here, take all the young people's jobs, bung up the NHS, overcrowd the schools, then they make a bit of cash and what do they do? Put it back into our economy? No — send it home to build a big house for when they leave.'

'Good heavens, Neil,' Ella couldn't keep the edge of annoyance out of her voice despite her best efforts, 'I had no idea you were so eloquent. Maybe you should stand for politics.'

'Maybe I should. Do better than the current lot, that's for sure. Anyway, if he's earning, why isn't he paying rent?'

'He offered, as a matter of fact,' Ella was determined not to sound defensive. This was *her* house, not theirs. 'I said no. I would rather have his practical help and computer advice plus the reassurance of having him around than ask him for rent.'

'Good deal for him.' How did he always manage to make it sound as if she was being taken for a ride when the truth was she loved having Wenceslaus here?

'And for me too. As a matter of fact, it works brilliantly. Far more people who want to stay in their own homes should do it. It's a really good solution. You get companionship, security and help with DIY all in one. In fact, now I've got Wenceslaus,' Ella added naughtily, 'I may never have to move. Now, isn't it time you got off to see the bank manager?'

She waved them goodbye, as she always did to her guests, standing under the elegant Georgian portico at the top of her front steps. As she was about to go back inside she heard Neil's murmured remark to Julia as they got in the car. 'Really, that bloody Pole's got far too much of a hold over your mother. You ought to watch him. With the access he's got he could get up to anything.'

Julia, for her part, was staring out of the window as if she didn't exist on the same planet as he did.

Ella shut the door, seething. But at least she'd just had another idea for a blog. She rushed upstairs, turned on her screen and began to write.

THE ANSWER TO BEING OLD AND LONELY IS INVITING A STRANGER INTO YOUR HOME

OK, so it might sound a bit weird, but she'd explain it in the blog and – she had to admit – it was certainly eye-catching.

Sal lay in bed feeling utterly exhausted. She hadn't really understood until now what cancer sufferers meant when they said it wasn't the disease that made you feel ill, it was the treatment.

Apart from how terrible she felt, her time at the magazine had been a big success. Rose and Michael liked her ideas, the staff seemed to accept her, and she was really enjoying taking something already good and making it better. Best of all, she'd discovered, it was fun to write for a market she was so in tune with.

Sometimes it was hard to explain to the young quite how heady the Sixties had been. Of course, to understand their dizzy liberation, you had to have experienced what went before – the unutterably dull and deathly decade of the 1950s. When Sal, Claudia, Laura and Ella had started university, it felt as if everything was changing: marriage, convention, what women did with their lives. It had been the birth of the Me Generation and now the Me Generation was growing old. Could she, Sal, help map out the route for them?

Suddenly full of energy at the excitement of it all, she got out of bed and looked out at the sunny winter's morning, feeling that life was good after all. She had a job, a flat, close friends. So what if she also had cancer?

She shampooed her hair and wrapped it in a towel to dry while she did her make-up, wondering what to wear. She had started a *New Grey* fashion page in the magazine, calling it 'I Shall Wear Purple' in homage to the wonderful poem by Jenny Joseph about growing old disgracefully, and had a few of the clothes to try out.

Just time to dry her hair. Sal removed the towel, got out her hairbrush and began to brush. When she put the brush down she gasped. It was full of strands of red-gold hair. She knew this might happen despite the cold cap, and yet she'd still prayed she'd avoid it. Sal dropped her head into her hands and wept, not even daring to look into her dressing-table mirror. It was so sodding unfair. Getting cancer at all and, even worse, getting it *now*. Would she even get the chance to grow old, disgracefully or not?

She opened her hands and looked at herself boldly in the mirror. 'You look like a red setter with mange!'

Reaching for the wig on its stand she carefully pinned up her own remaining hair, just as the shop assistant had done and pulled the wig carefully onto her head. It was remarkably convincing. If anyone at *New Grey* guessed and asked her why she was wearing a wig, she'd just tell them she had to look good as an editor and washing her hair every morning was too much trouble.

She had no idea how long she could keep up this charade. And yet she had to. Some people, like Rachel, might be able to wear their cancer with pride, and she admired them greatly, but she wasn't one of them. Others spent all day online, trying to find out every last thing about the disease, its treatments, which hospital or doctor offered the greatest hope, and she could see the attraction of that. But that wasn't for her either. For Sal there was only one sensible course: to pretend the whole thing wasn't happening.

She smiled crookedly at her own reflection. 'There's nothing wrong with being in denial,' she told herself out loud. 'It's stood me in good stead all my life and I'm not going to give up on it now.'

It was the final session of Relationship Recovery today and Laura was feeling amazed at how quickly it had gone. She had always been sceptical about the value of something like this, and wary both of psychobabble and touchy-feely emotional incontinence, but she had come to the conclusion that joining a group was valuable in itself. Maybe it was because you felt: *Oh my God, my life's better than X's* – or perhaps it was because in a group you were all in the same boat. It was also, Laura had found, much easier to spot other people's disastrous relationship patterns than your own.

But actually, working in the shop had done her just as much good, she was convinced, as coming to the group. And they paid *her* as opposed to the other way round.

'Right, everyone,' Suzanne clapped her hands, 'can we all sit down in the circle? We don't want to waste our last session, do we?' She looked eagerly round the group. 'I would like you all to say, in just one sentence, what you've got out of coming.' She smiled indulgently at her co-leader. 'It doesn't have to be flattering. Stephen and I are strong enough to take it, but it should be honest. Louise,' she addressed the amazing divorcing octogenarian, 'why don't you start?'

Louise thought for a moment. As she did so a ray of sunshine caught and illuminated the hairs on her chin. 'I suppose what I've learned, listening to you lot,' she seemed to be looking straight at Laura, 'is that people put up with too much for the sake of security. I did myself. Then I stopped. And do you know what, it's been absolutely fine.' The others began to clap. 'Except,' Louise added, 'that my daughter won't speak to me. But then she's nearly sixty herself and dull as a wet Wednesday in Wigan.'

Laura smiled at her. She was a wise old bird.

'What about you, Gerald?'

'Bloody waste of time, the whole thing. My wife was in the wrong, end of story.'

'She had a lucky escape, if you ask me,' Louise murmured.

'Rich, have you learned anything these last six weeks?'

'The thing is,' Rich replied with alarming candour, 'I don't really like women. I mean, I'm not gay or anything, but I just prefer the company of blokes, so I think I'll just stay out of relationships, if you know what I mean.'

'Laura, your turn.'

Laura found that Louise was watching her closely.

'The odd thing is,' Laura realized the truth of this as she said it, 'I don't feel bitter any more. Maybe it's because my daughter's going to have a baby and I'm still overwhelmed by that. I feel angry. I feel it's a waste. But at the same time I know my marriage wasn't as good as I'd told myself, so losing it doesn't seem as bad as it did. Maybe I just needed to believe it was good, as Louise says, because I wanted the security. I feel, almost, ready to – I loathe the words "move on" – but certainly to open myself up a bit, look forward, not back. That's it.'

'Lastly, it's your turn, Calum.'

Calum was looking at Laura. 'I must admit, I think Laura's an incredible woman; the fact that she can be so calm and philosophical—'

'Don't worry, Calum,' Laura chipped in, 'I still want his head on a plate.'

They all laughed.

Calum continued. 'I suppose I've learned that I'm quite egotistical.'

'Come again?' asked Rich.

'Selfish,' Calum stated baldly. 'I didn't really think about my wife's needs, only mine. If I was starting out again, I'd try to remedy that.'

'Good,' Suzanne congratulated. 'Remember the tools for your relationship recovery are in your own hands. I want you to give yourselves a clap!'

'Oh for goodness' sake!' Louise protested.

'Now I'd like you all to take each other's hands and, since it's nearly Christmas, sing "Auld Lang Syne" together . . .'

'I thought that was New Year,' whispered Louise.

'. . . to cement a long-lasting sense of friendship and trust between you.'

'Do you think you'll ever see any of these people again?' Louise asked with a wicked grin, taking Laura's hand as instructed.

'No, never,' Laura admitted, suddenly aware of Calum's gaze. 'You?'

'Me neither. For the sake of auld lang syne!'

As they shook hands with Stephen and Suzanne and hugged

the other members of the group, Laura noticed Calum waiting for her by the door.

'Fancy that coffee? Or are you serious about never seeing us again?'

Laura smiled and shook her head. It had been a mistake when she'd invited him. It was too soon. She was, as the members of Alcoholics Anonymous might put it, 'in recovery', but she wasn't recovered yet. And she didn't want to bounce from one mistake to another, even if Calum had acquired some self-knowledge compared to Simon.

'Not just now. I think we've probably got too much baggage.'

'Why don't you ask young Rich,' Louise suggested naughtily, 'he wants to spend more time with other men.'

After Calum had gone, Laura felt a sense of relief. She was only just getting back a sense of equilibrium, and it was such a wonderful feeling that she didn't want to risk another bad relationship.

'I think you made the right choice,' Louise murmured. 'For now. Get your balance back. But can I make a suggestion? If he asks you later, say yes. You're a nice woman and I think he may be quite a good bet.'

'For nice read doormat?'

'For nice read nice. Have a happy Christmas.'

'You too.' It was only now, only today, that she felt she could actually start looking forward to her first Christmas without Simon.

And she might be calm and philosophical but she still hoped he would have a shitty Christmas with his demanding new mistress.

Claudia stared into space, in two minds about what to do. She had decided to sign up for the choir and was wondering if she should encourage Don to do the same.

She was actually beginning to enjoy the village, especially the preparations for Christmas. There would be carol singing and a get-together to distribute everyone's cards, ending up in the pub. Most things in Minsley, she'd found, seemed to end up in the pub.

Don, on the other hand, seemed not to want to get involved. The only place he seemed truly happy was the dump. Ever since she'd sent him down there with a load of cardboard he'd fallen in love with the place. He had even made friends with the staff who had filled him with Fascinating Facts About Refuse, with the result that he was now busy completely reorganizing their rubbish disposal. 'Think about it, Claudia, each person in the UK throws away their body weight in rubbish every seven weeks! That's thirty-three million tonnes a year, enough each day to fill Trafalgar Square up to the height of Nelson's Column!'

Claudia tried to visualize Trafalgar Square buried in McDonald's wrappers and old pizza boxes. She'd already heard about 'fat bergs' of congealed grease in the sewers underneath. Minsley seemed even more attractive by comparison.

'And did you know, one glass bottle could power your laptop for twenty-five minutes?'

She had been going to try and persuade him to join her at the choir but since he'd announced his intention of constructing an ingenious system of boxes so they could start their new recycled life, Don, she could see, was a man on a mission of his own.

In a way it was a relief. For reasons she didn't want to explore too deeply she decided she wanted to keep the choir as her separate interest. The attractive choir master had nothing to do with it.

By the time she arrived at the school where the choir practised, the queue just to sign up for the term snaked right along the corridor and down the stairs. It was, as she'd expected, mainly women her age, but there were a few really old ladies, Betty included, and also a surprising number of young ones, in their teens and twenties.

Less than a third were men.

'That's pretty good,' confided Betty in a loud stage whisper. 'You don't get many men joining amateur choirs. Too busy telling other people what to think in the pub. Are you an alto or a soprano?'

Claudia nodded hesitantly. 'I don't know. I was never allowed to sing at all at school so I never got the chance to find out, but when I sing along with Abba my voice sounds quite high to me.'

'No Abba here. Actually, we could do with a bit of "Mamma Mia" sometimes. It can get a little bit serious.'

Claudia began to wonder what she'd got herself into. She'd been hoping for something jolly and spirit-lifting, rather than Wagner and Stockhausen.

'Hello, everyone.' Daniel Forrest smiled around genially. It was cold in the hall and he looked well-wrapped up in his cashmere with his tartan scarf still tied in the European way. 'Shall we get warmed up?'

He started them off with singing exercises which, to Claudia's novice ears, sounded distinctly odd.

All around her, voices began to sing: '*R-r-r-r avi-oli and spagh-etti! . . . 'R-r-r-r avi-oli and spagh-etti!' . . . 'R-r-r-r avi-oli and spagh-etti!*'

And then, equally rousingly:

> '*Maybe My Mummy Will Move to Miami*
> *And Maybe My Mummy May Not!*'

Self-conscious at first, Claudia soon found her lungs beginning to expand as she got braver and joined in with the best of them. To her astonishment, she could hear her own voice, surprisingly confident and clear, holding the note as it soared higher and higher until only the purest voices could follow it up.

'OK, very good. Let's do some work now. Has everyone got a copy of the score?'

'I haven't.' Claudia put up her hand.

'Ah, yes, today we're welcoming a newcomer. Would you like to introduce yourself?'

'I'm Claudia Warren and I've just joined.'

'And what attracted you to the Minsley Choral Society?' Daniel quizzed her.

Claudia grinned. 'The fact that I don't have to audition and you all go to the pub afterwards.'

Everyone laughed, including Daniel Forrest. He really did have rather nice eyes, Claudia decided.

The rehearsal passed quickly and was surprisingly enjoyable despite the challenging nature of the music.

When she heard herself definitely off-key several times, she whispered to Betty, 'I think this would be a lot easier if I could read music.'

'Don't worry, it's fiendish, isn't it? But next time, Dan says, we're doing *The Sound of Music*!'

She was flattered when Daniel singled her out at the end. 'Congratulations, that was no picnic, I can assure you. You did excellently to keep up when this is your first rehearsal, especially since the others have been singing it for weeks. I hope you're coming on to The Laden Ox with the rest of us, seeing as that was why you joined up?'

Claudia realized that to refuse would have been churlish, even if she had wanted to. She walked along the village street next to Betty who was riding the demon mobility scooter towards the village pub.

The pub was empty on a Tuesday night, so the choir members had it almost to themselves.

'What can I get you?' offered Daniel Forrest. 'I'm afraid they don't run to pink champagne, Betty. Tell me, did the gentlemen really drink the stuff out of your slipper?'

'Dan, dear,' Betty replied roguishly, 'You're thinking of the Cancan dancers at the Folies Bergère. I was at the Paris Lido in the 1950s! It was all dry Martinis and the occasional absinthe.'

'The Green Fairy!' Daniel sighed. 'Well, they won't have that here.'

'And just as well. It's made from wormwood and rots the brain. They didn't ban it in France for nothing, you know. I'll settle for a G and T. Large, now that you ask.'

'Betty!' Daniel teased. 'I'm shocked. How suburban! Not even a cognac? How about you, Claudia?'

'G and T will do me nicely too.'

'Ladies, you disappoint me. I suppose you want ice and a slice as well?'

'Well,' Claudia replied, 'we have an image to keep up. We are in Surrey.'

Daniel bought their drinks, then disappeared to circulate among the other choir members.

'Yes, he is rather dishy, isn't he?' Betty commented.

Claudia hadn't even realized she was watching him. She stirred her drink, embarrassed. 'I haven't heard that expression for years.'

'It's quite a good one for our Daniel, though. Daniel is like a gourmet meal, a treat for now and then but not the meat-and-two-veg of everyday. Though I've sometimes wondered what he'd be like if he met the right woman.'

Claudia was about to ask her what she meant when Betty produced another of the roguish looks she somehow carried off despite being over eighty. 'But then I have always found men rather a disappointment. The interesting ones are no good at ordinary living and the ordinary ones always bored me. On the whole I prefer dogs.'

When she got home, a little giggly after two G and Ts, Claudia was greeted by the delicious aroma of frying onions. Sausages were also sizzling away on the hob and there was a pile of mash as big as a pyramid on the hotplate.

'How absolutely delicious!'

'You're not as sloshed as Schlegel, then?'

Claudia giggled and put her arms round Don, resting her head on his shoulder.

'The diva returns. I thought singing might be hungry work. I've opened a bottle of red, if you fancy a glass.'

'Just as long as we recycle the bottle?' Claudia poured herself some.

'Sorry, I got a bit carried away earlier.' Don grinned.

'And I've been a bit of bitch. It's been even more of a culture shock than I was expecting. For both of us.' She raised her glass at the same time as he did. 'Let's have another go, shall we? To country living!'

Laura was replenishing the tins of Heinz beans, always a big seller at LateExpress, when the boss's wife suddenly appeared in the stockroom, on one of her lightning visits. It was early for Mrs A, who didn't usually surface until late morning unless she'd run out of milk or cat food for their enormous British Blue.

'Good morning, Mrs Minchin,' she perched herself, still in her quilted dressing gown, on a stack of boxes. 'How are you enjoying working for my husband?'

'Very much, thank you.'

'I have one question. How come posh lady like you wants

to serve in supermarket? None of my sons even agree to work here in holidays!'

'I needed a job,' Laura explained simply. No point in lying. 'My husband left me quite suddenly. My children are grown-up and I hadn't worked for a very long time.' Something told her Mrs A would share in the sisterhood of the stay-at-home wife. 'As a matter of fact, not for twenty-five years.'

'And then husband left?'

Laura nodded.

'For floozy?'

Laura couldn't help laughing. 'For a colleague.'

Mrs A nodded sagely. 'For floozy. It is sad world, Mrs Minchin. My husband says you are very good worker, also nice lady.'

'Thank you. He's a nice boss.'

It was true. Mr A liked to oversee what everyone was doing more than would be usual in another kind of business, but he was unfailingly cheerful and always had a kind word.

On the whole, Laura liked working here much more than she had expected to. It was the other side of town from her home so she didn't get her neighbours coming in and being quietly shocked at her doing something so menial. Simon's partners and the high-ups from his office had started to buy their sandwiches elsewhere, which was a relief. Fortunately, Mr A had not worked out the connection between the drop in his superior sandwich trade and Laura's presence. There was a camaraderie here she doubted she would have found in somewhere more aspirational.

She was just checking the day's delivery, and wondering how Simon would take it when he finally discovered that his daughter was due to give birth before his mistress, when she heard a commotion out on the shop floor and put her head round to see what was happening. She was greeted by a truly memorable sight.

Mrs A, every inch an operatic diva in her pink dressing gown, was confronting Suki Morrison, while her husband hung on her arm trying to deter and persuade her to go upstairs and leave the matter to him.

'Leave it to you, Mr No Balls? I just heard young lady there' – she pointed to an embarrassed Elaine, Simon's secretary – 'tell her friend that this is floozy who stole Mrs Minchin's husband! I am telling this trollop she can leave our shop. We have a rule here. No slags. No Jezebels. Out!'

Laura watched as her rival, wearing a quite unnecessary maternity dress, was ejected from LateExpress by the wife of the proprietor, to the sound of muffled laughter.

Laura had a good idea what the fall-out from this little scene would be, but what the hell.

She was enjoying every moment.

CHAPTER 17

Was it a brutal irony or an amazing gift, Sal found herself wondering, that she loved working at the magazine as much as she did, and that it was all going so well?

The very eccentricity of the place, which previous editors had found so hard to cope with, actually appealed to Sal. She began to see how much she'd hated working for increasingly large and faceless conglomerates, often run from Europe or the US. She had no objection to Rose McGill wandering in and giving her opinions, especially since, once she'd delivered her thoughts, Rose didn't seem to mind if they were followed up or not; she just liked to have her say. Occasionally, only she and Rose were left in the office, the last to leave, and she saw that they had something in common: two women alone. In fact, there were moments when she felt an overwhelming temptation to confide in Rose. Then she reminded herself of Rose's fearsome reputation, and that their relationship was professional, not private.

Her treatment seemed to be progressing well but it would mean a very lonely and peculiar Christmas. But at least she could just spend it recuperating. Claudia, Ella and Laura would easily be persuaded that she was going away as usual. It had better be somewhere cold or they would wonder about her lack of tan. Sal was a dedicated sun-worshipper who was perfectly happy to risk leathery skin for the sake of those blissful rays. She usually made the others jealous with her winter colour. Not this year.

What would happen, she asked herself as she packed up her work things, if the cancer didn't go, if it actually spread and she got seriously ill? There would be a time when she would *have* to ask for help.

Stop all that! She would recover. Breast cancer, she reminded herself of Mr Richards's words, was one of the good ones.

The prospect of Christmas not at some glorious hotel surrounded by hot and cold running waiters bringing her strawberry daiquiris but in her own flat was deeply unappealing. At this rate she wouldn't even be able to drink. Sal plonked down the fur hat she'd taken to wearing on top of her wig. She glanced in the mirror and saw she looked almost the same as usual. But she wasn't.

She would *not* cry.

It struck Sal that there was one person she'd enjoy meeting up with around Christmas.

Rachel.

Rachel, with her indomitable nature and utter lack of pretence about her condition. Of course she might be with her family, but it was worth a try. Stupidly, she hadn't taken Rachel's number. Even though she wasn't due for another session till January, she stopped off at the hospital's chemo suite. She knew them well enough now that they might bend the rules and give it to her.

'Excuse me,' she asked Lucy on Reception, 'but do you know if I could contact another patient I met here? Her name's Rachel Freeman.'

A look flashed between Lucy and a passing nurse. 'I'm afraid Rachel's no longer with us.' Lucy reached under the desk. 'As a matter of fact, she left this for you. I didn't want to give it to you around Christmas, but now you're asking . . .'

It was Rachel's pink wig. And this time Sal did cry.

Ella stood back to admire the vegetable wreath she'd just hung on her front door, complete with Bill's raffia bow.

It looked absolutely splendid.

The house on her left sported an enormous one made of fake golden apples, pine cones, dried orange slices and cinnamon sticks, complete with angels, baubles and a fake robin.

Her neighbours on the other side, ever the minimalists, had fashioned theirs from a few old birch twigs and a lone Christmas star. Viv and Angelo were still away, which was a pity, since they came up with a creative new design each year which the whole square eagerly awaited. Once it been made out of the serrated tops of old baked-beans tins; the next from torn-up white T-shirts, attached by rubber-band plaits; and yet a third, and possibly most memorable, a wreath made entirely out of old keys. Ella had assumed these were not to the front door.

It was a glorious day and Ella opted for a frosty walk down to the allotment which could do with one last tidy-up before Christmas.

The plan this year was that Julia, Neil and the boys were coming for Christmas Day and then Julia and Neil would head off to the other in-laws – probably a blessed relief. Cory was joining her to celebrate a Polish Christmas Eve with Wenceslaus.

The walk by the Thames always lifted Ella's spirits. She stopped to watch the rowers as they glided in among the occasional geese and swans that had stayed for the winter. The clouds were massing over the far bank, purple, grey, lavender, blue, with a touch of pink that heralded the beginning of sunset. Despite the planes that descended incessantly into

Heathrow like a row of divers queuing for a diving board, it was still heart-stoppingly beautiful.

How lucky I am to have all this, Ella thought. A lot of people might look at her life and imagine she was lonely, but it wasn't true, especially since Wenceslaus had come along.

The sight of a young mum pushing a buggy prompted a sudden memory of a line from Keats's 'Ode to a Nightingale': *No hungry generations tread thee down*. And it struck her that no matter how young she and her friends might feel, they would not live forever. They had seen amazing times, maybe unique, and they thought they'd never grow old like their parents, but the truth was they were no different. She had two grandsons and now Laura was going to be a grandmother as well!

Despite the lateness of the hour, the allotments were busy.

'Hello, boys,' she greeted Bill, Stevie and Les, who stood like three wise monkeys arguing over the finer points of potting compost versus well-rotted manure.

What Ella felt like today was a bit of digging to loosen up her muscles but the ground was so hard she had to abandon the idea and content herself with hard pruning and sorting seeds into wooden boxes. She had just sat down to admire her handiwork when Julia burst in through the gates. She looked as if she might have been crying. This was so unusual in unemotional Julia that Ella stood up and started walking towards her.

'What on earth's the matter?'

'Oh, God, Mum, it's all so stupid.'

'What's happened? Is it you and Neil?'

Julia looked away. 'It was all about the stupid camera!'

'What, *my* camera?' Ella felt a flash of decidedly unmaternal irritation.

'It was really dumb, but I turned out to have had it after all. I'd just downloaded a photograph – a really nice one in the woods — and Neil came across it and went berserk.'

'Where had you put it?'

'I'd transferred it to my phone.'

'Look, Julia, who was this photo of? I'm assuming it wasn't of me and there was only one other person there. Was it Wenceslaus?'

Again Julia looked away.

'It was, wasn't it?'

Julia shrugged in exactly the way she had always done whenever she was in trouble ever since the age of five.

'Anyway, there was this massive over-reaction from Neil and he threw my phone on the ground, and now it doesn't work.'

'Julia,' Ella insisted firmly, 'you are going to have to take responsibility for this. Why did you have a photograph of Wenceslaus on your phone?'

'It was just a really nice photograph.'

'No, it wasn't — well, it might have been, but that isn't the point. You've fallen for him, haven't you?'

'OK, maybe a bit.'

'Not a bit. I've seen how you follow him around. But, look, Julia, he doesn't have feelings for you, that's the point.'

'How do you know?'

'He said you were a very pretty lady but that you didn't smile because your husband didn't notice you enough.'

'You mean you've actually talked about me with him?' She thought Julia would be furiously angry but almost the opposite was true. 'What did he say?' she demanded. 'Did he really call me pretty?' She was blooming suddenly like a bud opening in the sunshine.

'That's all. That was all he said.'

'I knew he'd thought about me. I can see it sometimes when he looks at me.'

'Julia, darling, I'm so sorry to say this, but this is a fantasy.'

'What would you know about it anyway? You're over sixty. And you and Dad were comfortable together. There wasn't any passion between you, even when we were little. You didn't even go in for cuddling like other parents did.'

Anger coursed up in Ella. 'Of course we were passionate! I loved your father very much. And fancied him!'

'*Fancied?*' mocked Julia. 'What a ridiculous word.'

'OK,' Ella was shouting now, 'desired, wanted, lusted after. Is that clear enough for you?'

It was certainly clear enough for Bill, Les and Stevie who moved, as one man, up to the opposite end of the allotments in case Ella should turn her wanton woman's eyes in their direction.

'You have to stop this, Julia. You're behaving like a lovesick schoolgirl and it's clearly affecting your marriage.' She almost added: *Look, I'm no great fan of Neil's, but I can see his point*, but thankfully stopped herself in time. Words, once uttered, could never be taken back and went on to have a dangerous, corrosive life of their own.

'Julia, if you're unhappy in your marriage, I'll do all I can to support you. I'm your mother and I'll always be there for you. But don't throw it away for a silly fantasy.'

'I might have known you'd be like this.' Julia delved into her parka pocket and pulled out Ella's camera. 'Here's your stupid sodding camera and much joy may it bring you!'

For a moment Ella thought Julia would throw it on the ground but she shoved it into Ella's hand instead and disappeared off in the glowing light of the sunset.

Ella sat down, not sure if she were more angry or worried. All the time she'd been thinking she was going doolally, losing her new camera, Julia had had it. And this thing with Wenceslaus. He was Ella's lodger. Ella really liked having him around. He was helpful yet unobtrusive, friendly but never pushy, with an almost female instinct for when to talk to her and when to leave her alone. And now, because of Julia, she was wondering if she ought to ask him to leave.

She thought about it. She was sure Julia had got the wrong idea. Wenceslaus would never take advantage of a vulnerable married woman, she was certain of it. But had he somehow given out the wrong signal? Should she talk to him? Ask him if anything had happened, just to reassure herself?

'Don't worry, it may never happen,' a voice interrupted her thoughts. It was Bill, braving her woman's wiles with a nice cup of tea.

Normally she wanted to kill anyone who came up with this ridiculous platitude, but today it seemed rather endearing. 'Thanks, Bill. I don't think it will either, but I'm not sure my daughter agrees.'

Laura could hear the shouting as she parked in the driveway. Simon and Sam, head to head, were arguing in the hall. She stood for a moment, listening, trying to decide whether to go in and intervene.

'This is bloody ridiculous,' Simon was shouting, 'you can't just announce you never want to see me again. I'm your father!'

The louder Simon shouted, the cooler Sam became. 'I'm twenty-two. I'm a fully-fledged adult. I can make any decision I want!' Laura stood listening by the open front door.

'This is all your mother's doing. She's always been good at playing the victim. She's turning you against me. I'd heard this is what happens. It's why I stayed with her so long because I knew if I left she'd badmouth me to you and Bella.'

'Dad,' Sam's voice was calm but implacable, 'shut up. You're in the wrong. It would come better if you showed a bit of regret or apology. We might understand why you left if you tried to explain instead of blaming it all on Mum.'

'But some of it was her fault!'

'Maybe it was. Marriages don't always work. I get that. Half my class at school had divorced parents. And they nearly all behaved as shittily as you. Moving out with no warning, selling the house when it was the only bit of stability left, like Ben's parents did. I suppose you're intending to do that too.'

Simon was silent and had the grace to look chastened, as well he might. He ought to be proud of his son. Sam was terrific.

'Of course, you'll need somewhere for your new family.' The deadened tone in which Sam said *new family* made Laura want to weep.

'I don't want to lose you, Sam,' Simon said finally. 'You're still my son, you'll always be my son.'

'I expect you'll get over it when you have a new baby.' He paused, and if it hadn't been sweet, straight-talking Sam, Laura would have sworn he was being deliberately mocking. 'I'm told new babies are very time-consuming.'

'Yes,' Simon hesitated, 'well, to be honest, I hadn't planned that part. But Suki's never had a child so it's natural she'd want to have one.'

'You'll have to hope it's a girl. You'll be too old for football.' Laura could see that hit home, but then Sam was entitled to fight back, even if it was below the belt. 'I suppose fathers are older now.'

Laura noticed how tired and grey Simon was looking, his debonair charm wearing as thin as a cheap suit.

'Yes,' Simon attempted a wan smile, 'just don't mention Picasso. Everyone mentions bloody Picasso. Sam . . . will you come and have a meal with me? It'd mean a lot.'

Sam shook his head. 'Sorry, Dad. It's all a bit raw for me.

I thought you and Mum were happy, you see. Now I can't help distrusting people, especially you.'

'I'm sorry about that, Sam, you were always such a trusting person.' There was actually a catch in Simon's voice, though whether the emotion was for Sam or for himself, Laura couldn't tell.

'Was I? Well, I'm not any more. In real life love isn't the way it was in Keats and Shakespeare. They seem to have left out the bit about loving a woman till they're middle-aged then buggering off with someone thirty years younger.'

'Sam, don't be so cynical. Please.'

'Well, if I am,' for the first time his voice sounded genuinely angry, 'we'll know who to blame, won't we?'

Laura decided it was time she intervened.

'Simon. I thought I heard shouting. Are you all right, Sam?'

'He's fine.'

'I didn't ask you, Simon, I asked him.'

'What difference does it make if I'm not?' Sam demanded angrily. 'Is Dad going to change his mind and come home again and will we all play happy families?' He turned to Simon. 'Dad, I know you want me to forgive you, to say it's all OK, but it isn't. Bella and I feel replaced, as if we didn't count any more. That's probably why she—'

'Sam!' Laura interrupted. 'It's up to Bella.'

'What's up to Bella? You're all just trying to make me feel guilty, that's why I didn't try and explain myself before. But I *do* feel guilty. And I do love you both. But I have loyalties to Suki too and now to this baby.'

'Yes, Dad,' Sam said wearily. 'We get it. But it was a choice and you made it. I can't just say, "Don't worry, these things happen." I may not have been in love but I know whether it's OK or not to treat a friend badly just because it suits me.'

Simon looked helplessly from his son to Laura. He could

try and plead that he'd fallen in love, been bowled over by passion, but standing here in his old home, it didn't seem convincing or seem solid. 'I'm sorry you feel like that.'

'Yeah. Well . . .' Sam had said all he had to say. He left them both in the hall.

Laura watched, and realized she'd never felt more proud of her son.

'Time you went, I think,' she said to Simon. And then, when they were alone in the hall, added, 'Are you still going ahead with this unreasonable behaviour nonsense?'

'Yes. Are you going to defend it?'

'My lawyer says it's just a formality; it doesn't matter what the grounds are. We might as well get it over with. It'll be easier for Bella and Sam.'

He paused, looking around at the familiar surroundings almost with an air of loss. 'And you?'

'Don't mistake guilt for love, Simon. Love is a lot harder. It involves sacrifice to keep it going. Maybe you'll find that out one day.'

'And maybe I won't.'

How strange that in all these years she hadn't seen that it was only himself he really cared about.

As he walked to his car, she felt something lighten in herself. She saw that if she had to leave this house, she wouldn't mind that much after all, as long as the money she was left was enough to get somewhere big enough for her and Sam. The memories here were no longer the solid base of her life. It was time she created some new ones. And she was glad again that Bella's baby would not be born out of misplaced vengeance but as a new beginning.

Claudia looked out of the window and saw that the sun was shining. She decided to walk to her parents' house. Fresh air and birdsong were just the tonic she needed and Vito would enjoy the walk.

'Bye,' she called to Don as he sat in his usual chair doing the crossword. 'See you later.' At least he wasn't surreptitiously rooting through the house for more things to take to the dump. Claudia was beginning to think she'd have to nail things down.

It was a glorious morning, one of those days that lifted the heart. A pale yellow sun blazed in the hazy blue of the sky and a veil of mist still hung in the tree tops giving the scene a dream-like quality, as if the light were being filtered through net.

'Hey,' Claudia confided in Vito, 'if I'm not careful, I might find myself liking it here. At least on days like this.'

Twenty minutes later, humming 'As I walked out one midsummer morning', one of Don's old favourite folk songs, she rang her parents' doorbell feeling in better spirits than she'd been in since they'd moved here. The countryside, she had to admit, had its delights.

Silence. Then she remembered that this was the day the ambulance picked up her father for his weekly check-up. Still, her mother ought to be in.

She took out her key and went in, leaving the little dog in the hall. Her mother wasn't keen on muddy paws.

There didn't seem to be anyone on the ground floor. 'Mum!' she called up the stairs. Getting no reply, she ran up to her parents' bedroom and opened the door. The curtains were still drawn and she was about to go back downstairs when she heard a movement.

Claudia turned on the light to find her mother, still in her nightdress, sitting on the end of their bed, still as a statue.

'Mum, why are you sitting here in the dark?'

There was no response.

'Mum, what's the matter?' She sat down next to her mother. 'Have you been taking the tablets the doctor gave you?' This,

Claudia saw, was a stupid question. She manifestly had not.

Claudia went to look for them. They were, as she had expected, unopened. She started to run a bath, putting in some of her mother's favourite Floris bath essence. 'Come on, Mum,' she said gently, 'let's get you into the bath.'

Olivia still didn't move.

Claudia kneeled down and put her arms round her mother. 'Mum,' she held her tighter for a moment, 'I love you, Mum.'

Olivia seemed to wake at last and turned to her. 'I love you too, dear. I'm not sure I showed it enough. You were always your father's girl.' She took Claudia's hand in hers. 'I'm not well, am I? I feel like I'm drowning in mud; can't move, can't see, can't breathe.'

'The pills will help. Time to get up now. The bath's running. I'll make a cup of tea and have a bit of a tidy while you're having it.'

Her mother got up and began to move in a strange shuffling walk that wrung Claudia's heart.

She saw how much they'd all relied on Olivia. Her mother had been like a heat source, radiating energy. Now it seemed she could hardly drag herself out of bed.

At the bottom of the stairs she heard Vito bark, wondering what had happened to everyone. Claudia went down and picked him up. 'Oh, Vito, what am I going to do?'

The thought of Betty, wonderful, indomitable Betty, flashed into her mind. 'Tell you, what, Vito, I think we need a Bluebell Girl around here!'

She would enlist Betty's help tomorrow and maybe together, with the help of the medication, they could get Olivia to turn a corner.

There was one more thing Sal had to do before she could lie on her sofa and watch Christmas TV: go to the office party.

It was the last thing she wanted to do, but she knew how bad it would be for morale if the brand-new editor didn't show up. She wouldn't have to stay that long, just enough time for her presence to be noticed and for her to congratulate the people who had worked so hard.

Thank heavens, for reasons of budget, it was being held in the magazine's office, not some noisy night club with blaring music, strobe lighting and a hubbub so loud you couldn't hold even the most basic conversation.

Once upon a time, she would have been the last to leave, draining the last dregs of the free champagne, game to go on to whatever late-night club or dubious drinking dive was proposed next. She'd seen the sun come up over the river a fair few times as she hailed bleary cab drivers on their way to hearth and home. All in all, it hadn't been too bad a working life. She'd had a lot of fun over the years.

Bloody hell, her inner voice whispered, *you sound as if you're checking out!*

Sal pulled a stylish black sheath dress from her wardrobe and matched it with a pair of heels she hadn't worn for years. With the wig she actually looked passable as long as you didn't look too hard. She added a pair of sunglasses, to hide the fact that her eyelashes had departed down the bathroom drain after the last round of drugs. She'd managed to compensate for the loss of eyebrows by pulling the fringe of the wig down almost into her eyes.

On the spur of the moment she added the black fur hat and surveyed herself in the long mirror. It all came together with surprising dash, if a trifle over the top. She looked as if she'd escaped from the après-ski slopes. She could say it was her new Isabella Blow look. After all, better to be thought mutton dressed as lamb than mutton that had gone completely bald.

She swallowed her anti-nausea pills and had to sit down for a moment. People had warned her of one of chemo's more delightful tricks – that you could be starving and feel sick both at the same time.

Into battle! She spurred herself on.

Fortunately, a black cab was passing – this was no time for economy, she could always come home on the bus, but she wanted to arrive with a bit of éclat.

The party was in full swing when she got there.

'Champagne?' asked a waiter holding a tray.

Sal helped herself to an elderflower spritzer which at least had the advantage of looking, if not tasting, like fizz. 'I'm on antibiotics,' she told him, to explain her abstinence, then she worked her way round the room, chatting to everyone involved with *New Grey*, from the lowly office boy to Michael Williams.

By 9 p.m. she was dead on her feet, and had started edging towards the door to make her escape.

'You look terrific.' Sal turned to find Rose McGill in a purple shift designed for a woman a third of her age. Somehow Rose carried it off by sheer force of personality. 'Very Julie Christie in *Doctor Zhivago*.'

'And about the same vintage. Maybe we should get her to write for *New Grey*!'

'Have you had any luck with your mystery blogger?'

'Still pursuing her. She's very hard to get.'

'Maybe she doesn't want to be found.'

'Maybe she's famous!'

'Maybe she's Julie Christie!'

Sal eyed the door longingly. What acceptable excuse could she plead to leave this early?

'Rose, I'm afraid I must go. I feel I'm coming down with something and I don't want it to ruin Christmas.'

'Of course.' Sal felt Rose's X-ray vision examining her wig, her dark glasses and the lashless eyes beneath. 'You are all right, aren't you? Only sometimes you seem a little bit tired.'

'Just end-of-the-year exhaustion. Now, Merry Christmas to you and a very happy new year. I hope it's a prosperous one for us all.'

She leaned forward to embrace Rose and her hat and wig very nearly fell off. Sal clutched onto them in panic. 'I really must go,' she lied. 'I've got a taxi waiting downstairs.'

'Then I'll come with you,' Rose announced. 'I can't bear these noisy parties. Fun for the young, though.'

When there was no sign of a cab, Sal pretended to be furious. 'Always the same at Christmas. Probably didn't want to go north of the river.'

A distinctive red double-decker was approaching. 'Tell you what,' Rose enthused, 'we can go on the bus. I adore using my Freedom Pass.'

Sal, on the other hand, had been known to pay full price at the cinema rather than admit to being an OAP. How bloody stupid that felt, given what had happened to her since. For another half an hour, feeling like a dug-up corpse, her eyes itching and her nose running because her nose hairs had followed her eyelashes and brows down the sink, Sal fended off searching enquiries from the magazine's proprietor, conducted at maximum volume, and it was the most blessed of reliefs when Shepherd's Bush roundabout hove into sight.

'This is me. See you on the third of Jan.'

Back at her flat, Sal collapsed onto her bed, dragging off the hat and wig and falling asleep fully dressed.

Christmas passed for all four in very different ways: Sal spent it alone with a Marks and Spencer's individual Christmas pudding and frequent visits to the loo. Claudia persuaded her parents to come to her house and christen the new kitchen, even managing to get her mother to wear a paper hat. At Bella's and Sam's request, Laura cooked the same Christmas dinner she always cooked and stuck religiously to every familiar ritual from stockings on their beds to presents at midday and a chocolate pudding after the turkey. Ella had two Christmases. The first was cooked by Wenceslaus, ably assisted by Minka, on Christmas Eve, which they called *Wigilia*, the vigil, since, Wenceslaus informed Ella, Christmas Day is not the big day in Poland. Cory came too while Julia and Neil visited the other relatives, thank God.

Minka, dressed in her trademark stripper chic, kept glancing at Cory's subtle beauty, accentuated by a dark-blue velvet dress which matched her eyes, then glancing at Wenceslaus to see if he had noticed it too.

But he was entirely involved with making sure the table was laid correctly. 'At *Wigilia* there must be food from the four corners of the earth. Grain from the fields, fruit from the orchard, carp from the water and mushrooms from the forest.'

'I'm surprised you can face mushrooms after my sister almost poisoned you,' Cory teased him.

'Yes,' Wenceslaus laughed, 'I may forget the mushrooms this year.'

Ella watched, fascinated, as he laid straw under the tablecloth to remind them that Jesus was born in a stable, lit a candle in the window to welcome the Christ child and, last of all, laid an extra place at the table. 'For weary traveller or relative who is dead that you wish could be present here.'

Cory suddenly jumped up and ran from the table.

'Have I upset your daughter?' Wenceslaus asked, looking shaken.

'She's thinking of her father,' Ella explained. 'They were incredibly close.'

'I am so sorry. I should have remembered it was not so long ago.'

Ella was about to get up from the table and follow her when Cory returned holding a blue lamb's wool jumper.

'It was Dad's,' she announced and Ella saw she was not sad but shining with happiness.

'I thought we'd given all his things away.'

'I stole it from the pile and kept it in my room. I used to go to sleep holding it.'

Ella reached over and squeezed her hand.

'Don't worry,' Cory smiled back, 'it's fantastic. Now he's here with us at the extra place. I think this is a great custom. We should do it every year.'

They tucked into dumplings and herring, noodles with poppy seed, then gingerbread biscuits and spiced honey cake, washed down with a rather outrageous amount of Polish vodka.

The next night, with Neil and Julia and their sons Harry and Mark, was a penance by comparison. The boys played with their gadgets, Neil sulked and Julia, never the most entertaining companion, tried to keep the conversation going with no encouragement whatsoever from her family.

Tactfully, Wenceslaus had gone out to join Minka and a group of their Polish friends, which didn't stop Julia glancing round for him constantly, and Neil noticing her glances and sulking even more.

Merry bloody Christmas, thought Ella, *no wonder the divorce courts were busiest in the New Year.*

She was grateful when it was all over.

But just like a drinker addicted to gin or a junkie to their hit, before she went to bed she sneaked up to her computer.

CHRISTMAS, she tapped out, *BAH HUMBUG, I'M WITH SCROOGE ON THIS ONE.*

In her empty flat in North Kensington, which wasn't quite Notting Hill, Sal sat with her laptop on her knee and tried to watch the evening's irritatingly cheery Christmas television.

It had been the worst Christmas she could ever remember. Her eyes were itching, her nose was running constantly. She had eaten a chicken breast and a lonely chipolata and it had brought the happy legacy of constipation followed by diarrhoea. The newest surprise was night sweats and a constant feeling of cold so that she had to wrap up in a duvet when she wasn't at work.

Goodwill to all men and Fucking Peace on Earth.

It was quite the fashion for cancer sufferers to share their pain on a blog and Sal saw how helpful this might be, giving you a voice when you felt reduced and powerless, but she didn't feel like doing it herself, even anonymously.

Instead she went to her favourite MOAN FART DIE, where she came upon Ella's bad-tempered rant on the subject of disliking Christmas.

It instantly cheered her and made her laugh out loud. The anonymous blogger had such a wonderful wry and downbeat take on life, puncturing all the sentimental Yuletide saccharine that was peddled by the media.

Sal quickly tapped out a reply to the post:

Whoever you are, you are wonderful. Please please please contact me. I want to offer you a job. Is that too many pleases? If so I will add another. Please get in touch with me as soon as you get this message,

> *Sally Grainger, Editor of* New Grey *magazine.*

Contacting the mystery blogger gave her a lift.

Enough of this self-pity, she told herself, *get dressed and get out.* She looked at her patchily naked head in the mirror and tried not to flinch.

At least you haven't got a man to put off, she found herself thinking, before angrily correcting herself for such anti-feminist claptrap.

Her wig stood on its stand next to her dressing table but Sal reached into the drawer instead. After a bit of rummaging she found what she was looking for – Rachel's legacy to her, the pink wig – and put it on.

CHAPTER 18

Claudia's next choir practice was in the New Year.

She took extra care getting ready, even washing her hair and putting on a dab of perfume.

'You look nice,' Betty commented, with an ironic twitch of the lips. 'Red velvet on a Tuesday.'

'Trying to keep up the Christmas spirit.' Claudia avoided Betty's glance. 'How was yours, by the way?'

'Quiet but enjoyable. I went to my great-nephew's. Played lots of charades.'

'I bet you're a dab hand at those after all your stage experience.'

'Kicking your legs in public isn't that useful a training for charades, as a matter of fact.'

The singing exercises began and Claudia was finding them rather fun. At first she had felt self-conscious coming out with these nonsense words – 'Veh-veh-veh-veve-veh!' and rhymes about ravioli and *arrivederci* – but now she could feel her lungs expanding and could listen to her voice rising through the different keys. She began to see why people took such pleasure in singing. They worked their way through some Bach and Schumann, which were way beyond Claudia's capacity, and it was a relief when Daniel confirmed that they would definitely be tackling *The Sound of Music*.

'I loved that show,' Betty whispered.

'I'll be wanting to choose some soloists,' Daniel added.

'You'd be brilliant as the Reverend Mother, Betty.' Claudia nudged her.

After practice ended there was a buzz of excitement in The Laden Ox with everyone wondering who should be chosen for Maria.

Betty, by now on her second G & T, began reminiscing how, when she was young enough to play Maria, she had swum in a tank with dolphins that had been specially trained to undo her bikini.

'I know men who could do with that lesson,' commented one of the young girls.

'I hope you're going to be trying out for something, Claudia?'

Claudia turned to find Daniel Forrest at her side.

'*Me?*'

'Don't sound so astonished. You have a very good voice. I could hear it in rehearsal.'

'I'm really not sure . . .'

'Why did you join a choir if you don't want to sing?' He raised an eyebrow quizzically.

'I do want to sing. Everyone tells me it's good for the soul. But I have zero ambitions to do a solo. To be honest, I really joined because I wanted to be part of the community.'

'There are plenty of ways of doing that around here.'

Claudia grinned. 'I'm not really the church-cleaning type. Or the flower-rota type. Or the golf type. Or the bridge type.'

'What type are you, then?' His rather amazing hazel eyes bore into hers. 'Think you're above the good ladies of Minsley, do you, with your red dress and your London ways?'

She was about to protest when she realized he was teasing her.

'No, no. it's just that I'm looking for something a bit more challenging.'

Several of the aforementioned ladies were looking at her and Claudia wished she hadn't started down this route.

Daniel Forrest, on the other hand, was clearly enjoying her discomfort.

'Stop it, Dan,' Betty intervened. 'Leave off troublemaking and get some more drinks in.'

Later on, as the gathering was about to disperse, Claudia found Daniel at her elbow. 'You know your trouble? You're allergic to risk. Have a go at a solo. What's the worst that can happen?'

'I might embarrass myself.'

'So? Maybe you'll have fun. And then maybe you'll be up for something genuinely challenging. Like my charity.'

'And what exactly does your charity do?'

'It's called Sing Out. We bring music to kids who've fallen through various nets in society.'

'How, exactly? By singing them their favourite tunes? I'm a bit out of touch with rap.'

'Thank God for that. And don't be so patronizing.'

Claudia bristled. She could bet she knew a lot more about marginalized kids than he did. 'I was a teacher, remember. I don't think you need to lecture me about relating to kids.'

'Come along, then. Your experience could be useful. Better than tidying the house and walking your little dog.'

'I'll think about it.'

He was laughing at her again. 'Don't do anything *too* rash, will you?'

Betty was coming towards them on the demon scooter. 'Betty!' Dan appealed to her, 'Get Claudia here to join us at Sing Out.'

He turned one last time to Claudia. 'Prove you *are* different from the ladies of Little Minsley. With something like this, you think you're helping them, but it's often the other way round.' She could hear the commitment in his voice; clearly the charity was his real passion, not the choir.

'Why not?' She'd been looking for something to motivate her after all. 'I'd be happy to get involved.'

'Great. I'll be in touch. I don't think you'll regret it.'

Betty and Claudia watched Daniel's retreating back. 'The red velvet wasn't wasted, then.'

'Betty Wilshaw, you are a wicked, wicked woman.'

'I was,' conceded Betty. 'But there's only so much you can get up to when you're pushing eighty.' She smiled mischievously. 'So I'll just have to watch you, won't I?'

Don was still up when she got home, even if he was on his laptop. Claudia planted a kiss on his forehead.

He looked up, surprised. 'What was that for?'

Their marriage was hardly hunky dory when her husband needed an explanation for a kiss. She'd better take care.

'Maybe the music is going to my head.'

'How was it? The Minsley Choral Society?'

'Interesting. You should come along. The choir master's unusual. He runs a charity for deprived kids. As a matter of fact, he's asked me to get involved. Why don't you come along too?'

Don shook his head. 'I'm glad about the choir.' He shut his laptop with a snap. 'It's great you've found something here you really enjoy.'

Feeling peckish she opened the fridge and hunted for a Raspberry Ski. Damn, it was past its sell-by date. She chucked it in the bin.

'Claudia,' Don pointed out piously, 'do you know, in the UK we throw away one point three million unopened yogurts every day?'

Claudia bit back a rude reply. She was damned if she was going to feel guilty about yogurt.

'Are you coming up to bed?' She felt maybe they ought to have some sex. Even unspontaneous pre-planned sex that had more in common with Band-Aid than the Kama Sutra could still help bridge gulfs in marriage.

For a moment the question hung between them.

'Vito needs to go out,' Don answered eventually. 'I'll see you in a few minutes.'

Ella woke up, convinced that she could hear banging from the bottom of the garden. For a moment she felt the old fear of the house being broken into, then relaxed, remembering she had Wenceslaus to look out for her.

Drowsily she pulled back her bedroom curtains and was greeted with the sight of Wenceslaus up a ladder. Not only had he fixed the damaged boards on the garden shed but he had repainted it from top to bottom.

It had fallen into disuse for so long that Ella had forgotten how delightful it was, more summer house than shed, really, with lacy woodwork round the gables that were now gleaming with white paint.

When the girls were little, Laurence had loved gardening and they would often spend whole weekends at the bottom of the garden. He would give them rides in the wheelbarrow before accidentally tipping them out into the piles of new-mown grass. Ella stood looking out, almost able to hear their shrieks of delight as they ran naked through the sprinkler or chased each other across the lawn with the hose. If only she had known what was to come.

She repeated her mantra. *They are not long, the days of wine and roses.*

At least she'd had hers. More than some people.

She showered and dressed quickly. Wenceslaus often made a pot of coffee when he came down but today he was clearly too busy. She breakfasted on granary toast and delicious gooseberry jam, then made a pot big enough to share.

She poured a mug and carried it to the back door where she slipped on her outdoor shoes. Even though it was midmorning, the frost on the lawn was white and thick and her footprints left deep imprints as if Bigfoot or the Abominable Snowman had been an early visitor.

She was about to call out a greeting to Wenceslaus when she heard a sudden burst of laughter. Feeling like an interloper in her own property, Ella peered in the window. The shed had changed beyond recognition. Instead of old chairs and broken furniture leaning up against garden tools and the lawnmower, there was a table covered in a gingham cloth on which sat a kettle, cafetière and a basket of croissants.

Beyond that, a sofa was draped in brightly coloured rugs. The effect was charming and raffish, like one of the more bohemian homeware catalogues.

Had Wenceslaus done this with Minka?

Ella heard laughter again and realized what she was feeling was faint irritation that Wenceslaus had invited Minka, not herself, to join him in this little hidden world.

Surely, Ella asked herself, she wasn't jealous?

And then the door opened and a figure stepped out holding a brightly checked cushion and laughing.

Ella's irritation flickered into fury.

It wasn't Minka but her daughter Julia.

'Julia, for God's sake! What on earth are you doing here?'

Julia shrugged, holding the cushion like a shield against her mother's anger.

'Get off my case, Mum. Since Wenceslaus was doing up the outside of the shed I thought it'd be fun to do the inside. I don't know why you're making so much fuss.'

'Yes, you do.' Ella resisted the temptation to shout at her daughter. 'You know perfectly well why I'm on your case, as you put it. You have to stop this stupid involvement. You are married. You have children.'

'Believe me, I know.'

'I don't want to have to ban you from coming here. But I will if this goes on. If you and Neil are so unhappy, separate. But don't sneak round here pretending to play house with a man ten years younger than you and tell yourself it doesn't matter.'

'You're jealous! You like having him around to fill your empty life!'

Ella felt as if she'd been kicked.

'I think you'd better leave. And I'd like my house key back.'

'Oh for God's sake, don't be so petty! This is my home too.'

'No, Julia, I don't think it is. Your home is with Neil and the boys. If the marriage ends and you are homeless, that would be different, but I refuse to be involved in this underhand game of yours.'

Julia delved into her shoulder bag and almost threw the key at Ella, then stormed out of the side gate.

Ella took a deep breath and knocked on the door of the shed. A moment later Wenceslaus opened it, his blue eyes anguished.

'El-la, I very sorry. But maybe I think you have wrong impression. Julia ask me to help her make shed nice so she can bring her sons here.'

'If I have the wrong impression I think you do as well. I don't think Julia has the slightest intention of bringing her sons here. I understand that my daughter is forceful but she is also vulnerable. It is a combination that can prove dangerous – to you as well as to her. I think perhaps you are being a little naïve.'

'What is naïve?'

'Unduly innocent, too easily taken advantage of.'

'I understand. Would you like me to leave?'

'I have told her she may not come here again unless to see me. I am also locking this shed and removing the keys. Julia needs to sort out her life for herself. Agreed?'

Wenceslaus nodded.

Ella put the key in her pocket and walked back to the house.

To her horror she remembered that before any of this had blown up she had invited Julia and Neil to supper tonight. They would be coming on their own as Cory was busy and the boys had gone back to school.

That was going to be a fun little gathering.

Julia wouldn't mention anything about the confrontation, she knew, but Ella had better tell Wenceslaus she expected him to stay firmly out of the picture. Should she ring up Julia and cancel? Perhaps Julia would do so herself. But she knew her daughter better than that. Julia would bluff it out.

She was right. The doorbell rang at precisely 7 p.m.

'This is good of you, Mum,' Julia announced as if the scene that had taken place earlier had never happened. She kissed her mother on both cheeks and handed over a bunch of roses.

Neil eyed the three steaks sizzling on the grill. 'Yes, nice change for a Wednesday.' He sniffed the air like a bloodhound.

Ella handed them a glass of wine. 'Why don't you both sit down?'

Half an hour later they were seated round the table trying

to make conversation. The steak and chips were delicious, almost as good as in France, Neil said.

Ella was just about to plead an early night when their conversation was interrupted by the phone.

She got so few calls on the landline these days that she jumped.

Neil and Julia exchanged one of their deeply irritating 'Isn't Mum a hoot' looks while Ella answered it.

'Hello,' asked the caller, 'am I speaking with Mrs E. Thompson? This is the Fraud Prevention Department of the SouthWest Bank.'

Ella experienced a minor flurry of panic. Hearing from the bank's fraud department somehow made her worry that she had done something stupid, like leaving her bank card in the machine.

The agent from SouthWest ran through the usual security questions before informing Ella that her credit card had experienced some unusual activity. 'Did you, for example, purchase an Apple computer in Krakow, Poland?'

'No, I certainly didn't,' Ella replied. 'My laptop is an ancient Hewlett Packard.'

'Did you withdraw a thousand Polish zloty from the PKO bank in Warsaw?'

'Absolutely not.'

'One final question: did you apply for a credit card from Deutsche Bank, Warsaw, giving this address?'

'Apply for a credit card?' Ella repeated, shocked. 'From *Warsaw*?'

Even before she put the phone down she could imagine Neil's face.

He sat opposite Julia, gloating and gleeful, poised like a crow at the prospect of fresh carrion.

But before he could say a word they heard a key turning

in the front door. It must be Wenceslaus. True to their agreement, he started to go straight upstairs instead of coming into the kitchen.

Ella went into the hall to intercept him. Minka was at his side.

'Wenceslaus, could I have a word?'

He came back down, looking thrown at this change from the designated plan. Minka followed, tossing her long red hair.

At the sight of both Julia and Neil at the table, his eyes darted to Ella's face, trying to work out what the hell might be going on.

'The thing is,' Ella explained, 'I just had a rather strange call from my bank. Someone in Poland has been trying to buy stuff with my card – a computer in Krakow and a cash withdrawal in Warsaw. They even tried to take out a credit card – using this address.'

'Is horrible,' Wenceslaus replied, angry on her behalf. 'Internet scam, perhaps? They did not get away with it, I hope?'

'I don't think so. Anyway, the bank will cover it.'

'So you will not lose?'

'Convenient, eh?' Neil said nastily. 'Victimless crime. Except that it isn't victimless. Somebody ends up paying. Curious it happened in Poland, don't you think?'

Wenceslaus was about to leave the room when he suddenly understood what Neil was implying.

He turned towards him.

Ella saw that his whole body was taut as an athlete's. 'You think, because in Poland, is something to do with *me*?'

The final word hung in the air, sharp and dangerous.

'It seems quite a coincidence, I must say, given the address they offered was right here.'

Wenceslaus didn't look at Neil again. He simply bowed to Ella and announced: 'I go now', then ran upstairs.

From the top floor they could hear the sound of something being pulled across the floor. Ten minutes later Wenceslaus appeared with a large backpack. The movie posters he'd had on his walls were rolled up and tucked into the front pouch and he was holding a pair of walking boots in one hand. In the other was a key he held out to Ella.

'I thank you from bottom of my heart. I was weary traveller like at Christmas table and you let me live in your beautiful house. I will go now, El-la.' He held out his hand in a gesture of farewell. 'And I give so many thanks to you.'

'Wenceslaus, look, there's no need . . .' Ella began.

'Yes,' Wenceslaus nodded, and she glimpsed a pained sadness in his eyes that made her want to weep herself, 'there is need.'

'Very convenient,' Neil whispered under his breath. 'And I don't suppose you'll leave a forwarding address for when the police come.'

Wenceslaus looked at him and shrugged as if Neil were not worth wasting any anger on. 'I work at coffee shop in High Street. Easy to find me.'

'Unless you scoot off suddenly.'

The expression on Wenceslaus' face announced that this was not worthy of an answer.

'Goodbye, El-la. Goodbye, Julia.'

With great dignity he walked through the hall and down the front steps, calmly putting his stuff in Minka's car, while she ranged round the room, eyeing Julia with dislike. 'Wenceslaus is good man. The best.' She pulled herself up to her full five feet nine and stood her ground, with all the presence of a female leopard protecting her cubs. 'You all make mistake about him. I know men. Bad ones too. Wenceslaus is honest, if not honest, he be much richer man.'

'If he's so honest, why did he try and steal my wife?' Neil burst out.

Julia gasped.

'He did not try and steal your wife.' Minka looked at him pityingly. 'Your wife throw herself at him because you make her unhappy, never think of her, treat her like she not exist. Wenceslaus tell me this. He wish for her sake she were more happy.'

Quietly, behind them, Julia began to sob.

'Julia, for Christ's sake, deny this cobblers,' Neil insisted angrily.

Julia's head went up. Her whole body changed and she sat with sudden queenly dignity. 'How can I deny it when every word is true?'

Before she left for her shift, Laura knocked on Sam's door and took him in a cup of tea. He had another appointment at the dentist this morning and she didn't want him to miss it. She wondered how his online job applications were going. So far he hadn't even got a single interview, despite his degree.

She put the tea down beside him.

Only the top of his head was showing under the duvet, his fair hair sticking up like an old-fashioned corn stook. Laura couldn't resist stroking it, which brought the expected protest.

But at least it meant he was awake.

'I'm off now, don't forget your appointment at ten-thirty.'

She hurried off to the bus stop, feeling pleased that she was only doing a half-day today since she was meeting Bella to look at prams – well, not prams, since no one used prams any more, but buggies or car-seats that, like Sam's old Transformers, could be magically converted into buggies. It seemed very early days to Laura, since Bella wasn't yet five months pregnant, but though she might look like the bride of Frankenstein, her daughter had always been a planner, and she wanted to really study the different models before starting to save for her favourite one.

When Laura arrived at LateExpress, the proprietor's wife was paying one of her surprise visits to the shop. 'Morning, Mrs Minchin,' she greeted Laura enthusiastically. 'How are you? No sign of your husband's harlot today?'

Laura shook her head, trying to suppress a grin.

'And a good thing too. We wives need to stick together or you never know where husbands would be sneaking their trouser-snake.'

Mr A's trouser-snake, Laura suspected, would have no chance of escaping with so many unscheduled visits from his wife.

Laura spent most of the morning checking orders and bundling up the unsold newspapers to go back to the distributor, until it was time to supervise the midday rush for crisps and fizzy drinks that constituted lunch for half the school children who invaded the shop. Then she took off her Late-Express overall and said goodbye.

She'd arranged to meet Bella in Oxford Street and, since she was ten minutes early, had the opportunity to immerse herself in the brave new world of baby transport. This had changed beyond recognition since the days when she'd wheeled Bella around in a striped pushchair that rolled conveniently up until it was no bigger than an umbrella.

The stately lines of the Silver Cross hadn't changed much. They still looked like the sort of pram only a Norland nanny would be permitted to push. A Viktor and Rolf special edition made her jaw drop at the cost, as did the various 'Baby Joggers' for the active yummy mummy. One or two had a marvellous invention called a 'buggy board' designed for older siblings to hitch a ride instead of screaming the place down. She wished she'd had one of those for Bella and Sam.

The Bugaboo seemed to be flavour of the month, as wheeled by celebs everywhere, with a celebrity price-tag so that when Laura came across a no-nonsense Maclaren stroller, the asking price seemed almost a giveaway.

'Hi, Mum.'

Laura turned and had to do a double take. Bella was looking almost conventional. She still wore black, but the Miss Havisham-meets-Count-Dracula look had disappeared without trace. Instead, she had on a figure-hugging crepe dress, plus a silk scarf that completely hid her bump, and knee-length black boots. If she'd added a little pillbox hat with a veil she could have been a particularly ravishing Sicilian widow.

Drawing on years of experience as a mother, Laura didn't comment on the new look. It was, she had learned, safer to say nothing.

But today, contrarily, Bella seemed to want her to.

'What do you think?' She twirled around the baby department. 'All from Oxfam, the Notting Hill branch. The cast-offs in Portobello Road are from Dolce and Gabbana.'

'You look lovely, darling.'

Laura's eye was caught by a tiny knitted hat shaped like a strawberry in the baby section. 'Oh look, you had one just like that! Isn't that the sweetest thing? I suppose it would be bad luck to . . .'

But Bella wasn't listening. Her gaze was fixed on the maternity department where a voluptuous redhead was holding up an Isabella Oliver ruffle wrap dress in a glorious shade of amethyst. Standing next to her stood Bella's father Simon.

'Oh God,' muttered Laura as Bella headed straight for them, clearly relishing the encounter.

Simon, on the other hand, looked as if he'd seen the ghost of Christmas Past. He almost covered his ears to stop the chains jangling.

'We meet again,' Bella addressed Suki, who shot a puzzled look at Simon. The new Bella looked so different and they had met only once before, at night, and under somewhat stressed-out circumstances. Unsurprisingly, Suki had no idea who she was.

'Do we?' she enquired blankly.

'When's the baby due?' Bella persisted.

'The end of July.' Suki smiled, beginning to relax.

'That's nice.' She looked her father in the face, challenging his nervous grey eyes with her bold brown gaze. 'You'll be a grandfather for two months before you're a father, then. Congratulations, Dad.'

'Look, Bella,' Simon was clearly having to hold on to his temper. 'What is this nonsense all about?'

'Me. Your daughter.' She lifted the scarf, revealing almost five months of baby bump. 'I'm due on the twenty-fourth of May.'

Simon's face crumpled like a used paper bag. 'Oh my God, I didn't know!'

'No,' Bella replied calmly, 'I didn't tell you. Seeing as you're not part of this family any more, there didn't seem much point. Besides,' she pointed cheerfully at Suki, 'you've got a new family now. Come on, Mum,' she turned back to Laura who had been standing on the perimeter, not wanting to make things any worse, 'let's go and buy that baby buggy!'

She marched off, leaving Suki livid at being upstaged and her parent satisfyingly shaken, appalled that he was going to be a grandfather before he was a father again. Which was exactly what Bella had intended.

'Bella, darling,' Laura attempted, as they inspected the twentieth buggy, all of which seemed largely identical to her, 'you're not really going to ban your father from seeing the baby?'

'Too right I am. He has to see there are consequences to his behaviour.' God, how confident she was, how black and white the world seemed to her. Was that just the certainty of youth?

On the other hand, Laura could see why abandoned wives felt so bitter at a world that seemed so all-accepting. Your husband did the wrong thing and you were the one who suffered. But the law, and society with it, didn't believe any longer that falling in love with someone else *was* wrong, it was just seen as one of the messier aspects of modern life. And what power did children have when their parents walked away from a marriage? All they could do was stand helplessly by. Unless they were Bella.

Laura was exhausted by the time she got home. As she opened the front door, TomTom came and wound himself round her legs, but otherwise the house was eerily quiet. Sam must have gone out somewhere.

She went up to her bedroom to kick off her shoes. Oddly, the cat followed her and started scratching at Sam's door.

With a sudden lurch of panic she pushed it open. The room was in complete darkness and had that boy smell of trainers and unwashed clothes that men took so long to grow out of. As her eyes got used to the lack of light, she made out a form under the duvet.

'Sam! Sam!' She bent down and pulled off his covers. 'What on earth are you doing?'

'What does it look like?' was the gruff reply. 'Sleeping.'

'But it's five o'clock in the afternoon!'

'So?'

'Did you go to your appointment?'

He shrugged infuriatingly.

'That cost me forty-two pounds! Twice what I earned today. How could you be so bloody selfish?' She snapped on his bedside light. He seemed lifeless and dull-eyed as a cod on a fishmonger's slab.

'What's the matter with you? You haven't been taking anything, have you?' she panicked.

'Of course I haven't. Nothing's the matter. I just don't happen to like my life so there's not much to get up *for*.'

'Oh, Sam. Sammy. C'm here.' She tried to put her arms round him as she had when he was little but he shrugged her off.

'Just leave me, Mum.'

She still sat on the bed, feeling helpless, until he turned away from her, with his face to the wall, and she realized for the first time what that expression meant, how much despair lurked in those few simple words.

She stayed on the bed until his breath became regular and she knew he had fallen asleep. How long could a twenty-two-year-old young man sleep? What the hell should she do?

What she did was go back to her bedroom, shut the door, throw herself on the bed and weep. When she stopped crying she went downstairs, poured herself a glass of wine and got out her ancient Nokia. It was actually so old that it had push buttons and total strangers occasionally came up to her and smiled reminiscently as if, in an age of word processors, she had insisted on using a manual typewriter.

She sent a text to Claudia, Sal and Ella. It read: *Feeling shit, isn't it time we met up again? Grecian Grove Wed 16th at 6?*

Ella, who was alone in her kitchen, thinking about the unravelling disaster of her daughter's marriage, instantly texted back: *Yes!*

Sal, who was feeling sick and sorry for herself and wondering if she was the stupidest woman in the world, opened it and texted back: *You betcha!*

Claudia, who was sitting on the sofa in her dressing gown,

cuddling Vito, saw the response of the others and thought Halleluiah, which she translated into a text reading: *Hell yes!*

But before she felt like sharing a bottle with her friends, Ella had something else to do that had been on her mind.

She walked the ten minutes between her house and the coffee shop where Wenceslaus worked.

He was just wiping down a counter before finishing up.

'I have something to say to you. I should have stood up for you when my son-in-law was so rude to you the other night. I just wanted you to know that I didn't believe that tripe about you opening up bank accounts in Poland for a single moment.'

She turned and waved, almost shyly.

'Thank you, El-la,' he replied with a catch in his voice. 'This mean a lot to me. I hope everything work out very well for you. You are very kind lady.' He paused a moment as if not sure what to say next. 'And for Julia as well,' he added finally.

Sal dressed extra carefully in a nicely cut black dress with her best boots. She took longer than usual applying her make-up and she shampooed and blow dried the wig. The wig, she had convinced herself, looked better than her real hair.

She took one last look in the mirror and burst into tears. It was the first time they would have seen her since the cancer, and one glance would tell them something was desperately wrong.

They would guess she was ill the moment they saw her.

It was one thing fooling Rose McGill, but these were her oldest friends, the friends she'd known since she was eighteen, who had witnessed every triumph and disaster of her life. Except this one.

She slumped onto the bed. Would it be so terrible if she

told them? They would be supportive, sympathetic, full of offers to help.

Sal knew it would be hard for her friends to grasp why she needed to do it this way, but that was exactly why she couldn't tell them. Support and sympathy would undermine her resolve. She might even collapse. Strength was what she needed. Strength and the determination that she was going to pull through, triumphantly, and still have a means of supporting herself for the years ahead. And that strength was easier to maintain if no one but she knew the truth.

She put the wig back on its stand and texted Ella that she couldn't come owing to a crisis at work. She might share her friends' love-hate relationship with technology, but she had to admit it was brilliantly useful when you had to tell a lie.

Ella was the first to arrive. As she sat in their usual alcove at The Grecian Grove, she decided even the nymphs and satyrs looked pleased to see them. 'Business not been so good without us?' she enquired of the nearest nymph. 'Never mind, it'll pick up tonight!' She summoned a waiter and ordered a bottle of their usual wine.

Claudia rushed in five minutes later. 'Sorry I'm late. Don had disappeared with the dog.'

'How is he?'

'Don?'

'No, the dog.'

'The dog's great. Don, on the other hand—'

'There's Laura!' Ella interrupted.

Laura, looking pale and pretty, waved from the other side of the restaurant. 'Where's Sal?' she asked as she sat down.

'Not coming,' Ella replied. 'A crisis at work, she says, but I'm a bit worried. There's something funny going on. She cancelled the last arrangement we had as well. I suddenly realized that though I've emailed and texted her, I haven't actually seen her for ages and ages.'

'Maybe it's this new job,' Laura suggested. 'She's throwing herself into it because it was so hard to actually *find* a job.'

'Because she's OLD!' Claudia snapped. 'Do you know, for the very first time I've started to *feel* old?'

They looked at her, shocked at this heresy. It was their declared belief that they all felt the same as they always had.

'I was driving along the other day to Bruce Springsteen's *Greatest Hits*,' Claudia expanded. 'And I could hear this ticking sound. For half an hour I thought it was part of the music till a policeman stopped me to tell me my hazard lights were on!'

'Claudia,' Laura said solemnly, 'I'm worried about you.'

'I know,' conceded Claudia. 'I was worried myself. It's the sort of thing only old people do.'

'Forget the hazard lights. It's the music I'm worried about. Bruce Springsteen?'

'Let her be,' Ella protested. 'She just wants to strap her hands across his engine, don't you, Claudia?'

Claudia laughed. 'There are so many things I'm starting to notice that make me feel ancient. Hairs on my face. No one ever told me after the menopause I'd get a furry face!'

'Or forget my best friends' names.'

'Or why I went into a room.'

'Or that I'd get into a panic if I'm ten minutes late.'

'Or hate looking at my turkey neck in a mirror.'

'In fact,' Ella sighed, 'I'm beginning to feel not just old but *really* old. Proper old, like my parents were old.'

They both looked at her, silently. Ella was always so quietly competent, never making a fuss about anything. 'It's my daughter Julia.'

'They're not on at you to move again?'

'Worse. Julia has only fallen for my lodger.'

'The wonderful Wenceslaus?' Laura asked. 'He is rather gorgeous.'

'Yes, but Julia's married. I'm so annoyed with her about it. I still believe it's a silly fantasy, but she put a photo of him on her phone and her husband found it and was naturally livid. But even that didn't stop her; she's still been hanging round Wenceslaus. The thing is, I don't know whether she should stay with Neil or leave; I just know she seems so unhappy and I don't know how to help her sort out her life.'

'Isn't that up to her?' Laura asked gently. 'I sometimes worry our generation is too involved in our children's lives. Maybe it would be better that they had to sort things out themselves, like we did. Though who am I to talk? Sam won't get out of bed and Bella's having a baby and living in a squat while my husband divorces me.'

They all began to laugh. 'Let's have another bottle. Contrary to moralistic pronouncements, drink *is* the answer.'

'The thing is,' Ella pronounced, 'we may not *look* old, but the truth is, we *are* old. I wrote a whole blog on the signs of ageing and loads of people came back with their own lists. And they were all our age.'

She was so upset about Julia she'd forgotten her blog was supposed to be a secret.

'*You* wrote a blog?'

Ella realized Claudia and Laura were both staring at her as if she'd just announced she was a Martian. She had to own up some time and she'd hated all the secrecy.

'Yes. Wenceslaus showed me how. I wanted it to have lots of black humour so I called it MOAN FART DIE. Actually, I get quite a lot of hits.'

'*You* write MOAN FART DIE?' Laura demanded, stunned. 'But that's the blog Sal's always going on about! She sent it to both of us to read.'

There was an ominous pause. 'You wrote about why men leave their wives after twenty-five years!' accused Laura. 'When I read it I thought it sounded very like my situation but, Jesus, Ella, I had no idea it actually *was* my situation. And then . . . Ella, that blog about a friend of yours and their divorce lawyer saying adultery was commonplace – that was me too, wasn't it?'

'I know, I know, I'm so sorry.' Ella desperately hoped they'd understand. 'I just sort of wrote it and didn't believe anyone would actually read it, a bit like keeping a diary.'

'Don't be so bloody naïve!' Laura flashed, angrier than any of them had ever seen her. 'I told you that stuff in confidence. I mean, I didn't spell it out because I didn't think I needed to. Because we're friends! How could you? What if Simon reads it or his lawyer? Or Bella or Sam? For God's *sake*, Ella.'

'Why didn't you ask us if it was OK to use it?' Claudia seconded. 'Did you expect to make money from this blog? Sell lots of ads for plastic surgery on the back of Laura's divorce? Would my mum's mental problems have been next? Or Sal being too old to get a job? Is anything fair game? What about Julia's fantasy about your lodger, that'd make a good blog, you could make it really funny!'

'Oh God, you're right,' Ella wailed. 'You're both right. I see that now, but I really didn't at the time. You probably won't believe this but it was really a way of me learning to use the Internet.'

'Oh, that's OK, then.'

'And you lied to Sal! She asked you, I heard her, if you had read MOAN FART DIE and you said you hadn't.'

'She kept wanting me to write for her magazine.'

'Why didn't you just say no?'

'I didn't want her to know it was me.'

'So you could betray more secrets!' Laura was almost in

tears. 'Why don't you try trolling next? I gather anonymity's useful for that too! To think I came here tonight to tell you about my son who won't get out of bed and my unmarried daughter who's five months' gone and how we bumped into my husband with his pregnant mistress in John Lewis's baby department. They'd make good blogs, wouldn't they? Help yourself because I won't be telling you any of my private life in future!'

Laura reached for her bag and coat and stumbled out of the wine bar.

Ella dropped her head into her hands. 'Oh, God, Claudia, I've really screwed this up.'

'Yes,' Claudia agreed, 'you have. And, to be honest, I'm not sure how you undo the damage.'

Sal sat with the letter from the hospital in her hand, shaking. She had finished two cycles of chemo and had hoped she was making good progress.

Now the consultant wanted to see her again.

For the first time since she had had the diagnosis, Sal wasn't sure she could do this alone. She longed for sane and rational Ella to come with her and hear this next news.

She'd begun to delve into the depths of her very untidy bag looking for her phone, when she heard it ringing from the other side of the room.

'Hello there, Ms Grainger.' Claudia's familiar tones greeted her. 'Long time no meet for glass of bad wine. How's your work crisis? Ready to come out and play yet? We're all worried about you. We're wondering if you've secretly mutated into an alien. We'd still love you, you know.'

'The job's a bit knackering,' Sal replied cautiously. 'I don't have much energy left for socializing.'

'Don't say you're feeling old as well? My God, Sal, talking

of which – you won't believe this – it turns out that Ella, our Ella, is the writer of that blog you love.'

Sal listened, so stunned she forgot her predicament. 'You don't mean MOAN FART DIE?'

'Absolutely. We had a huge fight about it. Laura was really upset because Ella used stuff in it Laura told her in confidence.'

'But Ella can't be the writer. Why wouldn't she tell me, when I've been asking her to write for us? She knew how desperately I was trying to get hold of the writer!'

'She didn't want anyone to know it was her, she says.'

'My God,' Sal felt almost physically winded, 'I feel really betrayed!'

'Join the club. We all do. How can we tell her things if she's just going to use it in a blog? Sal? Are you all right?'

'I'll call you back later, Claudia. I just need some time to digest this.'

To think she'd just been about to call Ella and finally come clean about her cancer. That would no doubt have ended up in the blog too!

Sal sat down on the bed again, the letter still in her hand.

She really was on her own.

What was it John Donne had said – that no man is an island? Well, she certainly was. In her whole life she had never felt more friendless and stranded.

For a moment she was tempted to tear off her wig and throw it in the bin. If she were a Rachel, she might do it. If she were a Rachel, she might stride into work bald as a billiard ball. But she wasn't Rachel, she was Sal.

She placed the wig back on her head, reached for her sunglasses and headed for the office. Now that she knew Ella was the author of MOAN FART DIE she had better start looking for another star writer.

CHAPTER 19

Ella sat with the phone in her hand, staring out at the frosty sunlit garden. Her friends were right. She had been stupid and naïve. How could she have had the ridiculous fantasy that she was writing just for herself?

She had so enjoyed trying to overcome her fear of all things technological that writing the blog had seemed like her own private reward. The fact that she got responses from total strangers just reinforced this. The blog wasn't about her real life, it was something out there in the ether. If she had accepted Sal's offer of writing in the magazine, *that* would have been real, which was why she had never considered it. She would indeed have seen that as a betrayal. None of this, of course, made any difference to her friends.

She realized how dangerously seductive the Internet was, at once intimate and anonymous. She could see why people invented whole personalities and identities for themselves that had nothing to do with reality.

But the Internet wasn't a parallel universe. The offence she had caused was firmly rooted in this one. She had no idea what to do next, how to make it up to them. Just when she wanted their support over the Julia problem, no one even wanted to talk to her. And who could blame them?

For now she would go to the allotment and try and dig herself out of the depression that had descended on her.

*

Increasingly, Claudia was finding Tuesday was the day of the week she really looked forward to. The Christmas choir recital had been a big success and now they were deeply into *The Sound of Music*. If anyone had told Claudia the highlight of her week would be singing 'How do you solve a problem like Maria', she would have given them a withering glance. And yet it was true, and not only because of Daniel Forrest.

'I'll probably go to the pub after,' she told Don as she wrapped up in a coat and scarf.

'Fine. I won't wait up.'

And then she had added her guilty addition: 'Why don't you come along too?'

'What, and find myself cast as the lead in *The Desert Song*? I don't think so.'

Claudia kissed the top of his head in silent acknowledgement that, apart from his lack of voice, Don was the least likely man in Minsley to be cast as a seductive sheik.

The school hall was already full by the time she arrived. Everyone stood round the big stove at one end warming their feet, and there was the unmistakeable aroma of mulled wine in the air. What was it about mulled wine? Mostly she loathed the stuff and yet, if you were outdoors or on the ski slopes, it miraculously tasted magical and irresistible. Tonight was one of those nights.

Claudia breathed in the scent of cloves, cinnamon and lemon peel and decided everyone in the world should join a choir.

'You look happy.' Betty had left her scooter at the door and had taken to what she called her 'chariot': a walking frame on wheels.

'Probably drunk!' Claudia laughed. 'Have you tried this? It's really good.'

'Daniel brought it, I gather. Hmmm, he's never done anything like that before. Aye aye, here he comes.'

'My two favourite women, sharing a drink and a gossip. Not about me, I hope?'

'Don't be creepy, Daniel, we expect better from you, don't we, Claudia?' Betty reprimanded. 'We might forgive you because of your Glühwein. It's surprisingly good.'

'That's because I learned to make it in Austria. It's not as sickly as the stuff here. Now, Claudia, I've got the perfect part for you.'

'Not Maria, surely?' asked naughty Betty.

'The countess. You're the only one with the sophistication to carry it off.'

'Well . . .' Claudia began to reply.

'Excellent. I knew you'd agree.' He swept on to the next group to allocate more roles before Claudia could argue further.

'Come on, Countess,' Betty teased, 'let's get another before the drink runs out, or are you too sophisticated for a refill?'

'All right, Mother Abbess. I suppose you're about to tell me to "climb ev'ry mountain till I find my dream"?'

At the end of the practice they all crowded into the pub – except for Betty, who decided for once she was feeling too tired.

'Would you like me to walk back with you?' Claudia offered.

'With my demon scooter I'd be there before you got your coat on. Stay and have fun.' She raised an eyebrow. 'But not too much.'

The choir were a jolly bunch. She liked mixing with people who – unlike her own daughter – perfectly understood why she might like to sign up for singing once a week. It was fun trying new things and she even enjoyed watching other choirs sing the same songs on YouTube. Sometimes the choirs sounded just as amateur and occasionally off-key as they did.

By the time she decided to head for home, the night had

become colder and clearer. There was a moon high in the sky with countless clusters of stars surrounding it, some bright and distinct, others almost like silver dust sprinkled across the galaxy.

A voice behind her made her jump.

'One good thing about the country is the sky at night.' She turned to find Daniel walking behind her. He must have left very quickly to have got here so soon.

Try as she might she couldn't repress a small thrill of excitement. The whole street was silent and still and in the white light it had an air of unreality almost like a Hollywood stage set.

'Were you serious about Sing Out?'

'Sing Out?'

'My charity getting kids to start singing, remember? Keeping them off the streets? Stopping them mugging old ladies?'

'Yes, definitely. I'd like to.'

'Good for you.' He was serious for a moment. 'I've been trying to work out how to get them interested so they don't see us as irritating do-gooders. Have you ever been in a prison?'

Claudia shook her head.

'It's quite a shock. Even the young offenders' version.' He looked up at the velvety sky dotted with a million stars. 'A far cry from Minsley.' For the briefest of moments his eyes held hers. 'I'm glad you're coming.'

When she got home, she was surprised to find Don still up, glued to his laptop, but this time he made an odd furtive move to cover the screen so that she wouldn't see who he was emailing.

If Claudia hadn't been so thrown by Daniel Forrest she might have looked harder to find out.

'What the hell am I going to do about Sam?' Laura asked her daughter Bella. She was so worried and frustrated at her son's strange behaviour that she was considering professional help. The only thing was, how did you get help if your son wouldn't even get out of bed to seek it?

'Don't worry, Mum,' Bella advised her. 'I'm sure it's some kind of weird stage. Maybe he just needs some sleep.'

'Bella, he's been sleeping solidly for a week. No one can need that much sleep!'

'Actually,' contributed the normally reticent Nigel, 'I read this article about young guys in Japan who start sleeping for a day or two then gradually take to bed permanently. It's a huge phenomenon there. They call it Hikikomori.'

'Gosh, thanks, Nige,' Bella commented. 'But Sam isn't Japanese.'

'No, but the point I was making is that these guys aren't depressed or anything, they just want a break from the world's expectations.'

'Well, Sam can't have a break.' Laura wanted to tear her hair out. 'He's got to find a job or do some volunteering or do *something*.'

'I'll see if I can track down a new game,' Nigel offered helpfully, 'that might tempt him up.'

Funnily enough, the thought of her son endlessly playing computer games suddenly seemed a good thing – at least, compared with staying in bed permanently.

Laura's day just got better and better.

A letter arrived from Rowley Robinson advising her that Simon was pushing for a decree nisi which could mean he was definitely hoping for an order against the matrimonial home.

'To sell it, you mean?' she demanded as soon as she got Rowley on the phone.

'I'm afraid so. We have a date for the court case, but I strongly recommend we negotiate. Only about one per cent of petitions actually make it to court. After twenty-five years, he'll have to pay you a lump sum, even if you do sell the house.'

'What about the new woman? She seems pretty successful. Maybe she can support him and I can keep the house.'

'I'm afraid they've already thought of that one. Apparently she doesn't intend to work once she has the baby.'

Bloody typical. 'So you think we really will have to sell the house?'

'I'm afraid it looks that way.'

Well, that should cheer Sam up.

Mr A had asked if she could work all day today and she was actually quite grateful. Even stacking shelves and shooing off shoplifting children was better than moping around the house. She wished Sam could see that.

She was just replenishing the Pot Noodles, one of LateExpress's star sellers, and fantasizing about Suki coming in so that she could pelt her with cans of cut-price baked beans, when she saw a figure dodging in and out behind the confectionery. Suspecting another grab and run, a technique polished to perfection by the nimble-fingered school children, and which wouldn't bring a blush to the cheeks of the Artful Dodger, Laura ran round the corner and collided with the figure of Ella, buttoned into a frogged Russian coat, carrying a bunch of roses.

'I know you never want to speak to me again, but I'm sorry. Really, really, sorry.'

'Twelve red roses sorry,' commented Laura.

'I could make it twenty-four,' offered Ella sheepishly.

'I just don't understand how you could have done it.'

'I was incredibly stupid and naïve. I honestly never thought anyone would read them. I mean, why should they? Who am I? Some retired old boot who lives in Old Moulsford. It's not as if I'm Katie Price or Liz Hurley or someone who really wants to be in the spotlight.' She handed over the roses. 'And I always stuck up for you in my blogs.'

'In future don't even mention me. Or anyone who sounds like me.'

'Agreed.'

The truth was, Laura didn't think she could get by without Ella; Ella was a vital part of her support system. 'OK, I'll put you on probation.' She opened her arms and Ella hugged her so tight she could hardly breathe.

'I won't abuse it, I promise.'

'You'd better not. My son won't get out of bed and my husband wants the house sold, and I need you to listen to me blubbing and NOT PUT IT IN YOUR BLOODY BLOG!!!!'

Claudia made a cup of coffee and thought about Don's strange reaction last night. He had definitely been hiding something. She decided to have a furtive check of his laptop while he was out on another foray to his precious dump. He and the staff were all on first-name terms and last night he'd announced his goal that their household set itself a target of recycling every single bit of their rubbish!

Mutinously, Claudia threw the plastic milk container into the bin designed for compost.

Don's laptop was just sitting beckoning at her from the other side of the kitchen. Claudia hesitated. She shouldn't be doing this. She'd been burned before when Gaby was about twelve, opening her daughter's diary and discovering in glowing detail how much she hated her mother.

In for a penny. Maybe it would help her find out why he seemed to be finding it hard to settle in Minsley.

It didn't take long. Don wasn't a natural dissembler. Two months ago he had signed up to Friends Reunited and made contact with an old school friend called Marianne. Their communications, just a few at first, had grown and grown until they were emailing each other ten or twenty times a day. From reading the emails, Claudia was amazed to find that they hadn't actually met up yet. They were having a cyber-romance and it was fuelled by Don's revelation that his wife cared more about her friendships than her marriage.

She was so angry with Don that she could only just stop herself throwing his laptop out of the window. He'd been so keen for them to leave London and all her friends so that they could start again and now he was being unfaithful, at least via email, and, for all she knew, probably more than that soon. The thought that she wasn't behaving too well herself knocked on the door of her unconscious, but she wouldn't let it in.

Her next reaction was to pick up the phone to ring Ella. With a shock she remembered how Ella was off-limits because of her own bad behaviour.

What was the matter with everyone?

She grabbed Vito and dragged him out from his nice warm bed in the kitchen to go for a walk so that she could think.

She was halfway down the village street with Vito shivering behind her when she stopped dead and almost squashed him.

Coming towards her, in old clothes and an anorak, holding a bunch of flowers and a basket full of muddy-looking veg, which matched the rest of her, was Ella herself.

The sight of Ella, so out of context, and looking full of contrition, jolted Claudia out of her rigid mindset. Ella looked so ridiculous in her mud-caked clothes and boots, with arms loaded down with leeks and cabbages like a contestant on *Crackerjack*, that Claudia found she couldn't hold on to her anger.

'Ella!'

'Claudia! She filled Claudia's arms with the veg. 'It's so great to see you! I can't tell you how stupid I feel!'

'Quite right too. Have you said sorry to Laura?'

Ella nodded.

'Good. She was more hurt than any of us. Except maybe Sal.'

'Oh, God, Sal! She still won't return my calls. Do you think I should go and see her?'

'I suppose you could go to her office.' They walked back towards Claudia's cottage. 'Oh look, a snowdrop!' Ella pointed to a tiny clump of the delicate flowers that had just pushed their way through the hard ground by the garden path. 'Spring must be on the way.'

'Trust you to notice.' Claudia smiled. 'It must be all this messing about at the allotments.' She bent down and picked one. 'They are lovely, though. Symbolic. New beginnings and all that.'

'And has it been a new beginning?' Ella asked, standing back to admire the pretty cottage with its white wooden porch. 'Winter jasmine too. How gorgeous.' She pointed to the delicate sprays of yellow. 'You weren't exactly keen to come.'

'Dragged kicking and screaming, you mean. I am quite enjoying it, actually. I've joined a choir!'

'Claudia! I didn't know you could sing.'

'Neither did I but I'm not too bad. I'm going to be the countess in *The Sound of Music*!'

'Well, get you!'

'And I've signed up to help with a charity that takes singing to underprivileged kids. It's run by this charismatic choir master.'

'Is it, now? Good for you. And how about Don?'

'Oh, God, Ella, after all the song and dance he made, I'm

not sure he's happy. He won't admit it, but I think he misses his friends as much as I miss mine.'

'He probably needs a Grecian Grove. Men don't think friendships matter, but they do.' She gave Claudia a significant look.

'I think he's been passing his days linking up with an old school friend via some website.'

'Male or female?'

'Female. A Marianne.'

Ella raised an eyebrow. 'You want to put the lid on that before it boils up. They're really powerful, these reunion sites. People trying to rekindle all that innocent passion and one thing leads to another and the house burns down.'

Claudia took Ella on a tour of the cottage which took just five minutes flat. Ella listened for a moment. 'My God, it's quiet!'

'It's the country. Come on, let's see what we can find for lunch. With all those veggies you brought there ought to be something. And we could open a bottle of wine!'

By the time Ella left two hours later the bonds of friendship had been re-tied almost as strongly as ever.

Laura sat at her familiar kitchen table, the possessions that she had built up over the years all around her – a silver picture frame with a photo of Simon and her on holiday; a vase she'd been given as a present by Bella; a shell found on a faraway beach, the calendar made out of pasta by Sam aged six. Until a few months ago, these would have seemed the evidence of a happy and successful marriage. Now she hardly noticed them.

The truth was, she wouldn't really mind moving and starting again. Here there were memories round every corner waiting to pounce on her; things they'd bought together. Simon had been more interested than most men in choosing his surroundings. Most of her friends' husbands had left it all to their wives, considering a trip to a furniture shop as a living death, but Simon had loved Saturday visits to IKEA, even relishing the Swedish meatballs for lunch in the café, watching other couples fight over the self-assembly and blaming each other for forgetting the dimensions of the mattress they'd come to buy.

Sam, she knew, felt differently. His home really mattered to him; it was at least here, even if his parents' marriage had imploded.

Laura decided to do something Rowley Robinson had expressly told her not to do.

She called Simon and arranged to meet him in a coffee shop a long way from LateExpress or his office.

'The thing is,' she explained as she ordered the coffees, latte for her, macchiato for him, like they always had, 'I'm really worried about Sam. He won't get out of bed. Not at all. Ever.'

'Right.'

'I've tried everything. Threats. Bribery. Bella's boyfriend has bought computer games. None of it works. Simon, I think it might be to do with the house.'

'For God's sake, Laura, don't blackmail me.'

'Simon, my lawyer would kill me for saying this, but I don't really care about the house. Sam does, though. What I wanted to ask was, could we come to some agreement, nothing to do with lawyers, that I could stay there just till he's got over the split? A few months more. I mean, go ahead with the divorce, but just not sell the house yet.'

'Does he still hate me?'

'I think he's just confused. He can't see what went wrong, he says, and that's what's making it hard to accept.' She sipped her coffee. 'I didn't poison him against you, you know. I think that's despicable.'

'You didn't need to. I managed that all on my own.'

'I'm sure he'll come round. Eventually.'

He considered her for a moment, silently. 'You're a nice person, Laura.'

'Yeah, well, nice people finish last, as they say.'

'You haven't finished last. You made a stable home for them.'

'Perhaps.' Laura shrugged. 'Bella's having a baby with no job and no money and Sam won't get out of bed.' She gave him a small, wry smile. 'And here you are, starting again. Brave.'

'Or foolhardy.' For a moment he looked very old. 'About the house. I'll see what I can do.'

When she got home, Ella sat in her kitchen feeling grateful that she was forgiven, at least by Laura and Claudia. Sal would be far more difficult to convince because she felt even more betrayed.

Ella made herself a cup of coffee in the individual pot she'd hardly used all these months. Since Wenceslaus had left, the house seemed emptier than ever. She'd almost pressed him again to come back when she'd visited his coffee shop, but she knew he wouldn't accept. Pride went deep with him. Ella looked around at her familiar surroundings. She might criticize Julia for clinging to a fantasy but wasn't she doing the same with this house?

She was so deep in contemplation that she hardly even heard the doorbell as it rang through the echoing spaces, but as it persisted through several more rings, it finally penetrated her consciousness and she stood up and went to answer it.

The last person she expected to find on her doorstep was her son-in-law, Neil.

'Hello, Ella, may I come in?'

'Of course.' Ella knew her voice was frosty, but then it was Neil's fault that Wenceslaus had moved out. 'How is Julia?'

'It's about Julia, or rather us, that I've come to talk to you.'

Ella stood back, stunned. 'You've come to talk to *me* about your marriage?'

He smiled bitterly. 'I know you don't like me, Ella. You think I'm conventional and bigoted and probably selfish, and absolutely nothing like Laurence was.' He waved away any protest she might offer before she even made it. 'Let's be honest. You've never approved of me, and you hate the fact I've sent the boys to boarding school. You probably also think I've got a filthy temper. I jumped to conclusions about your lodger and probably quite a lot of other things. I'm sorry. The thing is, I'm really worried about Julia.'

She took him into the sitting room. He stood by the fireplace, with one foot on the fender, staring into the flames. In his tweed sports jacket, twill trousers, check shirt and yellow tie, he looked the picture of the country gent of thirty years ago. Ella wondered where he even found clothes that were so ruthlessly conventional. It was hard to see Neil as young, yet he couldn't even be forty.

'The thing is, I love Julia and I didn't know what to do about her and that bloody Pole . . .' It was as if he forced himself to put a name to his rival and accept him as a person. 'Wenceslaus. I knew she trailed about after him like a lovesick teenager.'

'How did you know that?' Ella asked nervously.

'I followed her.' He looked so miserable that Ella softened a little towards him. She noticed that his tie was twisted up under his shirt and almost reached out to straighten it as she would a small boy's. 'She stayed in that café for two hours. And then there was the photograph business.' He sat down across the table from her. 'Do you think his girlfriend is right?

That I pushed her into his arms, that I can't make her happy?'

'Neil, if it's any consolation, I think it's more of a crush, and I'm pretty sure nothing's actually happened between them.'

'That's not the point though, is it?' His answer surprised her. To many men it would have been exactly the point. 'She went to him for something she wasn't getting from me.'

'I hope you don't mind me saying this, but I think the problem is she's lonely.'

'*Lonely!* But she's got us.'

'Yes, but the boys are away and you're very busy.'

'She could get a job. Do some volunteering.'

'She has this notion of being a good wife. I think it's my fault.' As Ella said this, she saw that it was probably true. 'I was always working. My generation were the first to have careers. We were in love with the idea of proving ourselves, being women in a man's world. When I had Julia I went straight back to work. I only took a month or two off and then she had a nanny. She was quite a nice nanny, but she wasn't me. Years later, Julia told me how much she'd longed for me to pick her up from school.' The thought made Ella suddenly tearful. 'And then her father died, and I *had* to work then. I had this place to keep up.'

She glanced at her beloved home. 'Maybe I should have sold up, moved to a flat, given up work, but you know, Neil, when Laurence died it was work that saved me. Just having to get out of bed in the morning, put my clothes on, go to the office, think about something other than his stupid bloody wasteful death, got me through. But maybe I should have thought more of the girls. When they were children, funnily enough, Julia was the strong one, it was Cory who collapsed when Laurence died. Julia really helped Cory.'

'It must have been really hard for you all.'

She looked him in the eye and saw a Neil she hadn't glimpsed before. A conventional man, certainly, but not such a closed-off one as she'd imagined. 'So you can see why Julia might desperately want to make a proper home.'

'I was sent away to school at six,' he said suddenly. 'My parents got divorced and they quarrelled about who should have me. The funny thing was – neither of them wanted me.'

Ella glimpsed a sad small boy packed off in shorts and a blazer with a trunk, not knowing where he could call home. No wonder he clung to convention; perhaps it made him feel safe.

'And yet you've sent the boys off to school as well.'

'Not at six!' He looked out of the window. A young robin was sitting on the bird table, fluffing out its feathers in the cold. It looked tiny and vulnerable. 'You think you're doing the best for them.' And then he added, defensively, 'It's a really good education.'

Ella had no idea why but she suddenly asked Neil something. 'Actually, I've got a problem of my own. Maybe you can advise me.'

'*Me?*' Neil looked thunderstruck. 'Julia says I'm emotionally illiterate!'

Ella tried not to smile. She was glad they were at least talking about things.

'Now that Wenceslaus has gone, this house is feeling very empty. Do you honestly think I should sell it?'

Ella had expected him to simply rubber stamp the idea, but Neil seemed suddenly uncertain of everything. He was unexpectedly sheepish, his usual strutting demeanour seemed to have been left on the doorstep. 'I should never have accused him like that. I just wanted Julia to see he was no knight in shining armour who would rescue her. She was so obsessed with him.'

'Yes,' conceded Ella, but she wasn't going to forgive him.

'To be honest, I'm not sure I'm the best person to advise you. I thought it was madness that you wanted to go on living here, but you seem to love the place so much. I suppose I can see now that it's your link to Laurence and all your memories.'

'Perhaps it's time I broke that link. I'll still have the memories.'

'You were very happy with him, weren't you?'

'Yes, which is why I want you and Julia to be happy too. I didn't choose for my marriage to end and I suppose it makes me angry when people don't see what they've got.'

'I haven't tried very hard to make Julia happy.' The harshness in his voice made Ella look at him.

'Maybe it isn't too late.'

He smiled. It was funny, Neil was such a jerky, brusque character that she'd never even noticed he had quite a sweet smile. He would never come near the extraordinary beauty of a Wenceslaus, but for a conventional Englishman, he could be quite appealing.

As soon as he'd left, Ella felt emotionally wiped out. She had no idea if Neil and Julia would be able to save their marriage or whether she should stay on here alone.

For now she would have a bath. And a very large glass of wine.

CHAPTER 20

Sal had a message that Rose McGill had been looking for her when she got back to the office in Kensal Green.

Rose was often at general meetings, or those called to discuss company-wide issues, but she had never requested a one-to-one before and the news made Sal jumpy.

As far as Sal could tell, her editorship had been going well. Official circulation figures weren't out yet but the unofficial soundings Sal had made were good and subscriptions, previously in decline, were gently climbing. Their website was also popular and proving a useful tool for keeping in touch with their readers. Nothing to worry about that she could see.

'Sal, good to see you. Earl Grey?' Rose, resplendent in purple jersey, was proffering the teapot she always filled religiously at four every day.

'Thanks,' Sal sat down. She was wearing both wig and sunglasses, but these appeared to be accepted as a new look and rarely even remarked on. It was just assumed by the staff that they were an eccentricity in the Anna Wintour mould. Thank God she'd gone for the really expensive wig.

Rose, Sal suspected, had a sharper eye, but she didn't seem to be staring or studying Sal with extra interest.

'I asked you in because I wanted your opinion.' Rose sat in one of the two easy chairs opposite Sal. 'The thing is, we've had an approach.'

'What kind of approach?

'From Mayflower Publishing in New York. They've been watching *New Grey* over the last few months and they want to buy a stake in the company. The idea would be to start a US version, with our input of course.'

Sal was flattered and scared in equal measure. Flattered because it was a sign of their success under her editorship and nervous at what would be involved, especially given her precarious state of health. Had she been well it would have been a terrific opportunity for the magazine to branch out.

'And what do you think?' Sal asked cautiously. Rose was famously suspicious of conglomerates.

'If it had been any other group, I would have told them to take a running jump, but Lou Maynard is different. I know him from old. And Lou's already so rich he's not doing it just for money; he's genuinely interested in the idea of ageing.' She laughed. 'He's no spring chicken himself. He must be at least seventy.'

'What does Michael think?'

Rose shrugged. 'Michael's in two minds. He can see the appeal of making some money, obviously, but he's worried that in a big organization he'd be a smaller player.' She sipped her tea. 'It's true Lou would eclipse any other male on the horizon.'

'You sound as if you like him.'

'Everyone likes Lou.' Rose's laugh conjured up smoky night-clubs with jazzy music and heady cocktails, possibly in the company of this Lou Maynard. 'Now I shouldn't really be telling you this, but Jonny Wheeler isn't planning to come back.'

Sal gasped. Jonny Wheeler was the editor she was replacing.

'So you *might* find – no promises mind, and this is strictly between you and me and not an employment tribunal – you were offered his job. Which is why I'd like you to hop over to New York next week and meet Lou. See what your take on the idea is, whether we should progress it or not. I can't go, I'm too old, and Michael's too entrenched, so it'll have to be you.'

Sudden nausea overwhelmed her, and Sal got up and left the room, saying she would be back in a moment.

Once in the loo she dry-heaved over the lavatory pan, her chest aching with the effort and her head spinning. Should she tell Rose the truth?

Reality flooded in like a freezing dawn. If Rose knew she had serious cancer that would be it. Rose would have no choice but to find another editor, and just at the very moment when she was doing so well and might actually be offered what she had been dreaming of – the permanent editorship of a magazine she could shape and steer to real success – everything would evaporate and she would be left jobless and penniless again.

'Are you all right?' Rose asked when she sat down again.

'I'm coming down with some hideous virus, I'm afraid. New York's out for me. I'd be throwing up all over Manhattan.'

'OK,' Rose watched her closely, 'perhaps we can prevaricate for a little while. I'll keep you in touch.'

'Thanks, Rose.' Sal edged towards the door. 'I think I'm going to have to work at home till this passes. It all sounds very exciting.'

'Yes,' agreed Rose studying her more intently, 'yes it does, doesn't it?'

Claudia was feeling more cheerful. She had taken the decision to be nicer to Don instead of having a confrontation with him and to practice the dictum so beloved of agony aunts that they should spend more time together.

Her mother was a little better as well. The medication

seemed to be working and she had settled down. The only thing was, she was so much quieter than she had been and the irony was, Claudia still missed the old Olivia.

It was like the joke Woody Allen told in *Annie Hall*. A man walks into a psychiatrist's office and tells the doctor his brother thinks he's a chicken. When the doctor says, why don't you get him committed, the man shrugs and says, 'I would but I need the eggs.'

Somehow Claudia was finding the same thing. They needed her mother's manic energy like that man needed the eggs. Of course she couldn't admit this to anyone, not even to Don.

Instead of holding her mother back, she needed to find things for her to do. What with that and taking her dad to his physio appointments, plus the choir and the chance to get involved with Daniel's charity, life here was proving a lot busier than she'd expected.

She was about to leave to pick her father up when the phone rang. It was their daughter, Gaby, announcing that she was coming home for the weekend.

'How lovely,' Claudia said and meant it. It had been quite a while since Gaby had visited.

'How's Vito?'

'He's taken the country by storm. He was a wonderful present.'

'Not cowed by all the snooty setters?'

'He looks down on them from the basket of my friend Betty's scooter.'

'Mu-um . . . you're not turning that poor dog into a replacement child, I hope?'

Why ever not, thought Claudia, it was what most people did when their children left. She'd seen it time and time again. As soon as children stopped being a responsibility people got a dog and worried about that instead.

'By the way,' Gaby added tantalizingly. 'I've got a surprise for you.'

'A nice surprise?' Claudia wasn't sure she was up to a nasty one.

'*I* think so. You'll have to wait and see.'

Claudia put the phone down, bemused. There was a kind of suppressed excitement in Gaby's voice she'd never heard before.

'Who was that?' asked Don. There was a slight tone of anxiety in his tone. Had he thought it might be the mysterious Marianne?

'Gaby. She's coming home this weekend and she's got a surprise for us.'

'I hope she hasn't decided working for an architect's too dull and she wants to be an airline pilot or an astrophysicist. Did she give you any inkling?'

'None whatsoever.' She started to look for her car keys. 'I've just got to drop Dad at the cottage hospital. Then how about us taking Vito for a walk and a pub lunch later?'

'I'd love to but' – Don looked shifty – 'there's something I need to get on with.'

Claudia wondered whether to have it out then and there about why he was being so evasive all of a sudden but she would be late for her father. 'All right. See you later. Why don't we have supper early and watch a film?'

There was a moment's hesitation before he answered. 'Yes, that'd be nice.'

Her father's appointment went smoothly and he was declared to be making good progress. 'A bit more exercise would help, though,' insisted the physio. 'A short walk every day. Could you manage that?'

Len nodded but Claudia knew that without her mother's efficiency and energy to push him, he probably wouldn't. It was so sad that Olivia's energy seemed to be so tied up with her condition. They'd have to hope in time a happy medium could be achieved. For all their sakes.

Ella had spent a pleasant morning in the warm shed at the allotment wondering if it was too early to plant her sweet peas and thinking how best to try and make it up with Sal. The walk home was glorious with the real promise of warm weather to come. A swan was already building its nest on the bank.

She stopped for a moment watching a small bird with a twig in its beak that was almost bigger than itself.

The sun shone so brightly that she had to take her cardigan off for the first time this year.

Life felt good.

To her surprise she saw that there was someone sitting on the top of the stone steps outside her front door. It was her daughter Julia.

Her eyes were red and her hair unbrushed.

'For goodness' sake, darling, haven't you got a key?'

'You took it, Mum, don't you remember?'

Ella felt a flash of guilt that she'd been responsible for locking Julia out of her family home.

'Mum, I've left Neil.'

Ella's newfound optimism about her daughter's marriage evaporated like the morning mist. She'd really thought things might change for them. 'Oh, darling, come in. Quick!'

She opened the front door, too agitated to notice the usual aroma of beeswax mixed with the scent of lilies from the bunch on the hall table.

'Let's have a cup of tea. Come and tell me what happened.'

'Neil's just so petty-minded! He keeps watching me all the time as if I'm about to run off after Wenceslaus! He's like some little Hitler who just wants to guard his own possessions when he doesn't really value them anyway!'

'Aren't you being a bit harsh?' Ella was thinking of Neil's concern the other day for both Julia and their marriage. 'How do you know he doesn't value you?'

'Because he never bloody shows it! He's always out somewhere. I might as well be living on my own.'

Ella swirled the tea round in the pot. 'Have you said that to him, that you want to see more of him, spend some time together?'

'What's the point, Mum? It wouldn't make any bloody difference.'

'It might.'

'Why are you suddenly taking his side?' Julia looked at her suspiciously. 'You've never been able to stand him. You always made that quite obvious. Even the boys notice.' She stood up suddenly. 'You don't want me here!' she accused. 'I was always in the way! *Not now, Julia, I'm busy! Maybe later, Julia, now I just have to make this phone call.* Dad was the one who had time for us, not you!'

Ella cringed at the accuracy of that imitation of her. Poor little Julia.

'The thing is, he came round here.'

'Who came round here? You're not making sense.'

'Neil did. He came round to ask my advice.'

'Neil would never do that. You must have imagined it. What about, anyway?'

'How to make you happier, to try and keep your marriage together. Julia, he wasn't blaming you. I said I thought perhaps you were a bit lonely.'

'Well, it hasn't made a bloody bit of difference. He's actually disappeared off in the car today to close another sale.' Her eyes flashed with unshed tears. 'I'm not going back! If you won't have me, I'll find a bedsit or something.'

'Oh, darling, you can't have the boys in a bedsit!'

'You're beginning to sound like him! That's just the sort of thing Neil would say.'

She put her arm round Julia. 'You go and sit down. I'll see what I can rustle up for supper.'

But what she really wanted to do was scream: *'I'm too old for this! What is the matter with everyone? You should be looking after me!'*

But one truth was obvious to Ella and all her friends. Once you were a mother, you were always a mother.

After supper they watched TV and Ella noticed how Julia glanced at the clock and then at her bag, as if she expected her phone to ring at any time.

By 11.30 they were both yawning. 'Why don't you go up for a bath and I'll bring a hottie up to you?'

'Thanks, Mum, but I'm not a child, I'll be fine. Do you have a phone charger I could use now that you've joined the modern world?'

Julia found her iPhone charger and handed it over. She understood the hidden meaning in the request. Julia might say she wasn't going back to Neil, but she didn't want to miss a call from him all the same.

Once Julia had gone upstairs she made a hot water bottle for herself, the nights were still cold and it was the one indulgence she'd begun at Laurence's death to warm the gap left in their big bed.

Given Neil's concern at the state of their marriage, she was surprised he hadn't called. On the spur of the moment she rang their home number. Julia would kill her but then Julia wouldn't know. The tone rang and rang, not even switching to answering machine. Strange how desolate the sound of a phone not being answered could be.

Maybe Julia was right. Maybe the situation was beyond repair and Neil really had gone away.

She padded up the carpeted stairs and knocked on Julia's

door. When there no answer she opened it. Julia was fast asleep, the bedside light still on. Ella went in and sat for a moment on her bed. The trouble was, you might have a part in causing your children's problems but you could rarely solve them. What was it Larkin so famously wrote about your Mum and Dad fucking you up, even if they didn't mean to?

She thought of Harry and Mark, shuffled off to boarding school because their father wanted them to go, and how convinced he was that it would be the best thing for them. Why hadn't Julia put her foot down and said no, when she was the kind of mother who wanted them at home?

And was it their fault, hers and Laurence's, that Julia might seem strong yet hadn't been strong enough to fight against Neil's wishes?

When did the responsibility, or indeed the sense of fucking up, finish? When she was eighty and Julia fifty? Or would she still feel it on her deathbed?

The temptation to write a blog about it came down upon her and she had to shake it off sternly. No more blogging for Ella.

She kissed her daughter on the forehead and turned off the bedside light.

As she did so another thought came to her. She'd kept this big house not only for herself but for her daughters to come to if they needed a haven.

But was that altogether a good thing?

Laura woke up and instantly buried her head under the duvet. She was at a loss over what to do with Sam, and Nigel's breezy contribution about young men in Japan taking permanently to their beds had worried her more than she'd admitted. What if this was Sam's protest at how his parents had screwed up their marriage?

She sat up suddenly. There were unfamiliar sounds down-stairs. She could hear TomTom mewing to be let out, which meant that there was someone in the kitchen. Laura sniffed the air. Surely that was the unmistakeable smell of bacon frying?

For the briefest moment she thought maybe Simon had come back and was making one of his famous fry-ups.

Laura scrambled out of bed, dressed hurriedly and went downstairs.

The scene in the kitchen stopped her in her tracks.

Bella, her rapidly increasing bump camouflaged in an enormous sweater, sat at the kitchen table with TomTom, purring wildly, on her knee. Nigel, massive as ever and still Goth-like apart from the pinny he wore which bore the legend NEVER TRUST A SKINNY COOK, stood at the cooker in front of a frying pan, from which the glorious smells were emanating.

Also at the kitchen table, dressed in skinny jeans and a reasonably clean T-shirt, sat Sam.

The Cure's 'Just Like Heaven' blared out through Nigel's iPod dock.

'Hi, Mum.' Sam smiled, as if he hadn't been in bed for the last two weeks solid. 'Nige has got tickets for Bloody Dead and Sexy! To think, one of my favourite bands are playing in Hammersmith and I didn't even know!'

It took all Laura's strength of character not to fling her arms round Nigel's knees and declare him her guardian angel. She had no idea who Bloody Dead and Sexy were but she was grateful to them as well.

'Bacon butty?' enquired Nigel and plonked a doorstep of white bread filled with sizzling bacon on her plate.

Unsurprisingly, seeing as it was made by an angel, it tasted divine.

As she munched away, it suddenly struck Laura how misleading appearances could be. Simon, whom she had seen as a responsible husband and father, was off making babies with a work colleague, while an eighteen-stone Goth had taken the part of Victorian *pater familias*.

'And guess what?' Sam grinned. 'I've got an interview!'

'Sam, that's terrific,' Laura congratulated.

'Only trouble is, it's in Manchester.'

'Do you want me to drive you?' she asked between mouthfuls. This was such good news she'd go to any lengths to make sure he got there.

'Nige said he would.'

'In his van?'

It struck her that it was time Simon, Sam's actual dad, helped out instead of Nigel having to do it. After breakfast, when Sam had disappeared upstairs again, Laura rang him.

Reluctantly, Simon agreed he would come tomorrow and drive his son to his interview, moaning that he didn't see why Sam shouldn't get a train.

'But, Simon,' Laura pointed out. 'You're always saying you want to have more of a relationship with him.'

Even this one gesture of paternal responsibility clearly annoyed the hell out of Suki. Simon was hardly on their doorstep when she rang and shouted at him down the mobile.

'She wasn't very happy I'd agreed to do it,' Simon shrugged.

'I could hear that,' Laura replied. What a bitch, not even prepared to let Simon give his son some support after all he'd been through. Laura wished him good luck with her.

And Sam wasn't up yet, despite Laura taking him a cup of tea.

'Hello, Sam,' Simon greeted his son almost shyly when he did finally emerge looking surprisingly natty in a dark grey suit and narrow tie.

'Dad, what are you doing here?'

Simon looked nonplussed. 'Giving you a lift to Manchester.'

Sam shot a look at his mother.

'Sorry, Dad, but I'm going with Bella's boyfriend. He's coming any minute.'

He ran upstairs again to avoid arguing.

Simon looked livid. He turned to Laura. 'Did you deliberately set me up? I bet you knew he was going with that doofus all along.'

'I'm sorry, I thought it would be a chance for you to spend time together.'

'He clearly doesn't want to spend time with *me*. Thanks a lot. I suppose this is all about showing how important *you* are to the kids, while I'm the shit. Everyone's warned me about this, that you'd turn them against me and play the poor discarded wife. You can forget asking to stay here for his sake, I was a schmuck to even consider it. Suki was right. You're just preying on my emotions because it suits you. She was right about today too. She told me not to come, that I was just being used because it suited you.'

'Simon.' Laura lost all patience. She couldn't care less if Rowley had told her to be sweet and nice. 'Just fuck OFF!'

Simon turned on his heel and banged the door as he left, just as guilt and regret were beginning to sweep over Laura that she had let her temper make things worse for Bella and Sam.

'That went well,' commented Bella, who had been keeping out of sight in the sitting room.

'Yes, didn't it? Suki'll be happy, she didn't want him to come anyway.'

'How can she be so mean?'

'Either she's a cow, or she's not confident of him. Are you going with them?' she asked Bella.

'Nah. Boys' day out. I'm going to curl on the sofa and watch *Modern Family*.'

'Bella . . .'

'Yep?'

'Nigel's going to make a really good dad.'

'I could have told you that months ago, but you wouldn't have believed me.'

Laura put her arm round her daughter. 'You're right. I probably wouldn't.'

'Never mind,' Bella grinned, 'you're mellowing in your old age.'

'I'm having to challenge my assumptions,' Laura conceded. 'Take single mothers . . . I never expected at my time of life that I'd suddenly become one.'

'Join the club.'

Laura smiled. She felt so proud of her strong, feisty daughter. She had produced one child who would be all right no matter what. And maybe Sam would be all right too. Perhaps her marriage hadn't been such a complete waste after all.

'No word from Neil yet?' Ella wished she could do more to ease her daughter's unhappiness.

'No. Shows how much *he* cares.' Julia suddenly crumpled up on the kitchen table, her head buried in her arms.

Ella came and sat beside her and quietly began to stroke her hair.

'Have you tried ringing him?'

'His phone's switched off.'

'I'm sure there's some explanation. I'm certain he was serious when he was here the other day.'

Ella could hardly believe that she was actually trying to save their marriage. How many times had she loathed Neil and found herself wishing Julia would leave him? Now she had done so and Ella found herself pleading his case.

But Neil really *had* seemed to love Julia and want their marriage to survive. Maybe she should just keep her opinions to herself and let Julia and her husband sort it out for themselves.

'Why don't we do something nice and cheering? A walk by the river and a pub lunch? Or a spa day somewhere, if you'd prefer?'

'Mum,' Julia lifted her tear-stained face from the table, 'you can't cure everything with a spa day.'

Ella breathed in. She quite agreed and was just trying to be helpful, but she kept her mouth shut all the same. Neil was winning more of her sympathy with every moment that passed.

Sal looked at the sofa beckoning to her. She was still feeling sick despite her anti-nausea pills, and a morning curled up with daytime TV or a box set of the latest Swedish crime series was infinitely alluring. But she had some figures she needed to put together that Rose had requested. Reluctantly, she made herself a cup of disgusting green tea, said to be packed with immune-boosting substances, and settled down with her laptop.

An hour later she had finished and was able to turn to her printer with a sigh of satisfaction.

She had reckoned without the well-known malice of inanimate objects. As soon as she pressed 'Print' an error message informed her 'Printer Not Found'.

'Look,' yelled Sal, pointing straight at the printer, 'it's just there, right in front of you! Besides, you stupid fucking machine, don't you know I've got fucking cancer?'

Ella was wondering if she should take Julia a cup of tea or let her sleep when there was a knock on the front door. Still in her dressing gown, she opened it to find Harry, her eldest

Maeve Haran

grandson, standing on the doorstep, holding a bunch of 'Paper White' narcissi.

'Hello, Gran. Can I speak to Mum?' He leaned in to kiss Ella, towering over her, seeming to take up half the hall. Ella had forgotten how very tall he was, much taller than his father. And at nearly sixteen he probably had more growing to do.

'Hello, Harry darling, what a nice surprise! Your mum's upstairs in bed. I'm not sure she's awake yet. Are you starving? I've got some doughnuts in the kitchen.'

Harry was hesitating, torn between his mother and the doughnuts, when Julia dashed down the stairs and flung herself into his arms. 'Harry! What on earth are you doing here? Why aren't you at school?' She hugged him so tight he couldn't answer.

'Hi, Mum.' Harry flushed uneasily at all the unexpected emotion. There was clearly quite a lot of his father in him. 'Dad and I have been looking at sixth form colleges.'

Julia stood staring at him as the import of what he was saying finally got through to her.

'There's quite a good one in Chiswick, as a matter of fact; Dad and I really liked it.'

'But Dad's always been dead against you moving to day school for the sixth form.'

Harry shrugged. The ways of parents were always a mystery. 'He must have changed his mind. He was keener than me.'

Julia bit her lip, overcome with sudden emotion. 'Would you rather stay where you are?'

'I *thought* I would, but then I saw what a great place this was, just near home. The kids are really cool, and they get pretty good results, not as good as my school, but my school is a bit of a sausage factory. As Dad said, it isn't just about results.'

'Your dad said that?' Julia asked faintly.

'Do you disagree?' They turned to find Neil in the doorway.

'I'd have liked to have been consulted at least.' Julia's face took on the mulish, slightly petulant look her mother knew could lead to trouble. 'I mean, he is my son too.'

Harry looked anxiously from one parent to the other.

'Julia!' Ella decided that, popular or not, it was time to interfere. 'Stop it!'

She shooed Harry into the kitchen in search of doughnuts and left them alone together. If her daughter hadn't got the sense to accept this olive branch, then there was nothing more Ella could do. She just hoped for Julia's sake, and her own, that she would give her marriage another chance.

Laura, on the other hand, had given her marriage all the chances she felt it deserved. Maybe it had been a mistake to try and get Simon to take Sam to Manchester, but she had not done it to set him up, as he had suggested. How much of an unpleasant bitch did he take her for? He was beginning to think like this Suki. And as for her, what kind of marriage breaker resents her partner for taking the son he's abandoned for an interview? And now the whole plan to stay in the house for Sam's sake was up the creek. Terrific.

She was still fuming when she got to LateExpress.

'Hello, Mrs Minchin, top of the morning to you,' Mr A greeted her cheerily. Not eliciting the usual 'And to you too' response, he decided to give her a wide berth, a lesson he had learned from trying and failing to pacify Mrs A when she was in a tetchy mood and he was being bellowed at for his sins.

The result was that Laura had a reasonably peaceful morning, part of which she spent trying to calm her temper in the stock room. This largely worked, and she was more herself by the time she emerged for the school rush at midday.

Sadly, it didn't last. Mr A had tried various strategies to manage the sudden invasion by several hundred hungry and boisterous children who, despite Jamie Oliver's efforts to interest them in healthy fare, were boycotting school dinners for a Coke-and-chocolate-bar.

Two-at-a-time in the shop was partly successful but resulted in a long queue of noisy teens shouting and skittering about on the pavement. For some reason, today the commotion was greater than usual.

'Mrs Minchin, can you go outside to those children and reason with them?' Mr A requested. 'They only laugh at me and mock my funny accent.'

Reluctantly, Laura agreed. She could already see that the kids at the back of the queue were deliberately blocking the way of an old lady who was attempting to get to the cash machine, which happened to be the other side of the threatening river of schoolchildren. Another group, whose ringleader was familiar to her, had stolen a cabbage from the greengrocer next door and was playing football with it.

'Here, Tone, give us the ball!' shouted his mate.

Tone duly kicked the cabbage so hard it winded another spectator waiting peaceably in line.

'OK,' Laura took on the persona of her former headmistress, a bluestocking of the old school who inspired fear in every pupil, 'that is enough! You may think you're very clever but you may have noticed that this is the only shop within half a mile of your school – apart from the greengrocer next door, which only sells cabbages such as Tony here is kicking with such consummate lack of skill.'

They all laughed slightly nervously, not sure who to support, Laura or her antagonist.

'If we ban you all, which I can assure you we are seriously contemplating, you will be condemned to raw cabbage or school dinners. The choice is yours. But bhaji butties, Coke and Mars bars will be off the menu, so I suggest you start behaving in an orderly fashion.'

Out of the corner of her eye, Laura could see Tony get out a penknife and head towards Mr A's shiny BMW, the pride of his universe and his main reason for living. Laura whipped out her phone and in an outbreak of tech-savvy that would have impressed her own children, took a video of him, penknife raised.

She strode towards him. 'Right, you little shit,' she murmured so no one else could hear them, 'I've got you on camera. If I catch you making trouble here again, I'm handing it to the police, OK?'

Tony stumped off, tossing his head like a camp prima donna. One or two of the more daring clapped.

Laura, still disguised as her headmistress, decided on tactical withdrawal.

'Very good, Mrs Minchin,' congratulated Mr A, 'were you ever teacher?'

'To be honest, Mr A,' confessed Laura, 'I was always the naughty one at the back of the class.'

Laura hid herself back in the stockroom until the queue outside had dispersed then emerged to choose herself a sandwich. She was just weighing the merits of falafel versus fajita when she became aware of a well-dressed woman standing just behind her. A quick glance informed her that at least she wasn't from Simon's office.

'Hello,' the woman greeted her. 'I wondered if I could have a word?'

Suddenly Laura panicked. Had this woman heard her threaten that horrible kid? Was she a lawyer claiming Laura had breached his human rights? Or someone from the school, sent to complain? Maybe Tony had gone back and made an allegation against her.

The woman was still speaking. 'My name's Helena Butler. I work for the FoodCo Group. I was really impressed with how you handled that group of children out there.' Relief flooded through Laura. Thank God for that. 'I just wanted to give you my card. We have a lot of problems with kids in our inner-city stores and if you ever felt like a chat, we could see where it led to. What do you do here?'

'I'm an assistant.'

'I'm surprised; you're obviously management material.'

Laura almost giggled. She'd been in much more exalted jobs before she married, but then that was years ago.

'I only work part time. Family responsibilities.'

'Quite. Well, call me if you ever feel like a change. I can't promise anything but I'd do my best. The more women in management the better. Look, maybe I'll take your number, if you don't mind. You never know when something'll come up.' She smiled as Laura wrote it down, selected a sandwich with commendable decisiveness and said goodbye.

Laura watched her go, pretending to straighten the card stand. She turned to find Mr A looking at her thoughtfully.

Don and Claudia both stood on the platform at Minsley station waiting for Gaby to arrive. Minsley was looking its best; Claudia realized that she actually felt quite proud of it. There were snowdrops everywhere in the hedgerows and yesterday she had spotted the first primrose in the bank opposite their house. It was getting lighter and there was a sense of change in the air, of nature becoming busy and productive. That eternal, irresistible optimism was returning to the world.

The train, packed with commuters rushing home for the weekend, actually arrived two minutes early.

They looked out eagerly for Gaby's face among the crowds, three deep, swarming towards them across the platform.

They were beginning to wonder if, Gaby-like, she had missed it, when they saw her, at the very back of the crowd, walking along beside a tall, fair-haired young man. They were arm in arm.

'Hi, Mum, hi, Dad,' she sparkled at them, as fizzy as shaken champagne. 'I'd like you to meet Douglas. As a matter of fact, we've just got engaged, so I suppose I ought to say, Mum and Dad, meet my fiancé.'

CHAPTER 21

Laura stuck Helena's card up on the pin board in the kitchen, next to the reminders to buy cat food, and the one from the dental hygienist. She had to admit visits to the hygienist had joined waxing and massages as something that could be economized on. Pedicures and hairdresser's appointments, on the other hand, struck her as inalienable rights which could not be abandoned until total penury set in.

And now there was a letter from Simon's solicitors to look forward to. Laura decided a stiff drink was needed first.

Simon, it turned out, was as good, or as bad, as his word. His lawyers had lost no time in reminding her that as soon as the decree nisi was granted the house should be put on the market.

Harbouring fantasies of nailing herself in and refusing to move, Laura sat at the kitchen table with a calculator and pad. She needed to know exactly what she had, which was about eight thousand pounds of her own money, plus the money she'd invested for each child by putting their Child Benefit into a savings account. They didn't even know she had done this and she had intended to give it to each of them when they really needed it. In recent months the temptation to raid it had been severe, but so far she'd resisted. Apart from that she had a couple of savings plans of her own and a hundred premium bonds her dad had given her. Otherwise that was it. And out of that, plus whatever financial settlements they came to, she had to pay Rowley Robinson and meet any other costs.

It was time she stopped avoiding asking exactly how much it would be. Steeling herself, she dialled his office. 'Rowley, I've heard from Simon's lawyers. They want the house to go on the market after the decree nisi. Can they do that?'

'I'm afraid they can, yes,' Rowley replied.

'And when will the decree be?'

'In six or eight weeks depending on how busy the court is.'

Laura's stomach lurched. It sounded so soon.

'We need to get down to the financial settlement so I'll need all your household incomings and outgoings, investments,' Rowley explained.

'Ha!'

'Earnings . . .'

'Ha! Ha! I earn less than your cleaner, as you said. How does the court work it out?'

'Roughly according to your need and his capacity to pay.'

'Which he's already saying is reduced because the Sperm-digger doesn't want to work after the baby.'

Rowley ignored this jibe. 'They'll also consider your standard of living before the break-up, both your earning capacities, age, your right to a share of his pension, and come up with something fair.'

'Thanks, Rowley. By the way, I need to have a clear idea of what I'll be paying you.'

'Of course. I can give you an idea of how much so far. It shouldn't be much more after this.'

She put the phone down. What had she been hoping? That he would magically say, 'Laura, you're a mate of Ella's. No charge.' This was a man oligarchs consulted, for God's sake.

Laura decided to do a little research of her own. She was amazed to find a free website for separating couples called Wikivorce and even the *Huffington Post* had a whole section on the subject. How had she not known quite what a tsunami of separation there was out there?

Six to eight weeks.

In six to eight weeks she would have to put her house on the market and show happy couples round her home. And where would she move to? What would she be able to afford until the sale of the house had gone through and maintenance from Simon had been agreed which, she suspected, he would find every way he could to reduce? The job at LateExpress had been enjoyable and good for her confidence, it had helped her get through the pain of Simon leaving, but it was barely above the minimum wage. The cruel thing about marriage break-up at her age was that it reduced your life to the bare minimum. All the little luxuries: decent clothes, eating out, weekends away, the odd taxi, were stripped away.

For a wild moment she thought about starting a divorce blog, but she could hardly blackball Ella then do the same thing herself. The phone rang, jangling into her pleasant thoughts of revenge and ritual humiliation.

It was her daughter Bella, but with none of her usual feisty confidence.

'Mum?' She sounded panicked. 'Mum, I really don't feel at all well.'

Laura's maternal instincts kicked in, just as if Bella were a small child again. 'Where's Nigel? Is he there with you?'

'I can't get hold of him. He's got Parents Evening at his new school and his phone's off.'

'Tell me your symptoms.'

'My head hurts and I feel dizzy. And it's really weird, my hands are swollen. Mum, I just feel awful.'

Laura thought fast. She had no idea what this was, just that her daughter never complained and here she was pregnant and needing her help. 'Call an ambulance. I'll be right round.'

She grabbed her car keys and ran to the door. This was the first time, she realized as she drove to Bella's, that she'd seen the baby as a reality, but it was her daughter she was most concerned about. Giving birth was still one of life's most unpredictable experiences, no matter what the childcare gurus told you.

The ambulance was outside Bella's flat by the time she arrived. Bella, in grey jersey pyjamas, was being helped down the front steps. She looked terrifyingly young and vulnerable.

'Mum!' Laura almost wept at the touching relief in Bella's voice. 'Thank heavens you're here. Can you come with me to the hospital?'

To Laura's immense relief they didn't have to sit in A & E with the drunks, broken-limb victims and home improvers who'd chopped off half their thumbs, but were taken straight to the maternity area where Bella was given blood and urine tests.

'Pre-eclampsia,' pronounced the doctor when they finally got to see her. 'I'm afraid it means you'll have to stay in hospital so we can monitor you and the baby as well.'

Ella waved them off: Julia, Neil and Harry all together. She had no idea if the marriage would work out, but she was relieved they were giving it a try.

She also had to admit she felt partly responsible for some of its difficulties. She had recognized that streak of stubbornness in Julia, the inflexibility she'd had since childhood, and which Ella had always failed to confront because she was too busy. Neil might be difficult but Julia could be hard work too.

She was impressed that Neil had made such a major

compromise over their sons' schooling, and even more than that he had worn the sacrifice lightly, with no hint of blackmail or blaming. He was hardly Mr Darcy, but then Ella suspected Mr Darcy would have been a complete pain to live with. Jane Austen had saddled the nation's women with a fairly dodgy role model. All that stiff-necked pride and snooty superiority. Lovely Lizzie Bennet would have had her work cut out keeping him cheerful. Personally, she'd only have given them two years at Pemberley, one if her mother moved in.

As for Julia and Neil, Julia had to start engaging with her own life rather than fantasizing about another one with a stranger like Wenceslaus. A job might help too.

Ella found herself thinking about Wenceslaus. She had really enjoyed having him live here. Her daughters might have been shocked that she'd taken in someone random and unconnected to her, but that was precisely his appeal. She didn't have to feel responsible for Wenceslaus. And she could be straight with him without him going into a huff or accusing her of guilt-tripping. She wondered where he was living now. Maybe she'd pop into the café again and find out.

She glanced around. It was another beautiful day. Spring had definitely arrived. The catkins were out in the garden and the birds were singing their spring symphonies. She would put on her boots and walk down to the canal. Viv and Angelo had come up with the idea of her taking over the allotment permanently, if unofficially. She didn't think any of the others would shop her for circumventing the long waiting list. One of the aspects she most liked about the place was its easy camaraderie.

And another thing, the allotments had given her life a shape and a purpose it had needed. She had learned to see the annual calendar as a farmer or plantsman would: the autumn was the true beginning of the year when seeds were sown and bulbs planted. The winter wasn't dead but the time of hidden growth deep down in the cold soil. Spring brought the first gifts of fruition and also of promise. Summer was the high point, almost pagan in its light and abundance, the glory of sunshine and of shadow. Although, this being England, there hadn't been too much sunshine lately. And then there was autumn again, with all its Keatsian ripeness and oozings.

On top of that there was the joy of eating what you had grown yourself. Once she'd laughed at people for growing their own – why, she'd wondered, didn't they just buy stuff in the supermarket like normal people? But that was before she felt an almost maternal pride at her first knobbly carrot. And now she couldn't imagine life without the allotments. How had that happened?

As she let herself in through the gates and surveyed the busy, productive strips of land, she found herself intoning a silent prayer: let Julia and Neil be happy and let her find something to make her as busy and peaceful as this place has made me.

'Did you have the slightest inkling about this Douglas?' Don demanded as soon as Gaby had disappeared upstairs with him to take him on a tour of the house.

'None. Not a whisper. She's never even mentioned him before.'

'How long have they known each other?'

'I don't know that either; she's being incredibly mysterious about the whole thing.'

They looked at each other, struck by the same thought. Gaby had always been given to sudden starts and enthusiasms. Her endless string of jobs, not to mention short-term boyfriends, had left them wishing she would settle at something. Marriage hadn't exactly been what they meant.

'Do you think they're really serious about this engagement?'

Before Claudia had time to answer Gaby reappeared, holding her surprise fiancé by the hand. Claudia had to admit there was a glow about her that her mother had never seen before.

Maybe it's called Love and you've just forgotten what it looks like, Claudia mused. The sudden memory of Thierry and her heady days in Paris invaded her memory. But surely that had been mad infatuation, not love. Had she felt anything like that for her husband? He had been fierier in his youth, once he'd serenaded her with his own version of Dire Straits's 'Romeo and Juliet', but over the years she'd got into the habit of seeing him as Dependable Don.

Instead of stretching the planned supper to feed four, Don suggested they go and eat in the pub.

It proved a jolly evening. Douglas was, it transpired, a trainee architect who had completed about three quarters of his professional qualifications.

'We want to try and build our own house when we're married,' gushed Gaby. 'It'd be so much cheaper than buying one. *Your* generation got all the cheap property. If we could just find a little bit of land we could get started.'

'And when do you plan to get married? Or is that all a long way in the future?' Claudia imagined with Douglas's training taking another couple of years it would probably be a lengthy engagement which, given how short a time they had known each other, would surely be a good thing.

'June,' announced Gaby, standing back after she'd dropped the bombshell.

'*June?*' Both her parents echoed in unison. 'What, *this* June?'

'Exactly,' confirmed Gaby. 'And we'd like to get married here in Minsley. Douglas's parents retired to Australia and that's so far none of our friends would be able to come, so we thought Minsley would be perfect.'

Claudia was still recovering from the shock.

'Maybe we could nip down and look at the parish church tomorrow, Mum?'

'But Dad and I don't go to church.'

'Neither do we. I don't see what that's got to do with it. I just feel marriages in church are more likely to last. You got married in church, presumably?'

'Registry office, actually. We met in the Sixties, remember, or maybe it was the Seventies?'

'Your brain is probably addled by all those drugs. I'd forgotten you were dangerous radicals. Didn't Dad get arrested?'

'For legitimate protest,' Don insisted to Douglas.

What a long time ago it all seemed.

'You wouldn't want us to do that, though, would you?'

'What, get arrested?'

'Get married in a registry office. If it were church, your friend Ella could do the flowers; she's very into nature, as I recall.'

'Mainly vegetables, as a matter of fact.'

'Maybe we could have a vegetable theme; that'd be quite a laugh, wouldn't it, hon?'

'Yes, it would,' Douglas agreed, looking deeply dubious.

'Look,' Gaby offered generously, 'we'd like a smallish wedding in church with the reception in the garden, then, in the evening, you could invite all *your* friends – the coven would have to come – we'll have a *huge* party in the orchard full of all your oldie mates. That's fair, isn't it?'

Claudia could see Don was calculating the cost.

'That sounds lovely.' Claudia had to admit this was a generous offer, even if they were paying for it. How many people these days let their parents invite their own friends?

Claudia noticed someone waving from the corner by the bar. It was Betty. Claudia went over to her and invited her to join them.

'Betty, this is Gaby, my daughter, and her fiancé Douglas. They've just announced their surprise engagement.'

Claudia raised her eyebrow a millimetre and knew that Betty would instantly understand.

'Wonderful, this calls for champagne!'

'Betty, you mustn't,' Claudia began.

'Nonsense, I won at bingo yesterday. Though heaven alone knows what the champagne will be like here.'

'Betty knows a thing or two about champagne. She used to be a Bluebell Girl.'

'What's a Bluebell Girl?' asked Gaby.

'A chorus girl at the Paris Lido. All high-kicks and feathers. They were incredibly famous.'

'Wow. Cool. Like Kylie Minogue on tour.' The champagne arrived and they all toasted the engaged couple.

Claudia suddenly noticed Daniel was in the pub as well. He was raising his glass in a silent toast.

'Who's the handsome old geezer at the bar?' Gaby whispered. 'Not your secret lover, I hope.'

'No secrets in a village like this,' Betty boomed. 'Everyone knows who's doing what to whom even before they do it. Now,' to Claudia's gratitude she changed the subject swiftly, 'where did you two lovebirds meet?'

There was a brief silence before Douglas answered for both of them.

'On the Internet. It's where everyone meets these days.'

Claudia suppressed her shock. She'd always thought it was oddballs and losers who met that way. Sal had had various online romances and they had all been disastrous.

'You don't have to waste all that time meeting people in bars and then finding you don't like them,' Gaby enthused. 'When you meet online you can hook up with someone you're really suited to.'

'Ah.' Betty nodded. 'The trouble was, I never fell for anyone I was remotely suited to.'

'Who knows,' Claudia pointed out, trying to put a positive spin on things, even though she was shocked, 'our generation didn't do so well, did we, with all that divorce? Maybe finding each other on the Internet will be a better bet.'

'Yes,' Betty persisted, 'but what about eyes meeting across a crowded room and all that?'

'There's still Speed Dating, I suppose,' consoled Gaby. 'That's face to face.'

'I am very, very glad I'm too old for speed dating,' announced Betty.

The next morning, Gaby was as good as her word. Instead of staying in bed till noon, she was up by nine and sitting at the kitchen table with her iPad. 'I thought we could nip down and have a look at the church this morning and then check out this place that does amazing marquee hire. It's called the Flying Carpet Company. Look, Mum,' she pointed out the exotic desert tent on her screen, 'they can set up tents to seat a hundred, with bar and dance floor included, and it's only four thousand seven hundred pounds!'

Claudia caught Don's eye across the cereal. They hadn't even talked about who was going to pay for this surprise wedding, or how much it might cost.

If they were shocked by that there were more surprises in store. They were stunned at the sight of their daughter Gaby transformed into Bridezilla, devoting her every waking moment to venues and guest lists, party favour websites and bridesmaids outfits.

Claudia kept trying to find a chance to talk to Douglas and to get to know him a bit. 'Fancy a stroll with me and Vito into the village, Douglas?' she enquired hopefully.

Douglas said he had a few emails to catch up with.

'I'll come!' Gaby announced. 'Isn't he absolutely gorgeous?' she demanded as soon as they were out of earshot.

'He seems very nice, but how long have you actually known him?'

'Long enough to know that I want to spend the rest of my life with him. Look, Mum, this isn't one of my endless enthusiasms. He's fun, and serious, he cares about the same things I do, we talk endlessly, we both want children . . .'

Claudia had to admit that did sound promising.

'But why get married? Couldn't you just live together?'

'Get you; you really are an old hippie, aren't you? Most parents would jump at the idea of marriage. Look at the statistics: people who're married stay together longer than if they just live together.' She stopped and stared at Claudia. 'You're just frightened we'll get divorced, aren't you, and that'll be more hassle than if we just cohabit?'

This was so true that Claudia was embarrassed to even admit it.

'Well, we won't, OK?' And with that Gaby was able to turn her full attention to what really mattered: the search for The Dress.

'Do you mind if we come down again next weekend, Mum?' she asked gaily. 'There's a Wedding Fayre at Igden Manor I'd like to check out.'

Claudia gave a thought to the phlegmatic fiancé and wondered how he was taking all of this. She just hoped he didn't wait till the wedding day and then disappear off to an unknown destination. To be frank, she wouldn't blame him. She'd quite like to herself.

'How are we going to pay for all this?' Don asked Claudia in bed that night. 'There's been no mention of his lot chipping in, I see. I'd have thought in this day and age they might come up with half.'

'Traditionally, it's the bride who pays, or sometimes, if they're earning enough, the couple themselves, but that isn't Gaby or Douglas.'

'But we're old retired people on a fixed income,' Don moaned. 'Besides, she's only known him five minutes. How do we know the marriage is going to last?'

'We don't. We have to trust them. We'll just have to find it from the downsizing money. If I was prepared to leave London, even though I didn't want to, we should at least be prepared to pay for our daughter's wedding.'

'Well, I think she should pay for it herself.'

'Oh, Don, for God's sake, be realistic. Remember what they all tell us: we were the lucky ones who had cheap houses and lots of jobs.'

'Well, I don't feel lucky.' Don turned his back and when Claudia tentatively put a hand on his back to make peace, he shook her off.

Sal splashed cold water on her face, combed the wig and reapplied her make-up with extra care. One of her fellow patients had told her about eyebrow tattooing and she'd had her eyeliner done for good measure. It was expensive but so effective and morale-boosting it had to be worth it.

When she had arrived at the office in Kensal Green, she headed through reception at *New Grey* and on towards her office.

'Oh, Ms Grainger, Sal,' the receptionist called to her, 'there's a young woman to see you.'

'What's her name?' Sal wasn't expecting anyone and she certainly wasn't in the mood to chat with some hopeful who'd dropped in on the off chance of a job or a commission.

The receptionist consulted her log. 'Her name is Lara Olsen.'

Sal shrugged. She didn't know anyone of that name and she was much too busy; besides, she felt like the living dead. She also had an urgent meeting in less than half an hour. 'Could you tell her I can't see her? I'm very sorry, but I'm really pushed today. Ask her to make an appointment to come another time.'

Sal glanced across at the very moment the unexpected visitor looked up and smiled.

She was around forty, conservatively dressed, slim and neat, with blonde hair and startling pale blue-green eyes.

Sal thought for a moment she might faint, and this time it was nothing to do with the cancer.

They were eyes that she would never forget. Except that, back then, they had been on someone completely different.

CHAPTER 22

'Ms Olsen? Lara?'

Keep calm, Sal told herself, her heart beating wildly, *you could be imagining this.* Yet some deep and unshakeable instinct told her that she wasn't, that this was a moment she had been waiting for ever since she had left Oslo all those years ago.

She could see that the meeting room at the end of the corridor was empty and suggested they go there.

With quiet self-possession the young woman got up and followed her.

Once inside, Sal closed the door.

They stood for a moment in complete silence.

Finally, it was Lara who spoke first. 'I am so sorry to arrive like this out of the blue.' Her English was flawless, almost unaccented, only something in the rhythm could have indicated she was foreign. 'Only I wondered if I could ask you a couple of questions?'

'What about?' Sal felt panic rush towards her, knocking her from her feet, threatening to pull her under. It was too much! She wasn't strong enough for this.

'You will see. I am sorry to be so mysterious.'

'Ask away.' Sal's throat was drying up with the tension.

'Were you an au pair in Oslo in 1969?'

Sal looked away. She was ill. Maybe seriously ill. She was holding her life together by a thread. She had no energy or emotion to spare. Every last drop was needed just for survival.

'No.' She could see the desperate hope in Lara's eyes, yet couldn't respond to it.

'A language student, then?'

'No.' I'm *sorry, Lara, I can't do this!*

'You did not live with a family in Oslo named Bergsen?'

Sal was beginning to feel dizzy and feared she might faint. The old cruel symptoms of nausea and hunger were back. Her hands and feet felt like ice.

She shook her head.

Lara's eyes fixed on hers for what seemed an endless moment. Despite her self-possession, Sal could see the stark need, the lifelong desire for authentication and identity.

Lara held out a hand. 'I am sorry I have wasted your time. There must have been a misunderstanding.' She picked up her shoulder bag and her coat. 'Goodbye.' She held Sal's gaze for one final moment as if she might add something more. 'And good luck.'

As Lara walked quickly from the room, not looking back, Sal's hand half lifted in a gesture of protest and appeal, then fell back again. She sat down heavily, held on to the table and wept, unaware of time passing.

She wept for the fear she had tried so hard to keep at bay, for the loneliness of holding it inside and not sharing it even with Ella or Claudia or Laura, her closest friends, and lastly for the hole in her life where love and family might have been if things had been different.

And here, today, she had been offered a chance to fill that chasm and she had been too frightened to take it.

The insanity of her response suddenly overwhelmed her.

I've had poison pumped into my veins, I've lost my hair, felt worse than I have in my whole life, and now I've been offered this incredible gift and I turned it down; am I completely nuts?

She rushed out of the room to the reception desk at the front of the office.

'My visitor! Is she still here?'

The receptionist looked blank.

'Youngish, short blonde hair . . .'

'Ms Olsen? She left about five minutes ago. She asked for directions to the tube.'

Sal ran out into the street as if Lara might still be visible but there was no sign of her. She had vanished into the crowds and Sal had no idea where she was staying or even where she lived.

'Are you all right, Sally?' asked Michael Williams, who was on his way out to a meeting. 'You're looking incredibly pale.'

Sal willed herself not to faint. 'Yes, thanks, Michael, I'm fine.'

She walked back to her office, despair dogging her footsteps.

It was too late.

The rest of the morning passed in a blur of regret and misery, which she disguised, as she so often did, in intense activity.

Just after one, her assistant arrived with her order from the enterprising young man who came round on his bike every morning with a big hamper of freshly made sandwiches.

'I've brought fruit salad as well. Michael said you were looking peaky.'

Sal smiled her thanks.

The girl put down a dog-eared business card next to the fruit salad.

'What on earth's that?' queried Sal.

'The visitor you were trying to find. Liz on reception says to tell you she got it wrong. The lady didn't go by tube after all. She came back and asked for a minicab. Your friend Ricky had left his card so they phoned his lot. She said she'd meet him round the corner.'

Sal jumped up, leaving her lunch untouched and reached for her mobile. 'Ricky, it's Sally Grainger. Could you do me a favour? Find out who picked up a woman with short blonde hair near our offices this morning and where they took her?'

'Important, is it?' Ricky enquired. 'Only you sound a bit agitated. Mind you take care now.'

'You've always been my minicab driver in shining armour. I can't tell you what tracking down this lady would mean to me.'

'I'll do my best.' Ricky whistled. 'You do know we have forty drivers?'

Laura sat at Bella's bedside in the ante-natal unit and found herself sucked into the heightened reality of hospital life. It had been so long since she'd given birth that she had forgotten the camaraderie of the labour ward, with its powerfully female atmosphere, where the midwives were treated with far greater respect, and their opinions valued far more than any male doctor, no matter how eminent. Giving birth remained, as it had always been, a female rite of passage.

Bella, itching to be at home, and feeling much better, was a restless patient but as long as her blood pressure and urine levels remained so high, the obstetrician insisted she ought to stay in hospital to avoid risks either to herself or the baby.

The only treatment for pre-eclampsia, it transpired, was giving birth. Bella would have to stay in hospital till her baby came.

Mr A, probably leaned on by Mrs A, proved very understanding in letting Laura take time off so that she could stay at Bella's bedside.

The daytime ticked slowly by watching *Come Dine With Me* and DVDs on Bella's laptop. Sometimes patients from the other beds would gather round, and it was like a mini-cinema to watch with them. To vary the monotony, Laura ventured out and came back with biscuits and cakes and handed them round the small ward. Now and then Sam came in with a takeaway. He hadn't got the Manchester job but he seemed much more cheerful and more confident at last.

'I'd like to call Dad,' Laura announced, not sure how Bella would take it. 'I think he ought to know you're in hospital.'

'Your mum's got a point,' seconded Nigel, who came straight from work every day. 'He is your father after all.'

'No, he's not. Not since he left, he's not.'

Laura wished her experience with the baby might have softened Bella towards Simon but there was no point in arguing.

The other impact of her daughter being in hospital was that it took Laura's mind off the reality of putting the house on the market. Despite her anxiety, this was a welcome relief – for now at least.

Ella sat in the car, experiencing one of the most frightening moments of her life. She had sat down, put her bag in the well in front of the passenger seat as she always did and then for a split second she hadn't known what to do next. The memory that this was the brake, that the accelerator, this the gear stick, things as second-nature as breathing, completely deserted her.

And then, after only a matter of seconds, they came back and she turned on the engine.

Had she really forgotten, even for the briefest moment, how to drive a car? Maybe it was time to visit the GP and discuss her memory lapses.

A rap on the passenger window brought her back to reality and she realized that she had parked outside the allotments. She remembered now. She had taken the car because she wanted to bring home the strimmer to use in her garden at home.

Bill stood grinning at her in his bobble hat, which seemed welded to his head in summer and winter.

'In a bit of a dream, were you?' Bill asked, opening the door for her.

'Thanks, Bill. Yes, I was.'

'Are you all right? You look a bit pale-like?'

'It was the weirdest thing,' Ella found herself confessing. 'I sat there and I couldn't think what to do next.'

Bill took in her worried tone.

'And you wondered if you were going gaga? First signs of dementia and all that?'

'Yes, actually,' Ella admitted.

'The way I look at it is this. My old dad kept forgetting the name of things. He'd hold up a fork and say, "What's this called?" I got so worried I took him to the doctor and do you know what the doctor said?'

Ella shook her head.

'The doctor said to my dad, "Arthur," that was my dad's name, Arthur, "don't worry if you can't remember the name of a fork. Come back and see me when you can't remember what the bloody hell a fork's *for!*'

Ella grinned. 'Let's hope your dad's doctor's right. At least I can remember what a car's for.'

Claudia was doing her best to enter into the wedding madness. It was so odd the way generations reacted. Her own had rebelled against white weddings and dashed headlong to the registry office or decided not to marry at all, convinced that a piece of paper was no guarantee of enduring love. And now here was Gaby in full meringue mode, ready to spend three months' salary on a dress she'd wear once, enlisting four bridesmaids to clothe in matching tulle and spending hours on the Internet tracking down pistachio-coloured wraps that would match their shoes. She was even considering Vito as a ring-bearer.

Sometimes she worried about Douglas, the prospective bridegroom. She hoped it was the man Gaby was choosing, not the Flying Carpet marquee and the designer wedding dress. She knew a lot of Gaby's friends were getting married and that, just as there was something called a 'baby chain' when they all fell pregnant one after another, there might be a wedding chain. She hoped Gaby wasn't another link in it.

Don had reacted by decreeing a budget which he would pay for, then absenting himself from the proceedings. At least he hadn't railed against the waste and extravagance and worked out how many light bulbs could be run on the champagne or suggested they hold the reception at the dump.

'Mum,' Gaby wafted into the kitchen, bearing the white iPad that accompanied her every waking moment, 'you've got to look at this! For not much extra you can get a bridal boudoir for your wedding night! They kit it out like a sheik's tent in the desert. Wouldn't that be the most romantic thing in the whole world?'

'We're already pushing the budget to its limits with a sit-down dinner and dancing. I'm pretty sure it won't run to sheik's tents. Have you asked Douglas what he thinks?'

'Oh, he won't care. He's happy to leave it all to me. Come on, Mum, you only get married once.'

Claudia didn't snap: 'I think you'll find that's no longer the case. Especially when you only met five minutes ago on the Internet', but that was what she was thinking.

'You really can't help yourself, can you?' Gaby flashed, seeing her mother's expression. 'Just because you and Dad have been worried ever since you moved here, you can't imagine anyone else will be happy! I'm going to look at the bridal boudoir whether you're coming or not!'

Rather than scream in frustration Claudia grabbed the dog and headed off for a walk. Halfway down the village street she bumped into Betty who was on her scooter, accompanied by Daniel Forrest.

'You look down in the dumps,' Betty greeted her.

'Is it that obvious?'

'It's either that or you're trying to strangle that poor animal.'

Claudia glanced down to find that Vito's lead was caught round his neck and she was inadvertently throttling him. 'I'm sorry. It's all this wedding fever. It's driving me nuts. My daughter is planning to spend the gross national product of Brazil in a single day on tents and monogrammed napkins.'

'Come with us to Sing Out,' Daniel suggested. 'Nothing like meeting a bunch of young offenders to take your mind off marquees and menus.'

Claudia had a hundred things to do but she realized how much she wanted to go. It might restore her sanity. Besides, there was still plenty of time till the wedding.

'I'll just take the dog home.'

'Bring him along. He's just what we need to break the ice with the reluctant youth.'

'Can you take a dog into a young offenders' institution?'

'Probably not, but there's been a change of plan. We're meeting in a community centre instead.'

When they arrived at the dingy venue on the outskirts of Dorking, a dozen or so unenthusiastic teens were already waiting. They all wore Hi-Vis waistcoats in Day-Glo colours, apparently for their own safety as they'd just been litter-picking. None of them looked up.

Then one of the girls spotted Vito.

'Isn't he gorgeous!' she yelped. 'Can I pick him up?'

Claudia had never seen Daniel out of his rarefied middle-class element before and she was amazed. Not only was he right about Vito, but he also produced exactly the right tone, upbeat and friendly without being patronizing, to win over these spiky youngsters who had no reason to trust adults, most of whom had let them down or worse.

Daniel divided them into the ones who could sing along with their own music and the ones who could dance. He then threw the officials into a tizzy by swapping their waistcoats so that the singers had one colour and the dancers another. The waistcoats instantly became the badge of their group rather than an imposition by authority.

He got out his iPad, downloaded the lyrics for 'Officer Krupke' from *West Side Story*, and suggested they do their own updated version of this witty paean to anti-authority.

The version they came up with was both clever and funny. Claudia clapped and clapped. Seeing the energy and enthusiasm of these kids had been the perfect antidote. And so had spending time with Daniel.

'You ain't too bad for an old bloke,' congratulated one of the youths as they parted.

'What do you reckon?' Daniel asked as they headed for the car.

'Fabulous. I really enjoyed it.'

'You should come again next time,' he suggested. 'You're wasted in Minsley.'

'Yes,' agreed Claudia, ignoring the flashing signs of danger, 'I think I'd really like to.'

Sal came out of her bedroom after a sleepless night to find the doorbell ringing insistently.

'Yes, who is it?' she barked into the intercom.

'Delivery for you.'

Sal shrugged. She wasn't expecting anything. She opened the front door to find Ricky Reliable holding a bag from Caffè Nero. 'Breakfast,' he announced. 'And someone to share it with.'

He stood back to reveal Lara, plus suitcase.

Sal couldn't stop herself. She threw her arms round Lara and held close to her heart the child she had given away for adoption more than forty years ago.

Lara stepped back and looked Sal in the eye. 'I take it you were an au pair in Oslo after all.'

'Lara, I am so, so sorry. There are reasons . . .'

'You don't have to explain.' Lara's smile was warm and genuine. 'I shouldn't have just turned up like that. I was warned not to.'

'Are you ladies going in or not?' Ricky grinned, pushing Lara's case behind the door and handing over the croissants.

For a moment they sat in silence, Sal on the armchair, Lara perched on the edge of the sofa, the weight of the past a gulf between them.

'I can't wait to hear,' Sal gushed at last. 'Tell me all about yourself.'

'My name is Lara Olsen, obviously. I am forty-five years old. Born in Oslo, as you know. Married. And I am a journalist.'

'A journalist! How strange, so am I. How did you find me? Did you even know I was English?'

Lara smiled again. 'My job helped. You learn how to find people. I'd interviewed a wonderful woman – Mia – who tracks down lost families. I had never meant to look for you, but when I met her I thought: "This is Fate". It was she who found you, not me. She told me not to do this, not to come and see you out of the blue, but I was in London and I couldn't stop myself. She said it might wreck all my chances. You might refuse to acknowledge me.'

Sal felt herself choking up. 'And that was exactly what I did.'

'It is very common, Mia says. Women see their babies as being in the past, they have other lives now, they don't want to rake up the ashes.'

'Well, I do. I'm thrilled. I'm overwhelmed, but I'm delighted – no, that's too small a word. I'm overcome.'

She hugged Lara all over again. 'I want to hear all about you, every single detail since you were adopted.'

Lara laughed. She had a wonderful laugh that belied her cool and poised demeanour. 'That will take a long time.'

'How long have you got?'

'My plane is early this afternoon.'

'I should offer you something. Coffee?'

'That would be lovely.' She got up to help. She was wearing thick fluffy socks under her ankle boots.

'Do you get cold feet?'

'Like ice. My husband won't let me in the bed without socks.'

'Me too,' marvelled Sal. She had always suffered from cold hands and feet even before the chemo.

Sal took down the coffee from the shelf. 'Black or white?'

'Black, please. I always say milk is for cows . . .'

'Me too. And do you take sugar?'

'Three, please.'

'So do I.' She glanced at Lara's feet. 'Your second toe isn't longer than your big one, is it?'

Lara removed her sock and held up her foot for inspection.

They stared at each other, awed by these unsuspected similarities.

'You did not marry? Not ever?' Lara looked around at Sal's pared-down home with its smart but slightly soulless décor.

No, still a single girl, Sal almost replied, but it sounded pathetic and she didn't want Lara to pity her. 'I always had my career to consider.' That was a bit grandiose, but better than the truth which was that she had never found anyone. 'Maybe I was a bit burned by what happened. I was so young and naïve.'

'Tell me about it. I would like to hear it all.'

Sal poured the coffee and sat opposite her on the sofa.

'I was eighteen and ludicrously innocent. It was the Sixties. The world was changing. The press said it was all free love and flower power but I was just a naïve Northern girl who'd never even been abroad and my mother hadn't told me anything. I met your father and I just fell for him. I suppose I was crazily irresponsible but I was in love and I just thought everything would work out.'

'Tell me about him.'

'His name was Erik Jonsson. He was a philosophy student at the university in Oslo. And my ski instructor. . .'

Even after all these years, Sal almost blushed at how clichéd that must sound, falling for your ski instructor like all the other silly girls.

'My father was a ski instructor?' She could see Lara didn't know whether to laugh or be horrified. 'I suppose that explains my carved turns. Is he still alive?'

'I'm so sorry, but I have no idea. I haven't seen him since. He got scared when I told him I was pregnant and I never saw him again.' She knew she could never tell Lara about the disgust in Erik's eyes when she had told him she was pregnant.

'That was so cruel of him.'

'He was frightened, I suppose. He was only twenty. Too young to be a father.'

'And what happened then?'

'I went to work as an au pair and hid the pregnancy. When it became obvious, I was approached by a woman who asked if she could help. She said she was from a charity that helped unmarried mothers to have their babies adopted. I thought it might be a scam, that she was doing it for money, but it was a real charity, one of those anti-abortion ones I hate. She took me to a home for unmarried mothers and I had you in hospital. Then they came and took you away.' Sal got up to hide her tears at the searing memory, as fresh now as it was forty years ago. 'Before I left, they made me swear with my hand on the Bible that I would not look for you. They made it feel it was binding because they said it would be the best for you.'

She went to a cabinet in the corner of the room and came back holding a tiny vest. 'I kept this. I wasn't supposed to, but I had to have something.' She smiled at Lara, who was fighting tears herself. 'You didn't have any hair so I couldn't take a lock of that.'

'I've always had terrible hair.' Lara held up the tiny vest for a moment. 'I am so glad I've found you.'

They clung to each other, silently.

'And your adopted mother? Tell me about her. She was someone the charity found through the church?'

'Astrid. She was great. A really good mother.'

'What was she like?'

'Practical. Busy. A whirlwind round the home, cleaning, cooking, not such a career woman. But she was always there.'

The picture Lara painted was almost the opposite of Sal herself. Would she have been able to provide a child with that kind of unselfish love?

'She did have her romantic streak. She loved Omar Sharif in *Doctor Zhivago*. That's why I'm called Lara.'

Sal smiled at that. What had Rose said about her being like Julie Christie in her fur hat? How extraordinary the way things turned out.

'So she was a good mother?'

'Very good. But she was different to me. I am not such a homebody.' Lara's smile held a touch of mischief. 'I have a little bit of a wild streak.'

Sal laughed. 'So have I.'

'Maybe it's you I get it from.'

'And your wild streak, it hasn't stopped you being happy?' Sal realized she was referring as much to herself as to Lara.

Lara shook her head. 'Not at all. I have a husband of seventeen years.' She got out a small passport-type photograph of a dark-haired man with gently smiling eyes. Sal thought with relief that he looked kind. 'His name is Max. He teaches at the university.'

'Not philosophy?'

'Biology. In Trondheim, not Oslo.'

'He looks lovely.'

'And there are your grandchildren.'

'*Grandchildren?*' Sal closed her eyes and bit her lip to stop the tears falling. 'How many? What are their names?'

Lara handed over another photograph of two pretty girls and a tall, very serious boy. 'Angelika is sixteen, Martina thirteen and Martin is ten.'

'Martin was my father's name. Oh, God, Lara,' she stared at the happy, healthy faces smiling out of the photo, 'this is so staggeringly, amazingly wonderful. And your mother? Is she still alive?'

Lara's face clouded. 'No. That is another reason I wanted to look for you. She died. To look for you while she was alive would have seemed disrespectful.'

'And your adopted father?'

'He is dead now. He was a kind man. Rather serious but kind underneath. I had a happy childhood.'

'How did you find out? That she wasn't your natural mother?'

'She was always very open. I knew I was adopted from the start. In that way, I am like her. I don't like secrets. To me, secrets are bad. They create more problems than they solve. This is very Norwegian, I am told, to be so straightforward and direct.'

Sal hesitated, not sure she wanted the answer to the next question.

'How did she die?'

'Cancer. Of the adrenal gland. It was quite rare and pretty fast.'

'Lara . . .' Sal could hardly force herself to speak. 'I am so sorry.'

'Maybe she brought us together. She was a very generous woman.' Lara looked at her watch and stood up. Amazingly, two hours had passed. 'I am so sorry I must go because of the flight, but it has been so very amazing to meet you.'

'And we must meet again. Perhaps I could come to Oslo and see your family.'

'That would be wonderful. My children would very much enjoy having two grandmothers.'

And then she was gone.

Sal sat down heavily. The pain of loss was worse than any cancer symptoms. To have found her daughter was wonderful, amazing, but for her to leave so soon was like losing a limb and finding that it still ached after amputation.

I don't like secrets. To me, secrets are bad. They create more problems than they solve.

How right Lara was. And yet how could she tell her daughter that not only had her adopted mother died of cancer but also that her natural mother, whom she had found after a difficult and painful search, had the very same illness?

Sal went into her bedroom and sat down on the edge of

the bed staring into the blankness of the empty room. She ought to get ready for the hospital but felt as if all her energy had been drained like a battery that had gone suddenly flat.

Even the sound of someone banging on the door couldn't penetrate the depths of her isolation.

But the knocking persisted until finally she went to answer it.

Lara was standing on the threshold, the hood of her parka still up from the wind outside. 'I have one question.' Her direct blue gaze fixed on Sal. 'Do you have cancer also?'

Sal gasped. 'Is it so obvious?'

'To me, yes. Like Astrid, you are wearing a wig and you have no eyelashes from the chemotherapy.'

Sal almost wept as she stood back to let her in.

'Yes, I have cancer.'

'What kind of cancer do you have?'

'Of the breast.'

Lara looked relieved. 'That is not so bad. And what do the doctors say?'

'I have been having drugs to reduce the size of the tumour before they operate.'

'Neoadjuvant therapy. Yes.'

'I need to go back to the hospital this afternoon. My consultant wants me to meet his team and discuss what happens next. I'm so sorry, it seems so unfair when you have already lost your mother once.'

'Now that I know this, I will stay in London.'

'But what about your family?'

'They will understand.'

Sal took her hand and held it tight. She hadn't lost Lara after all. Lara would be at her side, and somehow that made it seem so much less frightening. 'Thank you, Lara, for coming back. I am so lucky to have you.'

Lara smiled. 'And I am lucky I didn't listen to Mia. And now we will face this illness together. By now I am good at asking the questions. But maybe we will have a glass of wine first?'

Sal found some Sauvignon in the fridge. 'What lie shall I tell my employers this time?'

'Why do you not tell them the truth?'

'Oh, Lara, because I am sixty-three and incredibly lucky to get this job. It is only for six months. How can I tell them I need to take time off because I have cancer?'

Lara didn't argue further but Sal knew she disagreed. Secrets were bad.

In the waiting room for the clinic the mother was there with her two pretty daughters. Sal could hardly believe she now had a daughter of her own. When she went in to see Mr Richards she introduced 'my daughter Lara' with such a broad smile that they must have thought her deranged.

There were four professionals on the other side of the table. Last time there had been only two. *Work it out for yourself*, as Rachel would have said.

Her tumour, it seemed, was not reducing in size as fast as they wanted it to.

'We would like to alter your drug regimen. At the moment you are on FEC.'

Sal felt a sudden desire to giggle. What had Rachel said about the cancer sufferers' joke? *You can all FEC-off.*

'To reduce the tumour more quickly we're going to start you on Taxotere as well. Then we'll begin to think about surgical options.'

'You mean I may not need a mastectomy after all?'

Mr Richards steepled his hands. 'I'm afraid your cancer is not suitable for breast-conserving surgery. A mastectomy has always been the only option. And we'll take some lymph nodes as well. Now, Ms Grainger, have you given any thought to breast reconstruction?'

Sal shook her head.

'Basically there are three options. The first is a silicon implant.'

Like a conjuror producing an egg from behind a spectator's ear, Mr Richards pulled a teardrop-shaped object from his top drawer. 'They come in silicon or saline solution.'

Sal had a sudden image of swimming pools on board ships that swooshed up and down.

'Inserting an implant will only take an hour on top of your operation and you'll wake up with a breast.'

'That has to be good.'

'Option two: the plastic surgeon would use your thigh, your tummy or your buttock. These are more major operations, but it is your own tissue.'

'Or – three – I could opt not to have reconstruction at all. After all, this is pretty major surgery.'

'Ms Grainger,' Mr Richards smiled at her gently, 'after what you've been through with chemo, the surgery will be a walk in the park.'

Once they were outside the consulting room Lara turned to her. 'I have one question.'

'Fire away.'

Lara shook her head, but smiled. 'Do you ever take anything seriously?'

Sal smiled back. 'Not taking things seriously is my way of taking things seriously.'

'In that case, I'm glad you're taking things so seriously.' She grabbed Sal's hand and held it tight. 'I am so sorry, just when I have found you, you must undergo this operation and lose your breast.'

But Sal was beaming as if the news had been nothing but good.

'Lara, this may sound crazy but I don't really care if I lose a breast. I long to get better, obviously. I can't wait to meet your husband and children,' she couldn't quite bring herself to call them her grandchildren yet, 'but something extraordinary has happened to me. Until you came, I tried to convince myself I didn't miss having a family, but now you're here I'm glowing with satisfaction.' She hugged Lara so tight that neither could breathe. 'My life is complete because you are in it. Thank you, thank you so much for coming to find me.'

Nigel was staying tonight so Laura, strung out and exhausted after almost three weeks at her daughter's bedside besides going back to her job in the day time, could go home. Bella's blood pressure was showing no sign of going down, and if it hadn't fallen soon, for the sake of both Bella and the baby, the obstetrician was planning a Caesarean.

As soon as she got home Laura poured herself a drink and tried to watch TV but nothing engaged her attention. She went online and browsed for a while on the subject of pre-eclampsia before deciding to go to bed at ten.

It was no good. Even though she was in her own bed she couldn't sleep.

Finally, at ten-thirty, she rang Simon.

He didn't answer on the first call and no message clicked in, so she tried again. Just as she was about to give up, he answered.

'Bella doesn't really want me to tell you this, but I feel it's your right as her father to know. She's got something called pre-eclampsia. At its most serious it could damage the baby or cause Bella a stroke, so if it's still an issue next week, they want to induce the baby or do a Caesarean.'

Simon's answer was a strange, guttural wail.

'Simon, don't worry,' Laura reassured, feeling panicked.

Simon rarely showed emotion of any kind. 'She'll be all right. Nigel's staying with her and they're monitoring her round the clock.'

'It's not just Bella,' Simon almost shouted, 'it's Suki too. They couldn't find a heartbeat at the hospital today. Oh, God, Laura, and she'll still have to go ahead with the birth!'

'Oh, Simon, how terrible for you both.'

'You don't need to pretend sympathy, Laura. I know how bitter you felt. Now you can see this as my just reward.'

Laura's hand crept to her face. She might have fantasized about revenge but listening to Simon just made her want to rush to Bella's side and stay there until her baby was safely born and lying nestling in its mother's joyful arms.

Claudia looked at the pale pink confection she was trying on in the changing-room mirror and shuddered. It was weeks since Gaby had broken the news of her surprise engagement and the wedding would be upon them before they could say the words 'Quickie Divorce'.

For the first time she felt sympathy for the mother of Kate, Duchess of Cambridge, when she'd married Prince William. It was no easy task being the MOB; as the mother of the bride, you had to look suitable, and not wear anything that could even remotely upstage your daughter, and you had to stay sober. At least she wasn't going to be watched by millions on telly.

No wonder her own generation had rejected weddings. Don and she had lived together quite happily and had only rushed down to the registry office when Claudia was in a fairly advanced state of pregnancy.

The thought of Don made her feel anxious. Was he still in contact with his long-lost girlfriend? He seemed to be in a good mood despite the cost of the wedding, which was strange.

His good humour certainly had nothing to do with Claudia's feeble attempts to get him to join the choir, take up bridge or come with her to Sing Out, since he'd resisted all of those. He had even stopped going to the dump daily. It had to be either because the wedding was keeping everyone busy, or because he was still enjoying emailing Marianne.

Maybe even meeting her.

Claudia wished she could make herself care more about the mysterious Marianne. The fact that she didn't was seriously worrying. And the reason for her insouciance was waiting for her downstairs.

When she'd told Daniel she was going to Oxford Street to buy her outfit, he'd said he'd be in town as well. Why didn't they celebrate with a glass of champagne?

So now, here they were, meeting in Selfridges' champagne bar.

I mean, Claudia told herself, *what could be wrong with that?* It was a department store, for heaven's sake. Perfectly innocent. *You'd hardly meet a lover in a department store, would you?*

Daniel was waiting for her in the balcony bar, in front of a large mirrored mural, staring down into the handbag department and laughing.

Claudia experienced a sudden *Brief Encounter* pang of misgiving. What did she think she was doing?

'Do you know,' laughed Daniel, 'that young woman has just spent a thousand pounds on a bag? Think what I could do for Sing Out with that.' He managed to sound amused, charmingly world-weary and non-judgemental all at the same time. It was a killer combination. 'Plain fizz or rosé?'

'Plain, please.' Claudia sat down, feeling divinely decadent, next to an artwork by Tracey Emin which had the effect of making her think of unmade beds and all that happened in them.

'Outfit bought successfully?' He eyed the large carrier bag. 'Let's see.'

Claudia hesitated, feeling oddly shy.

'Come on, I have quite good taste, apparently.'

'I'm sure you do. I'm just not sure *I* have.' Claudia laid the dress out on the chair next to him.

'Beautiful. Just right. Are you wearing a hat as well?'

'I loathe hats.' She produced the ivory feather fascinator she'd just spent the last half-hour selecting.

'Glorious. I shall henceforth imagine you in the Garden of Eden wearing that and nothing more.'

Claudia giggled despite herself. 'I don't think Eve ever wore a feather fascinator.'

'It's a nice thought, isn't it? Maybe adorned with serpents and apples?' He raised his glass to her in a silent toast. 'Have you time for lunch before returning to your mother-of-the-bride duties in Minsley?'

'As a matter of fact, I'm meeting my friend Ella who has been dragooned into doing the flowers – as cheaply as possible.'

'What a pity.'

Claudia felt the blood rush to her face at his caressing tone. It wasn't a pity at all, she told herself sternly. Lunch might sound innocent enough, but as every woman knew, lunch was the first step down the primrose path to extramarital entanglement.

She finished her drink with disconcerting decisiveness. 'That was delicious.'

'Fancy another one?' he asked hopefully.

'Absolutely not or I will be too sloshed to choose the centrepieces.'

'My, my, there are a lot of things to be decided on.'

The teasing tone made her giggle again and momentarily lose her resolve. 'OK, just one more and then I must go.'

While he was at the bar, the phone he had left on the table flashed a message: *You were supposed to be at rehearsal. WHERE ARE YOU?*

The blood rushed to Claudia's head again. He wasn't due in London after all. He must have come here specially to meet her. She knew she shouldn't be, but Claudia felt deliciously, dangerously flattered.

Once she'd finally torn herself away from Daniel and Selfridges Claudia found she had a message of her own. Ella was going to be an hour late. What should she do with the spare time?

Resisting the considerable temptation of running straight back to Daniel, she remembered that the hospital where Laura was watching over her daughter was only a few minutes away on the tube.

The Princess Lily was one of those huge teaching hospitals that embraced all the different medical specialisms. Claudia stood in reception trying to work out which part of the vast site she should head for when, to her amazement, she thought she could see Sal, of all people, coming out of a lift with a youngish blonde woman holding her arm.

She was about to rush over when a team of paramedics ran past her with a patient on a trolley. By the time they'd got into the lift, Sal had disappeared.

How odd. Maybe they had a colleague who had been taken ill? She must remember to ask next time she saw her. Claudia took the next lift up to the maternity and obstetrics floor and asked for Bella Minchin.

She was directed to a room on the left, but even before she got to it she could sense the sudden tension in the air. The door of the room opened; nurses were running, machines beeping. Claudia flattened herself against the wall to keep out of their way as Bella's bed suddenly emerged, pushed by sprinting orderlies. Laura followed, her face empty and strained as if all emotion had been sucked out of her.

'Claudia!' She looked momentarily confused, as if things weren't making sense.

'I'm so sorry,' Claudia hugged her, 'I've picked a terrible time. I was in London anyway and thought I'd take a chance. Are you OK?'

'They've just decided to operate even though she's nowhere near due yet. Something to do with the placenta which might harm the baby if they don't. Nigel's on his way. Poor little Bella!'

Laura, who had been trying to be strong for everyone, now collapsed.

'Oh God, Claudia, I hope they're going to be OK. I couldn't bear it if she lost the baby like Simon's girlfriend.'

'*Simon*'s girlfriend? You mean that sperm-digger woman?'

'The baby's stillborn. They're going to induce it.'

'Bloody hell. That's a bit biblical.'

'He said he supposed I'd be happy.'

'He really doesn't know you, does he?'

'All I care about is Bella.'

Claudia folded her friend into her arms. Under other circumstances she might have thought 'Serves him right', but here in this hospital, with all its anxiety and hopefulness, birth seemed so precarious that she could only feel sorry for them.

At that moment, Nigel ran in, still wearing the track suit he'd used for sports duty. 'Laura! Where is she? I came as soon as I got your message.'

A sudden wail stopped them both. Then a door opened and a smiling nurse beckoned to them. 'The baby and the placenta are both delivered. You've got a beautiful son,' she said to Nigel.

They all three flocked into the room to find Bella sitting

up, with the baby, not as tiny as they'd been expecting, already suckling at her breast.

'Bella, angel, I can't believe I missed it.' Nigel, despite his huge bulk, looked close to tears.

'There wasn't much warning. They gave me an epidural and it all happened so quickly.' The small head bumped off her breast. 'Here, you take him a moment.' She held out the small scrap of humanity to Nigel. The baby surveyed his father through inscrutable dark blue eyes from under a tuft of black hair which stood up like a cockatoo. 'Look at that, he's got a natural Mohican!'

Laura wondered if she could have a hold too, but didn't want to intrude on this precious moment of intimacy. She glanced at the still-smiling nurse. 'Will he have to go to special care?' She tried not to picture him covered with tubes and deprived of cuddles.

'We don't consider this premature. We may keep mother and baby in for an extra day or two but otherwise he's no different from any other newborn. He'll be fine.'

Laura almost laughed out loud with relief.

'Here, Grandma, have a hold.' Nigel suddenly held the baby out to her.

Laura held her grandson tightly against her chest, supporting his head with one hand as the memory flooded back of doing the same with Bella and with Sam. But with her own children the joy had been tempered by anxiety and the fear of her own maternal incompetence.

What she felt for her grandchild, standing here today, was pure, powerful, delirious love.

'You should have seen him, he was so incredibly adorable!' Claudia brandished the photo she'd taken of Laura and the baby in Ella's direction. 'Laura's in seventh heaven. She'll be an amazing grandmother. The second of us to be a granny. Amazing or what?'

'We've put it off long enough. In another era we'd all be dead,' Ella replied testily from her kitchen table, knee deep in lilies, freesias and bright green euphorbia, where she was arranging sample bouquets and centrepieces for Claudia to take back to Surrey and show Gaby.

'Ella, you'll never guess what's happened with Simon and the Sperm-digger. The baby's stillborn and she's still got to give birth.'

'Oh my God, what a terrible thing. I never thought I'd say this, given the misery she's caused—'

'*They've* caused,' corrected Claudia.

'. . . they've caused. But a stillbirth is the most tragic thing to have to go through. And don't say "Tough shit, they deserved it.'

'Ella,' Claudia grinned, 'I wasn't going to.'

'I bet you were thinking it.'

She went back to the flowers. 'How long is Bella in hospital for? I don't suppose Gaby would begrudge a few blooms if I made Bella up a bunch for when she gets home?'

'Forget what Gaby thinks. It's her mother who's paying. God, Ella, I don't know what's come over that girl. I'm looking forward to the honeymoon more than they are because it means it'll all be over. Two whole weeks of peace. By the way, the oddest thing. When I was in the hospital I saw Sal there. You don't think she's ill, do you, and not telling us? Only she has been rather elusive lately. It might explain why we haven't seen her.'

'Sal? Sal couldn't keep a secret if her life depended on it. She must have been visiting someone. Is she coming to the wedding?'

'She says she is but she's been very odd about arrangements

lately. Laura definitely is. And, amazing though it seems, Gaby and Douglas have told us to invite anyone we like to the do in the evening.'

'Now that *is* generous.'

'Most of his family's stuck in Australia so he's not got that many coming from his side. It's going to be quite a bash.'

'It's going to be a lovely occasion,' Ella agreed. 'Just what we old boots need, a bit of romance to cheer us all up. Remind us life is full of possibilities, not just memory loss and hip replacements.'

'Yes,' agreed Claudia, thinking how shocked they'd all feel if they knew how she'd spent the morning. In a champagne bar with a man who wasn't her husband.

CHAPTER 23

'Would you all like to come and stay with me for a day or two while Nigel gets everything sorted out?' Laura offered. 'I don't suppose he had time, what with you being rushed into hospital.'

Bella and baby were being discharged today and Laura was thinking of the spartan flat with its Blu-tacked posters and unappealing bedroom. She knew she mustn't convey any sense of worry or disapproval. Also she remembered from when she'd had her own babies that these first few days were a crucial time when you felt as if you were in a bubble of family intimacy when the outside world didn't exist, and she didn't want to spoil that for them. Posh people, she remembered, had maternity nurses who arrived on Day One, took the baby from you to get it into a routine and gave it back a month later. It had seemed like a shame to Laura. But her daughter's lifestyle was the polar opposite from that.

Bella shrugged. 'What do you think, Nige?'

'I think it's a great idea.' Laura was getting to like her giant son-in-law substitute more and more. Despite his scary image he was always sensible and reasonable.

They piled into Laura's car, with Bella and the baby in the back and Nigel in the passenger seat.

Last night Nigel had been given a lesson in bathing him. One of Laura's enduring images would be of this huge man tenderly holding his tiny baby, as if he were the most precious creation in the entire universe.

The weather was smiling on their homecoming. Brilliant sunshine lit up the streets, bringing happy looks to the faces of the grumpiest Londoners. 'You'll be able to sit out on a rug,' Laura pointed out. 'Such a lovely time to have a baby. They say summer babies are happy and more confident.'

'Won't you have to go back to work soon?' asked Bella.

'Yes, later today,' Laura conceded, sorry to miss out on the baby, yet glad she could give them the time they needed to be alone. 'I'll do a big shop first so you have everything you need. Nice for you to have some space for yourselves anyway.'

As she opened the front door, Laura had to move a big pile of post. In spite of the sunshine and the happiness of the occasion her spirits sank at the sight of another letter from Simon's solicitors. She wasn't going to bloody open that now and let it spoil everything.

TomTom was as thrilled as ever to see them, meowing wildly, and almost tripping them up.

'Will he be all right with the baby?' Bella asked anxiously.

'I'm sure he will. We could get a net, though, if you want, that's what all babies had in my day.'

'The days when you used to leave babies at the bottom of the garden to cry for hours on end?'

Laura almost repeated her own mother's dictum that it was good for the lungs but thought better of it. The modern granny kept her lip buttoned on the subject of childcare. God alone knew what the thinking was now anyway. It seemed to change every five minutes from feeding on demand to old-fashioned discipline. The realization suddenly struck her that her daughter was now a mother and would have to work such things out for herself.

And I'm a grandmother! That thought was equally amazing.

'Now, what do you want me to get you?'

'Don't fuss, Mum. I'll just order some stuff from Tesco. I'm part of the online generation, remember.'

'OK. I'll be off to work, then. I'm doing twelve till four. Any more thoughts about names yet?'

She knew this was a touchy subject but everyone at work would want to know.

'If he'd been a girl it would have been easy,' Bella replied. 'There's Siouxsie from Siouxsie and the Banshees, Candia from Inkubus Sukkubus or even Amy of Evanescence. But boys' names . . .' Bella sighed at the challenge of picking a suitably Gothic boy's name. 'We thought about Robert from The Cure, but at the moment we're veering towards Aaron of My Dying Bride.'

'Right,' Laura replied faintly. Whatever had happened to Roger and Andy? She supposed it could have been worse. Marilyn after Marilyn Manson, for instance. 'See you later. Just text me if you need anything.'

'Thanks, Mum,' Bella's sudden smile lit up her pale face chasing the anxiety away, 'you've been brilliant.'

Laura stored away these precious words to take out and enjoy later.

Babies were big news at LateExpress and everyone, led by an enthusiastic Mrs A, crowded round Laura wanting to see the picture on her phone.

'Aaah, he's maximum gorgeous,' cooed Mrs A. 'And a boy too. No messing about having to have three girls till you get your boy like my sister-in-law.'

Mrs A, despite her years in the UK, had not yet picked up the etiquette that decreed girls to be at least the equal of boys.

'What name will he have? Have they decided yet?'

'Maybe Robert or Aaron, but they're not absolutely sure yet.'

'Tell them Noah,' advised Mrs A. 'There are three Noahs in my son's class, one Muslim, one Christian and the other British National Party. Very good name for tricky modern world.'

Laura smiled. 'I'll pass it on. But at the moment I'm trying not to dish out too much advice.'

'Good policy,' endorsed Mrs A. 'Let them make their own mistakes. Then you can tell them "I told you so" when everything goes wrong.'

When her shift finished Laura decided to take home some basic supplies – nappies, wipes, milk and some pesto and pasta. She could always keep it if it wsn't needed.

She could hear Robert/Aaron crying even before she got out of the car, that primitive, penetrating wail of the newborn baby genetically designed to terrify the parent into never abandoning it.

Bella, pale and distraught, was on the sofa in tears.

'Why won't he stop crying, Mum? I've fed him till my nipples ache and changed him and burped him and he's still wailing the house down.'

Laura put down her shopping. 'Would you like me to drive him round in the car for a bit? I always found that worked with you, that and putting you on top of the washing machine.'

'You put me on the washing machine?' Bella demanded, horrified.

'In your baby seat. Yes. The vibration sent you to sleep in no time.'

'It didn't strike you as dangerous?'

'We never worried that much. I used to put a duvet on the floor in case.'

'Thanks a lot.'

The screaming, which had stopped for a moment, lulling them into temporary relief, started up again at double volume.

Bella dissolved into tears again.

'I'll take him,' Laura said firmly.

She carried the baby seat out to the car and carefully strapped him in, suddenly conscious of how precious he was. Curiously, she couldn't remember feeling this scared at driving her own children. She'd bowled happily along with them, music blaring, singing along with Bruce Springsteen or The Eagles. Laura was grateful that though childcare philosophies might have changed, the capacity of the combustion engine to lull infants to sleep had not.

In five minutes he was fast asleep, issuing happy little snuffles of content.

Laura drove round for another fifteen minutes, gauging corners and distances with the skills of a Jensen Button, so that she didn't have to slow down too much or stop at red lights, and risk the baby waking.

Once she got back, Laura knew the greatest challenge lay in how to stop the car and get the baby seat out in one smooth, seamless movement without waking him.

Bella was fast asleep on the sofa, a copy of *Grazia* magazine still clutched in her hands.

Laura put the baby seat gently down beside her and went to make herself a cup of tea. Miracle of miracles, he was still asleep.

Half an hour later the crying started up again, finally waking Bella from her slumber. She, too, began to cry. 'God, Mum, I don't know if I can do this, I really don't.'

'Yes you can.' Laura lifted the baby onto Bella's chest. 'All those classes about giving birth and no one tells you the hard part begins afterwards. You think it'll go on forever, but it doesn't. He'll soon settle down.'

Bella found her nipple and attached the screaming baby. A moment's blissful silence ensued. Until he fell off and had to be reattached.

'Breastfeeding's worse than childbirth, if you ask me.' Bella sighed. 'You keep worrying if he's had enough, and if he hasn't you know he'll wake again in five minutes. It's like living with a Middle-Eastern interrogator, only he wants milk, not information.'

Laura laughed. 'I remember.'

'How long does it last? I'm already suffering from sleep deprivation.'

'Not too long, but it feels like an eternity.'

'Thanks, Mum. How was work?'

'Fine, they all wanted to see pictures of the baby. Mrs A thinks you should call him Noah. Apparently it's acceptably global in our complex modern world.'

'Noah,' Bella repeated. 'Noah. I like Noah, actually. It feels solid. Makes me think of that wooden ark I had when I was little. I loved that toy. I'll see what Nigel thinks.'

'Where's he got to by the way?'

'Up a ladder fixing luminous stars to the ceiling. But he says he's going gangbusters and should be finished by tomorrow or the next day.'

'That's great.' Laura suppressed a pang at the knowledge that the little family would soon be off. But how long would she have a home to offer them? The letter from Simon's solicitors still sat on the kitchen table giving off the malodorous glow of bad news.

'I need the loo,' Bella announced. 'Here, you take him, Grandma.'

She handed the temporarily peaceful bundle to Laura, who sat on the sofa cradling his head and breathing in the milky new baby smell. It hardly seemed possible that this could be Bella's baby.

She kissed the top of his downy head, overcome by a wave of sudden, overwhelming protectiveness, and looked down into his unfathomable inky blue eyes. 'Hello, baby. Welcome to the world.'

When the doorbell sounded she jumped, so deeply was she communing with the new generation. Nigel must have given up on his wallpapering efforts. She stood up, still cradling the baby in her arms.

But the person who stood on the doorstep was Simon.

He was wearing an overcoat with the collar up even though it was a balmy night of early summer, as if he wanted to disappear into its expensive depths and never be seen again.

'Is that . . . ?'

She was about to say, 'Your grandson', but corrected herself; she wasn't sure why. 'Bella's baby. Yes.'

'Can I come in?'

Laura hesitated. She knew Bella hadn't forgiven her father. 'It's a bit difficult. Bella's here for a few days while they sort out the flat.'

'And she doesn't want to see me.' His tone was bleak.

'She found it hard to forgive you for leaving.'

The bleakness erupted into what Laura could only call desperation. 'Laura, I made such a mistake. I must have been bloody mad. And then there was the baby to think of and I was obligated, locked in, even when already I wanted to get out. Forgive me, Laura, please! The thing is, I want to come home. I genuinely, utterly, totally want to come home.'

If she hadn't been holding the baby, Laura might have slapped him.

In her private despair she had sometimes fantasized about this moment, when he begged to come back and start again, but Laura knew in that instant that she had changed. She was stronger now. She was angry.

'No, Dad, it isn't as easy as that.' Bella must have come

back into the sitting room without either of them hearing her. She took the baby from her mother's arms. 'We're going upstairs.'

'Bella . . .'

'Just saying you're sorry doesn't make it all right.'

Simon stared after her.

'What about Suki?' Laura asked. 'She must be devastated. You can't just leave her to deal with the stillbirth alone.'

She thought Simon was going to cry. 'She says it's all my fault. Something to do with my ageing sperm. She's gone home to her mother in Shropshire.'

Laura had a brief image of sperm in wheelchairs and Zimmer frames like some bizarre cartoon. If it wasn't tragic it would have been funny.

'Let's drop the divorce,' Simon begged. 'Keep the house. Sam and Bella will come round eventually.'

'But *I* won't, Simon. I'm going to put the house on the market as soon as Bella leaves. Start again. Find a flat with room for Sam if he needs it.'

'But what about Bella?'

'Bella will be fine. She has a home and partner of her own. She's a survivor.'

'Telling me.'

She wasn't sure even now if his sorrow was for anyone but himself.

'Time you went, I think, Simon. I'll keep in touch through the lawyers.'

He looked as if he might argue. Instead he straightened his collar, pushed his hands deep into his pockets and turned away.

Laura watched the door close on almost twenty-six years of her life. But this time it was she who was closing it, and she knew she would come through. She wasn't so sure what would happen to Simon. And for once she didn't care.

Gaby opened the back door to look for the sample flowers Ella had brought down for her. It was the most glorious day. The sun streamed down on the patio and high, fluffy clouds danced about in a bright blue sky.

'There's nowhere in the whole world like England when the weather's like this,' Gaby sighed, suddenly full of good humour and love of mankind. 'I just hope it stays this way for the wedding.' She retrieved the flowers and held them in a bridal pose.

It was a stunning arrangement. Ella had come up with the striking combination of cream calla lilies mixed with crème de la crème roses, secured with looped aspidistra leaves, glossily green and striped with white, the whole thing tied up with cream satin ribbon.

'What do you think?' Claudia asked.

Gaby put her arms round her mother's neck. 'I think it's gorgeous. Tell Ella I love it. It's a perfect bride's bouquet and I love the stripy aspidistra leaves. And is she happy making four mini-versions for the bridesmaids?'

'And six buttonholes for the bridegroom and ushers. Yes she is.'

'How much do we owe her for this lot?' Even Gaby was beginning to realize how much the whole day was costing.

'Ella says they're her gift to you. Plus all the centrepieces for the tables.'

'Oh, Mum, that's really kind of her!'

'Yes.' Claudia hoped a little chink of reality might be opening up. 'It is.'

*

'Sally . . .' Lara began.

'Sally? Oh dear, this must be serious. Call me Sal, everyone does. Sally sounds like someone else.'

They were in Sal's flat and Lara was making her a supper of gnocchi with tomatoes. With Lara here the flat didn't seem empty. She had a knack for adding unobtrusive touches – a couple of red tulips in a jam jar – a scented candle – that made Sal's flat of twenty years more a home than it had ever been before.

'I have to go back to Trondheim tomorrow. Max must spend some time at the university and I need to look after the children.'

Sal knew she must hide her disappointment. She'd been so lucky to have Lara here this long. 'Lara, you have been so kind, having you here really has made all the difference.'

'Max's mother is happy to take over again soon. I will come back next week.'

'You really don't need to.'

'But I want to.' Lara's bright blue eyes looked momentarily troubled. 'Am I interfering? Would you rather I didn't come?'

Sal laughed out loud. 'I love having you. I have never had anyone to look out for me since I was a little girl. Always the big independent woman, me. I didn't need a man. I didn't need kids. But when you get to sixty, life can start to feel a little lonely, and you're not as strong when something like this comes out of the blue. So, yes, I would love you to come back. If you really can come without too much disruption to your own life.'

'Max's mother, Hedvig, likes the chance to put right all my slack discipline,' Lara laughed. 'She gets them to sit up straight, do their homework, have good table manners.' She grinned wickedly. 'So when I get home again they are very, very pleased to see me. I do have one condition, though. Not condition. Request.'

'Fire away.'

'That you tell your employers the truth, that you are ill, that you are being treated for cancer. So that they understand and can give you the time off you need to get better instead of snatching a day here and a day there. It is too much strain. You worry they will not keep you on but I worry that with so much stress you will not properly recover.'

Sal closed her eyes. Lara's dislike of secrets had a remorseless logic. She had too many of them in her life.

This last occasion when she had needed time off for a hospital appointment, when another lie had been called for, she had not carried it off as easily as before. Lies needed confidence and all of a sudden hers was in short supply.

'OK.' She smiled at her new-found daughter. 'Done. I'll tell them as soon as I know when I have to go in for the operation. Lara Olsen, you are a miracle.'

'I bet you didn't say that when you did the pregnancy test.'

'Maybe not,' Sal conceded, thinking how weird it was that what should be the scariest, unhappiest moment of her life was turning out to be so wonderful.

Ella arrived before 5 a.m. at Nine Elms Market to choose the wedding flowers, impressed at how well organized it was, and how easily accessible it was to ordinary people like herself. She thought maybe she would need some special florist's pass to the biggest flower market in the country, but it was open to all.

The market itself was a little daunting with its acres and acres of stalls, some general, some specializing in particular varieties, all bustling and busy with crowds. It felt like every florist in London was here buying at the same time.

She wanted to find the very best choice for Gaby's wedding and place her order today for collection in time for the big day.

It was so hard. She had come for cream roses and lilies but other blooms kept tempting her with their velvety petals and exotic looks. Tiny white stephanotis with its seductive scent, palest pink hydrangeas, jasmine flowers, and glorious peonies – her favourite flowers – pink and dark red and creamy off-white.

She was just beginning to feel dizzy at the range of choices when someone caught hold of her elbow and turned her gently round.

'El-la!'

'Wenceslaus! What on earth are you doing here?'

Minka, her arms loaded with blooms, was standing behind him.

'We are having a goodbye party at the salon. Minka and I are going back to Poland for a few months to start a business there and we are saying goodbye – don't forget us – to Minka's customers.'

'So, are you closing the salon down?'

'No, not at all.' Minka shook her head. 'Is nice little earner, as you Brits say. We have opened another in Acton Town. We have one little problem. Our manager we have lined up has been poached by old boyfriend, you remember, one in Porsche? He do it deliberately to make trouble. Now we have to find new manager, double quick.'

'How about you, El-la?' Wenceslaus asked. 'You are very organized lady.'

'*Me?*' Ella was flattered that he had forgotten her leaving keys in doors, losing her car, and other examples of not being 'organized lady' at all.

'I'm too busy already with the allotment. Besides, I don't know anything about hairdressing.'

'Not that important. Stylists all self-employed. Just need someone to make sure salons well-run, have stuff they need, are nice to customers, not keeping all profits for themselves. Anyone who has brain could do it.'

'Well, I do have a friend who helps run a supermarket.' This was exaggerating Laura's role a tad but she was sure Laura *could* manage LateExpress if she got the chance, and why not the salons?

She'd just have to get Laura to meet them.

Claudia had said she could invite a friend to the post-wedding party, since it was outdoors and, unlike the select wedding and reception, designed to be big and noisy and more-the-merrier. She had a feeling Claudia would stretch it to two, especially if she knew why.

'Just don't put it on Facebook,' Claudia had teased, 'or all the disreputable oldies in the county'll turn up.'

'Look, I'm doing the flowers for a wedding in Surrey next weekend and there's a big party afterwards. I'll see if you two could come along.'

She quickly dialled Claudia's number. 'How's everything? This is a bit of a cheek so please say no, but could I bring two rather than one to the evening party?'

Apparently, since she was doing the flowers, she was very welcome to invite two friends along, Claudia insisted.

'Come to the dance and meet my friend Laura,' she suggested to them both. 'See if you hit it off.'

She wrote down the address and handed it to them.

Wenceslaus and Minka, with their boxes of blooms, waved and headed for the car park. It was only when they were out of sight that Ella remembered that, in her enthusiasm to find Laura a better job, she'd forgotten that among the other people invited to the party were her daughter Julia and her husband Neil.

CHAPTER 24

'Mum, you're not ready.'

This was an understatement, to say the least. Olivia had asked Claudia to take her shopping for her wedding outfit, yet here she was, still in her dressing gown, her hair unwashed, staring at her reflection in the triple mirror as if she needed confirmation of her own existence.

Claudia sat down next to her on the wide stool, and put her arm gently round her mother's shoulders. 'Have you taken your pills today?'

Olivia shrugged. 'I hate them, Claudia. I don't feel like me.'

'But you really need to, Mum.'

She almost wept at the cruelty of her mother's condition, that the mad bursts of energy that had worried them so much should be counterbalanced by such desolation as she saw in her mother's face today.

'You should go without me. I'm no use to anyone in this mood.'

'Absolutely not. First I'm going to get your pills.'

'I don't know where they are,' Olivia replied mutinously. 'I've forgotten where I put them.'

'I'll ask Dad.'

She found her father sitting in a deck chair outside the back door reading the newspaper. It was such a familiar image from her childhood that the years rolled away. 'Hello, Pops,' she greeted him, 'hiding out here as usual.' She sat down opposite him.

Len smiled, but she could see it was an effort, unlike the spontaneous good humour she was used to. 'Mum OK?' he asked anxiously.

'Not really. Is she taking the medicine? She says she doesn't know where the pills are.'

Len sighed. 'She hides them. Usually I find them and stand over her till she takes them. She finds different places to put them in. I wasn't up to it last night, I'd forgotten you were coming.'

'Will she be well enough for the wedding?'

Len smiled, some of his anxiety evaporating. 'Try and keep her away.'

'Good. Can you have a look in her usual hiding places? I'm not sure a shopping trip's a good idea. I'll wash her hair and maybe we'll see if she's already got something suitable in the wardrobe.'

Len put down the crossword. He'd aged years since her mother's diagnosis, as if their mental and bodily health were inextricably linked, which perhaps they were when you had been together as long as they had. Each gave the other a reason for breathing.

Claudia followed her father into the kitchen. He opened up various jars and tins. 'Nope. She's getting cleverer.'

He eventually found them hidden under a pile of hand towels in the downstairs lavatory. 'It'd be funny if it wasn't so sad.' He opened his arms and Claudia hugged her beloved father, realizing how much of his strength and twinkly good humour had depended on Olivia's glowing energy source.

She would have to get more involved with them, help them get back the balance that had sustained them over so many years. It struck Claudia with a sudden icy panic that she had lost the equilibrium that sustained her own marriage.

How easy it was for things to fall apart if all you did was stop making the effort to keep them together.

She'd been worrying about her mother and how to deal with her condition, and she'd been worrying about her daughter, hoping she hadn't fallen for the wedding rather than the man. But perhaps what she should be worrying about was herself and what was happening in her own life.

Sal sat at her desk at *New Grey*, surveying two very different communications. The first was a letter informing her of her mastectomy date. The second was the invitation to Claudia's daughter's wedding just three days earlier.

She wanted to get in touch with Lara and tell her at once. But first she had a promise to her daughter that she had to fulfil.

'Rose, do you think I could have a word?'

Sal had promised Lara faithfully that she would come clean about her illness, but she was dreading it all the same. She had decided to broach Rose first, even though Michael Williams was CEO, because she decided Rose would be more likely to be understanding. There was also, she had sometimes sensed, an affinity between Rose and herself. They both recognized in each other the strength and endurance of women who had taken on the world largely alone, and who had revelled in doing so, but who were beginning to see the cost to themselves.

Thankfully, the timing of her announcement was good. They had just had their latest circulation figures and *New Grey* had climbed noticeably under Sal's editorship after several periods of decline.

It was another glorious day and all the windows of Rose's office were open. As it backed on to a goods yard, with no buildings to steal its light, it was so bright they could almost be in the country.

Rose had succeeded in turning her office into more of a library, with oak bookshelves covering every spare inch of wall, a big old-fashioned desk and two wing chairs next to the real fireplace. 'I spend so much time here I like to feel at home,' she laughed, pouring them coffees from the cafetière she always used with her home-made shortbread biscuits.

'Do you make them yourself?' Sal marvelled. Nothing she found out about Rose would surprise her.

'Actually, they're from the café round the corner,' Rose admitted with a wink. 'I buy them in bulk every week.' She handed Sal a coffee. 'Right, what can I do for you?'

Sal sipped her coffee. 'Rose, there's something I need to tell you.'

'That you've got cancer.'

Sal almost gasped. 'How did you know?'

'My dear Sally, I'm almost eighty. Half my friends have had cancer. I recognize the signs.'

'Do the others know, Michael for instance?'

'Michael's a man. He only notices what's put in front of him, and what's been put in front of him is that the circulation's rising, we're getting more advertising and we're starting to be noticed on Twitter and other social media. I would say Michael is pretty pleased.'

'That's a relief.'

'More to the point, what kind of cancer?'

'Of the breast. I'm about to have a radical mastectomy.'

'Good. Best get the whole thing out of the way. Who needs breasts anyway? Any secondaries?'

'Not so far.'

'Even better. Now you'll be needing time off to recover from the operation.' It was a statement rather than a question.

'My friend's daughter is getting married in two weeks and my operation is on the following Tuesday.'

'I'll see if Jonny can pop back in and take over for a bit.' She flashed Sal a mischievous smile that deepened the runnels in her lizard-like skin. 'Otherwise *I* might have to have a go at editing. That would really annoy Michael, but I think I'd be rather good.'

'Rose,' a Niagara Falls of relief was flooding through Sal at the wonder of the woman, 'you are truly amazing.'

Rose chortled. 'Thank you. Now I'm assuming you want this treated with discretion, seeing as you've been to such lengths to disguise it.'

'I've never been much good at handing out pity and I certainly don't want to receive it.'

'I understand perfectly. I'd be the same. But the main thing is you get better, because we want you to keep running the magazine, to take it on to bigger and better things. Maybe even America. When do you want the time off?'

'Not till after the operation. I'll be fine until then. Thanks, Rose. I really do appreciate this.'

'No problem, as our American brethren say. Or is it the Aussies? I'll tell Michael and ask for his discretion.'

Sal found she was almost singing as she went back to her desk. She stopped for a moment and texted Lara: *You were right. No more secrets. Rose was wonderful. And so are you. Xxx*

The day was so blindingly beautiful that Ella, walking back from the allotments, stopped at the spot where the Grand Union flowed into the River Thames to watch the light on the water. It sparkled and danced under the bluest sky she could ever remember seeing. Crossing her fingers that it would keep up the good work for Gaby's wedding, she turned to continue her journey.

On the other side of the path there was a row of workmen's cottages she must have passed a hundred times, without really noticing them. Today the middle one caught her eye. It boasted a sign announcing FOR SALE BY AUCTION.

On a sudden whim she rang the number of the estate agent and made an enquiry.

The agent consulted his database. 'Must be Number three, Grand Union Cottages, due to be auctioned next week. My colleague's about to show someone around. Would you like a peek afterwards? No time like the present.'

Which was how, an hour later, Ella found herself looking out at the River Thames from the window of Number three, contemplating something she had never seriously contemplated before – a move from Old Moulsford and the house she had shared with Laurence and where she had brought up her family.

The cottage was a very different prospect from her present house. Three small bedrooms instead of five large ones, only one bathroom – though it was at least upstairs and there was a loo on the ground floor – a through sitting room, a small but pretty back kitchen looking into a lovely garden.

It also had several things to recommend it. First of all, the extraordinary views over the river; it was also near the allotments where she was spending more time now that Viv and Angelo had let her take over; finally, it seemed to be in surprisingly good condition, and, as it was in the centre of the row, it felt particularly safe.

Living here she wouldn't need a Wenceslaus to ward off burglars, she would have near neighbours either side.

'Any idea what it'll go for?'

'Maybe half a mill? You never know at auction, but look at the vista.'

What a strange world it was, Ella thought. These cottages

were almost certainly built for river workers, and would have been tied to their jobs. The rent would have been about ten shillings a week, fifty pence in modern money, and now they might fetch half a million pounds! The original occupants would have refused to believe it. But still, if Julia had been correct with her Internet investigations, her current home was worth enough to pay off the mortgage, buy this and give her daughters a sizeable lump sum each.

As she stared out at the sunlit water it made her smile that this was exactly what her daughter and son-in-law had wanted her to do all along. But now the boys were leaving their boarding schools and Julia and Neil seemed to be making a go of things, so it would probably matter less. And perhaps if she'd given them the money sooner Neil would never have seen how much it meant to Julia to have them home.

Of course she'd have to hold on to some money to fund her old age.

A question that had never occurred to her suddenly became real. *I wonder how long I've got?* She was almost sixty-four now, just like the Beatles' song. Would she have fifteen more years, which would make her nearly eighty, or maybe twenty? For God's sake, not thirty?

And would she be able to stay independent if she were somewhere small and cosy like this, or would the day come when she couldn't get up the stairs and had to be put in a care home? Surely the baby boomers, the Me Generation, who had been so clever at other things, could come up with something better than that?

Laura was also talking to estate agents, though, unlike Ella, with no idea where she might go instead. If it hadn't been for having to sell, she might have stayed on and filled the place with lodgers as her children moved out. She was sure of one thing at least, she'd been right to turn down Simon's offer of getting back together.

She didn't even think her children would want it. Certainly not Bella, and Sam rarely mentioned him.

Not surprisingly, there would be no trouble selling the house. Their part of town was still thought highly desirable, it seemed. Laura realized she'd have to curb her natural instincts to make the place as inviting as possible. Maybe she'd leave some dirty clothes in the sink, arrange Sam's stinky trainers about the place, take up smoking. Plenty of unwilling divorcees did their best to sabotage the sale, the agent confided. 'We had one who told every prospective buyer the place was haunted.'

She rather admired divorce-resisters.

Ten minutes after the agent left, the doorbell rang.

It couldn't be a prospective buyer already, unless the agent had tipped someone off unofficially and they were so desperate to get in first that they were already asking for a showing.

To her genuine surprise it was Calum from Relationship Recovery.

'Calum, how are you?' She had to admit he looked very well. The anxiety lines round his mouth had gone, he was suntanned and really rather attractive in old blue jeans and a loose white linen shirt.

'Not too bad. I remembered your address from when we had to write it down. Reading upside down is one of my more recherché skills.' He produced a bottle of champagne, all frosted and inviting, from behind his back. 'Decree absolute just came through and I thought it called for a celebration. How's yours going?'

'Just had the decree nisi, that's why I'm putting the house on the market. I thought you might be the estate agent or a prospective buyer.'

He shrugged. 'Just selling my own house. My ex-wife's found somewhere she likes, so that's good.' Laura led him through the house into the garden. 'Lovely place. Are you all right? About selling, I mean? Leaving behind all your memories?'

'Do you know, I thought I'd mind a lot more. I think the time's right. I've got this fantasy of giving everything I own to my kids or Oxfam and starting with a clean slate. Just keeping a very few things I love and trying to simplify.' She grinned at him. 'Plus I'm a grandmother!'

He smiled, surviving the shock with equanimity. 'You'll soon acquire plenty of clutter, then. Babies seem to carry the whole of Toys R Us with them these days. What is it, boy or girl?'

'Boy.'

'Name?'

'It was going to be Robert after the singer of The Cure, or Aaron from, would you believe it, My Dying Bride. But I think I've interested them in Noah.'

'Great name.' He opened the champagne and they sat drinking it with bees buzzing round them and the sun dappling among the delphiniums.

'Did you get much out of Relationship Recovery?' Laura suddenly asked.

Calum smiled. 'I met you.'

'Naughty, naughty. Did you *learn* anything useful?'

'I suppose I could see that the people who were doing best didn't let themselves get tangled up in bitterness.'

'Yes, I saw that too. I was struck by the quiz asking if you fantasized about reunions. I did. And then Simon turned up here and said it was all a terrible mistake, he should never have left and could he come home?'

'And what did you say?'

Laura smiled and raised her glass, meeting his eyes. 'I told him to fuck off back to his girlfriend.'

'Good for you. It's funny hearing you swear, you're so lady-like it's rather shocking.'

'Look here, Buster, I'm toughening up.'

'Don't toughen up too much.'

'I'm not going to be the silly little woman who doesn't notice her husband's having an affair again. The next man I meet will be too scared to be unfaithful.'

'I'll take that as a warning, shall I?'

Laura, who'd been enjoying herself, suddenly panicked. This was all moving too fast. 'I wasn't really thinking of you.'

'I'm sure you weren't, worse luck. Besides,' he mimicked her speech with a wicked accuracy, "The thing is, I'm not really ready for a serious relationship". How about an unserious one? We could forget how we met and pretend it was on the Internet like everyone else.'

'What, on one of those websites like Hot Granny Dating?'

'I was thinking more Guardian Soulmates. But now that you mention it, you are rather a hot granny.'

'You're not so bad yourself. Tell you what, my friend's daughter is getting married next Saturday in Surrey and I'm allowed a guest to the evening party. Why don't you come down?'

'I'd like that very much.' He drained his champagne. 'Time I left. In case you get another prospective buyer or change your mind about inviting me.'

Laura saw him out and they swapped emails. 'I'll send you all the details.' She waved him off into the early evening sunshine, asking herself, now that it was too late, if that wasn't a really stupid thing she'd done.

To expose Calum, whom she liked but hardly knew, to the

full glare of family, friends and The Coven – it would probably strangle any relationship at birth.

Maybe that was what she wanted.

'You haven't forgotten it's my choir tonight?' Claudia enquired.

Don looked up grumpily. 'Does that mean no supper?'

'Yes. Unless you make it.'

'And I suppose you'll be swanning off to the pub after with your pin-up of a choir master?'

'I might well.' She ignored the reference to Daniel. 'But I won't be late.' The wedding was fast approaching and there was still plenty to do.

Claudia walked down the lane to the school where they rehearsed and met Betty in the hall.

'Hello, Betty!' she greeted her old friend.

'I'm surprised you're here. Shouldn't you be out in the moonlight picking rose petals for confetti or turning napkins into swans?'

'There's plenty of time for all that.'

'Hey, Daniel. How about "I'm Getting Married in the Morning", just for Claudia here.'

'Oh God, not you too. I was hoping to get away from all that.'

'OK.' Daniel suddenly broke into a Fred Astaire routine, grabbing Claudia and gliding across the floor with her.

'I didn't know you could dance,' Claudia commented, impressed.

'Now, kids, keep it clean,' Betty scolded. 'Back to the serious music.'

They worked their way through some Bach, Schubert and George Gershwin before piling into the pub, where they were very welcome, Tuesday night being a quiet evening. The only customers seemed to be a couple of farm labourers, a tweedy couple sitting by the window and some invisible lovebirds in the L-shaped section round the corner.

'How's the outfit?' Betty asked.

'Pink.'

'I'm sure you'll look gorgeous in it. And very suitable.'

'*Suitable?*' echoed Claudia in disgust.

'I thought you wanted to look suitable.'

'Yes, but it seems such a depressing word.'

'Glamorous, then. Fabulous. Terrific. Sexy.'

Daniel joined them and they walked out into the balmy night, Daniel on one side of Betty, Claudia on the other.

'What an amazing evening,' Claudia murmured.

'Come on, lovebirds, time to go home to your nests,' Betty bore down on them, 'individually. Daniel and I are going in the same direction, aren't we, Daniel?' Betty reminded.

Daniel just laughed. 'Watch out, Claudia, there's nothing more disapproving than a reformed chorus girl.'

'That's because chorus girls know the cost of bad behaviour.'

'It's the rich what gets the pleasure and the poor what gets the pain?' Daniel teased.

'Something like that.'

Betty steered Daniel firmly in the direction of his home while Claudia continued the last few yards alone. She stood in the narrow lane thinking about him and smiling into the velvety silence of the night.

Except that there wasn't silence. There was shouting and screaming coming from somewhere nearby.

With a lurch of the heart Claudia realized that the source of all the disturbance was her own home.

CHAPTER 25

Don and Gaby were standing on the front path yelling at each other.

'What on earth is going on?' Claudia demanded.

Gaby, unearthly pale in the moonlit garden, turned to her mother, her face distraught. 'It's Dad. Did you know he was carrying on with some woman called Marianne?'

Claudia knew what was expected of her. Anger. Jealousy. A demand for an explanation. But what she actually felt was guilt. Guilt that she had known and done nothing, because her emotions had been tied up not with her husband but with Daniel Forrest.

'My God,' Gaby's face became a mask of shock and dislike, 'you did know!'

'I knew he was in touch with her, yes.'

Don, silent and drooping, turned to her. 'You never said anything.'

'You were unhappy here, lonely even. I thought maybe this woman might be helping.'

'He texts her all day long. He's just been doing it now!'

Anger finally broke through the paralysis that had been engulfing Claudia. Not just at Don, but at herself. She was as bad as Ella's daughter Julia. Worse, because she ought to have more sense at her age.

'I'm getting my friend Beth to give me away. It's archaic

anyway, being handed over by one man to another, and after this I don't want him to.'

'Gaby, darling . . .' Claudia tried to reason with her daughter.

'Why don't you ask your bloody choir master,' Don flung at Claudia. 'He's the one you're really interested in!'

They stood staring at each other as Gaby and Douglas watched in silent horror. 'If you two are an example of what marriage does to you, then I don't want to get married at all!'

Gaby ran down the path, sobbing.

Douglas surveyed them both. 'Well done, guys. Terrific timing. Let's hope she doesn't mean it.'

'I'll go and speak to her.' Claudia turned towards the house.

'No,' Douglas caught her arm to stop her, and she saw how very angry he was, 'you'd better leave this to me.'

Claudia and Don looked at each other hopelessly.

'Well, we screwed that up royally,' Don admitted.

'I'm not really involved with Daniel Forrest. I was just flattered he fancied me.'

'Marianne's a bit lonely. I think I'm a bit of fantasy to her. I could be anyone, to be honest.'

'Do you think Gaby means it?'

Don shrugged, looking suddenly older. 'I don't think she knows herself. It's late. Maybe she'll have got over it by the morning.'

Claudia lay awake, as far away from Don as possible, in their wide double bed, wondering what she would do if Gaby still did mean it. Perhaps they could cancel, even if it meant contacting all the guests, and the caterers, not to mention the Flying Carpet people who were due to arrive the next day to set up. It would cost a fortune. And then there was her already fraught relationship with her daughter to mend. Not to mention her husband. God almighty, what *had* they both been thinking of?

Sal had woken up with an exciting thought and was eager for morning to come so that she could follow it through.

Nights were not the cancer sufferer's friend and she often ended up propped up in bed wide awake trying to read a book listening to the World Service.

Since Lara was here and would be staying with Sal until after her treatment, she decided to phone Claudia tomorrow and ask if she could bring a guest to the wedding or at least the party afterwards.

By 8.30 she'd been awake for about four hours, and couldn't wait any longer.

Claudia's sleepy voice answered the phone.

'Heavens, Claudia, aren't you up yet? How's the wedding of the year going?'

'*Sal?* Oh, God, Sal, don't. We had the most almighty row last night. I even wondered if she was going to call the whole thing off.'

'Don't worry,' Sal soothed. 'Bridal nerves. We're always doing features on it. At least it wasn't the bridegroom, that's more serious. When they change their mind they usually mean it. She'll probably be fine this morning. My advice is pretend nothing happened. Just go on as normal.'

Claudia was grateful she hadn't asked the reason for the fight.

'Anyway, where have you got to?' Claudia demanded. 'You're harder to track down than the Scarlet Pimpernel. We've all been really worried about you. And you are coming to the wedding, aren't you? You replied ages ago.'

'Of course. Wouldn't miss it for the world. Claudia, I know this is very rude of me and weddings are tricky events, but there's someone I want to bring with me. I wouldn't ask normally but this is someone special, someone I'd really like you to meet. Do you think you could squeeze one more in?'

'I wouldn't even dare ask at the moment. It's been a very touchy subject. They can come to the party, though. Gaby gave us permission to ask as many as we wanted.'

'What time's that?'

'Eight till late, it says on the invitation. If it ever happens. I'll probably be spending the next day on the phone putting people off.'

'Cheer up, Claudia, I'm sure it won't come to that.'

'More to the point. Who is it you're bringing?' How amazing if Sal had a boyfriend at last.

'Just put Plus One.'

'Get you, Ms Mysterious. How are you, anyway? None of us can believe how long it is since we've actually clapped eyes on you. You aren't avoiding us because you've had a sex change or anything? Because, honestly, we'd still keep you in the coven.'

Sal laughed. 'Nothing so dramatic. It's always a thought though.'

Claudia suddenly remembered the glimpse she'd had of her at the hospital. 'By the way, what were you doing in the Princess Lily? I could have sworn I saw you there when Bella was having her baby. You were with a blonde woman.'

There was a beat of silence on the end of the line. 'Wait and see,' Sal announced infuriatingly. 'All will be revealed.'

Really, thought Claudia, irritated. She'd had enough drama recently to last a lifetime.

She'd just said goodbye and gone downstairs in her dressing gown when her father appeared, bearing a straw-filled basket full of eggs. 'A little pre-wedding gift for Gaby from my chickens,' he announced. 'New-laid. I hope she likes them.'

478

It was terrific to see her father properly mobile again. 'I'm sure she'll love them.' Her father, always intuitive, picked up the uncertainty in her tone.

'Something up?'

'Oh, God, Dad,' she leaned on his shoulder, feeling like a child again, 'we all had a terrific quarrel last night. I've no idea what'll happen today, whether there'll even *be* a wedding.'

Len opened his arms and Claudia surrendered herself to one of his big bear hugs. 'I'm sure it'll all come out in the wash.'

Claudia remembered that she was the one who should be taking care of her parents, not the other way round. 'How's Mum?'

'I haven't been finding pills hidden in the airing cupboard or down the back of the sofa recently. So that's something. I think she must be listening to you at last.'

'That'd be a change.'

'Cheer up. Weddings are always hell. That's why there are honeymoons, for the couple to get away from their families before they kill each other.'

'Douglas's parents must have arrived by now. They were only coming at the last minute.'

'Nice boy, is he?'

'Yes, he is. Quiet but with hidden strengths. Rather worrying how little time they've known each other.'

'I don't think that matters. I knew the moment I met your mum.'

Claudia smiled at him. 'I didn't know that.' But then you never really thought of your parents as people, young like you were and full of dreams and angst, falling in love and suffering rejection.

'I was a bit of a ditherer, scared of deciding unless I made a mistake. Olivia never had doubts about anything. She was magnificent.'

'That sounds like Mum.' Claudia caught the troubled look in his eye. 'She'll get better. I know she will.'

'Thank you, darling. I'd better pop off and take her her morning tea.'

'You're all right with stairs now then.'

He grinned, the old Len of her childhood peeping out again. 'I'm thinking of taking up hurdling, as a matter of fact.'

Ella breathed in deeply.

It was done.

She'd accepted an offer from the third prospective buyers who'd seen around the house. The estate agent insisted they were the dream purchasers: cash buyers who'd already sold and therefore weren't involved in a chain. To make it easier, Ella liked them. She couldn't actually bear to show them round her beloved home herself, but when she did meet them they'd made all the right noises. They understood the unique qualities of the place, loved the oak panelling and the sweeping staircase, even noting that the width of the skirting boards was exactly right for the period. Ella decided they wouldn't be the type to install basement cinemas or underground parking or an indoor swimming pool like a lot of London's newly rich. They were so eager they had already done an express search and were almost ready to exchange contracts.

She looked at her husband's photograph standing as it always did on the hall table. 'What do you think, Laurence?'

But Laurence had nothing to say.

'I'll take that as a yes, shall I?' She picked up the photograph and kissed it. 'We'll be all right if we get the cottage.'

Ella realized that she was talking to her dead husband and that if she wanted to actually get that cottage, she'd better damn well get moving.

She had been in luck when she'd been to see the bank about

a possible bridging loan. Although a retired woman with no income might be risky, the bank manager lived on the other side of the square and knew what a gem Ella's current home was, probably the best house in an increasingly desirable location. He also knew how rarely the houses came on the market. If these buyers fell through, others would take their place instantly. In fact, he counselled Ella, she could probably play buyers against each other and push up the price. But Ella didn't want to do that. She'd loved this house as if it were a person and she didn't want to feel guilty about how she'd behaved in selling it.

She'd got her finance.

The auction for the cottage was to be held in a church hall in the new part of Moulsford, near the flyover up to the motorway, far more directly under the Heathrow runway than Ella's house. In fact, the noise from passing planes was so great that everyone standing outside the hall waiting for it to open had to shout to be heard as they gossiped and joshed.

Ella glanced around the crowd, her interest sharpening. They were a mixed bunch: some nice older couples, the kind you saw at antique fairs, to whom house-buying was a hobby to be indulged in only cautiously when the right property came along; sober-suited businessmen; rough-edged builders still cleaning the paint from their nails; a sprinkling of cashmere-wearing developers from Eastern Europe, glued to their smartphones; a chic young woman who looked as if she might have a rich husband; and the rest fairly nondescript. She was the only woman her age, Ella noted. Good. With luck they would mistake her for a little old lady.

As soon as the doors opened they belted towards the registration desk to get their numbers, then headed for the few seats at the front where the auctioneer could get a good view of them.

Ella had done all her homework. She had studied the legal pack; commissioned a survey, which might be money down the drain, but which the estate agent had strongly advised; and she had almost acquired a lawyer, as the agent had also advised, before she had remembered that she *was* a lawyer. She might have specialized in employment, but it couldn't be that hard to bone up on conveyancing.

'I see Tim McAuley's here,' the man next to her whispered to his neighbour.

'Bloody shark,' endorsed Neighbour number two. 'He already owns half West London. There ought to be a quota or something.'

Ella glanced across the hall in the direction in which they were looking. A florid man in a grey chalk-striped suit caught her glance and tipped his catalogue in acknowledgement of her interest. Trying not to flush, Ella looked away.

Already she could feel her heartbeat quickening and the auctioneer hadn't even arrived. What if she didn't get it? Could she pull out of her own sale? It was one thing to sell her beloved family home, knowing she'd found an alternative she could love as much, quite another to leave it without knowing where she'd go.

Ella took a deep breath trying to remember all the advice she'd been given: have 10 per cent of the purchase price available in cash to put down as a deposit on the day; decide on a maximum price; don't get carried away; don't bid too soon; on the other hand, since it all happens fast, get ready to bid at the right moment. No wonder people said house-buying at auctions was daunting.

'Excuse me, could I squeeze in there?' A youngish man with a pleasant manner, casually dressed in chinos and a white shirt with a sweater slung over his shoulders, eased himself into Ella's row. A mother to the last, Ella caught herself checking him out for a wedding band in case be might be the type for her daughter Cory. Yes, he had one. Oh well.

And then the auction began in earnest.

Number 3 Grand Union Cottages was Lot 41, so Ella knew she was in for a wait. She decided to study other people's bidding technique. The florid man seemed to bid, in a loud, forceful voice, for almost everything. Clearly he was the spiv he had been branded. One of the nice older couples got the flat they were chasing and beamed. A rather hesitant man tried to make himself seen by the auctioneer and was overlooked.

'Probably sewn up already,' murmured the neighbour who had pointed out Tim McAuley.

What really struck Ella was how fast the hammer went down. She would have to place her bid quickly and assertively. There was one instance, though, when a sale was more drawn out. A dodgy-looking character in a sheepskin coat kept the auction going by throwing in last-minute bids. 'He wants that crap property like I want a heart attack,' mumbled Neighbour number one.

When the property sold at a much higher price than expected, Ella realized they were right. The seller had obviously employed the dodgy sheepskin man to artificially bid up the price. She hoped to God it didn't happen with her cottage.

By the time it came to Lot 41 Ella's palms were sweating.

The bidding started slowly: £100k . . . 120 . . . 130 . . . up to 200. Of course Tim McAuley was bidding. Damn. £220k . . . 240 . . . 260 . . . 270 . . . 300 – Ella held up her number and shouted 'Yes!'

'Three hundred?' enquired the auctioneer. 'Am I bid three hundred thousand pounds?'

'Three hundred and ten!' replied someone in Ella's row. She glanced along. It was the pleasant-looking man. Bugger.

'Am I bid three hundred and twenty?' asked the auctioneer.

'Three hundred and forty!' shouted her neighbour. He didn't seem so nice now.

'Three hundred and fifty?' demanded the auctioneer. The florid-featured McAuley raised his number.

Ella's fighting spirit began to emerge.

'Three hundred and sixty?'

The pleasant man next to her raised an eyebrow. It seemed to be enough.

'Three hundred and seventy?'

Another nod from Mr Red Face.

'Three hundred and eighty? Am I bid three hundred and eighty?'

By now the florid McAuley had dropped out and it was just Ella and her chino-clad opponent.

'Three hundred and ninety?' was the next request. Ella waved her number.

Now everyone was watching. It suddenly struck her that maybe he was buying it for his family home. Was she being unfair to outbid him? All the accusations from her daughters about nabbing the cheap property flooded into her head.

'Four hundred? Am I bid four hundred?' Ella's pleasant-looking opponent lifted his number.

'Four hundred thousand,' repeated the auctioneer. 'I'm bid four hundred thousand pounds by Mr McAuley for Number three Grand Union Cottages, in my view the property of the night. Any more takers?'

Ella did a double take between the florid-featured gent and the man she had mentally marked down as a potential husband for Cory. *He* was Tim McAuley, the property shark who owned half of West London.

'Four hundred and ten? Who will bid me four hundred and ten?'

Ella nodded again.

Somewhere at the back another punter clapped.

Tim McAuley directed a steely glance in her direction. 'Four hundred and twenty thousand!' he announced.

Ella was doing furious calculations in her head. If McAuley was a smart property developer he would need to get the cottage for a low enough price to modernize it, stick in the beige carpets universally adored by developers, probably a new kitchen and bathroom, as well as paint it throughout. He couldn't afford to go much higher and make a margin if the agent was right about the valuation.

He might do it out of sheer obstinacy though.

'Four hundred and thirty thousand?' The auctioneer was all attention. Ella waved, beginning to feel dizzy.

'Four hundred and forty?' demanded the auctioneer, beginning to visibly enjoy himself now. 'A prime riverside property! I wouldn't mind living there myself!'

McAuley nodded again, damn him!

'Four fifty? Am I bid four fifty now, ladies and gents?' People were craning round to watch now, like a poker game in Las Vegas.

'Four sixty!' countered McAuley.

Ella knew she had to stop soon. She should have stopped already.

'Four seventy?' It was Ella again. She could feel the electricity in the air. This was what she'd been warned about. She would go to five and that was it.

'Four eighty? Four eighty now. Am I bid four eighty?'

McAuley nodded.

'Four hundred and ninety? Will the lady bid four hundred and ninety?'

Ella raised her number, her arm shaking.

'Five hundred?'

The atmosphere was as silent and chilly as the wastes of the Arctic tundra.

'Mr McAuley?' enquired the auctioneer.

McAuley smiled at Ella. 'Five hundred thousand.'

Ella shook her head. She couldn't go any further. The hammer went down on the sale to Tim McAuley of McAuley Properties.

Ella had lost.

CHAPTER 26

Ella reached down for her bag. She was going to keep her head up no matter what. She certainly wasn't going to cry. Silly to think a newcomer like her could negotiate an auction.

'Here, missis,' hissed Neighbour number two. 'McAuley knows that was dumb. No way he'll get it back. Wait till he's calmed down and make him an offer.'

Ella hung around until the crowd had cleared. Tim McAuley was chatting to the florid man. Finally the conversation broke up.

'Mr McAuley . . .'

He turned round, surprised.

'Ella Thompson. I'm selling my house on Moulsford Green . . .'

'Moulsford Green? One of the eighteenth-century ones near the river?'

'That's right. Number twenty-seven.'

'The one in the middle next to the brass lamp post.'

'That's the one.' Ella raised an eyebrow. 'You seem to know a lot about it.'

He shrugged. 'It was the house I fantasized about living in when I got married. So it's going up for sale?' He seemed to think for a moment.

Oh God, thought Ella, *he's going to make me an offer and I've already accepted one from that nice couple.*

To her enormous relief, he didn't. 'So, what can I do for you?'

'When I sell it I want to move to Number three Grand Union Cottages – in fact, I'd rather set my heart on it. Now personally I don't mind living in a place where the plumbing's a bit old-fashioned. I even quite like unfitted kitchens. But I doubt anyone you sell on to is going to feel the same. It strikes me you'll have to spend at least a hundred thousand on it, and the agent tells me he very much doubts you'll get it back.'

'Does he now?' Tim McAuley grinned suddenly. 'And you'd like to do me the favour of taking it off me?'

'Exactly. Five hundred is my maximum, though. I've sorted out a loan with the bank until my house sells.'

'You're very confident it will.'

'The third lot of viewers to see it made me an offer. It has that effect on people.'

'Yes. I remember. A tall, friendly chap showed me around during a fair on the green. He knew an awful lot about the people who built the houses and where they brought their cargoes in down at the river.'

'Yes,' Ella bit her lip to hold back the sudden rush of memory, 'that was my husband Laurence. He was killed in a train crash soon afterwards.'

Tim McAuley looked stunned. 'I'm sorry.'

'Yes, well, I went on living there partly because I loved it and partly for Laurence's sake, because of what it meant to him. My daughters were forever on at me to downsize.'

'And give them the cash? I meet a lot of kids like that in my profession.'

Ella wasn't at all sure she liked this man. It might have annoyed her that Julia and Neil hoped for a windfall, but he seemed to be implying something genuinely nasty.

'Sorry, I'm sure your daughters weren't like that. About your offer, I'll think about it.'

'Thank you.'

'Anyway, it's a lovely house you're selling. I'd think about it for myself if I weren't just getting divorced.'

'Yes, it is. I'll certainly miss it.'

And this time she didn't even think about pairing him off with Cory.

The atmosphere in the kitchen was sullen and uncomfortable, as if a battle had been lost and both sides were counting their dead. There was a lot of banging of saucepans and abrupt swerving to avoid bodily contact. Douglas hid behind the *Daily Telegraph* while Gaby and Claudia avoided each other's eye.

Don, who loathed 'an atmosphere' and who had spent his childhood interposing himself between warring parents, was about to attempt another apology when the garden door burst open.

To everyone's astonishment it was Olivia. And not the Olivia her daughter had last encountered, staring desolately at her own image in the mirror. This Olivia had clean and neatly brushed hair and wore a rather smart print frock with toning suede court shoes.

'Chop, chop, everybody,' Olivia announced in ringing memsahib tones. 'You all need to get dressed. I have booked us in for croquet in the garden at Igden Manor.'

Claudia leaned on the kitchen unit, too stunned by her mother's sudden transformation to speak.

'Come on now, Claudia dear,' Olivia chivvied. 'No need to look like the village idiot. I didn't sign up for it with a voucher, so don't get your bloomers in a twist. I'm just popping home to get changed into sensible shoes and to sort out your father.

I'm sure you've got a lot to get organized before then. I'll see you all there at one.'

Without leaving them an opportunity to raise an argument Olivia disappeared like a puff of smoke.

Claudia looked after her, dazedly. 'I think Mum must have definitely started taking her pills, don't you?'

A fragile truce seemed to have descended, thanks to Olivia.

At 12.30 Don offered to drive the twenty minutes to Igden Manor. Claudia tried to make bright conversation while Gaby sat in the back ignoring her and Douglas glanced from one to the other unhappily as if he were observing a particularly tense game of ping pong.

No one mentioned the wedding.

Claudia wondered whether to at least ask when his parents would be arriving but judged it better to say absolutely nothing.

By the time they got to Igden Manor, Len and Olivia were already on the lawn sorting out mallets and balls. It was a beautiful day and the croquet lawn, between lush flowerbeds nodding with hollyhocks and delphiniums, was laid out before them like a bolt of green velvet.

'Are you playing, Gran?' Gaby asked.

'No, dear, Grandad's hip's not up to scratch yet. We'll sit on the terrace and watch the fun.'

Fun, it struck Claudia, was not the likely outcome.

'Right,' Olivia continued, 'two teams – Gaby and Douglas versus Claudia and Don. And I'm expecting plenty of inter-generational needle.'

'She'll get that all right,' murmured Don. 'I hope your mother knows what she's doing. If you ask me this is set for disaster.'

'All right, who knows the rules?'

'I used to play in my friend's back garden,' announced Gaby, 'but we never used any rules.'

'I know the rules,' announced Douglas. 'I played croquet a bit at college.'

'Hey, posh boy, you kept that quiet,' Gaby commented.

'Maybe I am a bit of a dark horse.' The silky mix of threat and promise in his tone brought a glint to Gaby's eye. Perhaps there was more to their prospective son-in-law than Claudia had suspected.

'OK, everyone, let's get on with it,' Olivia insisted. 'You'd better tell everyone how to do it, Douglas.'

Douglas launched into a colourful but brilliantly clear exposition of the rules of croquet which Claudia had always found impossible to fathom.

'Good man, that's it, get them going,' counselled Len from his seat on the terrace. 'I'll toss a coin to see who starts. Heads or tails?'

'Heads,' shouted Gaby eager to be in control.

'Tails it is.'

They all picked a mallet and lined up to start.

Gaby stood over her ball and began to swing like a golf player.

'Better if you stand like this.' Douglas moved his feet apart and thrust the mallet straight on from between his legs. 'A lot more accurate.'

Claudia and Don took his advice. Gaby stuck mutinously to her original stance.

Wisely, Douglas said nothing and they began the game.

At the first hoop they were all clumsy and self-conscious but soon the competitive spirit took over. At one point Don's ball disappeared into the herbaceous border. Claudia helped him look for it.

'Don,' she grabbed his hand as they hunted in the hedge together, 'I'm really sorry about the Daniel Forrest business. Nothing actually happened. Anyway, I'm giving up the choir.'

He looked her in the eye. 'It's not about the choir, is it? It's about us. Both of us. I shouldn't have contacted Marianne.'

Claudia spotted the ball nestling among the *Alchemilla mollis*. 'There you go.' She handed it to him. 'This is hardly the place to talk about it, is it? In a flowerbed?'

'I don't know. T. S. Eliot's always on about the rose garden.'

Claudia smiled. 'That sounded like the old you.'

'Hey,' came a shout from her father, 'what are you two up to? Haven't you found the ball yet?'

'Found it!'

The next half-hour passed in a flash. Don turned out to be rather good, unlike Claudia, who kept confusing it with Crazy Golf, and as the desire to win intensified, Gaby quietly abandoned her Arnold Palmer swing and copied her fiancé.

But the real star was Douglas.

'You know,' Olivia commented under her breath to her husband, 'I rather like that young man. I think he'll know how to handle Gaby.'

At the end Olivia stood up, clapping. 'Well done, Gaby and Douglas. It's a good omen for your marriage that you're able to compromise. Now, who's ready for tea, and don't worry, Claudia, it isn't even a two-for-one, so relax!'

To Claudia's relief, Gaby said nothing more about getting her friend Beth to give her away, and certainly nothing about calling off the wedding.

Across the tea table loaded with scones, clotted cream and cake, Claudia caught her father Len's eye. They both smiled with unspoken relief that her mother had emerged from the long dark tunnel.

After the last crumbs were polished off, Gaby announced that she and Douglas were heading for the pub.

Don raised an enquiring eyebrow at Claudia to see if she wanted to join them. Memories of Daniel jostled into her mind, but all she felt was foolish and embarrassed rather than sad or regretful. She shook her head.

'It's a lovely evening,' Don suggested, 'why don't we take Vito for a walk? They'll be an hour at least.'

They collected the dog from the cottage and strolled out over the fields. The corn was pale gold, rippling in the wind like billowing silk.

'It really is lovely here.'

Don looked at her in surprise. 'I thought you still preferred London, that I'd tricked you into leaving under false pretences and trapped you here against your will? Don't you regret leaving any more?'

Claudia turned to face him. 'No, Don, I don't. And neither should you. I think we should both start again. Together.'

He said nothing but kept on walking. Above them skylarks soared and sang their mysterious hidden melody.

'Like happiness,' Claudia sighed. 'Near but just out of reach.'

'Let's grab it, then,' Don replied, taking her hand. 'Soon we'll be old and ill. If we're ever going to be happy it had better be bloody now!'

'That's the most romantic proposal I've ever had,' Claudia announced.

'Come on, you old boot, beat you to that stile before we both need hip replacements!'

Together they ran, breathless and laughing, while Vito barked deliriously at this mad and unfamiliar new game.

By the time they got back to the cottage, they were surprised to find no sign of Gaby and Douglas.

'Must have stayed in the pub. Hang on, there's a note on the table.'

He picked it up, full of misgiving that the wedding would be cancelled after all.

'It's just a message. Ella rang; she'll be here at 8 a.m. tomorrow with the flowers. Ditto the Flying Carpet people.' He looked up, grinning. 'The happy couple have gone upstairs for a snooze and will see us later. Looks like there's going to be a wedding after all.'

The following day, respecting the fragile peace, they all kept out of each other's way. By the time Ella's hired van, loaded with flowers, pulled up outside their cottage, Claudia almost leapt on her.

'My God, am I glad to see you! I thought we weren't going to *have* a bloody wedding.'

'That's a relief since I've spent a small fortune on crème de la crème roses and calla lilies! Why ever not?' She handed Claudia a huge cardboard box to carry inside. 'Now where are we going to keep these? These are the bride's and the brides-maids' bouquets.' She indicated two more. 'That one's for the pew ends, the other is the centrepieces. The big decorations for the church are still in the van.'

'So why did you think there wouldn't be a wedding?' They were carrying the boxes of flowers into a shady outbuilding so that they wouldn't wilt.

'Oh God, Ella, where do I start? Gaby found out Don had been texting his old school flame and it turns out that he knew about my crush on the choir master all along. I think we both were just cross with each other and had stopped caring.'

'Are you and Don all right now?' Ella asked sternly. 'Out of the four of us, you're the only one who's still married, so get your act together, girl!'

'I think we're OK now. I *hope* so, which is at least progress.'

'In case you were thinking of leaving, can I tell you some-thing? It's quite tough on your own.' Claudia took the flowers from her friend. Ella was the last person to complain, even when fate had played the dirtiest of tricks. 'I don't advise trying it, unless you absolutely have to. Especially at our age. Look at it this way, women live a lot longer than men, so even if he has got annoying little habits like falling for someone he hasn't seen for forty years, he doesn't know that she has fur on her face, grey hair, and never lost her baby weight. Stick with him if you can. Right, end of lecture.'

Claudia felt chastened. Ella was so no-nonsense that they all tended to unburden themselves to her instead of wondering how she coped with life alone.

'And while you're about it, why don't you go away together, Paris maybe? Get the old radical Claudia back.'

'I think I was only a radical by accident. By the way, Ella Thompson, has anyone told you lately that you're a wonderful woman?'

'No one who isn't wearing a bobble hat and is up to his elbows in fertiliser.'

'Well, I'm telling you now.'

They went to fetch the last of the flowers from the van. Ella noticed her phone next to the driving seat and checked it for messages. Still no word from Tim McAuley. She'd better forget all about it or it would end up spoiling the wedding for her.

The excitement at the arrival of the Flying Carpet Company struck Claudia as akin to the stir caused by a medieval mummers' play. Everyone in Little Minsley came out to watch the drama. But then it wasn't every day that an Indian-inspired marquee appeared in an English village, complete with garlanded arches, birdcage chandeliers, brightly coloured rugs and acres of gold-tasselled velvet curtains.

And even she had to admit the result was highly dramatic. Down one end of the marquee round tables were set out, dressed in ruby and magenta silks, and at the other end a Raj bar, complete with a burnished brass counter top. In between was a small dance floor which would be rolled out and extended for the party afterwards.

Outside, in front of the marquee, a row of harem couches completed the exotic vision. And behind everything the unlikely setting of rolling English acres.

Despite her misgivings, Claudia had to admit it looked amazing.

'And you haven't seen the bridal boudoir yet,' Claudia whispered to Ella. 'It's a big secret, even from the best man, because you don't want an apple-pie bed in a boudoir. But sssh! and I'll show you.'

'Wait a minute and I'll bring some flowers. There're a few spare I brought to freshen the centrepieces.'

They sneaked away through the patch of woodland beyond the paddock where the marquee was sited, down an overgrown path into the dip beyond a nearby hill. And there, nestling in a hidden dell, was a jewel-bright Bedouin tent. Inside was a king-size bed, a table and two chairs, red and purple rugs and dozens of tea lights in coloured glass containers.

'They even come and light the candles for you later.'

'It's fabulous!' Ella congratulated, making Claudia feel better that she'd given in and agreed to it even though it had meant cashing in an ISA. 'Though why they all bother with wedding nights when they already live together, I don't know.'

'You're beginning to sound like my mother.'

Ella laughed. 'I'm beginning to *feel* like your mother.' She sat down on a stool and began arranging the posy she'd bought.

Claudia sat beside her. 'You're not feeling old, are you? You've always been like the bunny on the TV ad with the long-life battery.'

'Well, my battery's running down a bit. I think I'm ready for slippers by the fire and supper on one of those special trays in front of the telly.'

'Ella!'

'Is it breaking the Coven Code if I want to admit I'm nearly sixty-four and feeling it? I'm beginning to long for the days when sixty was sixty and not the new forty.'

'We'd better get back. The bride will be surfacing. Time to deck her out in all her non-virginal glory.'

Sal and Lara were sharing a leisurely breakfast at the comfortable country hotel two miles from Little Minsley which Lara had found on the Internet.

'So, when are you going to tell them about your mastectomy?' Lara handed over the basket of patisseries. 'Promise me one thing. You *are* going to tell them.'

'They'll probably guess anyway. Claudia saw me with you at the hospital, remember, and Ella's got a lawyer's eye for noticing everything. She's already been asking why she hasn't seen me for so long. I have to be careful, though. This is a wedding, it's supposed to be joyous, even when people only give the couple a month. I don't want to spoil things.'

'Tell them. They'll be angry if you don't. You have a major operation next week, for heaven's sake! They will want to stand by you.'

'I know. The trouble is, I should have told them at the beginning.'

'Remember your boss. She was fine about it. Maybe they will be too.'

'That's true.' Sal brightened. 'I will tell them, as soon as the right moment arrives. Now, which of my cancer-distracting outfits do you think I should wear?'

Sal had brought two: a bluebell-coloured trouser suit with

a Nehru collar and tiny buttons, and a fuchsia-pink sheath dress. 'The thing is, I want to wear the pink wig. In memory of Rachel.'

'Are you sure? The other wig looks more natural.'

'Screw natural! What I need today is *chutzpah*!'

'You'll certainly need that,' Lara replied dubiously.

Sal took her hand. 'Today I am intending to tell my three best friends that I have cancer and also that I have a wonderful, beautiful daughter. Wearing a pink wig will help me keep my nerve.'

'It had better be the blue trouser suit, then, or they'll think you are in – how do you say it in English – fancy dress?'

Laura was feeling too short of cash to indulge in a hotel and she intended to get a lift back from Calum after the party, but she did allow herself a new hat.

Trying on hats was one of those irresistible temptations she always indulged in whenever she was passing through a department store. Unlike most people, hats suited Laura. She had no idea if it was the shape of her face, the fact that people told her she was a 'pretty' woman, or the simple fact that she enjoyed wearing them, but she was definitely a hat person.

So she had spent a happy half-hour trying out feathered fascinators, enormous straw hats straight from *My Fair Lady*, and tiny pink pillboxes complete with jewelled veils. She settled on a taupe straw creation that perched jauntily on the side of her head, giving her the air of an optimistic wartime bride. It would go very well with the silky wrap dress she had last worn on that disastrous trip to Brighton which had heralded the end of her marriage. There was no reason to waste the dress just because the marriage didn't work out.

She paused for a moment in the shoe department that took up an entire floor and eyed the perfect suede slingbacks.

Then she saw the price tag. They'd probably only hurt her feet and she'd take them off anyway. Laura sighed. But she wasn't given to bitterness and bile, so she decided to concentrate on the thought that for the first time in months she and her friends would be together again. She hoped they would all be at the same table and that Claudia hadn't succumbed to that irritating hostess-like habit of putting them with interesting new people when all they wanted was to gossip with each other.

On the way back to the car she had to pass through the flower shop. A bunch of bright parrot tulips caught her eye. They were red and purple with exotic stripes of green and yellow. They were so extravagantly colourful, so shamelessly alluring, that she longed to buy them, but there was no way she could justify the cost.

If her marriage had continued, she could have had flowers like this in every room.

But all the tulips in Amsterdam couldn't compensate for a miserable marriage.

Her phone buzzed and she checked it. There was a message from Helena Butler, the woman who'd approached her at LateExpress, asking her to call back.

Maybe things were looking up.

Claudia looked up at the sky above the gloriously gaudy marquee. Thank God the weather seemed to be holding out. She and Ella were putting the centrepieces out on each round table. 'They're perfect, Ella. Thank you so much.'

They sat down side by side on one of the harem couches, Claudia's rollered hair hidden under a scarf. 'The bride's having hers done first, then all the bridesmaids. Why don't you and I have a glass of champagne while we're waiting?' She went and fetched a bottle and two glasses from behind the

Raj bar. 'We never went for all this wedding extravaganza stuff, did we? Don and I were hitched in the registry office then went for a curry.'

Ella took a slug of the champagne. 'Laurence and I didn't get married at all till after Julia. Weird how they all want to go rushing down the aisle in white dresses.'

'I'm glad I didn't. I look terrible in white, anyway.' Claudia looked at her watch. 'Eleven o'clock. I'd better get back and start behaving like the bride's mother. I wonder if Gaby will want all that something borrowed, something blue stuff.'

'Claudia,' Ella shook her head in mock disbelief, 'of course she will. It's in the handbook.'

Claudia picked up the bride's and bridesmaids' bouquets. 'Let's hope everyone's still talking to each other.'

Relative harmony seemed to be reigning when she got back to the house in time to help Gaby with her dress. The brides-maids had had their hair done and were dressed and waiting.

Gaby had opted to do her own make-up. 'I'd rather Douglas could recognize the woman he's marrying – which is more than you can say for most brides once the make-up artist's finished with them.'

Her veil was draped over a chair next to the circlet of fresh flowers Ella had made her. Next to it the dress, discovered by Gaby on the Internet, just as she had sourced her husband, rippled to the ground in a waterfall of ivory silk.

Claudia helped her to step into it.

She rested her head on Gaby's bare shoulder for an instant as they both surveyed the effect in the mirror.

'You look perfect.'

Gaby smiled. 'I'm glad we didn't call the whole thing off.'

Claudia grinned. 'So am I.' And she realized she meant it. 'Would you like to wear my sapphire earrings? They could be borrowed, old and blue all in one fell swoop.'

'And I'm wearing a new thong I just bought, so that's got that covered.'

The rest of the bridal party, still a little strained, had gathered outside to wait for the cars. Len and Olivia got in first, with Douglas's parents, followed by Claudia and the maid of honour, with Don and Gaby in the final one.

'My little Gabriella,' Don murmured, misty-eyed and unable to say more as Gaby appeared in all her bridal finery.

Ella stayed out in the sunshine drinking another glass of champagne, hoping things would be all right when Neil and Wenceslaus found they were both at the same party. She took one last quick look at the arrangements on the pew-ends to make sure they hadn't wilted.

No, they were beautiful.

The terrifying thought suddenly invaded her mind that she might soon be homeless. She could renege on the sale, but that would be against her personal code.

Maybe she'd better have another drink.

The wedding was at four and by three-thirty, following the maxim 'Never be late for weddings or funerals unless you're the bride or the corpse', the guests started arriving, just as Ella finished the tour of all her flower arrangements. She slipped out of the side door and ran back to Claudia's to change.

Finally it was all going ahead.

Claudia found she could breathe properly for the first time in days. She was seated in the front row, the music had started up and her only child was walking down the aisle on her father's arm in her perfect yet ludicrously expensive dress, looking blissfully happy while her bridegroom smiled at her over his shoulder.

And Gaby had been right about the church. While the Flying

Carpet Company might perfectly deliver an extravagant eastern fantasy for the reception, there was nothing like a small country church to provide the perfect mix of gravity and simple beauty for the wedding service.

'Great dress,' a voice whispered.

Claudia turned to find Ella behind her in a fetching feathered hat. 'Must have cost a bomb to look that simple.'

Pachelbel's Canon drew to a close and it was finally time for the exchange of vows. Gaby and Douglas in turn made their solemn promise to love each other 'for better, for worse, for richer, for poorer; in sickness and in health, to love and cherish, till death us do part'.

Throughout the church the congregation sniffed, acknowledging how very hard to keep these vows were, how they themselves had mostly failed, and, at the same time, hoping that this young couple might be different and manage it.

In the row behind, Laura was struggling to remain in control. The wedding vows, so familiar and yet so powerful, were proving too much for her. When she had uttered them to Simon at her own wedding, she had meant every word. She had imagined a life bound together through good times and through bad, with death, not divorce, as their only parting.

A hand gently tapped her, offering a handkerchief. Laura thanked the giver and was directed to someone who was watching her from two rows behind. It was Sal, and for some bizarre reason she appeared to be wearing sunglasses and a pink wig.

'I love you, Gabriella,' Don whispered to his daughter as she stood at the church door waiting to greet her guests, 'I think you've picked a better man than me.'

'Thanks, Dad.' Gaby blew him a kiss.

Outside in the churchyard a small group of musicians playing ancient instruments led the guests back along the village street towards the marquee while people all along the street threw open doors and windows and waved good luck to the newly wedded couple.

'Isn't this wonderful?' Sal squeezed Laura's arm, 'I feel as if I'm in some medieval woodcut of a wedding. Are you all right now?'

Laura nodded tearfully. 'I didn't even bring a hankie. I thought I'd seen through the values of marriage for good and all.'

Sal followed the happy couple with her eyes. 'I suppose every marriage starts with a pure heart.'

Laura glanced at her, surprised that for once she wasn't being ironic. She not only looked different, but sounded it. Sal was the least emotional person she knew.

They walked back through the village behind the musicians with the rest of the guests.

'This is all very amazing, isn't it?' Sal lightened the tone. 'I keep expecting the lord of the manor to sweep in and carry off the bride for deflowering.'

'I think he'd be a bit late in Gaby's case,' Laura pointed out. 'She's already living with the bridegroom. Claudia's a bit worried they haven't known each other that long, though I knew Simon for three years and you can see what difference that made.'

'How's it all going with the divorce?' Sal enquired.

'Just waiting for the decree absolute.'

'How's Simon the new dad coming along?'

'His girlfriend lost the baby then dumped him. His sperm are too old.' They laughed uproariously. 'Not funny, really, but you've got to laugh or you'd cry.' Laura dabbed her eyes. 'Come on, let's join in. Weddings are supposed to be joyous occasions.'

'Are they?' Sal grinned. 'In my family they usually end up with one half half-murdering the other.'

By now they'd arrived at the marquee and were being offered champagne in exotic-coloured flutes.

They looked round at the colourful gathering.

Ella, they noticed, was handing a waiter her empty glass and helping herself to a full one. 'Ella's knocking it back a bit, isn't she?' Sal pointed out. 'That's not like Ella. She's usually the well-behaved one.'

'Maybe she wants to break out a bit.'

'Ella? Hardly.' Laura considered their friend through the noisy throng.

'People may not be as easy to read as you think,' Sal remarked. 'Now, where are we sitting?' They headed for the seating plan posted on a board near the entrance. 'I hope we're all together.'

'Hello, you two!' Rather drunkenly, Ella put an arm round each of them. 'Sal, you're as thin as rake!' She turned to take a proper look but Sal had slithered out of her grasp and was seating herself at her allotted spot.

They were right near the front, close to the high table where both families were seated, with a clear view of the bride and groom.

'Claudia and Don look happy,' Laura said, waving to them. Claudia waved back.

'Actually,' Ella dropped her voice, filling her glass again from one of the bottles of wine on the table, 'Claudia says the wedding almost didn't happen.'

'Why ever not?' Laura asked. 'Was Gaby getting cold feet? I wouldn't blame her.'

'Laura, stop thinking about your own marriage and lighten up,' Ella replied tartly.

Laura and Sal blinked. 'What's got into you?' Sal asked. 'Apart from the champagne?'

'Sshh! They're starting the speeches.'

'I thought they were later.'

'Maybe they want to be able to drink afterwards.'

'Some people have got a head start already.' Sal shot Ella a sardonic look.

'Sssh! It's the speeches!'

Don began with a sweet speech insisting that they wouldn't have had to move to Surrey if they'd known their daughter would be leaving anyway, earning him a big laugh and a daughterly flounce from Gaby. He then got serious in a fatherly way about how much they loved her and how proud they were of their only offspring. Finally he welcomed Douglas to their family and handed him the mike.

Douglas, tall and serious, explained how Gaby had catapulted into his life and turned it upside down, but that he'd still been worried about making this final commitment.

'I said to Gaby: "What happens if we make a mistake and the marriage doesn't work out?" and she answered quick as a flash: "We can always put it on eBay," so you see, ladies and gentlemen, why I had to go ahead and marry this wonderful witty woman before anyone else does. Ladies and gentlemen, a toast to my wife!'

They all raised their glasses, then everyone sat down to the wedding meal of fresh asparagus followed by salmon, culminating in the cutting of the cake with a lethal-looking Indian war-sword.

'I wonder what's ahead for them?' Ella mused, beginning to slur a little. 'In fact, I wonder what's ahead for us all. At their age we were so hopeful and eager to change the world. But the world's much the same and I'm alone, and I'm getting old.'

'Old? Not you, Ella.'

Ella felt uncharacteristically sorry for herself. She was giving up her home and had no idea where she would move to. The idea was so frightening it made her sharp.

'Yes, I am. We all are.' She turned her gaze on Sal. 'Unless you're Sal with your pink wig and Jackie O glasses.'

Sal had suddenly had enough of Ella. Whatever had got into her, it was bloody annoying. She had cancer, she had been through hell, and she had done it alone, unlike Ella who had two daughters and a protected life in a huge house in Moulsford. 'I know exactly what's ahead for me, as a matter of fact, Ella. I'm having my breast removed next Tuesday morning. That's why I've got the hat and sunglasses. The reason you haven't seen me for so long is because I've been having treatment for breast cancer.'

Laura gaped and held out her hand. But Ella got angry.

'Why the hell didn't you tell us? We're your friends. We would have been there for you!'

'I didn't want you there for me. I wanted to deal with it my way. Alone.'

'That's so selfish.'

'*Ella!*' Laura replied, horrified. 'Stop it.'

'Yes, stop it, Ella!' endorsed one of the other occupants of their table. 'This is a wedding after all.'

'I'm sorry,' Sal apologized, 'I shouldn't have told you now, not at Gaby's wedding.'

'Too right,' agreed one of the guests.

'You can shut up!' Ella turned on them.

'Calm down, everyone,' Laura intervened.

'What if you don't feel calm, Laura?' Ella demanded, pushing back her chair and stumbling out of the marquee.

'I think we'd better get her a coffee,' suggested Sal, realizing that Ella would never behave like that sober. They followed Ella as she stomped off towards the house.

Claudia watched them anxiously from the high table.

Laura made some strong coffee and handed it to her friend. 'Ella, you never get pissed. What on earth's the matter?'

Before Ella could explain what a terrible mistake she might be making, they turned to find Claudia standing behind them with a tray of glasses. '*Hubble bubble, toil and trouble, cava fizz and champagne bubble!* What's the coven doing out here instead of at your table? I invited you all so you could have a good time and here you are as miserable as sin in the kitchen. What on earth's the matter?'

Laura decided it was time to tell the truth. 'Sal's got breast cancer. She's just told us.'

'Oh my God,' Claudia put down the tray and hugged her, 'so that explains the pink wig.'

'Ella thought it was me refusing to grow up and act my age.'

'Sal, I'm so sorry . . .' Ella mumbled.

'So you should be,' Sal agreed angrily. 'I've got enough to deal with without my friends turning on me. There's a reason I didn't tell you. I thought if I did it alone I'd find it easier to pretend it wasn't happening.'

'But why would you pretend that?' Laura demanded. 'Don't tell me you've been going to chemo on your own?'

'Actually, a rather wonderful minicab driver has been ferrying me back and forwards.'

'A minicab driver? For goodness' sake, Sal! When it could be one of us. You can see why we're a bit cross!'

'That was at first, but actually, lately, someone else has been taking me.' Suddenly Sal didn't care if her own personal drama upstaged the bride's big day. A youngish woman with blonde hair was walking towards them. 'And I think this is an excellent moment for you all to meet her.'

CHAPTER 27

'Girls, meet Lara Olsen, my daughter.'

'Your *daughter*!' Claudia was the first to respond. 'My God, Sal, you've never even mentioned having a baby!'

Sal grinned, removing her dark glasses. Lara had helped her fix on false eyelashes to compensate for her hair loss but, frankly, at the moment she wouldn't have cared what she looked like.

'It was when I was in Norway, during my year abroad. I was only eighteen. Erik, Lara's father, dumped me as soon as I broke the good news. So I decided to stay on, have the baby and come home. You know how good I am at compartmentalizing.'

'You can say that again,' murmured Ella.

'Shut up, Ella, you're pissed,' hissed Laura. 'So how did you find each other?'

'Lara found me.' Sal held out a hand to her daughter. 'She came along like a gift from heaven just when I needed her.'

'How did you know where to look?' Claudia asked Lara.

'I knew I was born in Oslo, that I was adopted, and that my mother was British, a student. My Norwegian grandmother let it out as an explanation for why I was so good at English. You know, nature rather than nurture. She tried to take it back but it was too late. I was only ten but I stored it away, and this year, when my adopted mother died, I decided it was time to look.'

'It gets better.' Sal delved into her bag for her wallet and brandished a photograph. 'These are my grandchildren!'

'Bloody hell!' Ella helped herself to another drink.

'I told Rose McGill about the cancer last week. The funny thing is, she'd already guessed.'

'Unlike your best friends,' Ella slurred.

'Someone take that bottle from her,' commanded Laura.

'I knew there was something wrong, there had to be a reason we hadn't seen you for so long.' Claudia shook her head.

More people were beginning to arrive for the after-wedding party. Gaby suddenly emerged from the crowd of guests, wearing a red organza dress with a corset top from which her breasts overflowed like a medieval wench's. 'Ivory doesn't go with the Indian décor,' she announced. 'Besides, I wanted to show Douglas both sides of my personality.'

'Who's a lucky boy, then,' remarked Ella.

'Ella,' Laura turned to her firmly. 'I really think you should stop drinking now. And why do you keep looking at your phone all the time?'

Ella stood up and walked off huffily.

'She'll be all right. Who'd have thought she of all people would get wrecked? I wonder what the hell's the matter? This isn't like Ella at all. She'll be mortified when she realizes what she's said.'

'Maybe she's tired of being like Ella,' suggested Sal, who was glowing with such happiness she could tolerate anything. 'Laura, who is that man waving at you?'

Calum was walking across the dance floor towards them, looking exceptionally attractive in a pale linen suit, holding a bunch of red tulips. They weren't the same as the ones Laura had yearned for in the florist, but near enough. 'These are for the bride,' he explained with a likeable touch of embarrassment.

'Of course, it struck me as I drove down here, what is a bride going to want with tulips? She'll already be surrounded with flowers she won't be able to take with her anyway.'

'Give them to Laura,' Claudia suggested with a smile. 'I'm the bride's mother, by the way.'

'Calum.'

'Sal isn't the only dark horse, then. To think I imagined it was the bride I had to watch out for today.'

Calum handed over the tulips to Laura. 'They made me think of you. Bold and colourful in this drab old world.'

Ella and Claudia exchanged a subtle glance.

'Hello, Claudia,' a familiar voice greeted Claudia half an hour later. It was Ella's daughter Julia and her husband. 'Have you seen Mum anywhere?' Julia was looking happy and pretty. Even her grumpy husband seemed to be smiling.

'She may have gone to have a little sit down somewhere. We think the champagne may have gone to her head.'

'Mum? Surely not? She could drink me under the table.'

'Not today she couldn't. By the way, she's left her phone.' Claudia handed it over to Julia who put it on the table.

'OK, I'll go and have a look. Neil, why don't you get us all a drink and then I must go and congratulate Gaby.'

The music started and it was time for the first dance. Everyone stood back to watch the bride and groom take to the floor while the DJ played Van Morrison's 'Brown eyed girl' while the guests hooted and clapped.

Claudia began to cry. 'I used to sing that to her in her cot. I was such a terrible mother I didn't know any nursery rhymes.'

Laura squeezed her hand. 'For a terrible mother you've produced a very lovely daughter.'

Don appeared out of the crowd and grabbed Claudia's hand

for the next dance. 'We didn't do too badly in the end,' he whispered. 'I think we may even like Douglas when we actually get to know him.'

A sudden commotion near the Raj bar made them turn.

Wenceslaus and Minka had just arrived. Minka, dressed in a figure-hugging sequinned dress that emphasized her statuesque curves, appeared to be having an acrimonious conversation with Julia's Neil.

'I think you are not nice man,' Minka announced in a clear angry voice, loud enough for everyone in the room to overhear.

'Minka, please . . .' Wenceslaus tried to stop her. 'Is wedding. Is not the time.'

Minka ignored him. 'You are Neil who accuse Wenceslaus of making fraud and cheating your mother of money when all he want to do is help her.'

Before Neil could utter a word of explanation or apology Minka had thrown her glass of champagne over him.

'Neil!' snapped Julia, ignoring the fact that her husband was dripping over the dance floor. 'Apologize to Minka and Wenceslaus this minute!'

'I apologize,' Neil produced meekly. 'It was grossly unfair of me to suggest Wenceslaus was in any way involved.'

'My God,' Claudia remarked to Sal, as Julia mopped the champagne from him with a napkin, 'where *is* Ella? She wouldn't have missed that for the world! Nasty Neil is doing what Julia tells him.'

'It's called marriage,' Sal replied merrily. 'Which is why I'm still single.'

'Goodness,' Claudia marvelled. 'We may have to christen him Nice Neil if this goes on.'

Laura and Calum glided past.

'And where did she find *him*? Not in the bargain section at

LateExpress, I bet.' Claudia shook her head, amazed at all the surprises her friends were capable of.

But there were several yet to come.

Calum had gone to get Laura more champagne when she almost jumped out of her seat. Bella, Nigel and baby Noah, all in their party finery, were coming towards her.

'Bella! You said you couldn't come!'

'I thought Noah was coming down with a temperature but he really perked up and Nige and I didn't want to miss Gaby's wedding so here we are. The only thing is . . .' A sudden look of anxiety clouded her features.

Calum had come back with the champagne. 'This is my friend Calum,' Laura introduced him.

'Oh shit,' Bella murmured.

'What's the matter?'

The answer had just emerged from behind the bar, holding a tray of cocktails. 'Here you are, everyone.' He put the tray down and began to hand them out. It was Laura's husband Simon, smiling as if he didn't have a care in the world.

He caught sight of Laura and Calum and froze mid-gesture.

'Simon! What the hell are you doing here?' Laura demanded.

'I came with Bella.'

Laura looked at her daughter incredulously.

'Dad's been round a few times lately,' Bella explained. 'He wrote me a letter asking to see Noah and I remembered what you'd said. He *is* my dad, the only one I've got. Maybe having a baby made me feel different. And I felt sorry for him in his situation. Gaby said he could come.'

'Aren't you going to introduce me to your boyfriend?' Laura could hear the danger tone in Simon's voice.

'He's not my boyfriend,' she could just imagine Rowley Robinson's reaction to this cosy little rendezvous, 'he's a friend. Calum, this is Simon.'

'Yes,' Calum replied evenly, 'I recognize the description.'

'And what the hell does *that* mean?' demanded Simon.

Laura shot Calum a warning look. What was the matter with him, for God's sake?

'I met Laura at counselling. We all talked about our partners a little. I heard how you marched off without a backwards look. On meeting you, that seemed to fit.'

Without another word, Simon took a swing at Calum, catching him a glancing blow on the chin.

A stunned silence spread through the wedding guests.

'Come on, Calum, we're leaving.' Even though she was almost as angry with Calum as she was with Simon, Laura grabbed his arm.

'No,' intervened Nigel, pulling himself up to his impressive bouncer's stature, 'you should stay. I'll take Simon home. It was a mistake to let him come. We're really sorry. We should have at least given you some warning. Noah will sleep in the car. Come on, Simon.'

Simon followed without a word to Laura.

'Sorry, Mum,' Bella apologized, looking distraught. 'I had no idea that would happen.'

Laura hugged her. 'It makes me doubly sure I'm doing the right thing.' She glanced at Calum who was sheepishly propping up the bar. 'I don't know what the problem is with bloody men.'

'Testosterone.'

'Yes, but Nigel doesn't go round knocking people down even when, with his size, he could.'

'Maybe that means he doesn't need to.' Bella smiled at him proudly.

'Gaby isn't the only one who's found a good guy.' Laura smiled at her daughter.

'Thanks, Mum.'

'Well, that's enough drama for one evening.' Claudia descended on Laura. 'Two fights and it isn't even ten o'clock. It must be a family wedding.'

'Claudia, I am *so* sorry . . .'

'Nonsense. A surprise daughter, a punch-up and an Anna Ford champagne incident, what more can a wedding ask?'

The sudden ringing of a phone on the table next to them provided the answer.

Tentatively, Laura picked it up, hoping it was Nigel saying he'd chucked Simon out and was making him walk home. 'Hello?' She listened a moment before switching it off. 'It's a message for Ella from someone called Tim McAuley. The deal's on, apparently. Do you think Ella's got into drugs? That might explain her strange behaviour.' Claudia looked round her, beginning to feel a prick of anxiety, 'Where *is* Ella, by the way?'

CHAPTER 28

They looked in the house first. Claudia and Laura hunted upstairs, Sal and Lara downstairs.

'She'll never live this down!' Laura joked, as she opened the door to the vast airing cupboard. It was getting late and there was a chill in the air. 'I wouldn't mind crawling in there myself.'

When Ella was nowhere to be found in the house they looked in the outbuildings and the cars parked in the drive, in case someone had left one open, and in Ella's hired van. They asked the waiting staff if they'd seen her but no one had.

'Where the *hell* is she?' Claudia was just beginning to get anxious.

'Could she have gone back to London without telling anyone?' Don asked.

Claudia shook her head. 'Her van's still in the drive.'

'I think we'd better get some more searchers,' Don suggested, picking up on Claudia's concern. 'I'll get Julia and Neil and the Polish boy. Don't worry, I'll be discreet so as not to break up the party.'

'Bugger discreet. The way tonight's going they'll probably kill each other in the woods.'

He disappeared to summon them while the others discussed the options of where Ella might have got to.

'I feel terrible.' Sal was beginning to look distressed. 'I was so rude to her.'

'Actually,' Laura pointed out tartly, 'she was bloody rude to *you*. I don't know what came over her.'

'She was, wasn't she?' Sal conceded. 'Oh, Ella, where are you?'

In the end it was agreed that Laura and Calum, Julia, Neil and Wenceslaus should all look in the woods while Claudia and Don stayed at the house in case she turned out to be there after all.

Don, ever practical, provided them with the torches but, in fact, there was a full moon which gave the search a curious sense of unreality.

They fanned out through the paddock beyond the marquee, passing the curious waiting staff who'd come out for a quick fag, and headed through the small wood which led down to- wards the river.

'You don't think she could have fallen in?' Laura whispered, panic beginning to rise in her for the first time.

Wenceslaus, who had followed a path into a small dell, suddenly shouted: 'Come, everyone! Look!'

They ran in the direction of his voice to find him holding open the curtain leading into a large and exotic canvas tent. On the vast bed in the middle of the floor, draped in bright fabrics and illuminated by hundreds of brightly coloured tea lights, lay Ella, spark out, clutching a pillow to her chest as if it were a lover.

'Oh, God, Mum.' Julia dropped to her knees, almost in tears. 'She's always slept like that since Dad died.'

'It's all right,' Neil comforted gently. 'She's fine. Thank God we've found her.'

'Mum,' Julia sat on the bed and gently shook her. 'Wake up now and come back to the party.'

Ella sat up slowly, blinking at the assembled company. 'What the hell's going on? And where the hell am I?'

'As a matter of fact,' Laura informed her, laughing with relief, 'I think you're in the bed intended for Gaby and Douglas.'

'Oh my God! The bridal boudoir! Claudia showed it to me this morning. How on earth did I end up here?'

The others just grinned.

'I suspect,' Julia was beginning to enjoy being the well-behaved one to her mother's naughty adolescent, 'it was something to do with you getting completely rat-arsed.'

'Thank God for that.' Ella climbed out of bed, relieved rather than insulted, and instantly began to smooth and straighten the covers until there was not the slightest sign left of her invasion. 'I thought it might be an attack of Alzheimer's.'

She stopped, sitting down on the perfect cover. 'I hope it was just a nightmare but I imagined I was incredibly mean to Sal.'

'Yes,' Julia informed her. 'Apparently you attacked her for being a bad friend when she said she had cancer.'

'Oh my God. How am I going to be able to face her? And did I break up the party?'

They headed back to the house where, to Ella's enormous relief, the party was still going on exactly as it had been before.

Claudia came rushing over. 'Are you all right? Where on earth had you got to?'

'In the bridal boudoir,' Laura answered for her. 'Passed out.'

'And what did your cryptic message mean?' Claudia demanded.

'What message?'

'We answered your phone. It was from someone called Tim McAuley. He said the deal was on. You're not going to end up as a drugs mule in Indonesia like Bridget Jones, I hope?'

Ella grinned. This was the news she'd been waiting for. 'I won't need to. I've sold my house and bought a dear little cottage right on the river by the Grand Union Canal, nice and handy for the allotments.'

Julia stopped dead. 'You've sold our family home?' she demanded, aghast. 'You've sold the house we grew up in without even telling us?'

Ella looked nonplussed. 'Julia, you've been on at me to sell the house practically every day for the last year.'

'That was when the boys were staying at boarding school. I grew up in that house! So did Cory! You might at least have warned us!'

'But, Julia, you told me a thousand times it was sensible for me to find somewhere smaller and more practical for my old age. Which I have done. Number three Grand Union Cottages, to be precise.'

'She's right, Jules,' Neil intervened gently. 'It is her house, after all. And it's a sensible move.'

'Besides,' Ella smiled at him gratefully, 'now that you are no longer nagging me, I may see fit to give you and Cory a nice lump sum, which hopefully will be sufficiently before my death to be free of taxes.'

Neil had the grace to look embarrassed.

Julia hugged her. 'Thanks, Mum. Sorry for being a pain.'

'We'd better get back to the house before I really spoil the party,' announced Ella, her usual briskness returning, 'and I think I'd better go and look for Sal.'

They made their way back through the darkened woods, following Neil with the torch.

Ella found Sal sitting with Claudia near the band.

'Sal . . .' Ella was rarely lost for words but she was on this occasion. 'I don't know what to say. I am so, so sorry.'

'You were outrageous,' Sal replied. 'It was entirely unacceptable behaviour.'

Ella looked like a dog that knows it has done wrong and is waiting for its master's judgement.

'On the other hand, if I didn't ever speak to you again I

couldn't remind you on every possible occasion of how badly you'd behaved. And that would be a pity.'

Sal opened her arms and Ella hugged her, then drew back, alarmed. 'I'm not hurting you, am I?'

'Ella, you really do know bugger all about cancer!'

'Then you'd better tell me, hadn't you?'

It was half an hour before Ella remembered she'd invited Wenceslaus and Minka because she wanted them to meet Laura, and so she went to look for them. On the way she found Laura looking cross in a corner. 'I suspected it might be a mistake inviting Calum, but that was because I thought it was too soon in our relationship, not because I thought he'd goad Simon into slugging him. Bloody men.'

'I thought he seemed quite nice. And he was right. Simon did behave like a shit.'

'Laura . . .' a voice interrupted them. It was Calum. 'Look, I'm really sorry. That was incredibly bloody stupid of me. It's just that when I saw him, I could tell he hadn't learned a thing. He'd walked away from someone as incredible as you are and he still didn't give a toss about any of it.'

'You still shouldn't have betrayed my confidence.'

'No,' Calum agreed, 'I shouldn't have. If I stick around and behave myself, dance with the bridesmaids, talk to old ladies, do I get time off for good behaviour?'

His smile, penitent yet charming, couldn't fail to disarm her.

'Depends how hard you try.'

'Just watch me.' He headed off towards Olivia to ask for a dance.

'Go on,' Ella advised, 'give him a break. There've been plenty of times I've wanted to take a slug at Simon.'

Laura laughed. 'Me too.'

She caught Calum's eye and smiled.

To her embarrassment he jumped exuberantly into the air and clicked his heels.

Laura hid her face in mortification.

'Well, I think he's lovely,' Sal congratulated, joining them.

'So do I,' Claudia seconded. 'How dare Simon swan in here as if nothing had happened?'

'Anyway, Laura,' Ella insisted, taking her arm, 'come and meet Minka. She has an interesting job to offer to the right person, running two hair salons.'

'But I don't know anything about running hair salons,' Laura protested.

'You go to one, don't you? Use your imagination!'

Ella led her over. Laura and Minka hit it off at once, as Ella had known they would.

'So. Are you going to take the job?' Ella asked her eagerly.

'I might. On the other hand, I've had a message from a woman who admired my way with disruptive school kids. The word "management" was mentioned.'

'Ooh, get you. Laura two-jobs Minchin!'

'Good night, dear girls.' It was Claudia's mother Olivia who had come to say goodbye to them all. 'It's been a lovely occasion and I gather the happy couple are still together.' She took each of their hands in turn. 'Claudia's lucky to have such wonderful friends. It's a very rare and precious thing.' She leaned in to Laura's ear. 'And so is being able to dance and talk to old ladies. Hang on to him, my dear.'

Calum was now jiving with the least attractive of the bridesmaids. When the music finished he thanked her and beckoned invitingly to Laura to join him for the next one.

'Go on,' Sal pushed her, 'you know you want to.'

But before she did, it suddenly seemed vital to Ella to gather all four of them together on the dance floor. 'Come on, while I can still remember your names,' she said as she herded them forwards. 'I am getting seriously forgetful. Maybe that was why I ended up in the bridal boudoir.'

'Ella,' Laura corrected her. 'You ended up in the bridal boudoir because you were completely pissed.'

'Well, I for one, have decided it's time to embrace old age,' Sal announced. They all looked at her, in shocked amazement. 'I've done a deal with God. I'm going to be fine providing I cut down on drinking and begin to act my age. He has also insisted on Ella writing a column in the magazine. As penance for her bad behaviour.' She grinned at Ella. 'He said it was part of the negotiation.'

'I'd better agree, then,' Ella conceded.

'What?' demanded Claudia in mock-disappointment, 'no more leopard-print playsuits, four-inch heels and unsuitable biker jackets?'

'I'm also planning to go to Norway and embrace being a grandmother!' She smiled across at Lara. 'As part of my convalescence. Work can bloody well wait!'

'I'm with Sal. Time to admit we're old,' laughed Laura. 'With the exception of hair colour — I intend to go to my coffin in L'Oréal Chestnut.'

'And mascara,' added Claudia.

'And knee-length boots,' Ella agreed, summoning a waiter to bring them all one last glass of champagne.

'To old age!' They raised their glasses. 'Do your worst!'

In the background the DJ began to play 'Forever Young' by Bob Dylan. Up till now it had been their anthem.

Ella, Claudia, Laura and Sal, friends for more than forty years, linked arms, not knowing what the future would bring, but grateful for a past in which all their lives had been so closely and satisfyingly intertwined.

If all else failed, they'd still have each other.

Forgetting their new-found acceptance of dignified old age, they kicked off their shoes and began to sing along.

Having It All

By Maeve Haran

The *Sunday Times* Top Ten Bestseller

'It will make you laugh, cry and rethink your life' Jilly Cooper

You work and you miss your children. You stay at home and you wonder if you're missing out . . .

Liz Ward has always believed you can have it all – career, marriage, children . . . So when she's offered one of the biggest jobs in television, she jumps at it. But she hasn't counted on the boss from hell, a rival who gleefully points out the baby sick on Liz's sharp suit, or a best friend who turns out to be a snake in the grass where Liz's handsome husband is concerned.

And when her son starts washing his hands ten times a day at nursery school, Liz starts to wonder: Should it be her rather than the nanny sitting on that rug in the garden with the children? So Liz decides she *will* have it all – on her *own* terms. But Liz's decision has a far greater impact on family and friends than she expects, shattering the myth they all live by.

In this funny and touching novel, Maeve Haran has movingly captured the dilemma of working motherhood.

978-1-4472-6094-3

Read on for the first chapter . . .

CHAPTER 1

Liz Ward, high-flying executive and creative powerhouse of Metro Television, woke to the unexpected sensation of a hand slipping inside the top of her silk pyjamas and caressing her left breast.

For ten seconds she kept her eyes closed, abandoning herself to the pleasurable feelings of arousal. As the other hand stole into her pyjama bottoms she arched her back in response, turned her head to one side and caught sight of the clock-radio.

'My God! It's ten past eight!' she yelped, pushing David's hands unceremoniously away, and jumping out of bed. 'I've got a nine-fifteen meeting with Conrad!'

She flung her pyjamas on the floor and bolted for the bathroom. On the landing she stopped dead and listened. Silence. Always a bad sign. What the hell were Jamie and Daisy up to?

Panicking mildly she pushed open the door of Daisy's bedroom. Jamie was sitting in Daisy's cot next to her, wearing his new Batman outfit, back to front, attempting to tie his Batcape around his protesting baby sister. Scattered on the floor were every pair of tights from Daisy's sock drawer.

Jamie looked up guiltily. 'We needed them. She's got to have tights if she's going to be Robin. Don't you, Daisy?'

'Me Robin,' agreed Daisy.

Liz repressed the desire to shout at him that it was eight-fifteen and he was going to be late for school, remembering it was her fault for getting up to no good with David. Instead she kissed him guiltily and sprinted back into the bedroom, grabbing her suit from the wardrobe and praying it wasn't covered in Weetabix from Daisy's sticky fingers. Women at Metro TV, from the vampish Head of Entertainment down to the lady who cleaned the loos, looked like refugees from the cover of *Vogue* and Liz was finding it tough going keeping up.

David had retreated under the duvet, his pride wounded. Mercilessly she stripped it off and handed him Jamie's school tracksuit. 'Come on, Daddy, you do Jamie. I'll change Daisy in the bathroom.'

She glanced at her watch again. Eight-twenty-five. Oh my God. The joys of working motherhood.

By the time she got downstairs, Daisy under one arm and the report she was supposed to have read in bed last night under the other, David was already immersed in the newspapers. As usual he let the chaos of the breakfast table lap around him, getting his own toast but never offering to get anyone else's. How could Donne ever have said no man is an island? At breakfast all men are islands, separate and oblivious in a sea of female activity.

Still sulking at her rebuff, he was even quieter than usual this morning, his nose deep in the *Financial Times*. Suddenly he steered the paper through the obstacle race of mashed banana, Coco Pops, and upended trainer cups towards her.

'Look at this. There's a piece about Metro. Conrad says he's about to appoint a Programme Controller at last.' Raising his voice to drown out the chaos of Daisy's shouts, Jamie's insistent demands to look at him as he climbed precariously up on his chair, and the nanny's radio tuned to New Kids on the Block, David shouted across to her, 'Why don't you pitch for the job?'

'Me?' Liz wished her reply sounded less like a yelp of panic. She'd only joined Metro Television as Head of Features a few weeks ago when they'd been awarded one of the commercial television franchises for London and she was looking forward to the three months before they actually went on air to settle quietly in and get her ideas ready for the launch.

'Yes. You. Elizabeth Ward. Talented producer. Deviser of a whole new style of programme making. Mother of two.' David warmed to his theme. 'A woman controller would be a brilliant publicity coup for Metro. None of the other TV companies has a woman in charge.' Fired with enthusiasm he jumped up and came towards her. 'The nineties is the decade of women, for Christ's sake! And you're the classic nineties woman. A glittering career *and* kids! You'd be perfect!'

No wonder he made such a good newspaper editor, Liz thought affectionately. Talking people into doing things they didn't want to was his great strength. But he didn't know Conrad Marks, Metro's tough American MD. Conrad thought women were only good for one thing. He had honed his chauvinism to a fine art back home where men were men and women went shopping. He would never hand over power to a woman.

'You don't know Conrad like I know Conrad.'

She winced, remembering the opening ceremony of Metro's stylish new offices the day before yesterday. Somehow or other Conrad had persuaded the Duchess of York to do the honours. Fergie had turned up in one of her fashion disasters, a low-cut peasant number which should have stayed on the upper reaches of Mont Blanc where it belonged. Conrad had spent most of the ceremony peering down her cleavage and she was barely out of earshot when he'd whispered loudly to his deputy: 'Did you see the tits on the Duchess? Lucky royal brats!'

Conrad would never appoint a woman to run Metro.

'But I'm an ideas person, not a tough exec.' Liz tried to gulp her coffee and stop Jamie wiping his nose on his school uniform. 'I don't have the killer instinct.'

'You don't push hard enough, that's all.' Liz could hear the exasperation in his voice. He was so different from her. So sure of himself. Thirty-five and already editor of the *Daily News*, Logan Greene's blue-eyed boy, heir apparent to the whole Greene empire. Occasionally, judging David by his boyish good looks, people underestimated him. Invariably they regretted it.

But then David had always known what he wanted. To get on. To get out of Yorkshire and away from his parents' council house. To succeed. And he had. Even beyond his wildest dreams. And he couldn't understand her reluctance to do the same.

Looking at his watch he stood up. 'It's the caring sharing nineties remember. Killer instincts are out. We're all supposed to respect the feminine now. Intuition. Sensitivity.'

'Bullshit. Try telling Conrad that.'

He leaned over and kissed her teasingly. 'No. *You* try telling him.'

Liz wiped the cereal out of Daisy's hair and, fending off the sticky hands that lunged for her suit, kissed the tender nape of her neck. Reluctantly she handed her over to Susie, the nanny, and tried to persuade Jamie to let go of her leg so that she could check her briefcase. As usual he wailed and clung like a limpet.

On the way out she glanced at herself briefly in the hall mirror. She wasn't too bad for thirty-six. She could do with losing a bit of weight, but at least it meant she didn't have any lines. Thank God she'd had a decent haircut last week which dragged her if not exactly into the nineties, then at least out of the seventies. And the smoky jade eyeshadow the hairdresser had persuaded her to try gave her eyes a sensual oriental look she was quite taken with. People said brunettes kept their looks longer. Well, brunettes said brunettes kept their looks longer anyway.

Looking at her watch, Liz felt a brief but familiar blast of panic: she was going to be late for the meeting with Conrad, the Hoover needed servicing and she'd just remembered that Susie wanted the car today. What had David called her? The classic nineties woman? Ha bloody ha.

There were, as usual, only two women at the weekly ideas meeting: Liz and Claudia Jones, Metro's Head of Entertainment. Having raced across London and run up three flights of stairs when she found the lift was full, Liz arrived out of breath and tense. Fortunately Andrew Stone, Metro's Head of News, was late as well so she managed to slip in and sit down without looking too obvious.

It meant doing without the coffee she would have killed for, but at least Claudia couldn't cast one of her usual withering glances at the clock. Chic, single and childless, Claudia turned Putting the Job First into a religion.

Glancing across the vast boardroom table at Claudia, Liz couldn't decide what she disliked about her most: the way she always looked as though she'd stepped out of Harvey Nichols's window, her blatant use of being female to get what she wanted or her complete lack of talent.

Claudia was the kind of person who kidnapped other people's ideas and took the credit for them. She loved being a woman in a man's world and wanted as few others as possible to be allowed to join the club. And Liz had a shrewd idea that included her.

There was also a rumour going round Metro that Claudia had the ear of Conrad Marks. And from time to time, so the gossips said, the rest of his body too.

'Nice suit,' Claudia congratulated her. Liz looked at her in surprise. Friendliness wasn't Claudia's style. 'Armani, isn't it?'

Every eye in the room looked Liz up and down with interest.

Claudia smiled unexpectedly. 'Pity about the back.'

Liz looked down horrified. Over the back of one shoulder, like some lurid post-punk jewellery, was half the contents of Daisy's breakfast.

In the Ladies there was nothing to wipe it off with. Toilet paper would disintegrate and cover the black suit with bits of tissue, and the roller towel was too short to reach. With a sudden inspiration she delved into her wallet and retrieved her American Express Card. That would do nicely.

By the time Liz got back into the boardroom Conrad had arrived. She slipped into her seat hoping he wouldn't notice. Some hope.

'I was just saying, Liz' – he didn't even bother to look in her direction – 'that no doubt you're all wondering who's on my shortlist for Programme Controller. There are two candidates, both internal. I assume you'd like to know who they are?' He looked round the room savouring the anxiety on their faces. 'The first is Andrew Stone.' There was a buzz of muted approval at the mention of the popular though disorganized Head of News. 'And the other is' – he grinned wolfishly, playing with them, enjoying the tension in the room – 'Metro's Head of Entertainment, Claudia Jones.'

Liz felt like a bucket of freezing water had been thrown over her, but it left her mind cool and sharp as a razor. If Claudia got the job that would be the end of Liz. She couldn't let it happen. She'd have to make a rival bid.

And yet, how could she? Programme Controller was a body-and-soul job, you had to give it everything you had. She had two small children and she saw little enough of them as it was, God knows. If she was running Metro she wouldn't see them at all.

Maybe Claudia wouldn't get the job, maybe Conrad would give it to Andrew. She glanced over at Andrew, bumbling and bluff, grinning ridiculously as he gathered up his papers. When he leaned forward she saw that his shirt was only ironed down the front where it showed and remembered that his wife had run off with an ex-colleague and Andrew was having to learn domesticity the hard way.

She saw that Claudia was looking directly at her now, smiling. Of course, she must have known Liz had been passed over. That's why she'd gone out of her way to humiliate her in front of the whole meeting.

And watching that confident, catlike smile she knew with absolute blazing certainty that Conrad would not give the job to Andrew. He would give it to Claudia.

A month ago, when she'd thrown up her promising job at the BBC to join Metro, it had been to help make it the most exciting network in British television. Challenging. New. Exciting. Different. And what would it be like under Claudia? Cheap. Derivative. Tacky. Predictable.

Liz sat motionless, gripped with panic. The drama over, everyone began to pack up their papers and leave, congratulating Claudia and Andrew as they stood up. The moment was slipping away.

Suddenly Liz heard her own voice, surprisingly calm and controlled, cut through the murmurs of excitement. 'Since you clearly think a woman Controller would be a good thing, Conrad, I'd like to pitch for the job too.'

Online and over fifty?

CONGRATULATIONS! You can now join the busiest little social network in town.

WWW.GRANSNET.COM

Amazing **competitions**, exclusive **web chats** and brilliant **experts on everything** from gardening to beauty.

Join in the party now and find the **kindest, funniest** and **most surprising community** on the world wide web ...

... If you are ready to **be surprised, inspired, amused, engaged** and tap into a world of wisdom, Gransnet is here for you.

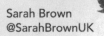

Sarah Brown
@SarahBrownUK
*Have just discovered gransnet.com - whole new world of Hola Español!, The Hungry Caterpillar and dust bunnies *random browsing**

Jane Pearce
@gransnet - I don't know what I'd do without you all - you have a wonderful line in banter - never see a tweet from you without a smile!

"Don't use Twitter or Facebook and always thought there were better things to do than chat to people via computer. Then I discovered Gransnet and I've had to rethink ..." Em

"Some of the threads have left me with a tear in my eye, while others have left me with tears of laughter rolling down my cheeks" Syberia

"Every time I walk around the house, I have a wee diversion towards my laptop in the kitchen - I don't want to miss anything exciting, like a good punch-up or advice on how to fillet a kipper" Gally

www.gransnet.com
Warning: This website occasionally allows rude, silly comments from clever, funny people. There may also be knitting. And sex.

extracts reading groups
competitions books new
discounts extracts extracts
competitions extracts
books new reading groups extracts events
reading groups new extracts events discounts reading groups
events extracts books
books extracts new titles reading groups
interviews events
reading groups books events extracts extracts events books
discounts new books events events interviews new books extracts
books new events new
discounts extracts discounts
www.panmacmillan.com
extracts events reading groups books
competitions books extracts new